A Twist of Fate

By: Emmarie Bee

Prologue

Thrax made his way down the spiral staircase, muttering spells to himself.

"*Míthas simo laúdas.*" He murmured, and tiny tongues of green flames danced between his fingers. The fires sputtered and died, shedding him in semidarkness. The candles flitted softly around each bend of the stairs, casting them in dim light. He scowled and repeated the spell until his hand cradled a large flame that bathed the area around him in a warm glow. He held the flame close until he reached his master's workshop.

"Master?" He called, knocking softly, in case she was deep in concentration.

"Enter."

Thrax pushed open the door to his master's workshop. Majora was slightly taller than him, with a slender body. Her long straight black hair went down to her waist, and her mage's clothes, a deep purple dress accented with gold, were decorated with chains and belts that held pouches of powders, herbs, and notes for spells. The dress was form-fitting at the bodice and loose in the skirt, with sleeves rolled up to her elbows and tied off with ribbon to keep them from slipping and getting in her way. She was leaning over a table, softly whispering a spell. Her brow was furrowed in concentration as the drawn-on runes glowed bright blue, illuminating her almond-shaped gray eyes.

"There you are, Thrax. I was wondering when I'd hear from you." She said, not looking up from her work.

"I wanted to show you, master - I think I got that spell right!"

She stopped her spell and turned to him, rubbing her sore wrists. "Ah yes, the portal spell! Why don't we start off with somewhere close, though, and work our way to somewhere further." She gripped his shoulder and closed her workshop door behind her. "Perhaps the Black Forests. Not even I've been there." She said with a playful smile.

Thrax grinned as he led her upstairs to his workshop. "I think I was writing the runes all wrong; it wasn't '*ayu*,' it was '*ayú*'!"

She nodded slowly. "Runes can be quite tricky. They never were your strong suit."

He pushed open the door to his workshop and bedroom, littered with books, papers, potions, spells, and a few scorch marks from his failed spells. The furniture had been shoved to the walls to make room for the significant rune mark drawn on the floor, surrounded by other failed marks and black charcoal notes he wrote around it.

"Thrax, how many times have I told you to keep your room clean? You'll have an accident here." She scolded lightly.

"It's only to make room for the spell! I promise I'll clean it up later." He insisted, rolling his eyes as he ran to kneel before the rune.

Majora stood over him, looking it over. She slowly broke into a proud grin. "This looks excellent, Thrax! Well done! You're becoming a fine wizard."

Thrax felt his chest swell with pride. "Thank you, master!"

Her hand gently pushed back some loose strands of his thick, black hair. "I know you've been working hard for so long…but it won't be much longer…you've gone eighteen long years working for this, but I'd say you'll be a full wizard soon enough."

"Since I was four, but who's counting?"

She laughed, and her gaze scanned his expression for a moment before she turned back to the rune. "Now, the question is, does this work? Try going just outside of the tower. I don't want to go all over Hevaña to find you." She laughed.

Thrax gave an embarrassed grin, thinking of the many times he had tried this spell and ended up miles from the castle. He put his hands on the floor and began chanting, "*Loñim herod, loñim herod,*" The rune began to glow faintly, and the wind started picking up. The loose papers rustled quietly, and Thrax's black cloak flitted in the breeze. As the light increased, the two wizards quickly realized something had gone wrong. Thrax's eyes widened as the light changed to red, with scarlet lightning crackling too close around his body. He cried out in shock and tried to jump away. As a blinding light filled the room, he put his hands out to protect his face.

Majora turned and shielded her eyes. She heard her student's cry of fear as the light swallowed him. Once it died away, she was horrified to see nothing left of Thrax or the rune but a black burn mark scorched into the floorboards.

Majora stood there momentarily as a loud silence filled the room. She felt her heart begin pounding as she slowly sank to the ground.

"Thrax…?" She murmured, her hands beginning to tremble and her breath quicken. She slowly reached out and touched the mark, running her hands over it as though she could summon him back. As Majora tried to assemble her racing thoughts, she heard a guard open the door, looking panicked. "Majora! The king needs you! It's an emergency!"

She tried to force her heart to settle down.

"Alright…I-I'm coming." She got up on shaky legs and slowly backed up, staring at the scarred floor.

Chapter 1

Gwen kicked the door to her flat closed behind her as she tossed her book bag onto the couch.

"Dad! I'm home!" She called. No answer. Heaving a great sigh, she approached the kitchen, where the fridge bore a note.

"Gwen,

> *I'm going to be home late tonight. The leftover soup is in the fridge to heat up, and I got you some of your favorite ice creams. Be a good girl; please, don't try to build another fire in the fireplace.*

Love,

> *Dad"*

Gwen groaned and rolled her eyes. "That was one time, dad." She jerked the fridge open for a can of pop. She let the door close, clicked the can open, then flopped onto the couch. Her gray cat, Billie Holiday, gave a loud purr as she hopped onto her owner's lap and pushed her head against her.

"Hello, Billie, love." Gwen scratched her cat's ear before turning on the tv and going to the newest episode of Coronation Street she'd recorded the night before. "Let's see what's happening, shall we?"

Gwen held her cat close to her chest as she watched the episode, enraptured, occasionally breaking between advertisements to look over her work for her Latin class. "I'm not ready for this exam, Billie." She sighed. "Whoever decided to make end-of-term exams a thing needs to be burned at the stake."

Gwen struggled through her studies between watching tv before giving a resigned sigh. "I'll finish this later tonight. Come on, pretty girl! Let's get a snack!" She cradled Billie like a baby and carried her to the kitchen. The cat gave a grumpy meow and batted at her owner's face with her paw. She opened the fridge and reached for a can of tuna, clicking it open before grabbing an apple. She slapped the tuna into her cat's food bowl before tossing the can and biting into the juicy apple. She held the apple in her mouth as she pulled some clean clothes from the dryer and began to sort through them.

"I can't wait to be done with school," she muttered as she pulled on some clean jeans and a mustard yellow off-the-shoulder sweater. "Why did I decide to go with a Classics degree, Billie? I don't even like doing all these readings. Latin alone will be the death of me."

The cat merely meowed in response, too focused on her treat.

"Yeah, I don't know either. Alright, let's see what we have for dinner." Gwen began walking back to the kitchen when she heard a loud thump down the hallway.

The twenty-year-old woman froze at the fridge as goosebumps ran up her arms. The front door had been closed and locked, with no signs of forced entry, and they had no back door; they were on the third floor of the apartment building. Was there a burglar in her flat? If there was, they were doing a terrible job at being quiet.

Gwen made her way to the silverware drawer as silently as possible, grasping the biggest knife she could find. She slowly crept down the hall to her dad's bedroom. She opened the door and saw no one. Nothing was disturbed; the window was still locked and intact.

There was another thumping noise, the sound coming from her bedroom. Her eyes widened as she made her way slowly toward the door, her sweaty hands

15

tightening around the knife. She silently grabbed the door handle and slowly turned it. Raising the blade in her hand, she threw open the door, preparing for the worst. There were no signs anyone had been in there, however. No busted windows, nothing disturbed; everything was just as she had left it that morning. Billie approached her owner, purring softly and rubbing Gwen's leg.

Another thump came, this time from her wardrobe, with a voice cursing.

Gwen bit her lip as she crept towards it, knife still raised, and threw open the door. Instead of a burglar, she got a very strange-looking young man.

He had shiny black hair, beautiful brown skin, and emerald-green eyes, wide and wild with fear. He was dressed oddly, too. He was wearing a chain with a gemstone and hoop earrings with a small green gem in his ears. His clothes looked like something out of a fantasy movie. They were dark green and black, trimmed with silver.

The boy's eyes locked onto the knife as she began to bring it down to him. He quickly leaped to his feet and held her wrist, his hand glowing with green flames. He grabbed her other arm, and a feeling of electric shock ran through her body. She yelped, dropping her knife and rubbing her wrists which were now red and raw from the flames and shocks. Billie hissed and took off under the bed, swiping his ankles as she passed.

The man grabbed Gwen's wrists in one hand and held them above her head. The other hand was filled with green flames that he had under her chin. "Where am I? What's going on here? What is this place?"

Gwen's eyes were wide with terror. "I think the question is, who are you, and what are you doing in my house?" she cried and threw her knee into his stomach.

The stranger fell, hunched over, gasping from the sudden attack. Gwen took the opportunity to grab the knife from the ground. She rolled over her bed, pointing the knife straight at him. "Stay back!" she cried.

He raised his hands, giving her a stern look, trying to stay calm despite his fear. "Listen, let's be sensible here. I'm just as confused as you are, okay? I have no idea where I am or why I'm here."

"Well, how did you get here, then?" she cried. Thrax paused and took a hard look at the girl. She was a short, curvy woman with long blonde hair in a braid. Her blue eyes reminded him of a deer frozen in place from fright. Her pink cheeks were flushed, and her trembling hands clutched desperately to her knife. The skin on her wrists was quickly becoming an angry red and swelling.

"I suppose I should start from the beginning. I'm Thrax Nightingale, the apprentice to the royal wizard of my kingdom. I was demonstrating a spell I thought I'd mastered, but something must have gone wrong, and now I'm here." His brow furrowed. He then turned to her. "Please, you must help me get back."

She jumped at his movement, holding the knife higher. "You're mad! Stuff like that doesn't happen in the real world!"

"Do I appear fake to you? Am I a specter?" he snapped. "I'm as real as you are, lady...?"

"Gwendolyn." she snarled through clenched teeth.

"Lady Gwendolyn. I am real." he moved to the wardrobe and began looking around, hitting the roof, sides, and floor. "Strange...you call this the real world. Does that mean you're not from the continent?"

"W-what the hell are you doing?" She said, lowering her knife only slightly.

19

"The continent. The land that my kingdom is in." He repeated. "Are you from there?"

"No, this is not "the continent." Guess that means you're not some weirdo from France. And what are you doing to my wardrobe?"

"I'm checking for some magic mark that might explain why I was brought here…but there doesn't seem to be one…very odd." he stood straight and turned to her quickly.

Gwen's heart leaped to her throat, and she raised her weapon threateningly again.

"Calm down; there's no need for that." he waved her away like he couldn't be bothered. "Now…there must be a reason I was brought here…why on earth was I brought to the room of a girl?"

She felt a twinge of irritation. "Girl? I'm at least as old as you!"

Thrax ignored her, continuing to think. Slowly, his eyes widened in realization. He looked at Gwen, examining her for a long moment. "Come with me."

"What? Hell no!" she cried, taking a hurried step back.

"I'm giving you about as much chance to decide as I was given," Thrax said sternly. "Look, I need to get back. My master might think me dead, and I can only assume I'm here for a reason, and you must be that reason. You are coming with me." he stepped closer to her.

"Stay away from me!" she shouted, pressing the blade's tip to his chest.

Thrax stopped and looked down at it mildly. He gave a resigned sigh and looked at her with an unreadable expression. "Lady Gwendolyn, I'd rather not have to act in a way that I will regret, so please, just cooperate, and come to my realm with me."

"No! Stay away! Leave me alone!" she repeated, causing him to sigh.

"Very well, you've left me with no choice." He grabbed her wrist, and a red flame engulfed their hands. She cried out in pain, dropping the knife. Thrax pressed her to the wall to restrain her, holding her wrists. His glare was full of fierceness. "Look, I don't want to have to act like this, but there must be a reason! Something has brought us together, and I must act on it, so just come with me!" he said, holding her wrists.

Gwen's heart pounded wildly as she jerked in his grasp, her mind racing. "You're not going to leave me much choice, are you...?"

"I'm afraid not," Thrax admitted. "I don't want to hurt you, but I have to know..."

"A-alright, then...I'll go...let's just not go crazy, okay?"

"Good." he looked around for a moment before turning to Gwen again. "Do you happen to have a piece of charcoal? Something for me to mark the floor."

"Um…yeah, sort of…" she kept her eye on Thrax as she walked to her desk and grabbed a sharpie, tossing it to him. "Here. It's not charcoal, but it should do the trick for whatever the hell you're trying to do…" she rubbed at her hands which were starting to blister and sting from the fire.

Thrax fumbled before grasping the marker firmly in his hands. He stared and prodded at it before managing to wiggle the cap off. "What a strange quill…but it should work."

He turned to the wardrobe and knelt, marking the floor with the teleportation rune.

"What are you doing?" Gwen peered over his shoulder curiously.

"This is the rune I used when I was brought here. It stands to reason that if I use this rune, it should get us back."

"Or you send us somewhere completely different."

"Well, that is a possibility, but we don't have any other options, do we? At this point, I imagine there must be some magic link connecting our two worlds here. What that means or how that works, I frankly don't know, but it's worth a try. There, done." he handed Gwen the marker and sat back to admire his work.

Gwen capped it and tossed it on the bed, staring down at the markings he had made. "Are you certain this will work?"

"I can't be certain of anything right now. Now, to be teleported with me, you'll have to hold on to me. Don't let go, no matter what."

"And what if I don't?" she stuck out her chin.

"Unless you want to be stuck in a magical void or appear in some other world, I'd suggest you get over it and hold on."

Gwen scowled as she hesitantly wrapped her arms around his bicep.

"Good. Now, let's begin." he put his hands on the rune and closed his eyes. "*Loñim herod, loñim herod,*"

The rune began to glow with bright red light, lightning crackling around. Gwen pressed her face into Thrax's shoulder as it grew brighter and screamed, squeezing his arm as a white-hot light engulfed them.

Chapter 2

Gwen yelped in pain as she and Thrax tumbled onto the wooden floor of what looked like a bedroom in a tower. Or at least what had once been a bedroom.

It was like a fiery tornado had passed through; burnt papers, broken flasks, strange liquids splattered across the walls, vials filled with odd substances spilled to the floor, and a tipped cauldron, dripping an orange-pink concoction, which held what looked like some sort of animal horn. Looking around, she saw overturned bookshelves, a desk with partially torn, burnt books, and a simple bed in the farthest corner of the room, broken in half. The walls were covered in deep gashes and burns. In the center of the room was a significant, black scorch mark. Thrax looked around and slowly got to his feet.

"What…happened here? My room…my work…it's…gone." Thrax gasped. His voice came out choked as his eyes began to turn red. "Everything…everything I've ever worked on…destroyed…" he touched some of the remaining papers, which crumbled to ash in his fingers. Slowly, he walked to the burn at the center of the floor, running his fingers over it. "This couldn't have been from the spell…something else caused this."

"What is this place?" Gwen asked tentatively.

"My workshop and room…this was where I lived…" he murmured. "Just out that door, down the spiral stairs, is my master's workshop." he knelt to scoop up what was left of one of the liquids into an intact vial. "This is my work. My…this was my life…this was…everything I knew…" his eyes slowly welled up with tears. "My life's work as a wizard…"

Gwen hesitated. She wasn't sure how to comfort him in such a situation. Slowly, she reached up and gently gripped his shoulder. "Hey…it's okay…we can…" she looked around. "W-we can still save what's left." she quickly began to move around the room. She grabbed the papers, and whatever wasn't destroyed. She bottled potions, gathered documents and books, and soon had everything she could save of his gathered into one pile.

Thrax watched before quickly wiping his eyes. "Gwen…thank you."

Gwen became quite bashful and looked away. "It's…no trouble." she quickly tucked a loose hair behind her ear before cleaning up.

"Wait," he reached out and grabbed her arm. She gave a sharp hiss as her burns stung. "Let me help with this first."

He held her hands in his and began to mutter, "*Sana akmad…incendit romar.*"

Gwen winced under his touch until the burning pain was replaced with a cool feeling like cold water, and a wave of relief washed over her. The swelling began to go down, and the redness and blisters on her skin returned to its regular soft, pinky color. She held her hands to her chest when he released her, shifting awkwardly. "Um…th-thanks."

Thrax opened his mouth to speak but stopped, his expression darkening. He grabbed her arm, putting a finger to his lips and looking toward the door. Gwen immediately fell silent, her heart leaping in her chest and her stomach somersaulting. Faintly, they could hear voices and footsteps climbing the turret tower's steps.

"Quickly." Thrax hissed, shoving her under one of the halves of the broken bed. She dropped the contents in her arms and scrambled around so that she could see. Thrax quickly crawled in after, keeping his finger to his lips. Gwen momentarily wondered if these people could hear how hard her heart was beating in her chest and clasped her hands to her mouth to quiet her breathing.

The door flew open, and a guard rushed in, breathing heavily, eyes wide. "Who's there?" the guard cried, looking around.

Thrax sighed, quickly crawling from his hiding spot. "Draeon! What's going on? What's happened?"

The guard whirled around and stared in shock. "By the gods…! Thrax, it is you!" he threw his arms around the wizard.

"Draeon, what's going on here?" Thrax repeated.

"It was an attack. After you vanished, a wizard came to our doorstep, claiming to be your half-brother! He killed the king and tried to attack the queen and prince!"

"What? What happened? Is Majora okay? Where are the queen and prince?"

"They're fine; they're hidden away! The queen and prince went east, I think. But we don't know what happened to Majora. We assume she followed the queen, but we don't know."

"Damn!" he hissed.

At this moment, the guard noticed Gwen getting to her feet from her hiding spot. "Thrax, who's this?" Draeon asked, pointing to Gwen.

"A friend of mine. Lady Gwendolyn," he said, waving vaguely toward her, his mind more occupied with his master's safety. "You say the queen and prince went east?"

He nodded, still staring at Gwen, who blushed in embarrassment.

"Then we should go to them. Do you know where they are?"

Draeon pondered. "I can't say for certain, but I believe they could be in one of the fishing villages along the river."

Thrax paused and began looking around frantically.

"What are you looking for?" Gwen asked, ignoring Draeon as he jumped and cried, "She spoke!"

"A spell...I know a spell to control air, but I need to be sure I have it correct, or rather than floating to safety, we combust into a pile of ash."

Gwen's face drained. "Yes, let's not have that happen, please."

"Aha!" Thrax held a half-charred scrap of paper. "Here you are!" He studied it for a moment before throwing it aside. "Draeon, I'm going to find the queen and the prince. Don't worry; I'll find out what's happening and fix this. Let's go!" He grabbed some of his saved materials and threw them into Gwen's arms. He scooped Gwen up again, holding her bridal style.

She cried out, one arm fiercely hugging his neck, the other clutching the saved materials and her things. "W-what are you-?" she gasped, but Thrax sprinted straight for the only open window before she could finish. "What the hell are you doing!" she screamed.

"Escaping!" he jumped straight out of the window, and they plummeted from the easily thirty-story building, rushing towards the ground.

Gwen closed her eyes, tightly clinging to Thrax, as she screamed at the top of her lungs.

Thrax stuck out a hand and yelled, "*Caeli*!" A blast of air burst from his hand and slowed them as they approached the ground, landing safely.

33

Gwen shook violently, her eyes still closed, refusing to open or get down. Thrax ran straight towards the forest, still carrying her. He could see people leaning out of the windows, yelling, and figures running through the castle to chase after them.

"I will see you again, master…I will find you again." Thrax vowed to himself. He didn't know why this had happened or why he was taken to this girl, but they knew they needed each other now for whatever reason.

Chapter 3

"Put me down, now!" Gwen smacked at Thrax's chest once they were hidden amongst the trees, kicking in protest.

"Suit yourself." He let her fall on her rump with a yelp.

"Ugh! Jackass!" she spat venomously.

"How ladylike. Is this how women in your world act?" he sneered, walking deeper into the woods.

Gwen jumped up and brushed the dirt off her. "Well, for your information," she jogged over to him. "Most women in my world aren't snatched up by wizards that fall into their wardrobes and burn them! I've been right peachy, compared to how most other women would have reacted! And slow down, damn it!" she cried, trying not to trip over tree roots.

"No. Besides, it'll do you good. People in your world must be terribly unhealthy if they're anything like you."

Gwen's face went beat red, and she put a hand over her stomach. She had never exactly been skinny. Her pudgy tummy and stretch marks were a constant point of contention throughout her life.

Thrax stumbled forward as a branch slammed into his back. "Ow! What the hell?"

Gwen stood there, the materials dropped in the dirt around her, and holding the biggest branch she could get her hands on. Angry tears filled her eyes as she glared at him. "Take that back!"

"What?"

"I said take that back, you absolute jackass!" she swung the tree branch again. "You had no right to say that!"

Thrax quickly jumped back and used his magic to levitate the branch from her hands and toss it. "Calm down, princess; I didn't mean it."

Gwen screamed in frustration and punched him in the chest. "Shut up! I don't care if you didn't mean it; you don't get to say those things! I'm only here because of you, and you have the absolute fucking gall to make fun of me? This is all your fault! I hate you! I wish I *had* stabbed you!"

The punch knocked the wind out of Thrax. He stumbled back, coughing as he tried to catch his breath. He quickly grabbed her arms, wrestling to hold her still. "Alright! I'm sorry, I'm sorry! I shouldn't have said that. Now, if you calm down, we may be able to find a way to solve this mess and get you back."

She wrenched her arms away and wiped her eyes. "Fine..."

The two fell silent as they started walking again.

"You know…you seemed pretty unbothered by that guy talking about another wizard."

"What? Oh, that…we can handle that later. The important thing is we find the queen and the prince."

"They must be important to you, then."

Thrax looked away. "It's…complicated. I'll tell you about it later."

She studied him for a moment and just silently kept walking.

Gwen leaned against a wall as she watched Thrax haggle with a horse owner, trying to ignore the curious stares she was receiving. Everyone looked like something from a Shakespeare play. She couldn't have felt more out of place as she shuffled her trainers and awkwardly tugged on her jeans and jumper.

"Remember, when asked who you are, you're a Gyrian traveler." Thrax had said before they got there.

"I don't even know what that means." Gwen retorted.

"Gyrian travelers are people who travel to hundreds of kingdoms. They're nomadic people who have split into multiple caravans with no homeland. So, no one will question your strange dress because they dress in all sorts of different ways."

"Can we not just get me some normal clothes?"

"Of course not. We need you in something for easy travel, and our clothes just aren't that. You would need wizard's clothes, and you cannot produce magic." he looked scandalized at the mere thought. "Wizards are often paid in exchange for their magical services. I can't have you making a fool of my practice by dressing in a wizard's garb and producing nothing." He also didn't want to admit he didn't have the coin to pay for new clothes and supplies.

Gwen rolled her eyes. "I promise, I was not intending to insult your wizardry." She mocked, waving her hands. Gwen had grown a quick temper and a short fuse over their journey. It had taken them at least three days to walk this far. She was grateful when they had arrived at the small market to buy horses and restock food for their journey as her feet ached like they never had before. Her irritability was not helped by how ravenous she was.

Thrax turned over his handful of gold to the owner and took two horses by their reins. As he walked toward her, he saw how awkward and out of place she was. She dressed entirely differently, her blonde hair in a plait, her blue eyes downcast and shifting nervously, while her fair skin was pink with nervousness under the watchful gaze of passersby.

"Lady Gwendolyn," he called.

She turned and smiled at the horses. "They're beautiful." she gently stroked the nose of a dark brown gelding.

"Do you ride?" he asked, tying their few belongings onto the horses' backs.

She nodded. "When I was younger…" she looked at the saddles. "But I've never seen a saddle like this."

"You will quickly get used to them. A true rider can adjust to any change, right?"

"I guess?"

"Do you need a leg-up?"

Gwen shook her head stubbornly. "I can manage." she slipped her foot into one stirrup and swung herself up.

"Well done, lady Gwendolyn." he nodded and mounted his horse.

She sat up a bit straighter. "I do know how to do some things, lord Thrax," she said the last part in an exaggerated posh voice.

Thrax relented with a chuckle, and the two began riding.

"By the way, you don't have to call me lady Gwendolyn all the time."

"Do people not call you that in your world?" he raised an eyebrow.

"Well, they used to say things like that many years ago, but not so much anymore. People call me just Gwen, and I prefer that."

Thrax's lips tugged slightly into a smile. "Very well, 'just Gwen.'" he teased.

Gwen rolled her eyes but relinquished a smile. "You know what I mean."

"Hey, it's not my place to question your strange ways." he gave a wolfish grin. "I'm just following your weird customs."

She kicked at his knee, making him squeak in pain.

"Serves you right." she giggled.

"Thrax, I don't know about this," Gwen murmured, holding onto his arm as he led her into a tavern.

"There's no need to be frightened. A tavern is the best place for us to receive information. If we're to learn of the queen and prince's whereabouts, it's most certainly here." he assured her.

"Yeah, and that makes sense, but can we not do that in a place that doesn't make me feel like I'm going to be skewered by arrows…?" she asked, looking around at the men and women dressed up in battle armor, scars, and war paint, with no less than three different types of weapons on each of them.

"What?" Thrax looked around confusedly. "I…don't understand. What's wrong with these people? They seem normal to me."

"Our definitions of normal are very different. In my world, when you go to a bar, no one wears body armor or carries weapons. You could be thrown in jail if you have a weapon with you." she explained.

Thrax gave her a look as though she were mental. "Your world is quite odd."

"Well, they're just different…" she murmured, eyeing a large man in full body armor, with a sword sitting on the table beside him. His eyes scanned her over his tankard, making her shiver with discomfort.

"Can we just get out of here?"

Before he could respond, someone cried out, "Is that who I think it is?"

The two quickly turned the voice and saw a group of people in wizards' robes and armor. "Thrax? Thrax Nightingale?"

Thrax beamed at the group. "Lady Midra!" he cried and pulled a reluctant Gwen towards them.

"Oh, my dear lad, it is you!" gasped a woman in long dark blue robes that hugged tightly to her waist and arms. Her skirt had a long slit, embroidered with silver designs. She had dark black hair pulled in a ponytail and glittering hazel eyes. She leaped up and hugged him close, stroking his hair. "We took you for dead! That accident with the spell!"

"Come sit with us, lad!" said a jovial man with vicious lacerations across his face. He grabbed a spare drink and slid it over to Thrax. "And you can introduce us

45

to your lovely traveling companion!" He winked at Gwen, who felt her heart jump nervously. She forced a timid smile.

"Everyone, this is Gwendolyn! She's a friend. Gwen, this is my master's sister, Lady Midra! She's a spectacular conjuration mage! She could summon anything by her side like that!" he snapped his fingers.

"You're too sweet." Midra smiled. "So where are you from, Gwen dear?"

"I-I'm-…" she paused to remember what Thrax had called it. "I-I'm a Gyrian."

"My, my! You must have many interesting tales about the lands your caravan has been to!" Midra beamed encouragingly.

Gwen immediately fell into nervous laughter. "N-n-not particularly…" she murmured.

"Gwen's rather shy, lady Midra." Thrax quickly jumped to her aid. "She doesn't enjoy telling long tales."

Midra nodded. "My apologies if I made you nervous." she reached over and gently patted her hand. Gwen was immediately fond of her. "So, Thrax, tell us, what happened?"

Thrax briefly explained what had happened, though he was sure to leave out specific details, and how he had returned to find the palace had been attacked.

"Yes, it was very upsetting when we heard…Majora was distraught. She thought she'd lost you and her home on the same day."

Thrax stared into his drink for a moment before looking up. "How long have I been gone?"

"Perhaps a fortnight?" she said sadly. "It felt like longer…."

"Was it that long…?" Thrax murmured, taking a long swig from his drink.

"Afraid so…and there's this business with this wizard."

"I know…Gwen and I are going to find the queen and prince Aaheer, but aside from that, we don't know what else to do."

"Well, if I were you, Thrax, I would begin to gather some followers and do everything you can to help you defeat this guy. From what Majora told me, he wasn't acting alone." the scarred man said with raised eyebrows.

"Noted. Now, when you say you saw Majora…" he began.

Midra gave a sad smile. "I'm afraid I know where she is about as well as you do, Thrax…my sister is very elusive."

"I see."

"Now, back to your plan," Midra continued. "You said you were going after the queen and the prince?"

"Yes. Do you know where they are?" he perked up.

"As a matter of fact," her smile grew. "I helped them go into hiding."

"Midra, thank the gods for you!" Thrax sighed happily.

She laughed and drew a piece of parchment from her robe. She waved her finger over it. A note in a strange language materialized on the paper. "Take this. It has the exact directions to get to the queen. You can read it, yes?"

"Of course," he assured her, taking the note. "Majora taught me all the arcane wizard languages." his eyes scanned the paper. "Thank you, Midra. You're a lifesaver."

"Don't worry, Thrax. You'll always have our support. If we find out more, we'll find a way to keep in touch with you." she gave a sly grin. "Consider us your first spies and allies."

He embraced her gratefully. "Thank you…" he turned to Gwen and nodded toward the bar. "Come on, this way."

Gwen nodded and hurried off with him to the innkeeper at the bar. Thrax slapped some gold down on the counter. "One room, please."

"Two beds or one?" the innkeeper didn't bother looking up from idly counting his gold.

"Two!" Gwen said, going bright pink.

The innkeeper raised an eyebrow and looked up to see her expression of indignation. "Very well." he shrugged, pocketing the gold. He led them to a plain room with two small beds on opposite sides, a single end table between them, and a dresser with a mirror on the opposite side. "There are night clothes in the drawer." The innkeeper jerked his thumb and went back to the bar.

Thrax was just about to go in when Gwen grabbed his shoulder. "What do you think you're doing?" she said.

He blinked. "Um…going into our room?"

"Oh no, mister!" she firmly pushed him back. "You're sitting right outside this room! I'm not going to let you hang out in there while I change!"

Thrax sighed and held up his hands in defeat. "Alright. Go ahead. I'll be out here if you need me."

Gwen scoffed and stomped past him. "Yeah, you wish…" she grumbled and slammed the door shut behind her.

Thrax was sitting outside their room, leaning against the wall, when Gwen poked her head out. "You can come in now." He got up and gave a long stretch.

51

"Do you want me to wait while you change?"

Thrax looked up and blushed a bit. The nightdress she wore was plain white but thin and short enough to make him uncomfortable. "No…I don't…I-I wouldn't want anyone trying to bother my travel companion."

"That's…very thoughtful of you."

"You sound surprised. Besides, I don't need night clothes." He kicked off his boots and set his amulet on the end table. He tossed his cape onto the end of the bed and began to remove his clothes.

Gwen turned around quickly to hide her embarrassment, pressing her hands to her flushed cheeks. She lifted the covers of her bed and screamed bloody murder.

"Gwen! What's wrong?" Thrax cried, quickly rushing to her side.

Gwen pointed a trembling finger at a dead rat in her bed.

Thrax gave a small smile and shook his head, grabbing the dead rat and throwing it out of a window. "Get used to that, my dear. You could have found one while it was still alive." he chuckled and tossed his doublet on top of his cape before crawling into his bed.

Gwen's lip trembled as she sat on the bed, hugging her knees to her chest, letting her silent tears fall. "Why did I ever let you pressure me into this." she whimpered.

"Because you didn't have another choice,"

"Yeah, you dragged me here, after all."

Thrax gritted his teeth and gave a small huff. "Well, I wasn't going to stay in your world. My people need me, anyways. What did you even have back in your world?"

Gwen sat up and glared at him, trying to keep her voice from trembling, "I had my own family. Believe it or not, I had friends, too. There were still people I cared about. But no, you somehow managed to fall into *my* room out of every other home in England!" she snapped before angrily tossing herself onto her side, away from him. "I wish you'd never come falling out of my wardrobe."

Thrax felt a stab in his chest at her harsh words. He sat up to retort before he heard her slight sniffle. He opened his mouth to speak before finally deciding to lie back down. He'd done enough damage for one night.

Chapter 4

"Midra said the queen and prince are just a village away from us," Thrax said, reading the note lady Midra had given him yesterday. "It's about three days from here."

"Three days…" Gwen muttered and shook her head. They had been riding since early morning, following Midra's directions, though Gwen sometimes wondered if Thrax honestly did know where he was going.

"It's best for them to be a decent distance away. This village is one of the furthest ones from the kingdom, and it's small," he explained, having his horse take the lead as he read and guided them. "She's in an inn called 'The Runaway.'"

"Fitting."

"We need to ask the innkeeper, Orag, for the runaway, and he'll take us to them."

"Sounds simple enough. You'd expect the queen to be hidden somewhere better than that." Gwen pointed out.

"You would think, but this is the best place for them. Orag is their protector and hears all news, gossip, and rumors from locals and travelers. He knows everyone and is wary of those he doesn't know, according to Midra. If dangerous strangers come, he'll be able to warn them and keep them away."

"I suppose you have a point." she followed him over a bridge.

"If anything, it'd be more dangerous for them to be away from people. If they run out of supplies, they'll have to leave their hiding place, and there's no one to warn them if someone's coming to look for them," he added, reading a sign at a fork in the road and turning left. "If they're at least in a small town, they'll have some eyes watching for them, and considering everyone knows everyone-"

"…They'll be able to warn them quickly."

"Exactly."

"And I suppose it's far less lonely than if they were, say, in a mountain cave or something," she noted. "It's quite lonely without friends."

"I'm glad I have you, then," Thrax said nonchalantly.

Gwen's cheeks heated up. "You…consider me a friend?"

He seemed put off by her reaction. "Of course. What else would I consider you?"

"Oh, no, it's just…I wasn't expecting you to say that. We haven't known each other long."

"Well, we'll have plenty of time to get to know each other now."

"Does Midra say which way to go?" Gwen asked, looking from the sign to Thrax.

"No…that's the problem. That wizard burned up all my maps." He groaned, searching desperately through his saddlebag for clues on where to go.

The pair had been traveling for almost two days and were currently stuck at a crossroads with no idea which direction to go. Midra's guide only told them so much, and the signs before them gave no further clues. It was heavily faded, and they couldn't tell where the roads led.

"Well, this is just great." She sighed. "Do you even remember the village's name?"

"Of course, I do, but these signs all have names of the major cities, and I don't remember which city it's closest to." he groaned, staring intently down each road. "Damn!"

Gwen also looked down the roads and paused. "Thrax…do you see that too?"

The young wizard turned and saw a figure hiding amongst the brush, growing closer. "Yes, I do…" he pulled his horse in front of hers. "Stay behind me, Gwen," he growled. "*Míthas simo laúdas…*" A warm green fire filled his hand as he stared intently ahead as the figure grew closer. A man burst from the brush wielding two long knives.

"Hand over all you have, and no one gets hurt!" The thief snarled, raising the blades.

Gwen gasped, her heart pounding, as she pulled her horse farther behind Thrax.

"I'm going to tell you this once, leave now, and I won't have to kill you," Thrax growled, glaring down at the thief.

He sneered. "You'll regret those words, wizard!" the thief rushed forward, raising his knives.

"*Ényo tumó*!" Thrax yelled and what appeared to be a purple lightning bolt shot the thief in the heart. His eyes became glassy, and he fell to the ground. Once he was down, Thrax dismounted to loot the thief.

Gwen's heart was still pounding as she slowly moved her horse closer. "Is he…?"

"Dead? No. I paralyzed him long enough to get this." he drew a map from his belt. "And I'll be taking these," he took the man's knives. "So, he can't attack anyone else." He held one up to Gwen. "Here."

"What? I don't want that thing!" she quickly held up her hands.

"Gwen, if you're going to come with me, you'll need to be able to defend yourself, especially if I'm not around. I won't allow you to get hurt." he insisted, pressing the knife handle in her hand. "Hopefully, you'll never have to use it."

Gwen sighed and reluctantly put the knife in her saddlebag. "Alright…just for emergencies, though."

He mounted his horse again and looked at the map. "The village is the way he came from." he pointed down the road, and they rode off.

The journey from that point was relatively straightforward. They had no issue reaching the small fishing village by a great river. The people kept their heads down and moved quickly from one place to another.

"Don't feel offended," Thrax assured Gwen softly. "The news of the wizard's attack had surely spread all over. They're most likely anticipating an attack from him and his men. He could be searching for the royal family and me in every village."

61

"I suppose I'd be concerned too…" she said and caught sight of a particular sign, where a pair of boots were painted under large red letters that read, "Thrax, look! The Runaway!"

"Good eye. Let's go." They dismounted just outside the little building and tied the horses up. Thrax held the door open for Gwen, who was greeted with a pleasantly warm building filled with lively music and laughter. A few women squeezed between the tables with drinks and food on trays. There was cheerful chatter amongst men who had just docked their boats, and Gwen even caught sight of a few couples, talking in hushed, giggly voices, and even a family, eating at the counter table with two small children swinging their legs happily as they tore at their bread. The lanterns and large fireplace gave the inn a soft, comforting light.

Thrax kept a hand on her waist. "It will be best to appear as though we are together…" he murmured in a barely audible whisper.

She went a tad pink and retorted, "Don't get too used to it." but followed his lead, leaning closer into his embrace.

"Orag?" Thrax asked the barkeeper, who was wiping down a tankard.

"Yes?" The burly man looked up.

"We're looking for the runaway." Thrax leaned closely, his hand tightening around Gwen's waist. "We're friends of Midra."

Orag almost dropped his tankard as he straightened up. "Y-yes, this way!" he said, leading them up a flight of stairs just out of sight. "They'll have been waiting for you." He opened the door to a winding staircase that led to a single room.

He led them up and gave a light knock. "You have guests, your majesty."

"Let them in."

In the room, a young man, barely younger than Thrax, leaned back in his chair at a desk, abandoning whatever he was writing. He looked at them and grinned.

"Thrax!"

He had the same upturned green eyes but golden-blonde hair and soft stubble. He also didn't have quite the same robust build or lean, muscular stature Thrax gave off. He, instead, appeared more bookish and lankier. The boy ran to him and threw his arms around Thrax. "We were afraid you were dead!"

"Your highness!" he sighed in relief, hugging him tightly. "I'm so glad you're safe! Gwen, this is Prince Aaheer."

"It's a pleasure." Gwen gave a little curtsey.

He gave a kind smile and bowed, taking her hand and kissing it gently. "It's an honor to meet you, lady Gwendolyn."

She blushed a bit and giggled. Thrax rolled his eyes so hard that Gwen wondered if they might pop out of his head.

"Thrax?"

They all turned to a woman standing before a mirror and now faced them. She was young, perhaps in her late thirties. Her light bronze-colored hair cascaded down to her waist. Her tired, teary green eyes gleamed at the sight of Thrax. She walked over and reached towards his face. Her lip trembled as she pulled him into an embrace.

"Oh, Thrax, my dear boy, you're safe!"

Thrax's entire face became as dark red as the queen's dress. When she released him, he stuttered terribly,

"G-g-Gwen, th-th-thi-this is h-her m-m-majesty, q-queen Myana…" he gestured to her.

"It's an honor, your highness." Gwen curtseyed to her.

"Did you help him get here?" she asked, taking her hands.

"S-sort of?" she also began to blush.

The queen quickly embraced her. "Oh, thank you, dear girl! Thank you for bringing my Thrax back to us!"

"Mother, please." Aaheer gently took her arm, making his mother step back.

"My apologies," her lip shook as she wiped at her eyes. "I'm just so happy to have both of my boys back!"

Gwen blinked in confusion. "Wait, wait, I'm confused…" she turned to Thrax, who was glaring holes into his boots, then to Aaheer, studying the features he and

Thrax shared with the queen. "Oh…you're…her son," she said slowly.

"Thrax, did you not tell her?" Myana smiled but couldn't hide the hurt in her eyes. "Yes, dear, I'm Thrax's mother. I was just nineteen, younger than he is now! His father and I were both so young when he was born." Her eyes grew misty for a moment before she plastered back on a wide smile. "But the king, my…former husband was not exactly…happy with his birth. He would let him stay on the condition that Majora agreed to raise my sweet boy as her apprentice until he could be the next court wizard, like her."

Thrax grimaced each time she called him "boy" or "son."

"He and my dear Aaheer have always been close, as only brothers can be. I'm just so proud of my sons!" she grinned. "Oh, Thrax, I'm so glad you found us!"

"Of course, your majesty…" he said and looked to Aaheer, who didn't appear any more pleased than Thrax was to listen to his mother's doting. "Aaheer, if we could speak to you,"

"Of course. This way." he led them to a wall, where he pressed a plank of wood; a false panel opened to a small, separate room. He led them in and turned to the queen. "We'll return soon, mother." he closed it behind the three of them.

The room had a table covered in books, stray parchment, quills, and inkwells. Above the table was an old map of what must have been Hevaña, with a few areas circled and marked.

"Thrax, I'm sorry about her-" Aaheer began, but Thrax held up a hand to stop him.

"Don't. You know as well as I that she's always been like this." he gave him a wry smile.

"So…I need to know, how did you escape? We all took you for dead."

"Something went wrong with a transportation spell I was practicing, and I was brought to a new place."

"My bedroom, to be exact," Gwen said.

Aaheer stared in bewilderment. "Excuse me?"

"I'm not from this world. Where I'm from, we don't have wizards, royals being overthrown, or people walking around in armor. At least not anymore. The royals, I mean. Not wizards."

Aaheer looked to Thrax. "Is she jesting?"

"I'm afraid not. I know it's strange; I don't get it either. But somehow, I was brought to Gwen, and we could come back." He paused and furrowed his brow. "How-…how long has it been?"

Aaheer pursed his lips and looked away. "It takes almost a week to get here from home, yes?"

Thrax nodded.

"It's…been almost a month since you vanished."

Thrax studied his brother and his unshaven face, tired eyes lined with dark circles. Thrax gave a heavy sigh and pushed his fingertips into his eyes. "I'm sorry, Aaheer…when I was in Gwen's world, we were only there for a few moments…I had no idea I was gone for so long."

"It's not your fault. The important thing is that now we need to devise a plan. I'm also coming with you, and nothing you say will convince me otherwise." Aaheer added quickly, sticking his chin out with a determined expression.

Thrax grinned, despite himself. "Who said I was stopping you? I'd be more upset if you didn't join us. Now, tell us everything that happened. I'm afraid we're still not quite sure what's going on."

Aaheer's face fell. "It was…all so quick and strange…we had no preparation. This man had burst into the throne room and just walked up to us. He didn't say anything at first. There was something…dark about him. He said his name was Zephrus Arimas, and he was here to claim what was his."

"And what did he believe was his?"

"Revenge. For his people, against you, my father," he muttered, darkly. "He's a Gyrian. He claimed to be the son of Thrax's father, but mother still doubts it. She said she knew Zephrus Arimas as a child and that he'd never act like this. He said he wanted to take Hevaña and make it a homeland for the Gyrians."

"But what about the revenge part?" Gwen asked.

"The house of Thornblade has persecuted Gyrian travelers for decades, leaving them barely able to make a living when they come through our kingdom. Jarkus never listened to my mother or me when we tried to make him see reason." He grumbled. "It's just stupid old prejudices. No one else even cares about such things anymore. Every other neighboring kingdom welcomes them. Father had been chasing them out, creating more bloodshed and tension. He never liked them."

"How awful," Gwen whispered.

Thrax clutched his fists so tightly that his knuckles turned white. "It only got worse after I was born…his resentment grew because of me," he growled, grinding his teeth.

"Stop that." Aaheer scolded, firmly tapping the table. "My father would have done those horrible things anyways! Don't you dare blame yourself! This is his fault!" Aaheer gave his brother a stern look.

"After Zephrus told us who he was, we called Majora for her help. Before she could do anything, he attacked and killed father. She got mother and me out, but he didn't even bother following us. It was while we were running that she told us about your accident with the spell." Aaheer's shoulders slumped with exhaustion. "Majora brought us here and vanished. We haven't seen her since."

Thrax's face fell. "I'm just glad you're safe, brother."

"The only thing we can do now is to find a way to defeat Zephrus before he makes things worse and creates a full war."

"And to do that, we need allies. Do you have any possible contenders?" Thrax asked, looking over at Aaheer's desk.

He pointed to the map. "In the past, I've communicated with those living in these woods." He indicated an area far from any major towns. "Many of these areas are filled with centaurs, elves, and sometimes druids or spirits, but this land is a rest spot for many Gyrian caravans, far enough from Jarkus's wrath. They might be willing to help."

"Isn't there a faun village in these woods?" Thrax asked, pointing to the same area.

Aaheer grimaced. "Yes. They're also home to the faun prince, Astricus…someone else I am quite familiar with."

"Why do you say it like that? Is there something wrong with him?" Gwen asked.

Aaheer looked at her and went quite red. "W-well, fauns are notoriously amorous creatures by nature, but the thing with Astricus is…the prince seems to have taken quite an interest in-…"

"The faun prince is taken with Aaheer and has tried to get into his bed many times," Thrax smirked, causing Gwen to giggle.

"How sweet! You've got a crush, your highness!" she teased.

Aaheer appeared quite flustered and cried, "Thrax! That's such a blunt way to say it! And in front of a lady!"

"She knows about sex!" Thrax snickered.

Aaheer cleared his throat. "We're getting distracted, anyways. Yes, the fauns do live here, but their numbers aren't as great as the caravans, which can spread the word to their fellows, as well as townspeople, although, if we do meet Astricus and his people, it would be in our best interest to gain their allegiance as well. We also must make friends with the centaurs. They would be our strongest allies, but will not give their trust easily, unless we get the fauns on our side." he said.

"Well, even if the numbers are small, we should take what we can get. We can go find the fauns and the centaurs and the Gyrians." Gwen insisted.

"Couldn't have put it better myself." Thrax nodded.

"You also mentioned elves, right? Why don't we go ask for their help?" she asked.

Aaheer hesitated as he pondered. "Well...the wood elves have a more amicable relationship with humans...but don't care about getting involved in our affairs, if they can avoid it. Frankly, I don't blame them. The dark elves live nearer to the fauns, but they don't care for us...if we find Astricus, though, they'll probably be more likely to listen."

"Well, wouldn't that be even more reason to find the fauns? We can ask them to help us speak to the elves and the centaur, and the Gyrians. We'd be getting four sets of allies in one forest."

"I'd listen to her on this, Aaheer." Thrax raised an eyebrow at his brother.

Aaheer sighed. "Alright, we'll leave early tomorrow to find them."

"Good." Thrax nodded. "We have Midra's help as well. She'll be able to keep an eye out for us."

"Then we'd better get some sleep so we can make quick time of it," Aaheer said, and the three separated to do just that.

"The sooner we get this done, the sooner I can go home." Gwen thought.

Chapter 5

For the first time in a while, Gwen could enjoy a full meal and was given access to the bathhouse to scrub off the layer of grime she'd developed. She was even able to wash out her clothes and finally brush her freshly cleaned hair. She felt refreshed and ready to continue their adventure when she returned to their room wearing her undershirt and shorts. Orag was warm and welcoming, ensuring she had everything she needed to feel comfortable.

Again, that night, Gwen had to sleep in the same room as Thrax, though to her great distress and Thrax's amusement, they had to share a bed.

"This is every fanfiction writer's dream."

When she entered the room, she discovered Thrax sitting on the edge of the bed, glaring at his hands, muttering spells, and watching the different colored balls of magic shine softly in his hand, reflecting on his handsome features.

"Thrax?" she gently touched his shoulder.

He looked up, letting the softly crackling purple lightning dissolve from his hand. "Oh, Gwen, there you are." His voice wavered slightly as he tried to seem casual.

She sat by him, tying back her hair. "Thrax, do you mind if I ask you something? Something personal?"

"Go ahead."

"Why is your name 'Nightingale' and not 'Thornblade' or 'Arimas'?"

The small smile that had been struggling to remain on Thrax's face immediately slipped away as he heaved a heavy sigh. "Well…it's a bit of a long story…you see, in our land, names have great significance. Take Aaheer, for example; the mere name of 'Thornblade' tells all he's from the Hevañian royal family. But my name…mine tells everyone without me even saying that I'm a bastard child…someone with no wealth, status, or power because I'm illegitimate. I can only gain it through working for the king's court, say, training as a wizard's apprentice…if I hadn't been born to the queen, I'd have been left with even less. No home, no prospects, struggling for everything to survive. I'm luckier than most bastards to be born in the royal court, but it's still not a happy life…" he explained. "When I was born, the king wanted to name me 'Mockingbird' because I would live in his court as though I were one of them when I'm not."

"That's so cruel!" she gasped. "You can't help how you were born! It's not fair of them to put that on you!"

"And you are very kind for thinking so, Gwendolyn." he gave a strained smile. "But I'm afraid I don't have such luxury."

She felt her heart ache for him. "You seemed bothered by your mother's affection. Why is that? Did she not care that you were being treated so badly?"

He gave her a severe and cold look. "Would you be fond of a woman who allowed you to be named a bastard? Who gave you up? Who tries to treat you like her child when she long ago disowned you?"

"I see your point…" she scooted closer. "But…did she really want that to happen?"

He sighed, his shoulders slumping. "When I was a child, nothing told me I was different. I never questioned my parentage. I had always known Majora as my master and true mother, so there was no need to question it. I even got to play sometimes with Aaheer when we were children, and have limited time around Myana. But, when I was ten years old, I was ordered to go to the injured soldiers and practice my healing spells on them. They were kind to me, friendly, and always glad to assist me in my studies." he gave a small smile. "I liked helping people. It always made me feel useful. But on my return, I heard a group of them discussing my name and how cruel it was that I was named 'Nightingale.' Of course, I went to my master to ask what they meant."

"What did she say?"

"Nothing. She scolded me for listening to their gossip when I should have been practicing. I needed answers, so the next day, while she was in the village, I snuck into her workshop and went through her journals."

"What did you find?"

"She was there when I was born. My mother had been nineteen when she announced she was with child, but the court wasn't foolish. They knew. My mother had been married to king Jarkus for only a few days, only slept with him on their wedding night, and had clearly been pregnant since before they got married. They knew what I was. But any hint of doubt was gone when I was born. Majora wrote how when I was born, the midwives and nurses all knew I was no son of the king. My black hair, my dark skin,"

"What happened?"

"As you can imagine, the king was livid, demanding my mother cast me aside and ordered to have me killed. She refused, and Majora stepped in. She offered to take me under her wing and care for me as her child. They agreed, but when the king suggested I be named 'Mockingbird,' Majora scolded the king, yelled at him even! Can you imagine my master, the king's wizard, yelling at him as though he were a disobedient child?" He laughed.

Gwen smiled. "I would have liked to meet your master." Thrax smiled gratefully. "So, what happened then?"

83

"Well…it answered many questions. My mother had me as Aaheer's playmate and kept us close. She always tried to give me the best in everything and tried to give me the same privileges and opportunities that Aaheer had. She kept me close, making Majora take me on their long journeys. I could then understand why she did those things, but it also made me realize other things."

"Such as?"

"What I was to her…I was her son, yes, but…after I learned that…I truly noticed how she looked at me. I was her eldest son, but I was also a black smear to her name. I was a disappointment. I was the son she had with a man she, hopefully, truly loved, but I don't know that. My father is dead. My brother was the son of the man that gave her power, luxury, and affection…I couldn't give her what she wanted; I was truly a mockingbird…a bastard son, acting as though he were royal."

"It wasn't your fault. You couldn't help how you were born." Gwen insisted.

"You're right. Majora wrote in great frustration, especially about the king. She hated how he threw me aside; I was expected to live and get by without my parents. She didn't write about my mother, but I think it was because they were once good friends. But I see what I was to Myana...I was just something to admire from afar and not get her hands dirty...Queen Myana isn't my mother. Master Majora will always be my true mother in my heart and soul." He said firmly and heaved a sigh. "I'm sorry, Gwen. Listen to me; I've been prattling on for too long about my own problems."

She shook her head. "Don't be sorry. I understand. That's not something you should keep bundled up." she paused and gave a sad smile. "I don't know much about being the illegitimate son of a queen, but I have an idea of what you're going through. My mother died when I was little."

"Oh...I'm so sorry."

"Don't worry, I was too young to remember her...there's not much to miss. But sometimes I feel like my dad treats me the way you feel Myana treats you...like he can't be truly bothered with me...like he doesn't know me...I'm glad you told me, by the way. I know that stuff can be hard to talk about."

He smiled softly. "I should be thanking you for listening to all of that."

"Of course! If I'm going to be on this journey with you, I suppose it's best we get to know each other."

He nodded. After a brief pause, he said, "So, what is your full name?"

"Grace. Gwendolyn Grace"

"Gwendolyn Grace…I like that. It's very fitting for you. Very elegant." he nodded, then gave a dramatic bow. "A pleasure to meet you, lady Grace. How gracious of you to graciously join our gracious event."

Gwen snickered and punched his shoulder. "Shut up. Come on, let's get some sleep." she crawled into bed and turned her back to him.

"Good night, Gwendolyn Grace," Thrax murmured as he turned away, drifting into a dreamless sleep.

The following day, Thrax woke with a start and felt his entire face heat up. In their sleep, he and Gwen had rolled closer together in the middle of the bed. They were now facing each other, close enough for him to hear her breathing. He swallowed hard, slowly detangled from her arms, and inched out of bed, trying his best to avoid waking her.

Once up, he went to the window to see the sun, not quite peeking over the hilltops. He looked out to the mountains he had crossed numerous times, but under such circumstances, the craggy rocks seemed ominous, looming threateningly ahead.

"Thrax?"

Gwen was sitting up, rubbing the sleep from her eyes, yawning widely. "What time is it?"

"It's daybreak," he murmured, picking his clothes up off the floor. "We have to hurry. Aaheer will be waiting for us."

She lethargically rolled out of bed and stretched rather cat-like. She tugged on her clothes, brushed her lengthy hair, and twisted it into a braid.

At that moment, there was a knock. "Come in!" Gwen called, and Orag entered.

"I've been instructed to give you both this," he handed them a sack of food. "And to tell you, Aaheer will be waiting in the kitchen to leave."

Gwen smiled. "Thank you, Orag. We appreciate everything you've done."

He smiled. "Think nothing of it, my lady. I'm glad to know someone is trying to stand up for their highnesses. I'll always be loyal to her highness." he nodded firmly before leaving.

"We should get ready," Thrax said, gathering their things. "I'll go meet Aaheer."

"Wait for me!" she threw on her shoes, hurrying after him. She slung the sack of food over her shoulder, holding it tightly. The two snuck down to the kitchen to meet the young prince.

Aaheer gathered more food into a bag when they came down and beamed. "Wonderful! You're here! There's no time to waste, the fishermen have already left, and if we don't hurry, the other villagers will soon follow. We have to make a clean escape."

He swung the bags of supplies over both shoulders as Orag opened the back door of the inn where their horses waited. Aaheer secured the packs to his gelding's back while Gwen and Thrax mounted their horses, securing their bags from Orag.

"Thank you for all of your help, Orag," Gwen said, gratefully squeezing his hand.

"Any time, miss. You lot make sure to return the prince safely," he said firmly.

Aaheer smiled. "You have our word. Please make sure my mother doesn't cause too much trouble."

He bowed. "Of course, my lord. You have no worries. Now hurry, you have no time to waste!" he waved them off as they rode out to the street.

Thrax looked at his brother, who pulled a map from his belt. "East." the prince instructed, and they rode out of the village into the forest, and their journey began.

"Thrax, please, use your magic! I'm no good at this stuff!" Aaheer begged, showing an empty fishing line tied to a tree branch for a makeshift pole.

"Magic is an ancient and noble art, Aaheer! I will not insult it by using it for fishing! Wait, where's your bait?"

"…We're supposed to have bait?"

Thrax slapped his forehead in frustration. Gwen stood from her spot by the campfire. "Look, we haven't got all night! Thrax, if it'll be faster, please, try it. We need to get as much food as possible."

Thrax growled low in irritation and set his fishing pole aside. He got to his feet and held his hands over the water. "*Nath loch morn*!" A giant bubble of water levitated up, with a few fish trapped in the bubble. Thrax floated the water over the grass before letting the bubble burst, and the fish fell, flopping into the grass.

"Eat up." He said, slumping over to the fire and sulking.

Aaheer hurriedly chased after the wriggling fish to prepare their dinner.

"Thank you, Thrax," Gwen said, raising a brow at his pouting. "I know you didn't want to, but we need the food, and your magic can help us."

He looked up in irritation. "My magic isn't made for catching fish, Gwen. I've been trained as a powerful court wizard."

"Well, they say it's better to know a little of everything than all of one thing, right? You're diversifying your magic! Won't that make you a stronger wizard?"

He hesitated and relented, "I guess you're right."

"Don't look so excited about it." she rolled her eyes. "Come on, grumpy. Let's get the fish, or I'm eating your half."

"Hey! I caught them, didn't I?"

"Sulky babies don't get fish, though! So shut up, and help me with this."

That night, the trio lay under the stars, warmed by the slowly dying embers of their fire. Thrax looked at Gwen beside him, his hands tucked behind his head. "Gwen?"

She opened her eyes, rubbing them blearily. "Hm?"

"Do…do you miss your realm?"

She propped herself up on her elbow and raised an eyebrow. "Of course, I do…that was my home. My father's there and everything I know."

Thrax mimicked her position. "Are you scared of my world?"

"Well…" she hesitated. "I won't try and claim that I'm relaxed here. But, no, I wouldn't say I'm scared of it. It's kind of cool."

"That's good…" he paused before locking his gaze with hers. "You know, Gwen…you don't ever have to be afraid in this world. I'll keep you safe," he assured.

Gwen gave a small smile. "Thanks…if I'm going to be here for so long, though, I guess I should learn how to defend myself."

"I'm sure Aaheer could give you some pointers. He's a swordsman, but he might know a thing or two about using a knife. Promise you'll keep it on you, okay? You're right, you need to keep yourself safe."

She nodded. "I promise."

"Good. Let's get some sleep. Good night, Gwen."

"Good night, Thrax."

Chapter 6

The trio trudged the next day, riding over bramble and brush, wading through rivers and streams, barely stopping to rest. The sun dappled through the lush green leaves that shielded them from its harsh rays, but they still had to wipe sweat from their brows and swat at flies that buzzed in their ears.

"How much longer until we find the fauns?" Thrax called his brother.

"It'll be a little longer. It's at least a three-day ride from Bonewell. We have to keep going.

"Well, isn't this pleasant…" Thrax growled moodily, wiping his forehead again.

Gwen gave him a look. "We appreciate all you're doing to help, Aaheer." She said, glaring pointedly at Thrax. "Perhaps it's about time we stopped to eat and rest. I think some people are getting grumpy. It sounds like it's their snack time." she huffed, bringing her horse closer to the front of the group.

"Gwen, you can just say if you're getting tired." Thrax gave a devilish smirk.

Gwen whipped around to him, her lips drawn into a thin line. "Thrax, if your mind and legs were as fast as your big mouth, then we might be a little farther along by now."

Aaheer covered his mouth to hide his laughter, avoiding Thrax's harsh gaze.

After a few minutes of walking and a few more snide remarks between Gwen and Thrax, they came across a stream, well hidden by trees and brush, for them to safely make camp.

"This seems as good a place as any. We can rest the horses here." Aaheer gave his horse his head, allowing him to bend down to drink. Aaheer opened his water skin and took a few large gulps.

Gwen reached for an apple in her pack while Thrax brooded over a piece of bread. She rolled her eyes at his grumpiness and took in her surroundings. "Is it always this pretty in Hevaña?" she asked, slipping out of her sweater, so she was just in jeans and an undershirt.

"Sometimes. It's a much nicer summer than usual, I admit," Aaheer said, from the stream, as he filled his water skin. "If you think this is pretty, though, wait until you see our autumns."

"What's it like? I bet it's beautiful."

"Well, here we get lots of colorful leaves. When I was little, I used to think the leaves were on fire." Aaheer smiled fondly. "The forests are filled with bright colors as far as the mountains. My favorite is when it gets cool enough to start wearing our cloaks outside and lighting the fireplaces. I love riding during the fall, too. The air is so crisp and pleasant."

"It sounds so lovely. Autumn has always been my favorite season. I'd love to see it here, I think."

Thrax watched her for a moment before sighing heavily. He went down to the stream, where he finished his food and splashed his face. As he cupped his hands in the water, he stared at them a moment before looking at Gwen, who was forlornly staring into the stream.

Gwen gasped and sputtered as a large splash of water suddenly hit her. She looked up in shock to see Thrax laughing as he removed his boots and rolled up his trousers, running into the water.

Gwen smirked. "Oh, so that's how it's gonna be, huh?" she took off her shoes and socks and ran in, splashing Thrax, who blocked it with his magic.

"No fair! You can't use magic!" she huffed but laughed as she got closer and splashed at his face.

He backed up quickly and splashed his brother. Aaheer promptly stepped out of the line of fire, but before he could successfully escape, Thrax grabbed him and pulled him into the water. The two wrestled for a bit, their laughter mixed with Gwen's yelps and giggles. They continued to run around, kicking, and splashing at each other, before they all collapsed against the bank, laughing breathlessly.

Gwen sat up and beamed to Thrax. "Thank you…I needed that…" she stood up and returned to the camp with a happy smile.

He smiled as he watched her walk away.

"What did you start all that for?" Aaheer asked.

"Well…she just looked sad." he shrugged. "I got her into this mess, so I thought I'd try to cheer her up."

"That's awfully nice of you." A sly smirk spread across Aaheer's face.

"What, I'm not allowed to be nice?" Thrax raised an eyebrow.

"No, it's just that I don't think I've ever seen you show such interest in a woman."

"I don't know if you remember, brother, but I don't have much of a track record of successful courtships. Besides, I'm not going to try to court someone I barely know." he rolled his eyes. "Wait, who are you to talk to anyways? I don't think I've ever seen you glance toward a woman romantically."

Aaheer suddenly went pink and looked away. "I don't have time for courtship. Besides, I'd rather take the time to get to know someone before properly courting them."

"You always were more old-fashioned about such things." Thrax laid back and looked up at the sky. "I dunno. It'd be awfully nice to find someone to consider courting me."

"You'll have time to think about such things later, Thrax. Come on, enough of this. We should go back to camp."

Thrax got up, smacking dirt and grass off his clothes, and followed his brother back to warm up by the fire. Gwen was standing with her horse, trying to brush off the dust while the mare grazed.

"You seem to be feeling better, lady Gwendolyn," Aaheer noted with a pleased smile.

"A bit, yeah. I needed a moment to get my mind off things. Also, call me Gwen. You don't need to be so formal with me."

The prince's cheeks flushed a bit, but he grinned widely. "Alright, then! And you can call me Aaheer."

Thrax sighed as he pulled off his wet doublet and chemise, tossing them aside. "Much better." he lay back in the grass, basking in the firelight.

"Thrax! Have some decency!" Aaheer cried and threw his brother's shirt at him.

"What? She's already seen me without my shirt!"

"Doesn't mean I want to see those scrawny arms," Gwen smirked.

"Oh, I'm scrawny, am I? Let's wrestle then and see who the real scrawny one is." Thrax challenged.

"Thrax, you brute! You would threaten to harm a lady? And I took you for a gentleman!" Gwen batted her eyes dramatically.

"Have you ever considered the theatre? You're quite the little actress."

"My dad always said I had a flare for the dramatic." She sat cross-legged in the grass and stared into the fire for a moment. "So what do you think it'll be like when we reach the fauns?"

"Oh, they'll be perfectly kind. Fauns are rarely hostile." Aaheer waved a hand. "I don't think prince Astricus has a mean bone in his body. Although, I don't think he fully grasps things like personal boundaries. As I said before, fauns are known for being very open with their affection. This can lead to some…awkward circumstances. While Astricus is quite sweet, I think he still struggles to understand the concept of…well…personal boundaries."

"He's speaking from experience," Thrax whispered, making her giggle.

Aaheer blushed deeply and huffed. "That's enough out of you!"

"Well, it sounds like it'll be interesting either way. I'll be glad when we get there, in any case. I'm still not quite used to traveling like this. My legs are still so sore from all this riding."

"You'll get used to it over time. Besides, you seem like a strong young woman. It won't be long before you're doing things even Thrax and I can't do!" Aaheer assured her.

"Kiss ass…" Thrax grumbled, making Aaheer throw his shirt at him again.

Chapter 7

"Damn!" Gwen cursed when another fish escaped the steely trap of her makeshift fishing rod. "Not again!"

"Did another fish evade your clutches, my dear?" Thrax smirked.

Gwen glared at him. "Well, if you're so good, I'd like to see you try and catch one of these slippery little bastards!" she glowered at the water.

"Step aside, dear Gwen." he rolled up his sleeves. "I'm more than happy to set aside my pride to remind you of the many ways wizards can catch a fish."

She gave a mocking bow. "After you, your majesty."

Thrax ignored her mocking and stood by the bank's edge, his hands hovering over the water. "*Nath loch morn!*" A giant water bubble rose, revealing a small fish swimming frantically around the bubble. The thing was so small that it could barely feed one of them.

Gwen snorted with laughter. "Oh yeah, Thrax, you're quite the master! At least the ones you caught last time were bigger than the bait! What was it you said about being too good to use your magic for fishing?"

He frowned at her and the fish but brought the bubble closer to him. The fish suddenly made a desperate leap, popping the bubble and causing Thrax to yell in shock. He scrambled to catch the fish as its tail smacked him in the cheek and bounced off his chest. He threw himself forward to grab it, and they both ended up falling face-first into the muddy bank.

Gwen was hunched over, howling with laughter till she had to wipe the tears out of her eyes. "Oh yeah, a real master of fish! You should use your magic to be a master fisherman! You're already so good!"

"What's going on?" Aaheer came down to the river, staring at Gwen rolling on the ground laughing and his brother, sitting in the mud, glaring at her. "Thrax, why are you in the dirt? I thought you were helping Gwen get food."

"The fish master here thought he would teach me, the poor, lowly peasant girl, how to "properly" catch a fish!" she said through her gasps for breath.

"I still caught one, which is more than you can say!" he sniped.

"Why don't you cool down in the water, fish-boy?" she smirked. "Now, while you're trying to catch dinner, I'm going to go and try to find some food that doesn't make me think of a fish market." she brushed the grass off her clothes and walked off, still wiping the tears from her eyes.

Aaheer looked over to his brother and shook his head.

"What?"

"You're such an idiot…" he sighed and walked

back to camp.

Gwen walked around a copse of birch trees, humming

softly to herself. "Good thing dad made me go to

Girlguiding." She murmured as she knelt, examined a

cluster of mushrooms, and began gathering them after

confirming they were edible.

She suddenly paused at a large rustling sound

coming from a nearby bush. She slowly got to her feet and

turned to it. "H-hello…?" she called out softly.

In a moment, something shot out at her and scooped

her up. She screamed, dropping her mushrooms, looking up

to see the strangest man she had ever seen holding her in

his arms. He was half a head shorter than Gwen, with pretty

hazel eyes, thick long brown hair, a scruffy beard along his chin, and no clothes except for a circle of golden leaves around his neck like a necklace and a belt with a dagger around his waist. Gwen then noticed the horns poking out from his head, and when she looked down, she saw, from his navel down, he was covered in coarse brown fur and had brown furry goat legs.

"I can't believe how lucky I am!" he cried with a huge grin. "I went for a stroll and found a beautiful maid instead."

"What the hell? Let me go!" she screamed, smacking him in the chest.

The faun gave a little yelp but obeyed and let her down carefully. "My apologies, my fair maiden. I didn't mean to startle you. Why don't you come back to my village with me and join my people for a feast?" he knelt and took her hand, sweetly kissing it.

Gwen blushed and yanked her hand away. "Back off! I don't know you! Who even are you?"

"Oh, how silly of me! I haven't even introduced myself! My name is Prince Astricus. I rule the village in this part of the forest."

Her eyes widened. "Wait, you said you're Astricus?"

"Oh, you've heard of me?" he grinned, and his tail gave a little wag. "I see my reputation proceeds me!"

She suddenly shoved him back into the grass. "Shut up! Prince or not, you don't get to go around grabbing random women! That's so inappropriate! What, were you never taught to keep your hands to yourself?"

The faun stared in shock before his eyes filled with pitiful tears, and he gave a little bleat-like blubber.

"Oh, calm down with the crocodile tears! You must learn to respect boundaries and not just swoop in on people! That's how you get punched!"

The prince gave a little bleat of fear and held up his hands to cover his face as though she was going to swing at him. "Please don't hurt me, miss! I didn't mean to hurt your feelings!"

"Gwen! What's going on?" Aaheer and Thrax ran into the clearing after hearing all the noise.

"Oh, don't mind me; I just casually found our faun prince after he scared the shit out of me!" she huffed, tapping her foot while the prince blubbered pitifully.

Aaheer sighed and pinched the bridge of his nose. "Calm down, Astricus, she's not going to hurt you." he pulled Astricus to his feet and wrapped an arm around him, patting his shoulder.

He gave another pitiful bleat and hugged tightly to Aaheer, looking up at him pitifully. "Oh my dear prince Aaheer, tell the mean girl I didn't mean it! I just thought she was pretty!"

"Then say it and don't sneak up on me and grab me!" Gwen stomped her foot, her face red with frustration. "What a way to introduce yourself!"

"You rather deserved it, your highness." Thrax glowered, standing next to Gwen with his arms crossed. "This isn't exactly the first time you've nearly been pummeled for this."

"I-I'm sorry!" Astricus whimpered, still hiding behind Aaheer. "I-I didn't mean to scare anyone! I just thought she was beautiful!"

"Consider this an excellent lesson in keeping your hands to yourself, your highness." Thrax huffed. "Are you alright, Gwen?"

"I'm fine; I just got scared out of my skin." She sighed and stepped forward. "Listen, your highness, I don't want to be your enemy, but you must respect boundaries, alright? If you do, then I don't mind being friends." she held out a hand to shake his.

Astricus watched her for a moment before taking it. "I am sorry I scared you. I'm still learning about what's too far for you humans," he admitted, a bit more of his confidence returning with their truce. "So…what are you all doing out in the forest? You don't usually come without a letter of notice, prince Aaheer and I've never met you. Gwen, was it?"

"Yes. Nice to meet you."

"Astricus," Aaheer gained the faun's attention again. His little goat tail wagged gleefully at the prince speaking to him. "We came to ask for your help. I'm afraid some things have happened in Hevaña, and we need allies."

Astricus's eyes widened. "What happened? Are you alright?" His gaze quickly scanned Aaheer's body for signs of injury.

"I was wondering if we could speak somewhere more privately, actually."

"Oh! Of course, how rude of me! You three must be exhausted. Gather your things and come back with me to my village. We'll have a feast, and beds prepared for you."

"That'll be nice," Gwen murmured as they returned to camp. Once everything was gathered, they walked with Astricus, leading their horses to the village.

They walked to a cluster of bushes, trees, and hanging lichen. Astricus clambered over the foliage and pushed it aside for everyone. They shuffled awkwardly into a deep, large valley surrounded by cliffs with more trees and brush guarding the ledge. Inside the hollow was a small, bustling village of tiny, wooden houses with the clangs of blacksmiths, the chatter of families, and children's laughter. Farmers worked in small fields, and fauns gathered water from the flowing stream from a small waterfall. Animals squealed and called as they were led to the market or food. A faun woman sat between two men, giggling as they kissed her cheeks while they weaved flower garlands. Two faun men bathed their child downstream. A faun woman kissed her wife as she left to work in the small market. A male faun put his daughter on his shoulders while his wife took down the laundry with her elder daughter. An older male faun guided an elderly human woman to her home.

Thrax raised an eyebrow as he looked around, but Gwen smiled warmly. "This is beautiful, Astricus!"

"Thank you!" he puffed out his chest with pride. "We were fortunate to have found this space. It's very well hidden."

The villagers suddenly cried out when they noticed them and rushed to their prince, surrounding him. They all chattered happily as they welcomed him back, quieting and shushing as Astricus raised a hand for quiet.

"My friends, I'm pleased to return to you with a group of friends returning to our village! Prince Aaheer, his brother Thrax, and our new friend, lady Gwen! We'll be welcoming them to the village to feast and rest! Please, begin prepping our festivities immediately. I will be in my home to speak with our friends."

The fauns cheered and immediately began preparations. Once they were gone, Astricus nodded toward the largest of the homes, the door decorated in ivy vines. Two faun guards with spears bowed deeply as they entered.

Once alone, Astricus relaxed with a sigh. "Now," he motioned for them to sit on cushions that circled a small firepit in the center of the home. "Tell me what's happening."

They all sat and began to explain the story as much as possible, filling in small details for each other.

"So we came to ask for your help. We need allies, and we're going through to speak with the fauns, elves, and centaurs. Once we've gone through the forest, we'll speak to the Gyrians. We need your help. We might lose our home. And if we lose it, I worry that this man won't stop."

Astricus sat silently through the whole thing, resting his chin on his interlocked fingers. "Hmm…of all the things you were going to tell me, I wasn't expecting it to be this." he leaned back and closed his eyes thoughtfully. "I want to help; I do. But I want you to remember, please; I have to think of what's best for my people."

Aaheer's shoulders sagged, and he looked down. "I understand. I apologize. This was a lot to ask of you."

"Hold on. I didn't say I wasn't going to help. I need to think about how to act on this. Listen, the fauns work together. If I go into this, my allies will join in. The thing is, you'll have a much harder time with the elves and centaurs. They're cautious and don't like humans. You need my help to work with them. Forest creatures tend to be allies to each other to protect their homes."

Aaheer pursed his lips. "Would you be willing to come and vouch for us?"

"Well…if what you say is true, I want to ensure my friends are protected and my people by extension. Alright, I'll come help." he grinned, tail wagging wildly. "I'll leave the village to my general in the meantime."

They all breathed a sigh of relief, and Aaheer gratefully took the prince's hand. "Thank you, my friend. I swear we won't let your kindness go unnoticed."

The faun flushed and beamed. Gwen feared that it might fly off if his tail wagged any harder. "Of course! I'm more than happy to be of assistance! Here, let me try to help build a proper plan before we feast."

Chapter 8

"I think I can help guide you toward the Gyrians. I'm afraid I don't know exactly where they might be, but I have an idea of where they might be. The centaurs might be able to give us a better idea. I'll help handle them. They're far less trusting of humans."

"That would all be most helpful." Aaheer gave a grateful sigh. "Do you think we'll get there before they reach the mountains?"

"I hope so. If we don't, we won't be able to reach them at all."

"Why do we need to find them so quickly?" Gwen asked.

"The Gyrians near Hevaña have a regular trade route they take yearly. When winter comes, they go to warmer countries before the mountains are blocked with snow. If we miss them before then, we won't be able to contact them until next spring, and their help is invaluable. Especially since this wizard claims to be one of them." Aaheer explained.

"He has no right to consider himself one of them," Thrax grumbled, crossing his arms. "The Gyrians in our kingdom would never do something so awful."

"Not all of them are alike, though, brother."

Astricus looked up at Aaheer with a cautious gaze. "And you can't exactly blame them, either. After all, years of poor treatment wouldn't exactly make many want to keep the peace."

Aaheer looked down, slightly abashed by Astricus's words, and Thrax quickly jumped in. "We'll find them, though, and make it work. It'll be alright. They can't hold it against Aaheer; he just wants to help!"

"I'm not trying to claim that he would do anything unkind." Astricus quickly raised his hands and blushed, smiling flirtatiously. "Our prince would never do something like that. He's too sweet and innocent." his tail went back to wagging wildly, and Aaheer turned away, leaning to the side to try and avoid Astricus's advances.

"Keep your hands to yourself, you damn goat." Thrax snapped. "You put your hands on my brother, and I'll turn you into a fucking roast."

"So mean!" Astricus whined and leaned against Aaheer, hugging his arm. "My sweet prince, tell the mean wizard to be nice to me!"

"Please, your highness, just leave it," Aaheer begged, his whole face and neck glowing red.

"Your highness," A faun servant poked his head in, bowing deeply to Astricus. "Th-the feast is prepared, your majesty, if you still wish to have it."

The prince immediately sat up and flashed his flirty smile. "Yes, I think we will. Thank you, Demias." He stood up and walked over to the servant, kissing the corner of his mouth. "Enjoy yourself tonight."

"Thank you, your highness. Please, all of you, come enjoy." Demias squeaked before trotting away, giggling sheepishly.

They all left the hut and found the clearing filled with music and dancing fauns, tables curving slightly under the weight of the vast amounts of food. "You can all sit here with me." Astricus gestured to the table at the head of the party. They all thanked him and took their places.

"Your people seem to be doing very well, Astricus." Aaheer complimented as the faun prince took his goblet as raised it to his lips. He paused and looked at him over the rim of his cup.

"Yes…they are, thank you…the Gyrians have been very kind to us, as of late…trade has been good for them…" he murmured, peering over his goblet at him. "You've done them some good, convincing your father to let them stay in these forests."

Aaheer appeared to relax slightly. "That's excellent news…I still fear we may not be able to convince them to join our cause, though…after all the terrible things my father did, I couldn't blame them if they spat in my face and turned us away."

The group was silent for a moment before Astricus put a hand on his and smiled. "Aaheer, the Gyrians are an understanding people, and your passion will make them see how much you're trying to help them. They will be glad to accept your friendship…I promise." he gently rubbed his thumb over his knuckles, making Aaheer blush as well, but he smiled in return.

"Thank you, Astricus."

Thrax mimed vomiting into his goblet, making Gwen slap a hand to her mouth to hide her giggles.

"Now, enough of this gloomy talk!" Astricus clapped his hands. "Come now, is this a feast or not? Go enjoy yourselves!"

Gwen grinned and drank from her goblet, almost choking. "Is this wine?"

The others stared at her, slightly startled. "Y-yes, is something wrong with it?" Astricus asked, his ears drooping in worry.

"O-oh, no, i-it's fine. I don't usually drink wine, so I'm not used to it," she assured him. Her cheeks went a bit pink, and she gave an embarrassed smile.

"W-we can fetch you something different!" Astricus cried hurriedly. "You fool, Astricus! I should have asked what you would prefer to drink. I'm sorry, lady Gwendolyn!"

"Astricus, please, calm down!" she quickly reached over and grabbed his hand. "I-it's alright! I-I wasn't expecting it! It's fine!"

"Are you sure?" his brows furrowed in concern. "I can ask for them to bring you something different."

"No, really, I'm alright. Please, relax." she smiled, helping him calm down. She couldn't help but appreciate his kindness and now found him to be rather endearing, despite the rather terrible first impression he gave her.

"Are fauns always this hyperattentive?" Thrax asked with a smirk.

The faun prince blushed profusely and wrung his hands. "W-well, it's a poor representation of a village if a guest leaves us dissatisfied…it's an old tradition, but one that fauns take very seriously."

"Well, you don't need to worry about that, Astricus. I'm very grateful for your kindness. Even if you did try to basically kidnap me the second you saw me." Gwen teased.

Astricus flushed and laughed. "I believe we agreed not to bring that up!"

"Oh, you're never living that down. But you're not the only one." Gwen snickered and dove into her meal. Gwen looked around at all the fauns celebrating as they talked and ate.

Beautiful faun girls with flowers decorating their hair grinned widely and swayed to the enticing music as they served drinks and food. Fauns stomped to the sound of the drums, horns, and fiddles, dancing about with their partners, laughing, clapping with glee, their shadows dancing amongst the light of the fires that illuminated the clearing. The men and women flirted with each other at their seats or from across the clearing.

"It's a beautiful sight, isn't it?" Astricus asked.

Gwen jumped, broken from her trance. "W-what? Oh, yes, it's beautiful around here! Your people seem very happy."

He grinned. "Do you truly think so? I'm pleased to hear it! Fauns take great pride in the joy of their people and guests." he looked out to the dancing fauns, their heads thrown back with joyful song and laughter.

"Well, I can assure you, they look pleased."

"We will embrace it while we can." his warm smile slipped slightly. "The days ahead are dark in the eyes of the forest. My people stand by Aaheer and Thrax and are ready to hold back the growing storm, but I fear we may not be as much help as we need."

129

"Hey," Gwen nudged him with her shoulder. "Don't look so gloomy. As you said, this is a party. We're all in this together."

"Of course. I worry for them, is all…" he kept staring at the villagers partying.

"Of course you are! You're their prince. Aaheer's probably worried sick too. It's to be expected. It shows you're a good ruler to care so much."

"You think so?" Astricus's smile returned.

"No shit! I wouldn't say it if I didn't mean it. We're going to be alright."

"Well, if you think so, then I guess it's only right to have more hope myself." Astricus nodded and turned to talk to Thrax.

Gwen felt a pang in her heart and stared down at her plate. She couldn't deny that a part of her was lying to her new friend to comfort him. She had no idea what would happen and struggled to keep up her hopes.

The following day, the group rose with the rising sun, sitting around a large map.

"Alright, so we're here," Astricus pointed a little from Bonewell. "And the centaur camp will be around here this time of year." He dragged his finger across the deepest part of the forest to a stretch of plains. "Like the Gyrians, the centaurs travel cyclically. They don't go as far, so we should have plenty of time to catch up with them."

"Excellent. Where is the elf kingdom?" Aaheer leaned closer to study the map.

"Well, that all depends. Which group would you rather speak with?"

"Which would you suggest?" Thrax raised an eyebrow.

"I," he dragged his finger along the map to the center of the forest depth. "Would go here to the dark elf kingdom. If we cut through the forest here, we'll be able to cross their path directly without taking so much time. While we're speaking to the centaurs, they can visit the wood elves over here." he pointed to a much further part of the forest, closer to a northern mountain range.

"Dark elves?" Thrax scrunched his nose at the suggestion. "How do we know we can trust them? It's tough to even get to their kingdom, and they've never been big fans of ours."

Astricus shot him a stern look that made the wizard jump. "I would keep your mouth shut and be grateful for any allies you can get. Dark elves are no worse than any other race. Well, except high elves, but that's a whole separate beast." Astricus rolled his eyes and waved his hand dismissively. "Don't be so flippant at the prospect of allies just because of what others claim about them. Old prejudices are not known to last with them. Now, crossing through here is it's not necessarily easy," he explained, tracing his finger along the map.

"Well, then, why don't we go around?" Thrax huffed, crossing his arms.

Gwen rolled her eyes. "Were you not listening? We can't go around, because the dark elves are in the forest, dummy."

"Exactly, Gwen. The path is not an easy one, and in fact, will take a long while. But, with a wizard on our side," Astricus gestured to Thrax, who puffed his chest out a bit. "And with my knowledge of the forest will be much easier and faster than any path around the forest."

Aaheer's brow furrowed as he studied the map. "Um…Astricus, I don't mean to question your judgment, but…doesn't this path lead us directly into-…."

"The Eternal Night." he nodded in confirmation.

"What's the Eternal Night?" Gwen asked, leaning closer to see.

"It's an ancient part of the forest filled with ancient magic. It's the heart of our forest. It's so old and thick that the trees block out the sun, and keeps it in eternal darkness. That's how it got its name."

"And," Thrax butted in with a growl. "It's extremely dangerous! I'd rather take the extra time to travel to the wood elves!"

Astricus's cheeks flushed as sparks of anger flew between their gazes. "And I said we'll be fine with your magic and my knowledge! The Night isn't dangerous as long as you respect it. But I suppose respect is too much to ask of *you*."

"What? What the hell did you say to me, you damn goat?" Thrax stood up, sparks of electricity dancing from his fingertips.

"Sit down and shut up you two!" Gwen snapped, yanking Thrax back on his butt.

"Ow! What the hell?"

"I said shut up!" The wizard went quiet under her scolding. "Look, if we're going to do this, we need to find the best way, and this seems to be that way! We have to trust that Astricus knows what he's doing. So, let's shut up and do what we need to do!"

"Who are you to talk?" Thrax jumped back up, towering over the shorter girl. "You don't know a thing about our world! You don't know how things work here!"

Gwen's face went bright red. She jumped up and stepped closer with her face in Thrax's, despite being a head shorter. He even stepped back a little at her furious glare.

"And whose fault is that, Thrax, that I'm in a world I know nothing about? You were the one who got me involved, so you're just going to have to deal with me! I have a say in this now, thanks to you!"

Thrax scoffed. "What's so great about your world anyways? Just look at what happened after I was sent to your world! It seems like your world is bad luck!"

Gwen's face was so red that the others thought steam might come out of her ears. "It may not have been like this place. We may not have magic, elves, or whatever, but it was *my* world, and I was relatively okay with it! But now I'm here, having to deal with an absolute man-child while trying to figure out how the flying *fuck* I'm going to survive this whole mess so I can go home!" she screamed so loudly that even Thrax seemed small when up against her rage. "It's *your* fault I'm here, Thrax Nightingale, so you're just going to have to deal with me! I will not just sit here and let you make every decision for me!"

A cruel smirk spread across Thrax's face. "As a matter of fact, princess, I don't have to take this at all. I could leave you in the middle of the woods to starve! And if you keep running your mouth like that, I might do that!"

Everyone stared in open-mouthed horror at him. The room was so silent that you could hear a pin drop. Tears filled Gwen's eyes as she swung out and smacked Thrax in the face with a sharp slap.

"Go to hell, Thrax Nightingale!" she screamed before storming out of Astricus's house. "Bastard!" She shrieked.

"Did you see that?" Thrax cried, holding his cheek. "She slapped me!"

"And it serves you right, you absolute ass!"

Aaheer's face was also flushed, glaring at his brother. "I'm ashamed of you, brother! How could you say such a thing? Gwen's right. *You* are the reason she's in this mess! This is all on you!"

"What? I didn't force her to come along!"

"But you were the one who took her from her home! What, is she supposed to sit around? She doesn't have anywhere else to go, Thrax! Of course, she's going to come with us, and of course she's going to have thoughts about what's happening." Aaheer stood up in a huff. "If Gwen hadn't done it, I would have slapped you myself. I thought you were smarter than this, brother. I don't even want to think about how disappointed Majora would be if she could see you now."

Thrax's mouth fell open as his brother ran out after Gwen. He gritted his teeth and glared over at Astricus. "What, nothing to say, goat?"

Astricus sat with his arms crossed, glaring up at him. "I have nothing to say that hasn't already been said. I don't even want to look at you." The faun got up and shoved Thrax out of his way. "While we talk to lady Gwen, you can sit here and think about what you've just said. Pray she forgives you."

Thrax glared at Astricus's back before scoffing again. He paced back and forth, holding his cheek. "Pray she forgives me…she should apologize to *me*!" He stood still and grumbled. "It's your fault I'm here, Thrax," he said in a falsetto, rolling his eyes. "Give me a break. Was I supposed to just stay there?"

He stood there, tapping his foot and stewing over his thoughts. As the minutes passed, he realized they weren't coming back. He felt his bravado deflate a bit and stepped back toward the map. Not a single spot on the map was something he thought might be remotely familiar to Gwen or her world.

"She really is all alone," he thought. *"And it's my fault."*

Gwen hiccupped as she wiped her eyes, trying to slow her tears.

"It's alright to cry, Gwen," Astricus hugged her, stroking her hair gently. "What Thrax said was awful."

"Absolutely." Aaheer held one of her hands comfortingly in his. "I'm truly ashamed of him. He had no right to speak to you that way."

"Thank you…" she croaked and hiccupped again. "I'm sorry for the trouble. He's right, in a way, really. I don't know what to do right now. I'm so scared and confused. I'm useless to you all. I guess that's what made me so mad at him."

"Stop that right now!" the faun prince hugged her tightly. "Don't you dare let him start getting in your head! You aren't trouble, and you aren't useless. You're in a new place you don't know, helping in a fight for people you don't know. You have more kindness and generosity for that than most people do in their left finger." he beamed, wiggling his pointer finger at her.

Gwen sniffed and gave a small giggle, then hiccupped again. "Thank you, you two…you're sweet to check on me, even when we've just met."

"Think nothing of it." Aaheer tenderly wiped her tears. "Things like this can make people fast friends. Even if we weren't, I wouldn't be able to bear leaving you alone when you're upset like this."

"Isn't he sweet?" Astricus cooed.

"Not the time, goat," Thrax grumbled as he approached. The three of them all turned and glared up at him.

"What do you want?" Gwen muttered, her voice thick from all her crying.

Thrax rubbed the back of his neck and looked down at his boots. "I…I want to talk to you. Alone."

"After what you just did? Fat chance!" Astricus stuck out his tongue.

"It's alright, boys," Gwen assured them and stood up, though her glare didn't simmer. "I want to hear what he has to say."

"If you're sure, Gwen. We'll be nearby if you need us." Aaheer took Astricus's hand and walked away, ignoring the faun's gleeful little bleats.

"So." Gwen crossed her arms and lifted her chin defiantly. "What do you want?"

"I…want to apologize," Thrax admitted, still looking down. "Those two were right. What I said was…horrible. I haven't treated you fairly at all. I'm ashamed of myself, and so should everyone else be. I even called you a friend, but I haven't treated you the way I should."

"Well, at least you're aware of that."

He gave a weak chuckle. "Yeah…and you were right, Gwen. This is my fault. It's my fault you're here. It's my fault you're involved. It's my fault you can't get back home. It's not your fault that I fell through your wardrobe; I wouldn't have ended up there if I had never tried that stupid spell. More importantly, if I hadn't been so selfish, you'd be safe back in your home right now. You'd be with your family and friends, in a more familiar place. I'm…truly sorry. Of course, you don't have to accept my apology, but I couldn't keep lying to myself. I was wrong."

Gwen's lip trembled as she gave another hearty sniff, wiping her eyes with the back of her hand. She suddenly reached out and held the cuff of Thrax's sleeve. "Would…you really consider abandoning me?"

The wizard's cheeks flushed, and he gently put his hand over hers. "No…and I'm sorry I ever said I would. I'm the reason you're here, so it's my responsibility to keep you safe. And if I ever forget that," he finally met her gaze and gave an apologetic smile. "You can slap the shit out of me again."

Gwen gave one more hiccup before finally smiling. "I'm going to hold you to that, Thrax Nightingale."

"I still have a lot to learn…and I hope we can continue to learn and work together as friends."

"I do too. Let's make a deal, you teach me how things work here and how to fight, and I'll teach you not to be an ass." she giggled.

Thrax's grin grew. "Deal. Be warned, though, I've been told I'm a problem student." he winked, making her laugh again.

The night air was warm as stars twinkled and crickets sang harmoniously with the musicians' songs. The fire and wine made Gwen's cheeks turn bright pink.

"How's the wine, Gwen?" Astricus called down to her.

"It's good! I'm getting used to it!" she giggled and looked out at the fauns dancing to the music. "They all look so pretty…I wish I could dance like that."

"Well, why don't you?" Aaheer raised an eyebrow.

"Oh, no, I've never been a good dancer!" she insisted quickly, waving her hand dismissively. "My friends always said I had two left feet and was never good at finding my footing. Besides, I'd probably find some way to mess up their fun."

The group was startled by Thrax putting down his goblet with a thunk and giving an exaggerated sigh. He stood up and held his hand out to her, not meeting her gaze. "Alright, princess, come on. On your feet."

"W-what?" Gwen pulled her hands close to her chest and leaned back.

"Look, you asked me to help you learn how things work here, right?"

"Y-yeah…"

"Well, here's your first lesson. Have a little more confidence in yourself, and enjoy yourself. You and I can both use the practice."

"Well…I-I don't know…"

"It's alright; I understand if you're too scared." He shrugged and smirked.

"What? Who'd be scared about going up against you in a dancing match?" a competitive fire lit up in Gwen's eyes.

"Well, prove me wrong, then." he held his hand out with a lopsided smile. "Come on. I'm tipsy enough to go out there and dance. Show me what you've got."

Gwen paused and stared at his hand before accepting it. The two joined the crowd, twirling and twisting their bodies, smiling, and laughing from across the circle of dancers. Neither of them was particularly good, but they'd drank enough that they didn't seem to care.

"At least they're getting along." Aaheer nodded.

"They do seem cute together." Astricus agreed. "Maybe they'll both be good influences for each other."

"Let's hope they can keep from arguing long enough." Aaheer's mouth twitched into a smirk.

Chapter 9

The morning was dim and cloudy with thick, gray clouds. Everyone packed in silence before making their way out. The group was greeted the following day with a silent parade. The fauns lined quietly outside Astricus' home, forming a path to the outskirts of the village.

Astricus sheathed a dagger in his belt and turned to the others. "Are we all ready?" His face was long and gloomy. Everyone agreed they were ready. "Very well. I'll lead you through the woods. Be warned, however. They can be dark and treacherous. We will probably need to rely on your magic at some point, Thrax."

He nodded and shifted his pack higher on his shoulder. "Just don't get us lost, goat."

Thrax rolled his eyes. "Come on. We should start heading out and get the horses."

Astricus looked over. "Horses? You won't be needing them where we're going. The land's not suited for them. The path is too small and easy for them to trip over the roots and twist a leg. We need to continue on foot. Besides, I can't exactly ride a horse." He said, tapping his cloven hooves together.

Thrax glowered. "You must be jesting. Is there truly no other way?"

"There are, but this way is the quickest and most well-hidden. Zephrus' men won't find you here, trust me. It's suicide in there without a guide." He explained.

"Then what do we do with the horses?" He asked through slightly gritted teeth.

"Have them released, of course. I had my fauns go and fetch them from your camp." He gestured to three of the fauns, who brought the horses stripped of their bridles, saddles, and supplies. "I had one of our scholars find an old spell that can create more space inside this satchel while it retains its shape." He took one of their satchels and a book from a faun, who handed it to Thrax. "We have no druids or wizards to cast the spell, so I'm afraid we must ask you to do it."

Thrax rolled his eyes and took the book. "Very well." He opened it and held out a hand, reading. "*Meithal tur yenä!*" A warm, swirling light twisted out from his hand and spun toward the satchel. The light encased the bag and seemed to soak into the leather.

Thrax took the bag and knotted it to his belt. "Alright." He rolled his eyes. "Let's go."

Astricus gave a triumphant little grin and nodded to the three fauns, who all released the horses and patted them off. They all galloped away, and Gwen heard Thrax sigh heavily.

She looked back to the villagers, whom all had tears in their eyes as they waved goodbye to Astricus silently, almost as though they were mourning. When Gwen looked at Astricus, his eyes were burning red as he fought back the large tears forming in his eyes, but he continued to smile and wave to his people.

Gwen gave the faun a kind smile and gently pulled him closer to the group. He returned it gratefully and trotted up to Aaheer's side, looping his arm through his. This time, though, Aaheer didn't try to pull away.

As the village fell out of sight, they returned to the river where they had camped before to ensure they had plenty of supplies. Gwen and Aaheer made sure their supplies were organized and they had plenty of food, while Thrax caught a few more fish, and Astricus ensured the water was filled. Once they returned, they all hoisted their packs and set off.

151

"So where do we go first?" Thrax asked.

"We head west. Centaurs put much stock behind the sun's strength, so they often camp in the direction it sets." Astricus explained.

"Why is that?" Gwen asked.

"Well, the west tends to be associated with fire. So, the centaurs follow the sun," he explained. "They sit in the west, opposite fauns, who sit in the east. There's no particular reason for it; it just so happens that in our forest, that's how things have worked out. It's to our benefit, however. It ensures the forest is protected from all sides. Add in the elves, and this forest is certainly one of the better-protected ones in Hevaña."

"Tell me more about the centaurs." Gwen insisted.

"The centaurs are powerful warriors and blacksmiths. Fire is very symbolic to them. Fire fuels the forges and their "warrior's spirit" or something like that.

It's a source of pride, too. Centaur royalty is often given a phoenix hatchling as a gift and symbol of their royal status. Remember how I said they tend to go west mainly? Well, phoenixes can sometimes only be found towards the west of certain areas. Fire's a big deal for them."

"Some also say their reverence of fire has become an internal part of them," Aaheer said. "Centaurs are very proud and can be rather aggressive. You wouldn't want to anger a centaur. They often have many weapons on their person and are certainly not afraid to use them. Although," he gave a small smile to Astricus. "I also wouldn't turn my back on an angry faun. Those horns can smart something awful."

The faun grinned, giggling softly as he blushed and his tail wagged furiously.

"How long will it take us to find the centaurs, Astricus?" Thrax called from up ahead.

"No less than a fortnight, but I expect it will still be quite a few days. The centaurs hide well. Very few are welcomed amongst them. We'd better be prepared for a long walk. Even with the shortcut, it will still be a long journey."

Chapter 10

"We should turn in for the night," Thrax said as the moon began to climb, peaking over the trees.

Since the group had started their journey that morning, the forest had grown quite thick. The trees were gathering closer together, and the leaves became so thick that the branches had begun to weave across each other. It was becoming harder to see, with sunlight struggling to break through the canopy of leaves. Though the sun was only now out of the sky, it had been darker for far longer as the light failed to pierce the leaves.

The group set their stuff out, and Thrax stood straight. "I'm going to find some wood."

"Wait!" Astricus cried quickly, grabbing his cloak. "You can't cut anything down!"

Thrax stared in astonishment. "Why the hell not, faun?" he scoffed, sharply tugging his cloak from his hands.

"You already know I mentioned the fauns protect the forest, but that's because we protect the outside, so nothing harms the inside. The deeper we go into this forest, the more alive it becomes. If you harm this forest, it will kill you and anyone else with you. An innocent human girl, a human prince, even a faun prince." Thrax's face blanched.

"You must gather what has already fallen or is already dead. Dead tree wood often lies around to make room for what is still living."

"O-okay…th-thanks for telling me," Thrax hesitated before going further into the woods, creating a little green fire in his hand to light his way.

"Is that true, Astricus? Is the forest really alive?" Gwen asked.

"All too true." he nodded solemnly. "I've seen the forest's vengeance take down many who doubted its power. This place is a powerful magic force. It's wise to respect it as such."

"Do the centaurs also protect it?"

"Very much so. They protect the outer forest just as much as the fauns do. The forest leaves trees that are alive but not quite, so the centaurs can create weapons and power their forges."

"What do you mean "not quite living"?"

"They are living, growing trees, but they have no magical force. They are normal trees."

"You mentioned the dark elves as well. They would protect the center of the forest, then?"

"Yes. They live in its heart, the Eternal Night. The elves have more magic than fauns or centaurs, so most know how to use at least runes to produce it, if not their abilities. The forest serves the elves with all they need as a thank you for protection."

"What do you mean?"

"The forest allows them to hunt or to use sick or dying trees as wood. The forest may even do more drastic things like divert a stream or grow medicinal plants around their village."

"How does it do that?"

"Don't know. We've never been told, as far as I'm aware. The dark elves might know, but it's a secret they're unlikely to share. Either way, I know that somehow, this forest has potent magic, and you do not try to mess about with it."

"If it's so dark, how will we know when we've found the elves?"

"Well, usually, they would find you. Any wanderers tend to be snatched up by them and based on their intent, they are either returned or…" Astricus gulped and looked away. "Used to feed their hounds."

"Oh,"

"Don't let him scare you too much, Gwen," Aaheer assured her. "The dark elves are also very kind and understanding. They know that sometimes people get lost accidentally or are curious about the forest. They're not monsters." He chuckled as though the thought was a little joke.

Thrax ended their conversation as he returned with armfuls of sticks and logs. "I was a bit surprised," he admitted as he dropped the wood and began building a fire. "I wasn't expecting to find so much dead wood."

159

"The forest helps those who respect it," Astricus smirked and nodded sagely.

"Yeah, I guess I should have listened. *Mithas simo laúdas*." Thrax lit the wood with green fire. The flames turned golden when they hit the wood and grew into a beautiful fire. "I remember master Majora telling me about magical forests, but I've never visited one. There are many across the country, especially around the border. They're a natural border protection. The forest houses fauns, centaurs, nymphs, or dryads, though those last two are more common in the spring and summer. There are also fairies, though those aren't as fun, and elves, of course. Sometimes you can even find the occasional siren in the rivers or lakes. We were going to visit the Black Forest one day, Majora and I. It's a range further east. I…suppose it'll be a while now, though, before we do that."

Thrax skewered some fish on a stick, handing one to each of them, and held it over the fire. "Astricus, are there not also forest druids? I remember a coven lived in the forest not far from the city."

"Forest druids have been gone for many years, so I doubt that what you saw was actual druids. I'd be surprised if there were any left at all. They used to be their protectors and sometimes even worshipped the forests. Our forests do not need druids, in any case. We have our own strength as protectors, and the magic within it is what we truly need. As more creatures fill forests to protect them, fewer druids are needed. I think, by now, they've just…left." the faun prince shrugged. "There might be a few more out there, but they're certainly not in Hevaña."

"How do you all know so much about this?" Gwen asked, finally.

161

"Faun princes are raised to know this sort of information. It is our duty to our village and the forest we reside in to know all we can to protect it."

"And human princes are raised to know as much as possible and interact with other rulers. Spending so much time with Astricus taught me about some of the forest's magic." Aaheer added.

"I've learned some forest magic myself," Thrax said, putting his hands to the ground, murmuring something, and revealing a single flower blooming from where he'd put his hands. Gwen gasped and grinned with excitement, making Thrax smile as well. "But I would have to become a forest druid to learn it all."

"I still think it's wonderful," Gwen said, making his cheeks go pink.

Astricus and Aaheer exchanged glances and smirked knowingly.

"So how exactly do we find the elves, Astricus?" she asked.

"Well, we're heading west, which will take us toward the forest's center. Because it's such a magical force, the forest will be able to lead us, as long as we-"

"Respect it?" Thrax repeated.

"Exactly! You're catching on, now. Fauns have learned to read the forest, but we must still be careful. We could still easily become lost, especially if the forest didn't want us to keep going."

"Then we'll just have to make sure we don't become lost," he said, checking his fish.

"I suppose it shouldn't be too hard when you put it like that." Gwen agreed. "If all it takes is respecting the forest and following the signs that Astricus reads."

"It's easier said than done, though." Astricus quickly jumped in. "The forest is only willing to help so much, and it's still hard to tell sometimes in such darkness. We need to make sure to remain vigilant and be careful."

"He's right. We should get plenty of sleep after we eat to cover as much ground as possible tomorrow." Aaheer said.

The group agreed, and after eating, they all stretched out and fell asleep, except Gwen. She couldn't help but remain awake, her mind swirling with the flood of information she'd received. She tucked one of the rolled-up blankets under her head as a pillow and looked up into the vast night sky. Even with the winding branches, Gwen could make out the enormous kaleidoscope of stars across a deep blue and purple sky and even what seemed to be a bat fluttering by.

"Can't sleep?"

She jumped slightly and looked over to Thrax, who was propped up on his elbow.

She shook her head. "You?"

"Well, I was, but my dreams woke me…" he admitted.

"About your half-brother?" she asked.

There was a long pause before he answered, "Yes."

"Do you want to talk about it?"

He shook his head. "No…I-…I want to know about your world…where does your king live?"

"We don't have a king," Gwen said. "Well…not really. There are some still around, but they don't have power."

"Really…? No king…?" He seemed almost hopeful at the thought.

"You didn't like king Jarkus, did you?" she asked.

"No, I didn't," he said firmly. "I loathe him. He's cruel and cold and deserves his punishment. I never felt any

165

love for him. When I heard what happened, I didn't care about his life, but I feared for Aaheer's,"

"You two are very close?"

"Yes, sort of…I know my mother wanted us to be closer, though…she didn't love the king but loved my brother and me."

"But you don't care for your mother," she said.

"I-…have a complicated relationship with her…I would miss her, but she frustrates me. There are many things I wish she did differently,"

"I understand…I feel the same about my father, sometimes."

"Tell me more about your world," he insisted. "You mentioned you don't have warriors?"

"Well, we have soldiers. But they no longer fight with swords, axes, or arrows. When you learn to use those things, it's usually for fun. Like falconry. Do you lot have that?"

"Yes, Aaheer and I both raised falcons."

"Well, our soldiers now fight with tanks, guns, and computers. We still have navies with ships and cannons, but they're metal, not wood."

"What are those things?"

"A tank is sort of a big metal shell with a gun. There are wheels on it to make it roll, and it can cross over lots of land. Guns are these sorts of metal sticks that shoot bullets. They're sort of like tiny cannonballs. I guess you could call a gun a handheld cannon. But they shoot much quicker than a cannon. Computers are…well, I'm not very good with them, so I don't know if I can explain them very well. You use it to…write things and look up stuff. Like a book, but without paper. There's a board with letters you press to make words, and the words show up on what's called a screen and show you what's happening."

"Fascinating…" he murmured, with genuine intrigue. "Do you not have books in your world?"

"Oh, we have plenty of books. Lots of libraries, and whole shops full of them. I love reading."

Thrax grinned. "I do too…I could spend all day reading…what about animals?"

"We have normal ones like you, cats, dogs, wolves, deer, rabbits, all that sort. But we don't have centaurs or fauns or druids. We call that fantasy. To our world, that's stuff you make up."

"Your world sounds so interesting."

"It's really not…it's quite boring compared to yours."

Thrax went quiet before saying, "Do…do you miss your home?"

"Well..." Gwen paused for a moment. "I will admit, I miss my father, but...there are only some things I miss."

"I'm afraid I've been horrible to you," he sighed. "I've forced you to a strange world that you never wanted to go to and have put you in a dangerous situation that you have nothing to do with...you must think terribly of me."

"Thrax, while I do admit I don't appreciate being snatched from my home," her eyes twinkled teasingly. "I don't think poorly of you. Though you've been stubborn, snarky, and a right prat, I don't think you're a bad person. I just...wish you'd be a bit kinder, I guess."

"I can't promise I won't stumble, but I will do right by you."

"Good. Or I'll insult you to death," she smirked.

"Your viper tongue knows no bounds!" he laughed, gripping his chest like he'd been shot. He smiled gratefully and rested his hand on hers. "I know I'll need your help, and I'm very grateful to have you by my side…besides, who else will pick at you if not I?" He teased.

She smirked and lightly shoved him. "Ass."

He flopped onto his back, snickering. "Before you return home, I would like to give you a chance to tour our country. When we're not under threat of war, of course."

"I think I would like that very much." She yawned and curled up under her blanket.

Thrax tucked himself in and looked over at her. "Thank you, Gwen…for everything,"

The group rose early when the sun was beginning to rise. Though it was hard to see, stretches of sunlight still peeked between the tree trunks, gleaming into their eyes.

Everyone stretched, rubbing sleep from their eyes. They ate a quick breakfast of berries and bread in silence.

"Let's head out. Lead the way, Astricus." Aaheer said, slinging his pack over his shoulder.

Astricus nodded and rose, brushing the dirt from his fur. "I will warn you," He noted as they began walking, clambering over roots, and ducking under limbs. "There will come the point where the forest is so large and tangled; we will need you to stand at the head, Thrax. You're the only one with magic, and we need it to light the way."

"Wonderful…" Thrax muttered.

The group was silent as they followed Astricus. Gwen looked around as the wind made the leaves rustle and strange animal calls echoed through the woods.

The further they went into the forest, the darker it became. Soon, the sun couldn't even peek between the tree trunks.

"This is the Eternal Night…we need your magic, Thrax," Astricus said.

Thrax swallowed and stepped forward with Gwen.

"*Míthas simo laúdas…*" A large emerald-green flame burst to life in his hand while he held hers with his other.

"We must stay close. If we get separated, we may be lost here forever." Astricus said, stepping closer to them.

Gwen gripped Thrax's hand and pressed close to his side. The last thing she wanted was to get lost.

Slowly, the group made their way through the forest, clambering over tree roots and feeling carefully around the trees.

"How long until we're there?" Thrax asked.

"I'm…not sure…it'll be more than a day, but no one ever truly knows…you don't know how time passes in the Eternal Night."

"Even more excellent," Thrax held his little handful of fire higher over their heads. He screwed his face up in concentration, and it blazed even stronger, lighting their paths. "There…let's get going so we can get out of here faster…everyone, stay close."

The four pressed into a single line, grasping hands, squinting into the forest's darkness. They all clambered over winding, black roots nearly reaching their knees, and trees swayed in a breeze that didn't reach the forest floor. The rustling of the leaves felt like angry whispers as the adventurers passed by.

"They see us," Astricus whispered.

"Who?" Gwen whispered back, feeling her heart leap in her chest as she scanned the trees.

"The trees…they see Thrax's fire…they don't like it. They won't hurt us if we stay out of their way, though."

"Why are they angry…?" Gwen asked, her voice quivering slightly.

"These trees are the most magical parts of the forest," Astricus gazed up toward the black, rustling leaves.

"They sense the fire and the magic from it. It's a risk of danger."

"Will they attack us…?"

"Not unless we attack first."

"At least we have that much, right…?" she tried to steady her voice.

"Well, yes, but we need to make sure we keep on their good side…" he explained. "We can't be waving it around."

"Will you two stop chattering like magpies?" Thrax hissed. "It's hard enough to get through here without you two making so much noise and making it harder!"

Gwen quickly closed her mouth. "Sorry…"

"Perhaps," Aaheer said. "This is a good sign that we should take a rest."

"Perhaps you're right." Thrax knelt and dug into the ground with a knife. He dug out a circle filled with markings and curves.

"What's that, Thrax?" Gwen peered over his shoulder, squinting in the fire's dim light.

"Runic magic. So we don't have to search for firewood and risk getting lost. I don't use it much because it takes so much energy, and it's quite difficult." Thrax put his hand over the rune and lifted the other that held the fire. "*Togál nke ignis.*" The rune glowed green, and the fire grew in size and light. Thrax pulled his hand away, slowly, leaving the flame suspended in the air. He stepped back, leaving the fire crackling brightly over the rune. "It should last us a while. Come on, let's rest a bit."

They all sat around the fire and stared into the green flames for a moment. The silence hung over them all before Aaheer finally broke the silence.

175

"I hope we find the elves soon."

"It shouldn't be long. If anything, they might find us before we find them." Astricus assured.

"How do we know we've found them?" Gwen piped up.

"It's sort of hard to explain, but just know that when we get there, you'll know."

"No offense, goat, but that doesn't exactly tell us what we need to know." Thrax huffed, tearing at a strip of goat jerky. "And it doesn't really make sense."

"Well, that's how I can explain it," Astricus growled. "Perhaps you shouldn't complain about your allies so much."

"You're not my ally; you're a horny sycophant chasing after my brother because he asked for your help, and you couldn't resist."

Astricus's face went dark red, even in the green firelight.

"Thrax!" Gwen snapped, jabbing his shoulder. "Don't you remember what we talked about last night?"

Thrax's cheeks went pink, and he choked slightly on his jerky. "I-…w-well, th-that was a private conversation between just us." he insisted, looking away. The two princes exchanged confused looks.

"You promised me you'd be kinder. I'm also asking you to apply that to your brother and Astricus. They're in this with us. Astricus left his village to help us! He's putting a lot at risk. We should all show some gratitude for that."

Thrax shrank into himself, avoiding everyone's gaze as Gwen scolded him.

Astricus smirked while trying to hold back his laughter. "Aw, that's so sweet of you, Thrax! I didn't think you cared so much or were self-aware of how you acted like an ass."

"Shut up!" Thrax's face went even brighter as he chucked a twig into the flames.

"Be nice, both of you!" Aaheer insisted.

"Astricus, if I'm going to ask Thrax to be kinder, I'm going to ask you to try not to antagonize him." Gwen pointed to him, making the goat wilt slightly at being scolded.

"I'm sorry."

"Good, now, let's all try to take five minutes to relax and come to terms with the fact we're going to have to put up with each other for a while now."

Thrax and Astricus grumbled slightly and laid down to close their eyes. Meanwhile, Gwen sat with her knees hugging her chest, staring into the dancing green flames of Thrax's fire.

"Isn't it beautiful…?" Aaheer asked, making Gwen jump slightly.

"Yeah…it is…" she murmured. "Do you ever wish you could do magic too?"

"Often…I remember how jealous I was of Thrax when we were kids." he chuckled. "I still am…he always had more freedom than I did…I wish I could be like him in many ways,"

"I think he'd say the same about you." Gwen pointed out.

"Probably. I don't blame him for that, but he doesn't get how hard it is to be a prince…he'll never know how difficult it is having to convince everyone I'm not like my father, that I'm here to help them, that I won't do what he did…I wish I could leave this accursed name behind."

"I'm sure Thrax wishes he could have a name in the first place."

Aaheer paused, tearing his gaze from the fire to look at Gwen. "You're right…I never did quite understand why Thrax was so angry at my parents. I only truly thought about how hard it was for me, not him. I'm angry at my parents too…especially my father. I don't like talking about how he was around Thrax. If he caused any trouble, my father would have brutally beaten him…and I didn't want-…" he paused and pursed his lips.

"You didn't want anything to happen to him?"

"Yes…I love my brother very much. We still have much to learn about each other, but we're each other's greatest allies…what about you, Gwen? What about your family back home?"

"Well…I don't think I have many allies back home. It's just dad and me. Dad tries his best, but-…well, he tries his best." She rested her chin on her knees and looked back into the flames. "We don't have my mother anymore to balance things out. He's just sort of…there. We can't even talk to each other because there's nothing to discuss. We're more like roommates than a family…he just doesn't listen."

"I think I understand." Aaheer leaned forward. "My relationship with our mother is very similar. She wants the best for us but so often misses the mark. I still love her dearly, and though he's loath to admit it, I'm sure Thrax does too."

Gwen grinned slightly. "I think you're quite right." she looked at his sleeping form. "He's so stubborn…but I know you're right…" she hesitated before reaching over to push a strand of his raven-black hair out of his face. He stirred slightly but didn't open his eyes.

Aaheer watched before standing up. "Let's get the toddlers up. We need to move before it gets much later."

"I'm awake." Astricus opened his eyes and sat up.

"Ah, so you were listening to us, then." Aaheer huffed, cheeks pink.

"I wasn't trying to," the faun insisted, his face solemn. "But if I got up or tried to warn you, I would have interrupted you. I…don't get to hear you open up like that often…" he looked down as he wrung his hands, his cheeks pink.

Aaheer looked away with a sigh. "It's… alright. Just warn us next time."

Gwen smiled softly and shook her head before poking Thrax's cheek. "Wake up, sleepyhead. We need to move. Got elves to find."

Thrax groaned and slowly opened his eyes. He rubbed the sleep out as he sat up. "You couldn't have given me a few more minutes?" he croaked. Even in the green light, Gwen could see the bags under his eyes.

"Sorry," she took his hand and stood up. "I'm afraid that's not up to me. Come on. You'll be able to get more sleep in a bit. Once we find them."

Chapter 11

The four had no idea how much time had passed since their last rest. With no sign of where the sun was in the sky, they could not tell how far into the day or night it was. Somehow, the forest had become even darker, to the point where without Thrax's fire, none of them could see their own hands in front of their faces.

"Astricus, are you sure this is correct? I fear we may never get out if we keep traveling in this." Aaheer whispered.

"I'm certain."

"Is…anyone else weirded out by the fact we haven't seen any animals yet?" Gwen whimpered.

"Oh…they're out there," Astricus answered ominously. "Just because you can't see them doesn't mean they don't see you."

"Thanks for the encouragement, buddy."

"Shut up, all of you." Thrax hissed, stopping suddenly.

Gwen squeaked as she walked into his back. "What the hell, Thrax?"

"I said, shut up!"

Gwen peeked around his back to see what he was looking at, considering that they couldn't make out anything in the thick blackness. Ahead of them was a faint, glowing light.

"What…is that?"

"I don't know…everyone, stay close." he carefully approached the light, keeping the fire close to him in case the forest saw them as too threatening.

They soon realized the light wasn't coming from an animal or another creature but from the plants.

"Since when could plants glow? What are these?" Gwen asked, reaching out to touch a large fern whose leaves glowed soft blue. The light where her fingers touched turned into a bright sky-blue color.

Astricus broke into a huge grin. "This, my friends, is the land of the dark elves. Welcome to the heart of the Eternal Night."

"It's beautiful," Aaheer looked up at the thick black trees that housed long, purple-glowing vines that brushed the tops of their heads. Strange birds with glowing golden marks and long, sea-foam green tails hopped between the vines, chittering and fluttering their wings at each other.

Enormous pink and purple plants quivered slightly as they passed. Little white bugs zipped and flittered from plant to plant. The trees rustled as they whispered, some leaves blinking gold, blue, and purple. The moss and grass glowed a faint teal with each step they took. When Thrax extinguished his fire, the world around them seemed to shine brighter. Swirling and twisting details revealed themselves on the colorful plants, and more small wildflowers showed their faces while distant creatures' glowing, multicolored eyes peeked between the brush to see them.

"This is…amazing…" Thrax gazed around in awe.

"Isn't it? I've only seen this thrice now. Each time is just as beautiful as the last." Astricus beamed as he spun around to take in everything.

"How big is it here?" Gwen asked.

"Not sure. It must be quite large, in any case. The dark elves have a sizeable kingdom and need space to hunt and farm, so it isn't a small territory. We'll run into them soon enough, I'm sure."

"How do we find them?"

"Oh, once we're in their territory, you don't find them. They find you."

"Come again?" Gwen raised an eyebrow.

"Calm down, Gwen. You look like, I mean, they're going to kill us or something." Astricus gave a little giggle. "They'll get the news from the forest first and will be led to us. Trust me; if the forest didn't want us to reach them, it would have ensured we didn't."

"Wow. You weren't kidding when you said it had powerful magic."

"So, how do we get their attention, then?" Thrax asked.

"Well…why don't we ask it? If the forest can alert the elves, couldn't we ask it to let them know we're here?" Gwen inquired.

"You know," Astricus's ears twitched. "I've never actually tried that. Usually, the elves sort of…show up. Maybe it'll help them get here sooner."

"Talking to a tree? Ridiculous." Thrax rolled his eyes.

"More ridiculous than being spoken to by a tree?" Aaheer quipped.

Gwen ignored them and stepped away. She pushed through some of the brush to the thick trunk of a black tree. She leaned against the trunk and held one of the glowing purple vines in her hands, running her thumb along the blue petals of a flower on its stem.

"Um…hello." she began awkwardly. "I'm…sorry to disturb you, but…well, my friends and I need help. We're looking for the dark elves, you see. But we don't know where to go. If you could…like…let them know we're here, that'd be very kind of you." Gwen explained.

189

"Bad people are trying to take over Hevaña. We need help stopping them. Would you please let the dark elves know we're here to speak with them?"

The boys fell silent as they watched her. The vine swayed slightly in her hand, and the trees began to rustle. The rustling sound became distant, and the area was quiet, aside from the sound of the animals.

"Did it work?" she asked.

"Suppose it did. I've never actually spoken to the trees here. They might be discussing it amongst themselves. I can't quite tell." Astricus explained.

"What do you mean?"

"Many forest creatures can understand the trees, but in the Eternal Night, it's completely different. Like another language. Come on, let's keep going. It's too pretty just to stand around."

This time their walk became more of a stroll. Gwen looped her arm through Astricus's while he explained different plants and animals to her, intermittently telling stories of his time visiting the dark elves. She listened in reverence.

"How long does it take trees to talk to someone?" Thrax asked.

Astricus and Gwen looked back with scolding looks. "In their own time, Thrax. They'll get here when they get here. If you're so tired, why don't we rest a moment?"

"Maybe that's a good idea since someone is being a grumpy goose." Gwen stuck her tongue out at him.

"How are you going to tell me to be nice when you're calling me a goose?" Thrax grunted.

"Maybe if we wait, it'll be easier for the elves to find us?" Aaheer asked.

191

Astricus opened his mouth to answer before pausing. His ears went up and swiveled around before he smiled. "No need! I hear them!" he pointed toward the forest. The three stared into the dim woods and soon heard the soft thump of hooves.

A group of deer marked with glowing paint appeared from the brush with dark elves on their backs. The group had gray skin with long, pointed ears poking out of their hair. The man in the lead was beaming, showing off pointy teeth. He walked his deer toward them and hopped off. He was built like a bear; broad shoulders, wide chest, and arms like tree limbs. He had a thick beard that went to his collarbone, tied-back shoulder-length dark brown hair, and red eyes.

"I see we have new travel guests. Welcome, friends." he bowed his head respectfully. "I'm captain Gunnalf. We were told that we had allies here to greet us."

192

The four all bowed, and Aaheer stepped forward. "Captain, my name is-…"

"Prince Aaheer. Yes, we were told your names." Gunnalf gave a soft chuckle. "Welcome to the heart of the forest. We will take you to our village to meet our leader if you accompany us. We weren't told why, but the forest told us you need our help, yes?"

"Yes, thank you." Aaheer practically melted with relief at their friendliness.

Gunnalf took his deer's reins and ordered the others in elvish. The four all followed the elves into the forest. Some birds gave loud squawks as they flapped overhead to nearby branches. Little golden birds sat in rows, watching them all walk by. They shook their feathers to reveal snowy-white ones beneath their wings. The group walked between black trees and managed not to run into enormous orange and yellow flowers almost as big as the deer. The

193

moss was now glowing sky-blue, and a hyena-like chittering was following them, the source hidden in shadows.

"Alosrin," Gunnalf motioned toward one of the elves. "Light our way, please. The black dogs are trying to interfere."

The elf nodded and muttered a spell, creating a ball of fire like Thrax's. The creatures around them hissed and their chitters faded away into the blackness.

"Much better. Our path will be much smoother now." Gunnalf motioned them all forward. Gwen yelped as she felt wetness on her feet and looked down at the black creek they had reached.

"Oh, I'm sorry. I forgot to mention that." Gunnalf chuckled and held his hand out to Gwen. She gratefully took it. The rest of the party was also lifted onto deer, though Astricus seemed less thrilled. He clung awkwardly to the rider and looked at the deer warily.

They waded down the creek before stepping through a row of thick trees and to an enormous tree in the center of a vast clearing. The tree stretched so high that they couldn't even make out the shape of its top branches. Silvery glowing vines snaked up the trunk and hung from its lower branches where enormous screeching birds perched or long-limbed creatures like monkeys climbed to pluck what seemed to be fruit from the tree. Surrounding the tree was the village, guarded by rows of trees and brush, lit by the glowing moss, plants, and mushrooms. The homes were covered tents where children darted in and out, squealing gleefully. Merchants sat on woven rugs, advertising wares on their mats or satchels. Weavers worked at their looms, mixing colorful, glowing threads to form their clothes. Blacksmiths worked by the vast central fire, pounding metal into weapons. A small herd of deer grazed in their enclosure, brushed down by their caretakers or laying in the grass while goats and chickens climbed over them.

"How beautiful!" Gwen beamed.

"I'm glad you think so!" Gunnalf nodded, trotting their deer toward the largest tent. "Now, you must meet our leader. Her name is Ethera, the Dark Mistress."

"Why is she called that?" Gwen asked.

"The Dark Mistress or Master are called that because they are our direct line to the forest. It speaks to all of us somehow, but if something is wrong or needs to be done, the forest sends the orders directly to Ethera," he explained. "Don't let the name frighten you. It's just supposed to be symbolic."

"I think it's cool. Makes it seem spooky." Gwen giggled.

They dismounted the deer, and Gunnalf motioned for them to follow him. He entered the tent and immediately bowed. "My mistress, I have brought the travelers." He hurriedly motioned for them to bow as well, and they obeyed.

"Please, Gunnalf, relax. You don't need to speak so formally. Stand, all of you." A woman said. Her voice was warm and friendly, with a smile to match. Her face was narrow with sharp features; almond-shaped red eyes, dark gray skin, snow-white hair, pulled back into a braid, and long pointed ears decorated with little gold hoops. She was dressed head-to-toe in black armor with two blades holstered at her waist. "Welcome, friends. I'm Ethera. It's an honor to meet you."

"You as well, my lady." Aaheer stood straight. "I am-…"

"I know who you are, Prince Aaheer Thornblade of Hevaña. I know who all of you are. The forest has told me. Come, sit." she motioned to a set of cushions surrounding a fire. "Gunnalf, be a dear and bring us wine."

"Yes, my lady." The soldier bowed and left the tent while they all sat.

"Now, I understand you came for our help. Tell me, what do you need of my little village?"

Aaheer heaved a heavy sigh. "Well, I'm afraid it's a long story." he went into the full detail of Zephrus's attack, his escape with his mother, reuniting with Thrax, and their journey to that point. "…so you see, we're trying to build up our army to take Zephrus down. With my father's death, I believe Hevaña can become something great, but with Zephrus attempting to take our territory, I fear what he may do to those that live in our lands."

"I see. This is certainly a lot to take in." Ethera took a long drink of her wine as she pondered. "Tell me; you have the elves and the fauns. Where do you intend to go now?"

"We are heading west to find the centaurs, following the last known path of the Gyrians. We'll catch them if we're lucky before the mountains snow. I sent word to some nearby villages before I left. They will likely answer our command."

"Hmm…" she leaned back with arms crossed over her chest. "Well…I suppose if the forest sent you to us, it believes there is something worth fighting for. That means something to us. We will help you. You will be provided a place to rest before you continue your journey."

The four looked at each other. "I-…don't mean to sound ungrateful, my lady, but I wasn't expecting you to agree so soon. A war like this is not easy to come to terms with."

"You're right, and I can't claim to be enthusiastic about the idea. But our people rely on the forest for everything. Its magic hasn't failed us for centuries. I'm sure you know that you wouldn't even be here if you were deemed a threat. If our forest trusts you, I will as well. Please don't make me regret that decision." She had a severely stern expression as she spoke. "I'm putting a lot of faith in your little group."

Aaheer swallowed. "Thank you, mistress. I don't intend to do anything to betray that trust."

"Good. Now, Gunnalf will lead you to your tents. Rest well, and we will wake you in the morning."

"How do you know when the morning is?" Gwen asked.

"The Chu-Chu birds return from their hunts at sunrise and leave at sunset. They're not exactly quiet birds." She smiled before waving them off.

Gwen grinned as she followed her friends, grasping Thrax's sleeve. "This place is so cool!"

"You think everywhere we go is 'cool.'" Thrax teased.

"Because it's nothing like where I'm from! I've only read about places like these!" She tilted her head to watch the animals jump between the trees. She was so enraptured that Thrax had to hold her arm to move her from running into people.

"A fair assessment. I also haven't ever been to a place like this. I suppose it is charming."

"Oh, look at that!" Gwen stooped to pluck a flower from the ground. It had enormous star-shaped glowing turquoise and lavender petals. She held it up to Thrax and tucked it into Thrax's ponytail. "You look so pretty!"

Before pulling the flower from his hair, Thrax relented a smile and even a chuckle. "I think it'd look much lovelier on you." He tucked the flower into the side of Gwen's braid, tucking back a strand of her blonde hair. "Yes. Much lovelier on you."

Gwen suddenly felt glad that he couldn't see the blush that had broken across her face. "W-we should follow them…" she murmured and scurried to Astricus, linking her arm with his.

Gunnalf led them to a pair of small tents by the large fire and motioned them to enter. "I'm afraid these aren't going to provide much space, but they should still bring you comfort. Sleep well, my friends."

Gwen sighed but smiled as she ducked into the tent. There was a mattress with a woven blanket across it and pillows. "It seems the universe is doing all it can to have us sleep in the same bed." She raised an eyebrow at Thrax. "You haven't somehow used your magic for this, have you?" she teased.

"Perhaps the forest is trying to play matchmaker." Thrax winked as he shed his pack, kicked off his boots, and rolled onto the mattress. "Please, lady Gwen, just come to bed. I'm too exhausted to keep teasing you."

"Well, I'm not, but I'll be nice." She removed her shoes and carefully placed her flower in one to keep it safe before dropping her pack and curling up on the bed, her back to Thrax.

He peeked over her shoulder to study the flower before looking at her. He hesitantly reached out to tuck that lock of hair back before pulling his hand back and shaking his head. "Good night, my lady. Sweet dreams," he murmured and blew her a kiss she couldn't see. He laid on his back and stared up at the tent. He suddenly felt an ache in his chest that he couldn't quite explain. It made him wish that he could talk to the others.

Thrax tossed and turned through the night. He couldn't remember his dreams, only what they made him feel. He felt pain and terror like he had never experienced before. Loneliness so dark and gaping he thought he might drown in it. It was like he was a child again, alone in his tower with no one to speak to or comfort him. For the third time that night, he woke with a sharp gasp, sitting straight up. His face was slick with sweat. He growled to himself and got up, throwing open the tent flaps. He wandered through the woods until the village's light was just a pinprick amidst the glowing foliage.

With a huff, he sat on the moss, watching little bugs zip from one plant to the other while birds swooped between branches, chittering at each other or pausing to pluck out pinfeathers.

"Thrax!"

He turned to see his brother pushing through the brush. His face was sweating, and he was breathing heavily.

"There you are! What the hell were you thinking?"

"What are you doing out here?"

"Looking for you, of course! You woke Gwen, and we couldn't find you anywhere! We thought you got lost or worse! I can't believe you'd go wandering off like that. You don't know your way around!"

"What were you so worried about? I'm fine. I can take care of myself."

"Gwen was looking all over the village for you. We wouldn't have even known you were gone if it wasn't for her waking us. We should get back before she starts tearing the forest apart to find you."

"Oh, that's it, is it? Gods forbid we make Gwen worry. Of course, she's the one to let you all know where I am."

"What are you on about?"

"Would you be out here looking for me if Gwen hadn't been so worried?"

"Why would you say that? Of course, I would."

"Oh really?" Thrax stood up quickly, making Aaheer step back. "Where I see it, all you and that damn goat do is worry for her. Even the other night, Astricus was happy to make as much fun of me as he could until Gwen shut him up. He listens to Gwen even more than he listens to you. And don't get me started on you always with the "lady Gwen" shit. You both listen to her like she's the final say in everything."

"Thrax, how could you talk about her like that? She wouldn't even be here if it weren't for you. It's more than right we make sure she's okay with what's happening."

"Yes, that's right! Blame me! That's what everyone does. *I* ruined the royal marriage! *I* ruined my father's life. *I* ruined Zephrus's life. *I* ruined Gwen's life! I ruin everything, don't I? No wonder I have no fucking family, right? Because I ruin everything, so who gives a fuck about Thrax Nightingale!"

"What is your problem? I care! I'm your brother, Thrax!"

"Brother." Thrax spat the word like venom. "Some good brothers do me. At least you and Zephrus had a father. At least you have a mother! I have no one! No one cares about-!" He was stopped by Aaheer slamming his fist into the side of his face.

"How fucking dare you?" Aaheer screamed, his eyes turning red as he swung at him. "I've *always* tried to be there for you! Do you think I wanted that monster as my father? Do you think I was much better off? You act like Myana, and I were frolicking through flower fields holding hands, right? Well, guess what? I could barely even speak to her!" Angry tears welled up as Aaheer lunged at him.

Thrax grabbed his wrists, but Aaheer grabbed his shirt collar and yanked him to the ground. The two wrestled until Thrax was on top, trying to pin him down, but Aaheer still writhed and swung at him, trying to move his legs to kick him in the groin.

"We were under my bastard father's thumb until he was murdered! I may not know what it was like for you to grow up as you did, but I have *always* been your brother, Thrax! So don't talk to me about not caring!"

"Thrax! Aaheer!" Gwen, Astricus, and Gunnalf burst into the clearing. Gunnalf pried Thrax off Aaheer while Astricus wrapped his arms around the prince's middle, trying to pull him back.

Thrax pushed Gunnalf's arms to break free. "Then why were you never around?" He shrieked.

"Because he would have fucking killed you, you dumbass little melodramatic bitch!"

"I don't care! Most of our lives would have been better off without me here!"

"Thrax!" Gwen cried, grasping his arm as tears formed in her eyes.

"Shut up! Just shut up! Shut the fuck up! Why the hell would you think I want to live in a world without my older brother?"

"Because I couldn't even be a brother to you!" Tears began to fall down his face freely. "I wanted so badly to be a brother to you! I never felt like you *could* care that much because I never got to be around! Sure, we care about each other and are allies, but I don't even feel like I can really call you my brother because I don't have the right to!"

Everyone stood still. Aaheer finally pulled Astricus's arms off of him and walked toward Gunnalf. He made the elf let go of Thrax, and Aaheer shoved him hard before stepping back. "You are so stupid, Thrax. Of course, you're my brother. And if I have to spend the rest of our lives reminding you of that, so be it. I'm not going anywhere. I want to have you in my life."

Thrax rubbed his chest and looked away. "Why?"

Aaheer gave a hint of a smile. "If Jarkus thought something was bad, it must have been pretty damn good, right?"

A smile tugged at Thrax's lips as he scoffed. "Damn straight." He finally turned and hugged his little brother. "I'm sorry…for what I said. I want to be in your life, too."

"Good. You wouldn't be able to get rid of me anyways."

When the brothers let go of each other, everyone walked back. Astricus held onto Aaheer's arm, whispering to him. From how Aaheer patted the faun's arm, Thrax figured he was trying to calm him down. He looked behind him and saw Gwen lingering back. She was staring at her shoes and hugging her arms. Thrax drifted back to walk beside her.

"Are you alright?"

She didn't answer. Thrax didn't press her. They got to the village, and Thrax gave Aaheer another tight hug before they separated into their tents. Gwen was still silent as she crawled into bed, her back to Thrax. He sat beside her and rested his hand on her shoulder.

"Gwen…what's wrong? Talk to me."

"Why would you say that?" her voice was choked.

"What?"

"Why would you think we'd be better off without you?"

He jerked his hand back like she was suddenly made of fire. "I-…Gwen, you're in a totally different place because of me. You're stuck in a war. My father is dead because of me, and my mother is…well, was stuck in a loveless marriage while my brother…" he paused for a moment like he had a sudden realization. "My brother had no one beside him. I just thought…"

"Well, you thought wrong!" Gwen turned to him with a trembling lip and fat tears rolling down her cheeks. "We all care about you, Thrax! We want you to have support and be loved and feel cared for! I thought I made you feel cared for. I thought we were friends! Even if it meant I couldn't go home, I thought at least I had a friend."

"Gwen…I'm so sorry…I didn't even think-…"

"You've got that right." She turned away again, crossing her arms over her chest.

Thrax pulled her close to his chest, wrapping his arms around her waist. "You're right…I was stupid. You've had my back in all this as much as my brother has. But I haven't had the chance to appreciate that truly. I honestly don't know where I'd be without you two. I…don't have anyone else but you two. You've…become my biggest support. Even with all the trouble I've caused. Thank you, Gwen. Thank you for supporting me and caring for me. I will do what I can to return your kindness tenfold." He turned her chin to kiss her cheek before wiping her face dry.

213

Gwen threw her arms around Thrax with a hearty sniff, burying her face in his chest. "Don't you ever repeat such awful things, Thrax Nightingale."

Thrax sighed as he laid back, holding her close. "Wouldn't dream of it, Gwendolyn Grace."

They lay there in silence, with Thrax petting her hair. When she finally grew quiet and began breathing steadily, he slowly and carefully untangled himself from her arms, cursing as he had to work a lock of his hair from her iron grip. He finally pulled away and carefully tugged the blanket to her chin, tucking it around her. He lay in his bed, serenaded by the distant chirps of birds and the reassuring sounds of Gwen sleeping peacefully; Thrax felt his body fully relax. He stared back up at the tent, and this time, instead of the feeling of gaping loneliness, his heart felt light and warm. Like he finally had something more than "principle" to fight for.

Chapter 12

Thrax's eyes snapped open as horrible shrieking cries ripped through the sky.

"Wuzzat?" Gwen sat up and held up her fists like she was ready to start punching.

"That," Gunnalf poked his head in with a mischievous grin. "Would be the dulcet tones of the Chu-Chu birds. Come, friends, have your breakfast before you set off."

"Still think this place is so beautiful?" Thrax grumbled as he yanked his boots on.

"Nothing is beautiful to me so early," Gwen whined and rolled out of bed. Ensuring her back was blocking Thrax's view, she took the still-glowing flower and tucked it into her pack before carefully pulling it on. "I hope it doesn't take us much longer to get out."

215

"Good morning, you two!" Astricus was beaming widely, little tail wagging.

"Not so loud, will you, goat?" Thrax scowled, rubbing his eyes as the faun sat next to Aaheer.

"Gunnalf was kind enough to get us breakfast." Aaheer smiled, sipping from a small cup.

"It's just a cornmeal mush and coffee, I'm afraid, but it's better than nothing." He chuckled.

"It's still very nice of you." Aaheer insisted, offering a bowl to his brother.

"Aye, it's better than nothing." Thrax shrugged and took a bite. He shrugged again and took a cup of coffee. Gwen took her meal but choked on her sip of coffee.

"Gwen! Are you alright?" Astricus cried as Thrax thumped her on the back.

"I-I'm fine!" she croaked, eyes watering. "I-I just don't usually drink it black."

"I'm afraid it's all we can offer." Gunnalf gave a sympathetic smile. "We don't have much sugar or sweets."

Once breakfast was finished, Gunnalf and his guards led them out of the heart of the forest into the blackness of the Eternal Night. "Continue heading this way. The forest will lead you out eventually. Stay safe, my friends. If you find yourself lost, ask the forest for aid."

"Thank you for everything, Gunnalf." Aaheer shook the general's hand. "Give our thanks to Ethera."

"Gladly. Safe travels, friends!" He waved before they all disappeared amongst the foliage.

"Well, I'm afraid we won't have such a delightful time from here on." Aaheer sighed as they all took each other's hands and walked carefully through the forest.

"Let's just hope we get out soon," Thrax muttered, raising a handful of green flames.

After another full day of traveling, the adventurers finally reached the end of the Eternal Night. Sunlight was slowly breaking through the dense cloud of leaves, burning their eyes as they adjusted to the light.

As Gwen was reintroduced to the sun's warm glow, a soft breeze like a whisper glided through the forest, making the leaves dance around her feet. "These trees seem more welcoming than in the Eternal Night." She pointed out to Astricus.

"Of course. The trees of the Eternal Night are one of the forest's greatest protectors." He beamed to the trees, patting their trunks. "We'd be lost without its magic."

"Hey, goat," Thrax looked back. "Are you gonna stop jabbering like a crow and get us to these centaurs?"

"Oh! Of course!" he trotted up to the front of the group.

"You're sure you know where you're going, right?" Thrax raised an eyebrow, making Astricus scoff.

"Of course I do! We're through safely, aren't we?" Astricus gave him an irritated scowl.

"I'm merely checking." Thrax gave him a look. "You're such a flighty thing. I had to make sure your brain was still in your thick skull."

"How dare you!" his face began to turn red. "Listen here, wizard, there is absolutely nothing that tells me I have to be polite to you other than the kindness in my heart! So, I'd watch your tongue if I were you!"

"If I were you, faun," he sneered. "I wouldn't be so quick to challenge a wizard." His hands clenched into fists, and Gwen noticed sparks forming around his fingers.

"Alright, that's enough!" Aaheer stepped in and pushed the two apart. Gwen approached Thrax and pulled him back closer to her. "Listen, you two, we've all been traveling for a long time and are tired, so let's take a breather and keep going."

Astricus's eyes suddenly lit up. "I know! I'll sing to calm things down!" he cried enthusiastically. "Fauns are known for their musical skills!" He began to lead the group, belting out in his warbling, bleating voice,

"Oooooooo!

Old faun king Fredrick had a fair love!

Hoo-rah hey! Hoo-rah ho!

A fair human princess with golden hair!

Hoo-rah hey! Hoo-rah ho!

The princess's father hid her away!

Hoo-rah hey! Hoo-rah ho!

To be married to the wizard, Feridai!

Hoo-rah hey! Hoo-rah ho!"

Gwen held onto Thrax's arm as he glared at Astricus. "If I have to hear that goat bleat for much longer, I will kill him."

"Come on, Thrax," Gwen lightly shook his arm, trying to encourage him. "It's not so bad. I'd rather have him singing than you two fighting."

He looked down at her. "How can you keep trying to see the best in situations like this, Gwen? Astricus's singing is enough to turn any man toward murder."

"Well, I suppose it starts with getting kidnapped by a mysterious wizard and taken to a mysterious world where you find out you're not sure if you can get back, then everything else seems rather casual, honestly." she gave a sly grin.

"Are you ever going to let up on that?"

"Nope, don't think I will." her grin widened. "It's far more fun to pick at you, anyways."

221

"Well, I suppose the damn goat isn't bad as long as I have you to keep me company."

Gwen felt her cheeks grow pink, quickly recomposing herself. "Thrax Nightingale, are you flirting with me, you great pervert?"

"Oh no, dear Gwen, if I were truly flirting with you," he pulled her hand up to his lips and pressed a kiss to it, gazing at her through hooded emerald-green eyes. "You would know it,"

Gwen felt her throat go dry, suddenly unable to find a way to respond, her whole face going pink.

"Oi, you two, are you done flirting over there? We have places to go!" Astricus called from the top of a hill.

Thrax held Gwen's gaze for another moment before he followed his brother and Astricus. "You know, Aaheer, I'm feeling rather peckish. Fancy trying some goat leg? I hear it's delicious when roasted just right."

Astricus bleated fearfully and clung to Aaheer. "You won't let your mean big brother cook me, will you, my sweet prince?"

"Perhaps make a greater effort to play nice, and I might not need to protect you." His lips twitched in a playful smile as they kept walking.

Gwen pressed a hand to her chest, feeling her pounding heart, then down to the hand that Thrax had kissed. It felt like her skin was tingling where he'd touched it. She quickly shook herself and ran after the group, his powerful look still seared in her mind's eye.

"And the fair lady decides to join us." Thrax gave a sly grin.

She did not look him directly in the eye, hoping he wouldn't notice how flushed he'd made her. "Did you think of that all on your own?"

223

Aaheer and Astricus snorted loudly. "I knew there was a reason I liked her," Astricus said.

"You are a wit, lady Gwendolyn," Thrax smirked as he passed her, leaning closer. "If it's wit you want, consider this a war, my lady," he whispered in her ear, his breath tickling the hair on the back of her neck.

Gwen felt her breath catch in her chest as she quickly turned to him. His green eyes danced with mischief as his lips turned up in a crooked smirk. She swelled up to retort but couldn't think of anything, so she quickly walked toward Astricus and Aaheer, pretending she didn't hear Thrax's low chuckle.

"That was quite a display for one with no romantic interest in someone." Aaheer pointed out as he and Thrax bathed in the river where they'd stopped for the night.

Thrax scoffed quietly. "I don't know what you mean, brother."

"Oh, I was merely imagining you kissing Gwen's hand and whispering in her ear earlier today?" The prince raised a knowing eyebrow at his brother.

"What Gwen and I do is none of your concern," he said, turning away from him as he dipped his head back to wash his hair. "We were speaking of private matters."

Aaheer scoffed. "Oh, private matters indeed…look, I am not judging you, brother. Lady Gwendolyn is a beautiful girl. Though, as you know, she is not the person I would court-."

"Aaheer, you *don't* court. I've never seen you show interest in a woman and barely so with men." Thrax chuckled. "Honestly, sometimes I wonder if my baby brother will ever marry."

"Perhaps I will. But you already know I have no time for some of the nonsense that comes with marriage, let alone courting. I've just never felt romantically towards anyone."

"You do seem to need to take your time." Thrax agreed, stepping out of the river and drying his body with a towel. "And I say good on you for it. I imagine it'll save you a lot of unnecessary heartaches, and there's no harm in going at one's own pace."

Aaheer joined his brother on the riverbank and took the towel from him. "You're avoiding the point at hand, brother."

"What point is there to make? Gwendolyn and I weren't flirting. There's no romance between us. Even so, I don't have time for nonsense like love at a time like this. The safety of the kingdom is more important. Finding the centaurs, finding master Majora, finding out who the hell this bastard really is, and getting him out of our kingdom and you at your rightful place." Thrax pointed out, pulling his hair back, and dressing.

"That may be true for the time being. But this will also change many things, Thrax. Perhaps it's about time you finally start living for yourself rather than how others want you to live." Aaheer raised an eyebrow at his brother before fixing his crown back on his head and joining the others at camp.

Thrax felt his face grow hot. "What does he know? Gwen doesn't belong here with us and our troubles. Once this whole mess blows over, I'm sure she'll be clawing to get back to her realm and away from us." He tossed his cloak onto his arm and trudged his way up the bank to camp.

"So how much longer until we reach these centaurs, Astricus?" Gwen asked as Thrax reappeared.

"We should find them tomorrow. I will have to warn you; the centaurs are a very proud and wary people. I will meet them when we get close to their herd and signal you to follow. It's far safer for them to see a familiar face, and my village has excellent standing with the royal family. You will need to stay out of sight during that time. They would see you as threats, and trust me when I say you do *not* want to go against a centaur. They begin training their children when they're old enough to leave their mother's breasts, boys and girls. They often carry many weapons with them and seldom miss their shots. They can catch a squirrel a league away." Astricus warned. "So, if you see any of them while I'm gone, stay hidden, or there could be serious trouble."

Gwen nodded hesitantly. "Are all centaurs so vicious…?"

"Oh, no, not vicious!" Astricus shook his head. "They're just incredibly protective of their people. But once you befriend a centaur, they're your friend for life."

"I think that's enough storytelling, faun," Thrax said and sat on his bedding. "The sooner we wake, the sooner we find them."

Astricus huffed. "Are you always so moody? Sometimes I can barely believe you're Aaheer's brother."

The following day, the group rose with the sun, following Astricus across plains and trees. "We're getting close to the herd," Astricus said. They had approached a large open meadow and were hiding along the edge of a copse of trees. "You lot stay here. I'll be back. Stay out of sight." The faun ordered sternly before racing across the meadow as fast as his goat legs could carry him.

Everyone sat in silence, interrupted only by the wind on the plains. "I hope he hurries up…I hate just sitting here…" Thrax grumbled.

"Enough of your mutterings, Thrax," Aaheer said shortly. "We should be grateful that Astricus can help us in the first place. Imagine how much harder this would be if he weren't here."

"Imagine how much more peace we'd have…" he countered with an eye roll.

Gwen sighed before spotting a large, orange bird burst from the trees across the meadow. "Look! What bird is that?"

The boys both turned to look where she pointed, and Aaheer gasped while Thrax leaped to his feet. "It's a phoenix." The wizard murmured. "I've never seen one this close before…it's beautiful."

"Aaheer," Gwen pulled him back beside her. "Didn't you say that phoenixes were given to centaur royalty? Could that phoenix belong to a member of their royal family?"

Aaheer grinned. "If we keep watching, we'll get that answer."

Not moments later, a large party of centaurs burst from the woods, led by a tall, beautiful centauress with a chestnut-colored horse's half and a black tail, while from the waist up, she had dark brown skin and tight ringlets of jet-black hair, blowing freely in the wind. Her face was painted with black war paint. She wore a gold circlet set with a ruby, a gold armband, rings, and a collar necklace. She had a leather gauntlet on her arm that, when she stretched it out, her phoenix swooped around and landed on it. She had weapons strapped around her middle, holding daggers, swords, and an axe. The rest of her party had a similar number of weapons. The ones towards the back had rabbits, smaller birds, and even a fox and deer tied to their waists.

"That must be the princess," Aaheer whispered.

"Some use Astricus is…he probably ran right past her," Thrax grumbled and stepped closer to get a better look.

"Thrax, no!" Gwen hissed. "Astricus said stay put!"

The phoenix on the princess's arm looked directly toward their hiding spot and shrieked, flashing his wings and taking off. The princess turned her attention to the trees and yelled at her hunting party, following the bird.

"Fuck!" Thrax gasped.

"We need to run!" Gwen grabbed the boys, trying to pull them into the woods.

"It's too late; we can't outrun them!" Aaheer cried as the centaurs all thundered to them and circled the group, pointing arrows and swords at them.

"Well, well, well," The princess stepped forward, glaring down at them. Up close, they could see the fierce glint of her hazel eyes. "Looks like we have a couple of trespassers."

"Please, my lady, we mean you no harm!" Aaheer quickly held up his hands in defense.

"Silence!" Growled the largest centaur in her hunting party. "How dare you speak so candidly to the princess?" He stomped a hoof almost as big as a dinner plate, drawing his bow more tightly. Thrax quickly moved Gwen and Aaheer behind him, raising his hands.

"What are you doing in our territory?" The princess demanded.

"We're just passing through, honest!" Gwen cried, clinging to Thrax's cloak, pressing her face against his back.

"You know our friend, please, just wait-!"

"I don't take orders from little humans like you!" The princess roared. "Tell me why you're here, or you get skewered!"

"Back off!" Thrax warned, sparks of lightning flickering in his hands. "We're not here for a fight!"

"It sure doesn't seem like it!" Another centaur growled.

"Wait! Hold your fire!" Astricus cried, scrambling from the meadow, tripping over his hooves, and getting between Thrax and the princess.

"Astricus? What on earth are you doing here?" She asked, her eyes widening in surprise.

"Princess Dyael, these are my friends, Thrax Nightingale, Gwendolyn Grace, and Prince Aaheer Thornblade. We're here to ask for your help."

Dyael's eyes widened as she held her hand up. "Drop your weapons! These are our friends!" She then turned to the others. "Why didn't you say so?"

Thrax scowled. "We tried…" He grumbled and got a sharp jab in the ribs from Aaheer to silence him.

"Come along, then." Dyael waved to her hunting party, who quickly moved behind the group so they could follow the centaur princess. "I'll take you back to the rest of the herd to speak to my father."

"Thank you, dear friend," Astricus said as he walked next to her.

"You know I love your company as much as any, Astricus, but what brings you so far from your village? It's not typical for you to seek out the centaurs except when something is deeply wrong."

"Well, I'm afraid something *is* wrong, princess." He explained. "There's an evil in the continent. A wizard has attacked Hevaña, overthrown the king, and is threatening the safety of us all."

"I don't understand. Why does the happening of a human kingdom have to involve my people?"

"Because, your highness, it seems he won't be stopped. I fear that if we don't have a greater force, we may be in terrible danger, and our ways of life may be threatened. He won't stop at the capital city. I fear he'll go after all Hevañian territories."

The princess listened intently, occasionally nodding. "You may have a point, Astricus...I'll take you all to my father immediately to tell the full story. I'm sure he'll be able to find a way to help."

"Thank you, Dyael. Your help is greatly appreciated."

"Um, excuse me, your highness?" Thrax piped up. "How much farther until we reach the herd?"

Dyael looked back to him, then to Astricus. "Who is this insolent man?"

"This is Thrax. He's a wizard," he gestured to each of them. "This is Prince Aaheer Thornblade of Hevaña, here to help, and this is Gwendolyn. She's not from our world. It's…a long story."

"Well, you can explain when we reach my father. We're almost at the herd." she waved a dismissive hand towards the others, continuing to speak in a low voice to Astricus.

Thrax scowled slightly. "What's up with that?"

"Well, not only is Astricus already a good friend to her, but he's not a human. I get the impression that it's easier for her to trust non-humans, and I don't blame her in many ways." Aaheer whispered back.

"Don't get your feathers ruffled just because you're not getting attention, Thrax." Gwen teased, bumping his hip and giggling softly.

Thrax looked at her with a chuckle. "Perhaps you're the one grouchy. I'm not giving you more attention, my lady."

Gwen flushed but shoved him playfully. "Ass…"

"Enough of that, you two," Dyael called from ahead of the group. "We're almost at the herd now. Look alive."

They walked over a high hill revealing a large camp. Centaurs worked at forges, practicing their fighting skills and preparing food, clothes, and weapons. As they grew closer, they all stopped what they were doing and turned toward Dyael, stepping aside to clear a path for their princess. "Your highness…" They murmured and bowed deeply as she passed. Their homes were large tents, easy to take down and put up.

"Dyael," Gwen jogged ahead to speak to the princess. "Are your people nomadic too?"

"Yes. Centaurs follow food and supplies. We tend to circle certain areas of the plains year-round. We don't have many creatures that come out this far."

Gwen grinned. "That's cool!"

Dyael looked at her, slightly confused, but smiled. "Well, here we are." She gestured to a large red and gold tent where a much larger red and gold phoenix sat on an outside perch, ruffling his feathers and eyeing the approaching strangers cautiously. "Don't mind him," Dyael assured them. "Go on in."

Gwen nodded though she still tilted her head a little lower from the enormous phoenix as she followed the others into the tent. A centaur stood over a map of the forest. His lower body was a dark chestnut draft horse. His upper body was covered by leather armor, and he had swords, daggers, and an axe strapped to his body. He turned toward the group, and Gwen was struck by how much he looked like his daughter. He had the same dark skin, black hair, and sharp features, but his eyes were acid green. His face was covered in deep battle scars, and he had a thick black beard.

He watched everyone file in with narrowed eyes. At the same time, Dyael and one of the larger centaurs from her hunting party followed behind her, a man with a dapple-gray draft horse body, russet-colored skin, dark brown hair that was shaved on one side, a face full of black war paint and a long scar that went from his jawline to his cheekbone.

"Dyael, you've brought me more weary souls for me to protect?" He growled.

"Father, please…you remember prince Astricus, right?" She gestured to the faun, who bowed low.

"A pleasure to see you again, your highness."

The king responded with a grunt.

"And," Dyael looked irritated. "These are his friends, Prince Aaheer Thornblade of Hevaña, Thrax, and Gwendolyn. This is my father, king Cyrian."

He scowled at Aaheer for a moment. "I knew your father…Jarkus…he was quite the bastard."

"I'm afraid he was like that to all, my lord." Aaheer didn't look up to meet the king's eye. "I hope you will not hold my father's actions against me…I am not the man he was."

Cyrian looked almost impressed with Aaheer for a moment before looking at the others. "And the rest of them?"

"Oh, they're all with me, your highness." He assured him, gesturing to Thrax. "My brother, Thrax, was training to be our court wizard."

"Brother?" Cyrian raised an eyebrow. "You two look nothing alike."

"Um…w-well…that's-…" Aaheer looked taken aback.

"I'm a Nightingale, your highness, not a Thornblade. Aaheer and I share a mother, queen Myana." He explained stoically.

"Ah…queen Myana…the magical world holds a certain respect for her…I will accept this."

Gwen made a face. "Though he shouldn't have to explain, your highness. If they're brothers, then they're brothers. It's not really your business, is it?"

The king whipped around to look at her, and all three boys looked horrified, though Dyael smirked and nodded in approval. Cyrian walked over and tilted her chin, glaring down at her. Gwen met his gaze defiantly, despite feeling her heart pound against her ribcage.

"And who, my dear, are you? Your attire is too drastic, even for the Gyrians, to be one of them, nor does it resemble any court I would know of."

"I'm not from this place." she pulled her face back and glowered at him. "Where I'm from, we don't act like you."

"Well, that certainly explains your quick defiance…no one here would be so stupid to speak to a centaur king as you have…I'm afraid, my dear, that mouth of yours could get you in quite a bit of trouble."

She crossed her arms, refusing to back down. "Then I will handle it as it comes."

Dyael broke out in a grin. "I like her!" she laughed.

Cyrian glared over at his daughter. "Dyael, hold your tongue." He walked back over to her and Astricus. "Now, faun prince, why have you come to me?"

Astricus explained the situation as best he could, with Aaheer and Thrax filling in occasionally. Gwen and Dyael stood to the side with arms crossed, glowering slightly, as the king refused to ask for their comments or opinions. He questioned them for nearly half an hour before finally making up his mind. "Very well. I will send two of my soldiers with you. They will call for us if you need us in battle. You may stay one night with our herd, but you must leave in the morning." He ordered. "You may go."

The boys all looked at each other, unsure what to do, but began to leave the tent.

"Father," Dyael stepped up to him. "I would like to join them."

Everyone stopped and stared at her. Cyrian looked rather outraged. "Dyael, what put such an absurd notion in your head? This is out of the question. You will stay here with your people. I will send my best men with them."

"But father, please, I *am* one of your best men! I'm one of the fiercest hunters; I've been in battles since I could carry a sword. No centaur can outrun me. Please, father, let me help them!" She begged.

"Why on earth do you want to help these humans?" He demanded, his face growing redder with irritation.

"Because if this evil succeeds, the whole territory is in danger! I'm tired of just staying here and being a good little princess. I want to *do* something! Please, let me fight for our people!"

"Out of the question." He stamped a foot. "You are my daughter and will stay here with our kind! Let the men handle this."

245

"You must be joking!" She raged, pawing angrily at the ground. "Mother would have let me go-!"

Cyrian slammed his hands down on the table that had the map. "That is ENOUGH, Dyael! Do NOT bring your mother into this! You will stay here with the herd, which is-…!"

"Your highness," The other centaur that had come in with Dyael stepped forward. He had been so silent that the others had forgotten he was even there. "If I may, the princess is restless in the herd. She needs a chance to spread her wings and grow. The best way to protect the herd is to learn how to defeat future threats. If she is kept here all her life, she won't have the opportunity to learn things that will only benefit our people."

"General Borbyr…" Cyrian growled. "You are crossing the line."

"I know, sire." he bowed his head. "But I've grown up with princess Dyael. I've watched her become the strongest warrior. She is powerful, my lord, but she can't grow into a queen unless given a chance to prove herself. If it helps to ease your mind, my liege, I can join the princess."

Cyrian growled softly. He looked between his daughter, the general, and the four friends, all watching from the tent's entrance with bated breath. "Very well. You may join them. Keep my daughter safe, humans."

The princess's face lit up, her tail flicking joyfully and her hooves tapped anxiously, but she forced herself to stand still. "Thank you, father…" she bowed and kissed his cheek before she followed the others out of the tent, Borbyr behind her. Once they were far enough away, she reared up, whooping with joy, punching her fists in the air. Her phoenix screeched and swooped over onto her shoulder.

"Oh, thank you, Borbyr!" she hugged him tightly. "Thank you so much!"

He smiled softly. "I must ensure the princess is happy."

"Welcome to the group, your highness." Gwen grinned.

"Please, call me Dyael." she insisted. "We're friends now!" her entire demeanor had become relaxed and joyful.

"I'm sorry if I'm stepping out of line but is your father always-…" Gwen paused, not sure how to ask without sounding rude.

"A grumpy old bastard who looks down on women?" she rolled her eyes, smile falling a little. "Afraid so. He thinks centauresses must put their duty with the herd, raising young. He still lets us fight, but that doesn't change the fact that he follows more "traditional values." It got worse after my mother passed. After she died, he was even more hesitant to let me leave the camp for hunts or to stretch my legs." she heaved a heavy sigh. "I am sorry he was so rude to you, but I loved watching someone get under his skin! Few ever stand up to him! Don't worry; the number of centaurs who still think like him is slim. Most who think centauresses can't fight are considered fools."

Gwen gave an awkward laugh. "Well, I won't deny I was kind of scared…your dad is rather intimidating."

She scowled more. "He's being foolish…he refuses to listen to me. It makes him furious that I won't be compliant with him."

Gwen's grin grew. "Well, we can be uncompliant together."

Dyael grinned down at her. "You know, lady Gwendolyn, you'd make an excellent centaur."

Gwen's smile faltered in confusion at the odd compliment. "Um…thank you." she hesitated but was glad to see Dyael so happy. She hoped she'd now have a new friend.

"The princess seems to be quite fond of you," Thrax said, tossing aside his jerkin.

"I suppose." Gwen slowly ran her fingers through her hair as she undid her plait. "She seems very kind. Her dad's an ass, though."

"He reminded me of Jarkus. Considering how alike they are, I'm surprised he hated him so." he pulled off his doublet, revealing his chemise.

"Jarkus sounds like a real charmer." she laughed, pulling her sweater off, so she was just in her camisole.

"You have no idea…I can say that while my mother was less than perfect, she stood up to him. Jarkus was one of the worst humans I ever knew. It honestly frightens me a little to think about how this Zephrus must be if he could easily kill the king."

"Do you think Zephrus is your half-brother?"

"Truthfully, I can't say for sure. I haven't seen him, so I don't know. My mother won't talk about my father, though I don't think that was her choice." He admitted. "For all I know, he could be, but it makes me question what kind of man my father was."

Gwen looked over at him with a furrowed brow. "So you know nothing about him?"

He sighed heavily and nodded. "The only thing I know is that he was also a wizard and died right after my mother gave birth to me. Master Majora told me that much, at least." He fell silent for a long moment before he turned toward her. "We should get some rest."

"Y-yeah…" she sounded far less confident now. The centaurs had given the group tents for the night. Gwen once again found herself sleeping in the same bed as Thrax, though she tried to push the thought out of her head, not letting her sheepishness show.

He chuckled softly at her blushing face. "Still not used to sleeping beside me, Gwen?" he teased.

She scowled slightly. "Shut up…" she climbed into bed beside him but didn't turn away from him.

He laughed softly and climbed in, propping himself on his elbow to look at her. "You look beautiful."

"What is it because it's so dark?"

Thrax frowned slightly. "Do you think I'd say that?"

Though Gwen hadn't truly been scowling before, she was now. "You haven't been very kind about my looks since we met." she reminded him.

Thrax flinched slightly, grimacing at the memory. "Well…I don't think I'll ever be able to apologize enough for what I said…I don't think that at all, and you can slap me all you wish if I should say it out of a mean spirit. I would honestly understand if you hated me for how I treated you at first…" he whispered and tilted Gwen's chin up to make her look at him. His thumb gently rubbed along her jawline. "Do you despise me, Gwen?"

She couldn't hide the blush rising to her cheeks nor tear away from his emerald-green eyes. "I-…no…I don't think I could."

"Good…" his shoulders relaxed a little. "I don't think I'd know what I would do if you despised me."

She hesitantly reached up and touched his face. "You're my friend, Thrax…I care for you too much…I can't despise you…"

He seemed to flinch at her words, his brow furrowing more. "Is that all you see me, Gwen…? Just a friend…?"

She paused even longer as she stared at him. "What do you want me to say, Thrax?"

He gently cradled her hand and pressed his lips to her palm, gazing at her with striking eyes. "I want you to tell me what's in your heart, Gwen."

She stared at each feature of his face for a long moment before gently cradling his whole face. "I-…I'm not sure…I think…I want to know you better for now. Can I have that, Thrax? Just a friend for now?"

He gently brushed her hair back. "Of course…it's the least I could do for you."

"Thank you…" she leaned forward and rested her forehead against his shoulder.

Thrax pulled her closer, one arm looping around her waist while the other cradled the back of her head. "It's been a long adventure so far. You should rest. I'll keep you safe…"

She couldn't help the small smile that crept across her face. "Thank you, Thrax…"

Chapter 13

The following day, the group of adventurers left with the rising sun. The herd gathered at the edge of camp to say goodbye to their princess and general. King Cyrian kissed his daughter on both cheeks and handed her a hunting horn. She stared at it for a moment before looking up in shock.

"Father…this is-…"

"The horn of the chimera passed down to each heir to the throne. Guard it well, daughter. When your enemy hears it, may they quake with fear knowing the great princess Dyael is on the battlefield…" He gave a sad smile as he pulled his daughter into a close, tight hug.

When they eventually let go, she whipped around, wiping her eyes. Borbyr walked slightly behind her, resting a reassuring hand on his princess' shoulder. He bowed to the king, who grasped the general's shoulders.

"Bring my daughter home to me, general."

"I would give my life to protect her, your highness."

Dyael smiled and playfully shoved his shoulder. "Don't act like I didn't beat you up all the time when we were kids."

The general rose, smiling as well. "I would never suggest you can't hold your own, old friend."

As they left, Gwen approached Dyael's other side and gently took her hand, smiling encouragingly. The princess squeezed it in return. They left the herd behind and were silent until they were entirely out of sight.

"So, we're off to find the Gyrians now, right?" Astricus asked.

"That's right." Aaheer nodded. "Dyael, do you know where they might be?"

"They drove by our herd a few days ago. We should be there within the day if we ride fast."

Thrax groaned. "Well, we don't have horses."

Dyael raised an eyebrow and heaved an irritated sigh. "Just this once, we can carry the group close enough to the nearest town. Don't get used to it." Dyael and Borbyr got down so the others could get on.

Gwen thanked her friend as she and Thrax hopped on Dyael's back. Gwen kept her arms wrapped tightly around her waist, and Thrax did the same, though he added an extra squeeze that made Gwen blush and swat at his hand. He snickered and rubbed his hand.

Aaheer got on Borbyr's back, ignoring his grim expression at having to let someone ride his back. Astricus stood still, hesitating.

"Astricus? What's wrong?" Gwen called.

"Oh, that's right…" Dyael sighed. "Fauns don't ride horses. It's uncomfortable and painful for them."

"I'm sorry, Astricus, but there's no other way," Aaheer called. "Come on!"

Astricus groaned softly but clambered awkwardly behind him, clinging tightly to the human prince and pressing his face against Aaheer's back, making him blush.

"Alright, you lot hold on. We'll be there soon." Dyael reared up, and they all took off through the forest. Gwen could hear Astricus's shriek of fear, even over the rushing wind in her ears. Thrax held firmly to her waist, and Gwen squinted against the wind.

"Are centaurs faster than horses?" she cried, leaning closer for Dyael to hear her.

"It depends! Most centaurs can outrun horses in short bursts of speed. Others have more stamina, in any case! Borbyr is the best on those long-distance runs. I have the speed, though!"

Gwen's grin grew. "Show us!"

A devilish grin spread across Dyael's face. "I knew I liked you, human!"

"Wait, Gwen, what are you-? Oh, fuck me!" Thrax screamed as Dyael reared up and shot across the fields, leaving Borbyr in the dust. Thrax clung to Gwen, pressing his face against her neck. Gwen laughed loudly as she held Dyael's shoulders.

"This is incredible! You're amazing, Dyael!"

They reached the edge of the fields and slowed down, Dyael panting hard. "You two still hanging on?"

"I am! What about you, Thrax?"

The wizard was silent, and Gwen could feel his knees shaking slightly. "Never do that without warning me again…" he hissed. His black hair was blown askew, half hanging out of its ponytail.

"You look ridiculous!" Gwen snorted.

"Oh yeah? Well, your hair looks like a snake that swallowed a hedgehog!"

Gwen looked at her braid, which was puffed and frizzy. She felt the chunks of hair that fell out fall into her face. She just laughed as she began to fix it.

Borbyr soon came into view with a panicked Astricus clutching a blushing but awkward Aaheer. "There you are, Dyael. Do you need to catch your breath before we continue?" the corners of Borbyr's mouth twitched.

"No!" she snorted defiantly, pawing at the ground. "I don't need to rest! We need to keep going anyways."

"Yes, please!" Astricus squeaked. "The sooner we get to wherever we're going, the sooner I can stand on solid ground again!"

"What's his name?" Gwen asked, stroking Dyael's phoenix as he preened his feathers, perched happily on his master's back. The group was sitting and resting after the long ride through the forest. Dyael and Borbyr, though they were too stubborn to admit it, were quite exhausted. They were all sitting around their campfire as the meat from their hunt that evening cooked over the flames.

"Ea." She smiled at the bird. "I've had him since I was a little girl." As he plucked a bent feather from his wing, the bird gave a warble. "He was such a tiny thing. His forest was destroyed, and he was the only survivor of his nest. I feel sure his parents had been hunted down as well." she explained. "Father found him, just a wee flightless baby bird with no feathers, no family, and brought him back to me. I raised him myself."

"He seems to adore you."

"I'm all he's ever known." Ea cooed affectionately and nibbled Dyael's curls.

"Could you tell me more about the centaurs?"

"Well, what do you want to know? Don't you have centaurs in your world?"

Gwen shook her head. "Nope. Just horses."

"What about phoenixes?"

"Nope. We have big birds like him, but they're not magic."

She pursed her lips slightly. "Well, what's the fun in a world with so little magic?"

"Not much!" Gwen laughed. "That's why I want to know as much as possible while here. If I return to my world, I want to ensure I never forget this…" she ran her hand across the thick, green grass, smiling fondly. "So tell me about the centaurs! Do you have lots of herds?"

"Absolutely! There are herds all over! Almost every magic forest has a centaur herd to protect from any threat that may get past the forests' defenses."

"Do phoenixes always live near centaurs? I know that royals get centaurs given to them."

"Well, phoenixes do tend to nest close to our herds. They can often flock to us in times of trouble. I'm not quite sure why, however. I think they just like the free food access and our forges. They're drawn to the warmth."

"That's so cool! You guys are like forest guardians or something! Could you tell me a little about Borbyr? You said you've known him since you were kids."

"Hmm? Oh, there's not much to tell that I haven't already said. He always said he'd become general to protect me, and he did! I'm proud of him. Plus, it means we get to stay close as friends."

"He seems sweet." Gwen agreed. "If a little quiet."

"Oh, he's always been like that." She waved her hand. "It's just his personality. Tell me about your world, Gwen!" she leaned closer. "I want to know more!"

"Oh man, where to begin? What questions do you have?" she asked as the princess began enthusiastically rattling off questions for her to answer.

The group sat around the fire as evening fell, talking in low voices. "I can send Ea to scout the village. He'll be able to tell me if Zephrus's men have reached this far." Dyael explained.

"What should we do if they have?" Astricus asked.

"We attack," Borbyr grunted.

"That would be unwise." Aaheer piped up quickly. "If Zephrus's men have reached this far, they must still be scouting for us. We ought to keep out of trouble and not draw attention to ourselves. Perhaps we can find a way to spy on them, maybe get some information from them. If we sneak to the caravan, they can help us more and maybe provide a disguise."

"I'll do it." Gwen volunteered.

"Out of the question!" Thrax stood up quickly. "I'm not letting you put your life at risk!"

The group fell silent as they stared at him, and Gwen glared bright blue daggers at him. "And why on earth not?" she growled softly.

"This isn't your fight, Gwen! I can't ask you to do something so dangerous! Unlike the rest of us, you aren't skilled in stealth, magic, or weaponry. I'd rather you be safe here than on the front." he explained, reaching down to touch her face.

Gwen glared and slapped his hand away. Everyone fell even more silent as they watched them. Even Ea was staring between them.

"Thrax Nightingale, I cannot believe you!" she huffed, standing up. Despite barely reaching his chin, Thrax shrank back at the look of pure anger she gave. "After all that talk about learning how to protect myself! I didn't ask to be here, but I'm here now! I'm not going to keep complaining about it or hide like a little kid! You gave me these to protect myself!" She quickly drew the long dagger she still kept in her belt. "So I'm going to damn well learn how to use them and fight! I'm going to do what I can to stop these awful people! I won't let you keep acting like I'm some helpless little girl."

Thrax clenched his fists and stood tall, though Gwen didn't shrink back. "And how exactly do you plan on learning? None of us are masters here. I've been training as a wizard all my life, and there's still so much I don't know! We don't have time for you to master something, Gwen! The threat is here, and it's coming for us! You can't act like you'll be perfectly fine or that you know exactly what's happening! This isn't a game; this is real!"

"You think I don't know that?" she laughed derisively. "I'm more aware than you could believe! I know

I might never go back to my old home! I might never see my dad or friends or do the things I wanted to do again! But I'm going to learn to be okay with that! I'm as involved in this as you are! I'm going to make the best of it, and I won't let some little wizard who thinks he can do whatever he wants or get me to swoon into his arms with just a word treat me like I'm some fragile, helpless little thing!" she jabbed her finger sharply into his chest, backing him up against a tree.

"Gwen," Aaheer began to stand up, holding his hands up to calm her.

"No, I'm going to say what I have to!" she shouted. "When I came with you, I told myself it was because you were making me, but I know much of it was I wanted a change! I wanted an adventure! I got my wish, and sometimes I regret it, but here I am, so I might as well work with it. I won't let you push me to the sidelines and be your pretty little girlfriend while the rest of you are risking your lives! I'm fighting with you all, and you better get that into your thick skull damn quick, Thrax Nightingale!" She turned on her heels and stormed off.

Everyone was silent, watching her stomp off and out of sight.

"Well done, wizard…" Borbyr grunted, crossing his arms over his chest.

"Yeah, you messed that one up." Astricus sighed. "But she has a point, you know."

"Oh, what do you know, goat?" Thrax snapped. "I just don't want her to get hurt!"

"We know, Thrax…" Aaheer put a hand on his brother's shoulder. "But if she's going to be here with us, she must learn to defend herself."

"But what if something horrible happens to her? She could get killed." he wrung his hands nervously.

269

"Well, it seems like a risk she's willing to take," Aaheer explained gently. "I don't think it'd be very fair not at least to give her a chance."

As the boys talked, Dyael quietly got up and followed after Gwen. She found her yelling and wildly swinging at a tree with her dagger.

"Stupid, stupid, stupid Thrax!" she screamed, tugging aggressively as it stuck in the tree trunk. She yelped as her hand slipped, and she fell on her butt. "Damn it!"

"You'll dull the blade like that," Dyael said from the trees.

"Dyael! What, come to tell me I should apologize?" she scoffed.

"No," Dyael trotted over to the tree and yanked the dagger free. "I came to help you." She helped Gwen to her feet and pressed the dagger's handle into her hand. "You're right; you need to know how to defend yourself. We don't have much time, but despite what Thrax thinks, we do have a master." she smiled slyly. "Centaurs are trained in hundreds of different weapon styles. I'll teach you how to use dual daggers for now. When we're through, Gwendolyn Grace, you'll practically be a trained assassin."

Gwen broke out into an enormous grin. "Thanks, Dyael."

Dyael chuckled. "Don't mention it. Now, are you ready to start your training?" she asked, holding a second dagger to Gwen.

Gwen's grin grew as she took it. "Yes, ma'am!"

Chapter 14

"Dyael, where are we going?" Gwen yawned, rubbing her eyes. The sky was only becoming dark gray with the early dawn rise.

"We are going to keep training. We'll be working on your stealth and perceptiveness."

"How?"

"We're going to sneak into the village and keep an eye on Zephrus's men."

"What?" Gwen gasped. "I thought we were trying to stay out of sight!"

"That's exactly what we're doing, though." she chuckled. "The point of this is to learn to hear and see without being seen. It helps that we're both women, and while a woman traveling alone is odd, two women traveling together is more common than a man alone. No one will think twice about us, even if we are a human and centaur.”

“Alright…” Gwen still seemed apprehensive. “If you say so…”

Dyael led her through the forest and over streams until the sun began to peak over the trees.

“Dyael, are you sure you know where we’re going?” Gwen had to reach out to stop a branch from snapping into her face.

“Of course I do.” she looked back at her. “Keep up, Gwen, you’re falling behind.”

Gwen grumbled slightly as she tried to jog closer, nearly tripping over a tree root.

“There’s a farm just past this copse of trees, and they’re less than half a mile from the…the village.” Dyael stopped as she pushed away the tree branches. Gwen caught up beside her friend and gasped in horror.

They had come to a broad meadow where there was nothing, but the black remains of what would have been a log house and a small barn, with crop fields burnt charcoal black. There was a man and a woman with their three children, all tossing the destroyed remains of their home into a wagon with a single withered, sickly donkey at the head.

"Oh my…" Dyael whispered. "This is…horrible…" she approached the family, and Gwen followed.

The children saw her first and cried out, running to hide behind their mother. In Gwen's eyes, none of them could have been older than ten.

"What do you want?" The father cried, raising his axe to them. "We won't have more trouble here, you understand?"

Dyael quickly raised her hands to them. "I'm sorry if we startled you. We mean no harm. My friend and I were merely passing through to the village and wondered if we could help."

"What could you do?" he cried. "Can't you see we've already gone through enough? Leave us!"

"Please," Gwen stepped forward. "What happened here? Who did this to you?"

The husband and wife looked at each other for a moment before he seemed to cave from weariness. His arms fell, and the whole family hung their heads as the mother hugged her children, who began to cry. "It was horrible…the soldiers of some bastard in Hevaña, somethin' with a z. They claimed he killed the king. I thought it was nonsense. No one would dare to mess with Hevaña with that mad king and that mage of theirs, but they said it was true. They came demanding we tell them about some apprentice to the court wizard and the prince. I've no clue why they were after the apprentice or were coming to

275

us about it. I told them we knew nothing, but they wouldn't leave. Demanded we give them gold or jewels. I told them we've barely enough to live. They got angry and destroyed everything. Burned the fields, our home, our barn…stole our livestock…and worse, they took our boy…our eldest son…said he was old enough to fight for them…he's only fifteen!" The whole family began to sob.

Gwen hugged the mother while Dyael comforted the father. "How long ago was this?"

"Just yesterday. We fled to the woods and just got back. We've nothing left of value." He explained, wiping his cheeks.

"I want you to listen to me very closely. Take this to the village." she pulled a loose feather from Ea's tail and handed it to the mother. "Selling a phoenix feather can get you enough coin for food and a place to sleep at the inn. We will get back your son."

276

The couple gasped and gripped each other's hands. "Oh, thank you, miss…!" They cried.

"Dyael, how will we even find him?" Gwen questioned.

"Simple, Gwen. It will all be part of your training," she smirked. "We must go, but don't worry, your son will return to you in a few days." She assured them and walked with Gwen back to camp.

"I thought we were heading toward the village?"

"Change of plans. We are getting the boys and scouting out these bastards. We find out where the boy is and return him to his family. We can't do this alone."

"What are we going to do to get him back?"

"Well, we're going to figure that out."

By the time the two returned to camp, the boys were already up, except for Borbyr, who was missing.

"There you two are! We were wondering where you slipped off to!" Thrax said as he stamped out the breakfast fire he'd made.

"We were doing some training. Where's Borbyr?"

"Running about like a headless rooster looking for you," Astricus explained as he rolled up his bedding.

As he spoke, Borbyr came thundering into the camp, his face flushed from running around and his eyes wide with fear. As soon as he saw Dyael, he sighed in relief and ran over to her. "Dyael! Thank the gods; you're safe!" The general hugged her and gripped her shoulders, scowling. "Don't run off like that! You'll cause my death before my thirtieth spring!"

She smiled and put her hands on his. "Borbyr, you silly thing, you should know better. I've always been trouble, and I always will be."

Borbyr smirked and chuckled. "I suppose that's what I can expect from being your guard."

"Hey, folks? Sorry to break this up, but we need to talk." Gwen jumped in. "We found something on our way to the village…there's a family that had a run-in with Zephrus's men… they had everything taken from them."

Thrax's face began to grow red as he clenched his fists. "What did they do?" he growled.

Gwen wrung her hands and shifted between her feet. "They…they burned everything down and took their eldest son…" she murmured.

Thrax got up and ran his hands over his face. He gave a small, derisive laugh, pacing for a moment. He stood still and grabbed a rock, lobbing it as hard as he could into the trees. "DAMN him!" he screamed and kicked at a nearby tree repeatedly. "Damn him! Damn him! Damn that bastard to hell!"

"Thrax!" Aaheer grabbed his brother's shoulder, forcing him to calm down. "It'll be alright…take a deep breath…"

Thrax gave a deep, shaky breath and gripped his brother's arm. "I'm sorry… I lost my head for a moment…" he ran his hand through his hair. "Did you run into the men?"

"No. We came back here right after to make a plan."

"Perhaps for the best…" Thrax rubbed his chin thoughtfully. "Strength in numbers and all…what do you propose we do?" he asked Dyael.

"Well," Dyael tossed her head and pawed at the ground. "I say we hunt them down and beat what we need out of them!"

"That," Aaheer quickly stepped in. "Would be incredibly unwise! Did you forget what we discussed last night? Dyael, the point of hiding out is to avoid drawing attention to ourselves. If the men are already in the village, that's even worse. Zephrus could be right on our tail, or they may have more reinforcements nearby. We need the advantage of stealth."

Borbyr stepped up, growling softly. "Are you questioning the princess's leadership?"

"Stand down, Borbyr." Dyael waved a hand to her friend. "He did nothing wrong. Aaheer is right."

Borbyr gave the princess a grumpy face but obeyed, muttering to himself.

"Alright, so how do we keep the 'advantage of stealth?'" Astricus asked. "It's hard not to notice a prince, a faun, two centaurs, a wizard, and a human."

"What if we disguised ourselves?" Gwen suggested. "We could dress up like the locals and look for the men in the village during the day when there are plenty of people.

In the evening, we go through the taverns to listen in. I'm sure they'll be drunk out of their minds and spill some secrets if we wait and be patient."

"What are we going to do to disguise ourselves, though?" Borbyr jutted in, arms crossed over his broad chest.

"Well, we can hide most things that would identify you three as royalty," Thrax gestured to Dyael, Astricus, and Aaheer. "Gwen," Thrax took off his cloak, clasped it around her shoulders, and tugged up the hood, partially hiding her whole body. "We hide you in a cloak, and I," Thrax ran his hands over his face, and when he moved them away, his features had become sharper, his eyes turned brown, and a thick black beard formed across his jawline. "Can use a spell to disguise us a bit." He pulled his hair out of its ponytail and let it fall loose.

Gwen gasped in awe and touched his face, her hands running along his chin to feel his beard. "Woah! Can you do this all the time?"

Thrax blushed and smiled softly. "No…I can only hold this spell for a limited time, and my skills aren't great enough to change my features too drastically. Just enough that people won't initially recognize me."

Gwen smiled. "We should set out now while it's still morning."

"Let's get changed, then." Aaheer took off his crown. "Thrax, could you help me?"

The wizard regretfully pulled away from Gwen to go to his brother, with Borbyr following close behind.

Astricus trotted to the other girls and removed the gold leaf necklace around his neck. "Could you hide this for me, Gwen?"

Gwen took the necklace and slipped it into her pack. "I guess you don't need to do much."

"No, most humans don't care to look closely at fauns unless they have more outstanding features." The prince explained as he braided his wild hair.

"It's a little harder as a centaur," Dyael noted as she carefully removed her circlet from her thick curls. "Our markings are symbolic. Washing it off is like asking us to remove a limb." she pulled off her gold armbands and the rest of her jewelry. "Many would be unwilling to remove their symbols. They're significant to us."

"Would they be able to recognize you from them?" Gwen asked.

"No, I don't think so. While we may recognize them, they may not unless we encounter some human expert on centaurs. I will still remove them to be safe."

"Thank you." Gwen took her friend's hand. "I can help you get them off and put them back on if you'd like."

Dyael smiled softly and squeezed her hand. "That's very kind of you, Gwen. Some help removing them would be appreciated." The two girls walked to the river, sat, and carefully washed off Dyael's face paint.

"It feels odd to take it off," she admitted.

"What do you use to put it on? Maybe we can find some later to put it back on."

"We use black flowers. We dry them and crush them to make the paste. I…couldn't leave home without a few," She admitted and reached into a small pouch on her belt, where she pulled out the heads of some of the dried flowers.

Gwen smiled softly. "When we get back, we'll make more." She promised.

Once they were done, the girls walked back to camp, where the boys waited. Gwen felt odd seeing Dyael and Borbyr without their paint or Aaheer and Astricus without their gold jewelry. Thrax was shifting their features. Aaheer's face was sharper, with no facial hair. He also now had hazel eyes. Astricus's scruff was much longer, and his eyes were a different shape. Borbyr's face was less chiseled and given a curved nose and gray eyes.

"Are you going to change us too?" Gwen asked.

"Yes. It'll be good for all of us. Come here." his hands gently cradled her face as he ran them over her features. Gwen felt like her face was melting and cringed. Her face was rounded out, and her eyes were wider, with a brighter blue color. Freckles had also been splashed across her face. Dyael's face was made to look more angular, and she was made to look as though she had more scars and a blinded eye.

"We're all ready." Thrax pulled up the hood of his cloak to hide Gwen's face. "Do you have your daggers?"

She nodded, patting against the belt where she kept them sheathed.

"Excellent. Let's get going, then."

"We'll take you again." Dyael and Borbyr knelt. "The sooner we get to the village, the sooner we find those bastards."

"Good idea." Thrax and the others got on their backs. "We ought to think of a way to pay you both back for this." His lips twitched up in a grin.

"Buy us an ale, and we'll call it even," Borbyr grunted as they took off the way Dyael and Gwen had walked that morning.

The town was quiet as they entered. People kept their heads down and moved quickly. There was no desire to stop and chat.

"Doesn't seem like we'll be able to stop and question anyone," Aaheer noted.

"If we find where those bastards are, then maybe we can get something." Thrax pointed towards the tavern. "Come on. I have a feeling that'll be our best place to start."

They all silently walked into the tavern, where plenty of people were chatting, but not as jovially as one might typically hear. When they entered, everyone became quiet to watch them before turning back to their companions.

"Friendly…" Borbyr muttered, crossing his arms.

"Let's try to keep the attention off of us, Borbyr. Come on, let's get a drink." Dyael led the group to the bar.

They all took a seat and ordered their drinks, scanning the crowd.

"Notice anything odd?"

"You mean other than a faun and two centaurs in a bar? Not yet…"

"That sounds like the start of a bad joke."

"We are a joke. It's too crowded in here."

"Calm down, Astricus; we'll be gone soon."

"But what if they're not here?"

"These human seats are humiliating."

"Easy, Borbyr…"

"Thrax, how long are we staying here?"

"Shut up, all of you…" Gwen hissed, glaring towards a corner. The group followed her gaze and spotted a group of about ten men sitting around a table, laughing raucously and drinking heavily.

"Did you hear how that little rat squealed?" Guffawed one.

"And his simpering mother trying to keep him away! You sure showed her, Andro!"

"Yeah, there's not a soul in this dinky little village that could stand up to you!" Crowed one of the men. He slapped the back of the man at the center of the group, the largest and burliest of them. His arms were covered in tattoos and scars, and a smug smirk stretched across his face.

"If lord Zephrus is gonna ask us to find that rat wizard, we might as well have some fun, right?" They all chuckled and nodded in agreement.

"Too right!"

"What do you plan to do with that little farm runt we got yesterday?"

The group at the bar fell quiet, trying hard to listen to them.

"Hmmm…" Andro stroked his chin. "Might use him for the front lines. 'Least if we have to fight, we get rid of the useless ones first!" The men all burst out in raucous laughter and got up to leave.

"Oi! Pretty missy!" One of the drunken men grabbed Gwen by the shoulder as he swayed past the bar. "Hey, hey, I'm talkin' to you, little lady! The least you can do is say 'ello! Why not give us soldiers a kiss for our trouble?" he jeered.

Thrax moved to grab him, but Gwen swung and planted her fist in his jaw, sending him into the tables and to the ground. Everyone fell silent and stared in shock as she picked him up and shoved him toward Andro and his cronies.

"Fuck off and lay off the drinks," she growled.

Andro watched her for a long moment before he stood slowly. "Come on, boys…I think that's enough for one night…" He growled.

Once they were gone, Gwen sighed, shaking her hand where her knuckles had started to bruise. "That was dumb of me…"

"It was, but pretty neat." Astricus grinned.

"We should follow them." Dyael nodded towards the door. "At least enough to get an idea of where they're going."

"No. It's risky. If we follow them, they could spot us or attack the child. We need to head back to camp and plan. There's no way they're that far from the village, and I'm certain they come in regularly."

"Thrax, we can't let them get away with this. We have to confront them, take them down!" Gwen begged.

"I know, but there's only so much we can do…" he rubbed at his chin in thought. "There's only six of us, and we don't want to risk drawing attention. If Zephrus learns we're here, it could hurt the townspeople and get us captured. As much as I hate to admit it, we need to be cautious."

Gwen felt her anger flare. She planted her hands against his chest to make him stop. "I'm so sick of hearing you lot say that over and over again! I say we're long past being cautious and leaning toward cowardice! It's time we act! People are suffering, Thrax! That little boy has a family who is grieving for him, and unless we stop them now, there will be others like them left in their wake."

Thrax's eyes burned as he tensed, squaring his shoulders. "You seem to be under the constant idea that I don't know this. Of course, I want to get that boy back to his family, but if we raise hell, it'll put Zephrus on our trail, and that's not what we need right now!"

"How do you expect us to stop him if we keep hiding? You can't keep running away, Thrax!"

He clenched his fists, his green eyes burning. "Running? *Running?* What do you know of me running, Gwendolyn Grace? You don't know me as well as you think you do! I'm doing what my master would wish and doing my best with what little I have. I'm no prince; I don't have strong allies. I'm not a general; I can't command an army. I'm just a bastard who's a wizard's apprentice, barely able to perform a more complex spell! You seem to forget that I'm terrified! I may be strong in your world, but I'm nothing here. I'm doing what I can with what I have because the truth is if I had been a better student and been here for the attack, none of this would be happening." he roared, his voice cracking as he fought back the tears burning his eyes. He angrily wiped his face and turned away. "The truth is, without my master or Aaheer, I'm completely alone, Gwen. I can't face Zephrus head-on because I can't fight him…if I face him now, I die, and nothing stands between him and my brother's kingdom."

Gwen hesitated before reaching up and grasping his shoulder. "Thrax…you're an idiot."

He raised an eyebrow and sniffed. "Is this what passes for encouragement in your world?"

"No, I mean, you keep saying you're alone and can't do anything, but that's not true. You've got many people on your side, Thrax, not just Aaheer or your master. You have Astricus, Dyael, Borbyr, their armies, your mom, your master's sister, Midra, and-…well, I may not be much," she took his hand and locked her fingers with his. "But you have me."

Thrax relinquished a small smile and reached out to gently touch her cheek. "You're right. I do have you."

"You also shouldn't doubt yourself so much as a wizard. You're strong and don't need to be a leader to fight. Speak with Aaheer more and help each other. He carries a heavy burden too. You need to learn to trust in yourself and us."

He closed his eyes and took a deep breath. "You're right…you seem to always be right…" He couldn't help a small chuckle. "I'll talk to my brother more. It's time we act." He assured and pressed his forehead to hers.

"Thank you. Come on, let's head back."

Chapter 15

Gwen carefully pulled Thrax's trousers on and tied them so they wouldn't fall. She slowly pulled on her shoes, ensuring her movements wouldn't wake the others.

"Ready?" Dyael whispered.

"Hold on…" she pulled his cloak back on and ensured both of her knives were sheathed in her belt. "Alright, let's go."

"Are you sure about this?" Dyael strapped her weapons to her as they walked toward the village.

"No, I'm not. But we need to do something, and the boys aren't moving quick enough." Gwen pulled her hood farther over her face.

"I don't disagree," Dyael nodded. "You have been coming along excellently in your training. You could even face at least some of them on your own."

Gwen felt her heart thumping and her stomach flip. "Are you sure about that?"

Dyael's lips twitched in a grin. "Well, not really," she teased. "But I'll be there beside you, and I don't think these men are exactly Zephrus's finest."

Gwen giggled. "So, we go get the boy once we take them out, right?"

Dyael nodded. "They'll regret stepping foot in this village before today is over."

Gwen walked slowly down the side roads of the village, one hand on the handle of her knife at all times. Dyael followed in the shadows, just out of sight, with Ea perched carefully on her shoulder.

Gwen turned toward a dressmaker's shop where a man cried out and was thrown into the muddy street.

"Come on, old man, cough up the gold, or we won't
be so generous anymore!" Andro stomped out with his men
behind him. They snickered cruelly as he scrambled back.

"P-please, th-that's all I have! Th-there aren't many
travelers coming through anymore!" he cried, holding his
gnarled shaky hands up to guard his face.

"Shut up!" He kicked him in the ribs. The man cried
out and collapsed, moaning in pain.

"I'd stop now if I were you." Gwen shoved Andro
back and stood protectively over the older man.

"Who're you?" Andro growled.

"None of your business. Just let him go." she kept
her head lowered.

"What does a little woman like you think you can
do to me?" he scoffed. "Stand down, girlie, and let's have
some fun instead." He reached out to touch her face.

Her heart pounded against her ribcage, and her palms began to sweat. Without thinking, Gwen drew her blade and stabbed it into his hand. Andro shrieked and stumbled back, staring at the hole in his hand.

He was left panting before he gave a shaky laugh. "So that's how it's going to be, eh…? Alright, girlie, we'll have a different kind of fun." he stepped back, and one of the men drew his sword and raced to her.

He roared at Gwen, who stumbled out of his path. The man pivoted and lunged, but Gwen stepped away again and stabbed the knife into his shoulder before quickly wrenching the blade down his arm. Her heart still pounded, but now from adrenaline.

"Die, you little whore!" A man screamed as he shot his crossbow. Gwen tucked forward and rolled toward him. She kicked him in the shin, making him hunch over with pain. Her knee flew up and connected with his nose as she scrambled to stand. He shouted, clutching at his face, and Gwen took another chance to stab him as deeply into his back as she could manage.

"Kill her, you bunch of fools!" Andro yelled, backing away.

The men charged her, raising their weapons. Gwen ran forward and rolled between the two of them. Her ears rang with the sound of her heart pounding so hard that she thought it might burst from her body. At this point, she acted instinctually, dodging, swinging, and stabbing at any inch of the men's flesh.

She was suddenly grabbed from behind, one of the attacker's hands squeezing around her throat. Gwen gasped and clawed at his hands desperately as he pressed, feeling his hot, putrid breath on her ear as he laughed. Ea swooped low and grabbed the man's face in his claws, a mix of screaming and angry screeching as they clawed at each other.

Dyael cantered out and shoved away Gwen's attacker, drawing her sword. "You've learned well!" she grinned and swung her sword, relieving the next villain of his head. "Keep quick on your feet! I've got your back!"

Gwen beamed, launched herself over Dyael's back, and kicked square into a man's chest, knocking him down long enough for her to plunge the daggers into his chest, feeling the blade chink into bone.

"If we get Andro, we can go find the boy! I remember where they were hiding!" Gwen called.

"Then let's finish them off!"

"You know," Andro's raised voice cut through the noise of battle, making everyone pause and turn to him. He was grinning widely, one hand gripping the farm boy by the throat while the other held a dagger to his chest. "It's not wise to discuss plans in front of your opponents. It takes your edge."

The boy whimpered softly as fat tears rolled down his cheeks, his thin body trembling. His hands were still bound, and he appeared too weak to fight back. "Please…h-help me…"

"Shut your fucking mouth, boy!" Andro hissed, pressing the tip of the blade harder into him. The boy hissed as a tiny bit of blood stained his shirt.

"Stop!" Gwen cried. "Don't hurt him!"

"Then you do exactly as I say! Stand up and hold your hands where I can see them. Slowly, now. Little boys are so easy to break, you know."

Gwen did as she was told and lifted her hands beside her head. Dyael stood straight and did the same.

"Now, drop your weapons. Right on the ground in front of you. Stay standing. I don't want any tricks."

The two exchanged glances but continued to follow orders. Dyael even whistled for Ea, though the phoenix was reluctant to obey.

"Very good…now, kneel to me and swear your allegiance to Zephrus. I'm sure he'll find some excellent use for good fighters such as yourselves." his grin widened with self-satisfaction. As he spoke, Gwen noticed a flicker of light amongst the trees. Her heart leaped in her throat. It had to be the boys. She and Dyael caught each other's eye again, and neither of the girls moved.

Andro's grin was quickly replaced with a scowl. "What, are you deaf or just stupid? I said bow!" he roared, his grip tightening on the boy.

"We don't bow to villains." Gwen snarled.

"What? What did you say? You stupid little bitch! You will die with this worthless little- AH!" Andro suddenly released the boy as an arrow was plunged into his shoulder. Another flew into the back of his legs, causing him to fall into the muck.

"Gwen, grab him!" Dyael cried, grabbing her sword and launching Ea after Andro's men.

Gwen scooped up her blades and ran to the boy, lifting him into her arms. "You're safe, now!" she whispered, running for the tree line. Once the fighting broke out again, people Gwen didn't recognize poured out of the woods, running to their aid. Two women in cloaks met her halfway from the trees. One took the boy while the other pulled Gwen back toward the battlefield.

"He'll be safe now! Let's focus on the fight!" she held out her hands, and purple fire burst from her fingertips.

"R-right!" Gwen ran to defend Dyael but felt a hand grab her ankle.

"You're not getting away that easy, girlie!" Andro's face was shiny with sweat and caked with mud from his fall as he clutched at her leg, trying to get to his feet. "Don't think this war is over if you defeat us! Zephrus has an even bigger army on his side! Can your puny prince say the same?" he got up and grabbed her cloak, wrenching her closer. Gwen felt her heart leap into her throat at the mention of Aaheer.

"Your eyes went all big…" he laughed darkly. "Oh yeah, I know just who you are, girlie. You're with that wizard boy and his little prince, aren't you? Zephrus won't tell us why he wants him so badly, but he's a dog to that puny prince, so I'm ready to see them both die, bloody and bruised! You tell him for me, girlie, even if you kill some of us, more will come!" He raised his dagger to attack.

Gwen quickly grabbed his wrist and punched him in the jaw. He tumbled back and spat. "Still think you can beat me? You're just a little girl! None of you even stand a chance! Just roll over and die!" Andro leaped forward, swinging his dagger wildly.

Gwen yelped and tried to dodge it. She hissed as his blade sliced her cheek and arms. Quickly, she grabbed him by the hair and tried to plunge her weapon into him. He caught her arm and pushed her back, her arms waving to regain her balance. Andro leaped for her again, but Gwen quickly threw herself to the side, making him land deep in the mud. She quickly jumped onto him and raised her arms to plunge her weapon into his chest. Andro grabbed her arms, and the two wrestled for a moment before he punched her in the jaw. Gwen fell to the side with a gasp, her weapon flying from her hands. She quickly drew her other one, and as they leaped for each other, she buried her knife to the hilt into his chest while his sliced into her shoulder. Andro's eyes widened as one hand clutched at the wound while the other covered his mouth. He gurgled and sputtered. Blood splashed down his chin and leaked between his fingers before he collapsed, wheezing and bleeding into the dirt.

"You did it!" Dyael cried, trotting up to her. "Your first battle! I'm so proud of you!"

"Huh…y-yeah, thanks…" Gwen's whole body suddenly felt heavy, and her knees wiggled like Jell-O, making her sink to the ground. A rush of pain hit her as she grasped at her wound.

"We should get the boy back to his family," The mysterious woman said, kneeling to examine Gwen's injury. "Then get you to your friends. You can stay with us."

"Wait," Gwen grabbed her cloak. "W-who are you?"

Gwen saw the woman smiling from under her hood. "I'll explain everything soon. For now, let's just get your friends."

Gwen stared at her hands as they rode to camp. The woman had been kind enough to give her a horse to ride and bind her shoulder but still wouldn't explain who they were. The boy had been returned to the joy of his parents, who thanked the mystery woman for "everything her people had done," which only raised more questions. Gwen pondered in thought as she tried to make sense of everything she was feeling.

"You fought well…" Dyael murmured. "Was that your first fight?"

"Huh? Oh…well, sort of…I had a fight or two at school, but it's…nothing like this."

"Well, even for a beginner, you're learning very quickly…" she rested a hand on her friend's knee. "I'm glad you're okay…"

Gwen stared harder at her hands, which were soaked in blood and dirt. When she had been fighting, she had been so focused on not dying that she hadn't noticed the aches in her limbs or cuts on her body. "Yeah…just some scrapes…they said my shoulder isn't that bad. Hurts like hell, though…."

"Something is troubling you…more than just our situation…" Dyael lowered her voice.

"What? Oh, it's just-…I don't know…I don't know how to feel about…all this…I've just-…I've never killed someone before, Dyael…I know it's necessary, but that doesn't mean I have to like it, right?"

Dyael pondered for a moment before resting a hand on her wrist. "Gwen, when centaurs fight, we never disassociate. We fight with the full knowledge that our opponents are living creatures. We don't take fighting lightly. When we go into battle, it's with the knowledge that what we're doing will help many in the end…though it doesn't mean there won't be mourning for others…does that help a bit?"

Gwen gave a slow nod. "I think so…thank you, Dyael…"

They returned to camp where Thrax was standing towards the edge, arms crossed moodily, wearing his blanket tied around his waist. He turned around and scowled at the girls. He watched Gwen as she dismounted and walked over to him.

"You took my pants," he grumbled.

Gwen couldn't help her small giggle and quickly tried to cover her mouth. "I'm sorry…"

Thrax shook his head slowly and pulled her close. "I'm just glad you're alright…I wish you would listen to me for once…" he held her face, his thumb barely brushing the edge of the cut on her cheek. "You're hurt…"

"Oh, right…don't worry about it," she assured him, reaching up to hold his hand to her cheek. "I'll be fine…"

It was then that Thrax noticed the people that had come with them. "Who's this?"

"She wouldn't tell me…"

The woman who helped Gwen stepped forward and reached up to pull back her hood. She had short blonde hair, matching emerald-green eyes, and golden-brown skin. She smiled warmly at them. "Hello, Thrax. My name's Inanna."

Thrax and Gwen exchanged confused glances. "How do you know me?"

"I'll explain along the way. For now, we need to head back to camp. Gather your things, and please, put your pants back on."

Chapter 16

"As I said before, my name is Inanna Pryor. I know your name is Thrax. You're the bastard son of Queen Myana. Zephrus is going after you, but I'm sure you don't know why. At least not in depth." she explained as she led them through the woods.

"How do you know all of this?" Thrax asked.

"I'm your cousin. My mother, Deidra, is your father's sister. Your father, Saedon Arimas, was one of us, a Gyrian."

"Oh!" Aaheer exclaimed. "You're the Gyrians! We were looking for you!"

She beamed to Aaheer. "Coincidently, your highness, we were also looking for you. All of you."

"So…how do you know me? I never knew my father, and my mother was kept away by Jarkus. No one was supposed to know about me."

"Well, I knew your mother when I was growing up. She would come to visit us often. She and uncle Saedon were so in love, and she was so happy when she visited our caravan." Inanna explained. "But, when you were born, uncle Saedon had already died, and she had been made to marry king Jarkus."

Aaheer became incredibly quiet and stared at his hands.

"My mother wanted to take you with us, but we couldn't go to Hevaña without risk of being killed. Mother kept in touch with Myana through your master, Majora. She would write us letters on her behalf to keep us up to date."

315

"Huh…" Thrax murmured. "Majora never told me this. I guess she wouldn't have been allowed."

"What name did you end up getting?"

"…Nightingale…"

Inanna went quiet for a moment. "If you'd like to…you could always start using your father's name. You have as much right to it as any."

"Well…" he hesitated. "I don't know…I'll think about it…"

"Uh-…" Aaheer moved his horse closer to Inanna. "I'm a little worried, lady Inanna-…"

"Please, just Inanna."

"R-right, sorry…um…is it wise for me to join you all at your caravan? I wouldn't want to make your people uncomfortable because of my father."

She waved her hand, shaking her head. "Don't be ridiculous, of course. You're welcome with us. Anyone with any sense would know that you're not your father. We've heard the stories of you defending our people." she beamed at him. "You are welcome among our people. Queen Myana should be very proud of you both."

Aaheer's cheeks went pink, and he relinquished a grateful smile. "Thank you…"

"We're almost there," Inanna assured them as they crossed a river. Once across and over the next hill, they saw a circle of beautifully decorated caravan wagons. Fires lit all around, and the sound of music, joyful laughter and chatter floated up to them. The infectious joy from them made the group all beam.

"Come on; tonight is one to celebrate." They followed Inanna down to the valley.

Once they were in sight, the Gyrians cheered and hurried toward them. The others who had joined the fight were reunited with friends and family, while many ran to Inanna.

"Thank goodness you're back, my lady!"

"Who are they?"

"Is that the prince?"

"It must be! Look, he has a crown!"

"Oh, a faun! He's so handsome!"

Aaheer looked away sheepishly, trying to hide his blushing face. Astricus went a bit pink but hugged close to Aaheer and comfortingly held his hand. Borbyr protectively put himself between Dyael and the curious Gyrians. Thrax and Gwen kept close to each other's side.

"Alright, alright, enough! Give them their space!" Inanna called, shooing the people back toward the circle. Once they moved away, Inanna beamed to the group, pointing toward a wagon. "That's my wagon. It should have enough space for at least you four," She gestured

318

toward Astricus, Aaheer, Thrax, and Gwen. "To stay in. I need to stay with my mother."

"Oh, no," Aaheer gasped and held his hands up. "We don't want to put you out!"

"Don't be silly!" she insisted. "You're one of us, now. Oh, and don't worry, we will get you two a place as well!" she said to Borbyr and Dyael.

"Don't bother. We'll be perfectly happy outdoors." The princess assured her.

Inanna nodded. "That's settled, then. Now, I think you lot have earned a chance to relax and celebrate! Come, sit, eat! We have much to discuss!"

Gwen, Thrax, and the group all followed her as the Gyrians cheered and began to line up in front of a large cauldron of what appeared to be a meat stew. They all received a large bowlful and a slice of buttered bread.

"Do…you typically have such small meals with your celebrations?" Astricus asked, trying not to sound impolite. He was, after all, used to celebrations being much larger and more extravagant.

"Oh, no, our more important celebrations have a much greater feast to go with it! But, we almost always find a reason to celebrate each day." Inanna smiled warmly. "Keeps spirits up even when times are dark."

Aaheer's grin grew. "I like that. It's a good way to keep the people happy."

"Well, enough of that for now. Come, eat!" Inanna gestured to the table where she sat in the middle, looking over her people. The group all followed and were served wine and food. Once everyone was seated at the tables, Inanna raised her wine glass. A hush fell over the circle of people, broken only by the sounds of nature around them.

"Today, we celebrate a victory over our enemies, but today, we also celebrate the return of a brother," Inanna gestured to Thrax. "Thrax Nightingale, son of Saedon Arimas. He joins us with his brother, prince Aaheer Thornblade, of Hevaña, and their friends." she gestured to each of them in turn. "Lady Gwendolyn Grace, prince Astricus, princess Dyael, and her guard, general Borbyr. We welcome you, brothers and sisters. May the gods of victory, Syna, and Loroth, bless your path to defeat the great evil."

The other Gyrians raised their goblets and cheered. As Inanna sat, they all looked away and began to talk amongst themselves, singing and laughing, as a small group began to play music.

"Your words are of much comfort, my lady." Thrax nodded his head to her.

She waved her hand dismissively as she took a long drink of her wine. "Oh, don't go all mushy on me, cousin. We are family, after all. Of course, we welcome you back. What, do you think we'd turn you away?" she couldn't help giving a teasing grin.

"In any case, my lady," Aaheer leaned across his brother. "I am truly grateful for the warm reception. I know it's hard to give to the son of a murderer," his brow furrowed slightly. "But I'm truly grateful for your kindness."

Inanna sighed and waved her hand to Aaheer as she did Thrax. "My dear prince, answer me this, do you condone your father's actions?"

Aaheer blinked and leaned back slightly. "I-I-…n-no, of course not, my lady." he knitted his brows in confusion. "B-but I don't think I understand."

"You say you do not stand by your father and his actions, yes? Then there is no need to thank me. Why imagine there to be bad blood when there is none, my young prince?" she leaned back in her chair and propped her feet up on the table. "You are no more responsible for who your parents are than Thrax or I. Let sleeping dogs lie, your majesty."

Aaheer leaned back a little and looked into his bowl of stew, but Gwen could see his grateful smile and swear she saw him wipe tears from his eyes. "Thank you, my lady."

"If I may, Inanna," Dyael leaned over to look at her. "It seemed you knew those men we fought earlier. Were they members of your caravan?"

Inanna hesitated, her brow furrowed and her spoon just at her lips. She slowly set it back in the bowl before she spoke again. "Yes…those men were once members of our

323

caravan…at one point, they were like brothers to me…Andro…was always…dark. He never cared much for anyone. I often remember him finding an excuse to fight or cause pain. Once Zephrus showed his true colors and tried to recruit our people, Andro was quick to side with him. Zephrus gave him a perfect opportunity for him. Overthrow the king he hated so terribly and hurt people. I guess it was a chance he couldn't refuse," Inanna shook her head. "Then his friends joined him. He even got a few of the younger boys to come along. Now look where it's gotten them…" she looked up toward the sky. "I hope the gods don't judge the younger ones too harshly. They barely knew what they were getting themselves into."

Gwen rested her hand on Inanna's. "I'm so sorry…I can't imagine how hard it was to fight people you grew up with."

"We did what we had to…" she sighed. "I couldn't just let them continue their actions. Besides, the fewer men in Zephrus's ranks, the quicker he loses what little hold he's gained."

"What do you think Zephrus will do if he gets control of Hevaña?" Astricus asked.

"Well, I suspect his first act will be to make it a permanent homeland for Gyrians. This isn't a terrible idea in theory. Gyrians have a long history of being denied any place for us to call home. But it also ignores our long history of taking in all deemed unworthy and unwelcome by their society. We make friends and families wherever we go. Our entire being is to take on so many cultures and peoples that we become unique. When all's said and done, we don't want to take Hevaña. We merely wish to live peacefully without being attacked. We want to care for our families, children, and elderly peacefully. I'd say most Gyrians don't want what he is after."

"Do you think we can stop him?" Thrax asked as he drank from his goblet.

"I won't claim it will be easy. But I think we can build an army and bring him down. But first, you will need to be taught more about your powers, Thrax, and quickly. We don't have the luxury of teaching you to master these skills, but you must learn them. It could be the key to you defeating him."

Thrax stiffened a bit. "When you say taught about my powers."

"I mean, you must learn many new spells quickly and how to increase the strength in your spells. You must also learn about your family's past. It will be vital in understanding Zephrus and how he came to be where he is."

"I understand…"

At this moment, Inanna looked at the young wizard and wrapped her arms around him in a comforting hug. "I know it's not easy…none of this is…I know you miss your home and your master…I promise you we will do what we can to take him down and find Majora."

Thrax gently gripped her arm that she put around him. "Thank you, Inanna…" his voice cracked slightly. He quickly straightened up and cleared his throat. "Will we meet your mother soon? I want to meet my father's sister."

"I'm afraid not tonight. Mother isn't feeling her best. I'm afraid performing spells and making potions are taking a greater toll on her than they used to. You will get to meet her soon, however. I know she will be very pleased to see you. You'll also get to meet my brother, Tan. He'll be returning from a hunting trip."

"It seems I have many family members I didn't know about," Thrax said rather sadly.

"I'm afraid so." Inanna frowned. "We've all wanted to meet you for so long now…I only wish it could be under happier circumstances…and I won't deny a bit of disappointment that we also can't see Myana again. We were very close to her at one point." Inanna gave a sad smile. "But I'm afraid that time is long gone. We can't dwell on the past anymore. It's time we stop Zephrus as I should have long ago."

"We're by your side now, Inanna," Gwen assured and gently squeezed her shoulder. "Plus, your people would stand by you no matter what."

Inanna's smile grew. "You all are very kind…I'm grateful we're able to join forces. I know our armies together will make a formidable opponent."

Chapter 17

Zephrus Arimas stood looking out the window of the king's chambers. He ran his fingers through his long, black hair and pulled his robe tighter over his brown skin, laced with deep scars from battles and spells gone wrong. He lavished on the fact that he could spend his nights in the king's room, the king's bed. That bastard Jarkus, who lounged around like the fat, happy tyrant he was, leaving a trail of pain and misery in his wake, getting to live in comfort while his people scraped to get by, was dead by his hand.

A woman slipped out of bed and walked over to him, pressing her naked body to his back as her soft, delicate hands slipped under the robe to run across his chest. "Why don't you come back to bed, love?" She whispered, placing soft kisses on his neck. Her dark brown hair hung down to the waist of her ochre brown skin.

Zephrus cradled them in his, running his finger over her knuckles. Her sweet, brown eyes danced with affection when she looked at his face.

"My apologies, Sigyn…my mind is elsewhere, love…" he turned to her, resting his hands on her hips.

She gave a slight pout and slowly slid one of her hands up his chest and across his shoulder. "Why don't you come to bed, then? Perhaps I can…ease your mind?" she offered.

Zephrus's sharp hazel eyes bore into hers. "What do you suggest, my love…?" he gently stroked her cheek with the back of his hand.

Sigyn leaned into his touch, gently cradling his hand against her face. "Why don't you let me show you, my lord?"

A devious smirk crossed his lips. "Consider me intrigued…" he tilted her chin up to look at him. "Please, do elaborate."

She grinned and took his hand, pulling him towards the bed. Slowly, she slid Zephrus's robe off his shoulders and let it pile on the floor. Sigyn lay back on the bed and held her arms out to him to hold her. He climbed over her, one hand planted firmly on the side of her head while the other slid through her dark hair and pulled her closer.

Sigyn wrapped her arms tightly around his neck and pulled the wizard in for a deep kiss. Her leg slowly ran up his body to his waist when they were suddenly interrupted by a rapid knocking.

They broke the kiss, and Sigyn saw her lover's eyes flash with rage. He got up and pulled his robe back on while Sigyn crawled under the blankets.

Zephrus stormed to the door and threw it open. "What do you want?" he snarled through gritted teeth.

A boy of about fourteen stood on the other side. He jumped slightly and swallowed because of his anger. "M-my apologies, lord Zephrus," he quickly bowed and held out a scroll. "I bring word from Terra Vale."

Zephrus seemed to perk up at this as he took the scroll. "Is it from Andro?"

"I-I'm afraid not, sir."

Zephrus was silent as his eyes slid across the scroll. His face twisted with anger, grinding his teeth as he viciously crumpled the scroll and threw it across the room, lighting it with bright red flames and an angry roar. "THAT FUCKING WHORE!"

"What's wrong, my love?" Sigyn sat up, holding the blankets to her chest.

"It seems the boy has found some little bitch as a travel companion, and they befriended the centaurs. The bitch and the centaur princess have killed Andro and his men." he spat these words like venom. His fists were clenched so tightly that his knuckles turned white, and fiery red sparks jumped out between his clenched fingers. "It seems my dear *cousin* found them as well."

"Inanna?" Sigyn's eyes widened. "No…I thought they had left the kingdom by now!"

Zephrus roared again, grabbed the curtains of the nearest window, and ripped them violently down. The young boy who brought the scroll jumped, his face going pale.

"You're dismissed, dear." Sigyn quickly waved him away.

The boy didn't hesitate to turn and run from his enraged lord. Sigyn hurried to close the door behind him before going to Zephrus's side. "Darling, please…" she placed small, comforting kisses on his face and neck. "Please…it'll be alright…they haven't won yet…they may have Inanna, but we have an army."

Zephrus put his hands firmly on her arms. Inanna pursed her lips, feeling the stiffness in his grip and words as he spoke, "Oh Sigyn…you still have so much to learn of war."

He turned and sat on the bed, but Sigyn quickly sat beside him and wrapped her arms around him. "My love, what does he have? Nothing compared to you. This is a boy we're talking about, who hasn't even learned all about his powers yet, and whom does he have beside him? A prince, a centaur, a woman, and Inanna. That's it! But," she pulled herself onto his lap and made him look at her, cradling his face in her hands. "We have the powerful Zephrus Arimas leading our army of wizards, Gyrians, and all who were scorned by that fool Jarkus. Not to mention, we have leverage against him. We have his master." As she spoke, she ran her fingers comfortingly through his hair, touching his thigh, kissing his face to calm him.

At the mention of Majora, Zephrus's face calmed, and his shoulders slumped. "Ah…you're right, my love! Sigyn, you're right!" He took her hand, eyes wide with realization. "Yes, yes! That's what we'll do! We'll move his master to the village and have her executed! That will draw the little rat out right into our trap! Sigyn, you're brilliant!" He took her face and kissed her.

"You won't hurt her, will you? You promised you'd only kill Jarkus." Sigyn raised an eyebrow.

"Of course, my love, of course! We'll fake her execution to draw him out! Oh, my beautiful Sigyn, you are brilliant!" Zephrus cried and kissed her deeply.

Sigyn couldn't help giggling. "Does that mean you'll come to bed, my king?" she purred, laying back on the pillows.

A lustful look crossed Zephrus's face as he threw the robe back off and crawled over her. "Of course, my queen."

Zephrus sat in bed late that evening and looked to ensure Sigyn was still asleep. He took a moment to admire her sleeping peacefully beside him before he got up and silently pulled on his clothes. He slipped out of the room and held up a handful of bright red fire to light his way through the castle halls, broken only by the full moon filtering through the windows.

Zephrus made the steady descent from the king's quarters to the front door of the castle keep. Once outside the keep, he hurried to the stables and down the hall to the largest one where his horse was kept, a large, black horse. Zephrus patted his nose before he went to a large pile of hay. He waved his hand, and a gust blew it away to reveal a trap door. Zephrus opened it and climbed down a ladder, ignoring the thick smell of rot and mold, into a black room. Once he reached the bottom, Zephrus held his hand over his head.

"Lux…"

The red fire leaped from his hand into a stone basin that stretched down the room and was filled with oil. The little flame burst into a great fire that illuminated the whole room.

The small room held a desk and chair, with rows of bookshelves surrounding it. The shelves were filled with leather-bound books with peeling gold lettering, bowls of herbs and stones, pestle and mortar, and glass vials. The table was darkened with the amount of black ash used to make runes, and stored under the desk was a small black cauldron colored with dried blood.

Zephrus began waving his hands, muttering quietly to himself. "*Indol magicae…laúdas…traeon…teñomas pater…fumus…interitus…otrusom…*"

Books flew around Zephrus's head, their pages flipping around. Zephrus pulled out the discolored cauldron and took a stone from the shelf, gripping it in his fist. When he opened it, the stone was lit with a small, red flame which he placed beneath the cauldron. As it began to heat, he levitated bottles of potions over to him, cut and crushed herbs, and magicked a spoon to stir the mixture. He pointed a finger to the fire and raised it. The flames grew, and soon, the mixture was steaming and came to a boil. Zephrus scanned the pages of one of the books, bound with black leather. The words were written in dark red ink.

"Here…"

Zephrus reached the shelves and grabbed a small bowl filled with black powder. "A pinch of ash from a phoenix feather…" he dropped some of it into the mixture, which turned a golden yellow.

"And deadly nightshade."

Two heads of the purple flower were thrown into the cauldron. Zephrus held his hands over the pot and began chanting, "*Darkness, decay, black moonless night, bring my father back to the world's bright light!*"

The potion began to bubble more as it turned to a dark purplish-black. Dark smoke billowed through the room. Zephrus turned away, shielding his face with his hands as the cauldron violently shook and fell with a loud clang. Once the smoke faded away, he stood straight with a growl. "Damn…! It wasn't right! It wasn't the right book-…!" his words trailed off at the sight before him.

The cauldron was toppled over, its contents still lazily bubbling, small plumes of black smoke still puffing out, but this time, the smoke took form; the dark, smoky shape of his father, Saedon Arimas.

"Father…" Zephrus gasped and slowly stepped around the desk before sinking to his knees. "It's you…it really is you…"

The wizard's eyes pooled with tears as he reached for his father's hand, but it fell right through. Zephrus felt his joy drop slightly, but even this was better than nothing. "Father, I-I have so much to tell you! So much has happened since I last saw you!"

"Yes, my son…you have changed very much since I last saw you," Saedon's voice wasn't quite the same as Zephrus remembered. It sounded like him, but when he spoke, it was like two other voices mingled with it, one soft and feminine, the other deep and masculine.

"Oh, father…I've done it! I've finally begun to avenge you! I've been practicing my magic so much since I was a boy! Look, look!" Zephrus held up his hands to his father, his hands filling with a small red flame before pooling into water that turned into a blooming rose. "I've been studying, and now I've finally overthrown the tyrant, father! I've killed Jarkus Thornblade! I've vowed to take down all that took you from me, father, and to become as great a wizard as you! Aren't you proud?"

Though Saedon's eyes had no pupils, Zephrus could see their sadness. "My poor boy…" his hand gently touched Zephrus's cheek. It felt like Zephrus had stuck his face in a cloud of smoke.

"You have gone through so much pain…for that, I am so sorry…I never wanted you to suffer so…but, you must stop this…the path you have chosen is one full of darkness and death…nothing good will come from this."

341

Zephrus got to his feet and took a step back. "What do you mean? Is…is this not enough for you? Haven't I already suffered enough? I lost my father! It's because of them that I lost you! Are you honestly telling me I need to forgive them?"

"Myana did nothing wrong, Zephrus. You know that. Jarkus is already dead. Please, let this be the end. Let everything be returned to peace. Don't take this out on your brother."

Zephrus clenched his fists and ground his teeth angrily. "Don't you *dare* call that little bastard my brother! He is nothing to me but the reason for your death! If it weren't for that harlot, Myana, and her little bastard son-…!"

"*Zephrus!*" The black smoke billowed thickly from the cauldron, and a dark shadow briefly crossed the room. "Do not speak of them that way! I loved Myana, and at one point, you loved her as she loved you. Thrax is my son just as much as you are. He *is* your brother, no matter how much you deny him. Zephrus," Saedon touched his son's face again. "I loved your mother and Myana very much. Please, do not do something you will regret. Let this end here. Let Myana and the royal family come back to Hevaña. There can be much-needed change! Please, son, do not go down this path. I know there is still good in your heart. Don't do this. Don't tear this family apart anymore. Perhaps this is the time when you should finally meet your brother. You have both suffered enough."

Zephrus's heart pounded against his ribcage, and blood rushed to his ears. "He…isn't…my…*brother!*" he roared and turned, throwing the desk onto its side, the books flying, potions and herbs being thrown askew. "He is nothing to me; do you hear me? Nothing! He has no right to call himself an Arimas! He hasn't even mastered his powers yet!"

"Neither did you at his age. You mustn't forget how similar you two are. Please, Zephrus, there's still hope for you. This path won't give you what you want. You won't become a great wizard through slaughter."

Zephrus's ears were ringing, and he saw red. His chest heaved as his breathing quickened. He gave a terrible roar of fury and threw handfuls of red fire at the cauldron, blasting away the smoky image of his father.

"You know nothing, old man." he snarled as he kicked the cauldron aside and grabbed the remains of phoenix ash. He knelt on the ground and began frantically tracing runes on the floor with the ash. "I will do what must be done…no matter what."

He summoned the black book to him, flipped to a particular page, and began chanting. The runes started to glow bright purple, and a dark grin crossed his face. "I will

plunge this world into fire and chaos."

Chapter 18

"Are you sure it's okay for me to have these things, Inanna?" Gwen looked at herself in the tall mirror of her caravan.

"Of course, dear! If you're going to pose as a Gyrian, you need something more fitting! Although," she touched the sweater laying on Gwen's side of the bed she and Thrax now shared. "I must say, this is a charming thing."

"I think I'd much rather wear this!" Gwen happily twirled before the mirror. The dress was lightweight and comfortable. The bodice hugged her waist though not uncomfortably so. The sleeve hung off her shoulders and draped delicately around her body. The skirt was hemmed, so the front reached her knees while the back brushed the top of her heels. The dress and sleeve were emerald-green, while the bodice was a lovely light brown color.

"Here, dear," Inanna stood up, undid Gwen's plait, and ran her fingers through so her light golden hair fell in lovely waves. Inanna pushed some of her hair behind her ear and tucked it in with a beautiful pin with a bright purple and pink jewel flower.

"There. Now you truly look like a Gyrian."

"Thank you, Inanna, it's beautiful! I hope it's not any trouble. I don't want you to feel like you need to give up your clothes!"

Inanna shook her head. "Stop fussing, Gwen, it's a gift! We'll have more clothes made and brought to you soon. After all, we can't have you stealing Thrax's trousers every time we go into battle." she winked and gave a teasing grin.

Gwen flushed and giggled. "Thank you, Inanna. I appreciate it. Is there anything I can do to help?"

"Well, I think it would be a good idea for you to begin to help out around the camp if that's alright," Inanna suggested. "Being able to pass as a Gyrian would also include blending into our camp. If our camp were to be invaded, the idea is that you would look like any other one of our people."

Gwen nodded. "Of course! I'd be happy to help!"

"Thank you, Gwen! I know Teyana could use an extra hand, if you don't mind. She usually watches the children."

Inanna led her to the camp toward a young woman, about Inanna's age, with long, thick hair pulled back from her face and held in place by a red and white jeweled hairpiece. She wore a long red skirt that stopped at her ankles, no shoes, a flowy white wrap top with long trumpet sleeves, and a short hem exposing her midriff. She also wore a black shawl around her shoulders. She looked at them and gave a warm smile with brown eyes that radiated warmth and kindness. She had a baby in a sling on her back and held a toddler on her knee. Children happily ran around her, though they never strayed too far.

"Teyana, I have a helper for you!"

"Oh, thank goodness! These children are almost too much to handle!" The woman gave the children a mischievous grin that made them giggle.

"Gwen will be learning about our camp. She'll be helping you with the children today."

Teyana turned her warm gaze to Gwen and gave a slight bow. "How do you do, lady Gwendolyn?"

"Oh-…" Gwen quickly did a little curtsey in return. "Um, alright, thanks."

"Thank you, Inanna. I'll make sure she doesn't get into too much trouble."

Inanna chuckled and bent over to kiss her cheek. "Behave, you two." She waved as she left.

Teyana waved the children over. "Come say hello to lady Gwendolyn!"

The children ran over, little boys and girls of varying ages, the youngest being the baby strapped to Teyana's back and the eldest being no more than thirteen. The children all had vastly different features, but all seemed to share the same happy grin as they bowed and curtseyed to her.

"Lady Gwendolyn will be playing with us today. Isn't that lovely? You all make sure to mind her, alright? We'll go to the stream today and look for food."

The children cheered and assured Teyana they would. She got up and walked beside Gwen, balancing the toddler on her hip. "Has your journey with Thrax been difficult?"

"Yes and no. The constant travel has been the hardest thing, I'd say. I…didn't grow up traveling around a lot."

"Ah, so you're not from another caravan then?"

Gwen shook her head. "I'm from…somewhere very far from here. Somewhere very different."

"Then I'd say you and I have a lot in common!" Teyana grinned. "I come from a kingdom very far east of here. I started traveling with Gyrian caravans when I was about your age. I was an orphan and had nowhere to go, so I was adopted as a Gyrian."

"What exactly makes someone a Gyrian?"

"Well, all you have to do is find a caravan to take you in. Because Gyrians travel worldwide, they find people from multiple kingdoms. They come to the caravans,

351

usually looking for a home amongst our people. It's not an easy life, but you'll want for nothing here." Teyana beamed happily to the children as they reached the stream. The children kicked off their shoes and stockings, if they wore any, and lifted their skirts and pants, running happily into the water. "A Gyrian family is one of love."

Teyana stopped to lift her skirt and tie it so she could wade in the water. Gwen took her dress and followed suit, kicking off her boots and wading with the children.

"So tell me, Gwendolyn, where did you learn to fight?" Teyana asked as she held a child's hand while they waddled into the water.

"I learned from Dyael. I still have much to learn, though." She admitted, jumping as a fish tickled her foot.

"Have you thought of working with a sword?"

"Oh-…um, not really, to tell you the truth." Gwen rubbed the back of her neck a little sheepishly. "I honestly haven't thought of it much…I don't exactly enjoy fighting."

"From what Inanna tells me, you're quite skilled, considering what you've learned so far."

"Sh-she said that?" Gwen felt her face grow flushed. "I'm not a great fighter, though."

"I'm afraid you'll probably learn to be better. If it's not too forward," Teyana looked at her. "I think I can guess why you fight. It's because you care about people, isn't it?"

"I'm not sure I know what you mean."

"I mean like these children. Our little village. This kingdom. You know so little about them, yet you're ready to pick a weapon for them. You've heard our stories, and you want to protect us. You want to set us free again. Isn't that right, my lady?"

Gwen looked at the children playing in the river. She thought of everything she'd heard and seen on this journey, all the stories of the horrible things Jarkus had done and how Zephrus terrorized people and tore families apart. "Yes…I suppose that's right…I just…want to help…I-…I think I can't help but feel for you…I know what it's like to be in a place that's not your own and to build a family with the people you meet along the way."

"Sounds to me like you're already a Gyrian by now." Teyana gave a mischievous grin.

Gwen giggled. "Do you think so? Reckon I'd be any good at it?"

"I think you'll fit in with us just fine, dear. I know Inanna would welcome you without a second thought."

"Do I have to ask her to accept me? Is there some ceremony?"

"Oh no, dear. You're just sort of…brought in, truthfully."

"I think I'd like it here. It seems so…peaceful and happy. Plus, I imagine it's wonderful to see so many places."

"As I said before, it's not an easy life, but I don't think any of us would truly have it any other way."

"I like it! We don't travel like this where I'm from. It's very different there. We don't have caravans like we used to, and it's tough to get so many different people to live together like this."

"Oh, we have our clashes, dear. Make no mistake about that. But we're struggling people that have learned to keep together. I can't tell you how we have, but we have, and I couldn't be happier with the family I've found here." She gave her a big grin. "I even found a wife. Inanna."

"You two are married? I suppose I should have guessed that, though."

355

Teyana giggled. "Yes, Inanna and I met when our caravans crossed paths one spring. I ended up staying behind, and here we are. But what about you, Gwendolyn? Tell me more about your family."

"Well…" Gwen paused. "I only have my father. My mother passed away when I was young."

"I'm so sorry, dear," Teyana said gently as she lightly bounced the baby, whom the playful screams of the other children had woken. "Were you very close with her?"

"Well, I was when I was a girl. I don't know if we would be now."

"I think your mother would be very proud of you for standing up for others. I think all truly good people would be proud to have a child that would do such a thing."

"There you are, Gwen!" Dyael trotted over the hill toward them. "We were looking for you!"

"Oh? Does Thrax need me?"

"No, I asked Borbyr if he might help me with your training some more."

"Oh…" Gwen looked at Teyana and the children. "Well, I promised Teyana I'd help her look after the children."

"Don't worry about me, dear." Teyana waved her hand to her. "You go do what you need to do."

Gwen beamed and thanked Teyana before she ran up to Dyael. "Let me change my clothes, and I'll meet you at the training grounds."

"Come on, Gwen! Put some force in your kick!" Dyael shook her fist, watching Gwen with her two daggers duel with Borbyr and his sword.

"There's only so much I can do without hurting him!" Gwen huffed. Her forehead gleamed with sweat, and her muscles screamed with exhaustion.

"You won't hurt him! You have about as much training as a centaur child at this point! Hit him! Give him all you've got! Don't underestimate our power! Think of it like a battle! The enemy won't hold back on you, so don't give them the satisfaction of holding back on them! Not giving it your all can get you and others hurt! Fight! Look for ways to get around him! Learn, observe, adapt, improvise!" She stomped a hoof, pawing at the ground.

Gwen tried to catch her breath for a moment. Borbyr didn't let her, in any case. He reared up and charged at her.

"*Observe...adapt...*" Gwen thought and quickly rolled out of his way as she looked around.

Borbyr quickly turned, digging up dirt as he charged back at her. Gwen then noticed the large boulder almost right in Borbyr's path. She ran straight toward it, making the centaur slow momentarily in surprise, giving

Gwen enough time to jump up, using the rock to launch herself on Borbyr's back. She grabbed him in a headlock and pointed her dagger at his neck.

"Enough!" Dyael called, and the two released each other. "That was very good, Gwen!"

A loud bark of laughter caught their attention, and the three looked up. Thrax was lounging in a tree, watching them with a cat-like grin. His hair was free from its ponytail and swaying with his cloak in the light breeze. "I wasn't aware you could be so easily beaten by a girl, Borbyr!"

Gwen hopped off his back and put her hands on her hips. "Why don't you get out of that tree and face me, then, Thrax Nightingale? You may think it's easy to beat a girl, but you'll find a woman's not so easy to beat!"

He scoffed and hopped down, using his magic to float him safely to the ground. "Gladly, lady Gwendolyn," he smirked and tied his hair back. "I'll be happy to show you up."

"Tough talk for someone who's going to get his ass handed to him." Gwen twirled her blades in her hands.

Thrax scoffed and held his hands out. "*Míthas simo laúdas*." His hands were enveloped in green flames. "Enough talk, lady Gwendolyn. If you want to spar, don't be angry at me when I beat you."

Gwen didn't speak. Instead, she shot forward towards Thrax. She rolled under a swing from Thrax. She sent a low kick to the back of his knees, making him stumble back onto his backside. Quickly, she held down his shoulders and straddled his waist, smirking.

"Gotcha."

Thrax gritted his teeth and threw her off. He grabbed a stone that began to glow faintly. "*Glador armis*!"

The stone in his hand stretched out into a stone sword. He gripped it and ran toward Gwen, swinging it.

She gasped and used her daggers to block his blow, gritting her teeth as she fought to hold him back. "Not bad, magic boy," she kicked him in the stomach, making him stumble around. "But not good enough."

She looked around for a moment before running towards him. Thrax used his stone sword to block, but she, instead, leaped up and grabbed his head, pulling herself up and using his body to launch toward a branch where she was totally out of his reach.

He stumbled back, rubbing his head where her foot had used it as a launching pad. "How do you expect to reach me from there, lady Gwendolyn?" Thrax called and held his hand up, shooting a red light toward her.

Gwen gasped and jumped down as the branch was sliced off the tree. She landed right on Thrax's chest and pinned him, with her dagger at his throat and a big sly grin across her face. "You were saying?"

Thrax scowled and pushed her off of him. "You got lucky." he stood up and beat the dirt off his pants.

"Oh, is that what I did? That's quite a way to describe being destroyed by a girl." Gwen laughed as she wiped off the dirt on her body.

Thrax scoffed. "You won't be so lucky next time, Gwendolyn Grace."

"You might need to do a little more work then, Thrax Nightingale," Gwen smirked proudly as she stepped closer to him, one hand on her hip, the other resting against his chest. "It looks like you still have some work to do."

"Oh, you think?" he said, a little more quietly as he stepped closer. "I'd say you do as well…" Thrax gave a soft chuckle and tilted her chin up. "You still haven't seen the true power of a wizard."

"Oh? Well, when you find one who can show me, you be sure to let me know." Gwen whispered, trying to ignore the way her heart skipped.

"Look, if you two are going to kiss, at least wait until I leave." Dyael groaned, breaking them from their banter.

Gwen went bright pink and quickly took a step back. "Sorry, Dyael! Is there anything else you wanna try?"

"No, I think you did enough today, Gwen. Come on, let's go wash up." The two friends giggled happily as they walked away.

"So, you have your heart set on the lady Gwen?" Borbyr asked as they walked back toward camp.

"W-what? N-no, it's not what you think!" Thrax went bright red.

"Do not insult my intelligence, Thrax." Borbyr sighed. "I could see your intentions for each other even if I was blind."

"W-well, what about you? Are you interested in someone?"

"Nay, I have no prospects of courtship at this time. I merely wish to aid the princess. Her resolution to fight beside you all keeps me here."

"Oh, come on, think of it as something between friends! There's gotta be someone!"

Borbyr remained stoically silent, staring ahead as they walked.

"Okay, um, is it Astricus? Is it…is it Gwen too? What about Inanna? Aaheer? The princess? At least give me a hint!"

"I told you, I have no intention of courtship. Why are you humans so stuck on the idea?"

Thrax gave a disappointed sigh. "You're no fun."

"Thrax! There you are!" Inanna was in the center of the camp, helping prepare the evening meal. "Come here; I need to speak with you."

"Did I do something, Inanna?"

"No, I simply wanted to talk to you about your powers."

"What about them?"

"Well, I imagine this was due to outstanding factors, but it seems you couldn't cover some of the bigger pieces of magic with Majora, were you?"

"Well…not really," Thrax admitted, awkwardly rubbing the back of his head.

"Don't worry, dear, I'll be able to teach you what you couldn't finish." Inanna gestured for him to follow her.

She led him to her wagon and pushed open the door. It was filled with so many beautiful things; little figurines, flowers drying from ropes strung across the ceiling, potted plants growing on the windowsill, a handcrafted quilt draped over one of the four chairs that sat against the wall of the caravan, handmade wooden furniture decorated with gold paint. There was a small fireplace with a crackling fire, filling the home with a soft orange glow and heating a cauldron filled with a mysterious dark green mixture. On the mantle above were glass jars filled with all sorts of herbs and parts of animals and half-melted candles of multiple colors. An orange tabby cat slept on the wooden tabletop. She blearily opened her eyes and stretched before hopping down onto the colorful woven rug and jumping past the curtains that separated the sleeping area.

"Mother," Inanna walked over and peeked into the curtains. "I've brought Thrax with me."

"Oh, bring him over! I want to see his face!"

Inanna turned and motioned Thrax over as she pulled back the curtains. He obeyed and observed the woman shifting, so she was sitting on the edge of the bed. She was in her fifties with dark brown hair turning gray and tied into a loose braid down her back. She had brown skin like Inanna's but with more wrinkles from age and hours of being in the sun that crinkled with her wide smile. Her hazel eyes sparkled with wisdom and a youthful spirit. She put her hands to her mouth when she saw Thrax's face and motioned for him to come closer, holding her hands out.

"Oh, Inanna…you were right…he looks the spitting image of your uncle…" The older woman cradled Thrax's face and turned him so she could view his profile. "Oh, my dear boy…I don't think you'll ever truly understand the joy it brings me to meet you."

Thrax gave a gentle smile and put his hand to hers. "I think I have some idea."

She chuckled and motioned to one of the chairs. "Please, sit, dear. Inanna, stir that pot and put the kettle on, please."

Inanna nodded and did just as her mother requested. Meanwhile, Thrax's aunt stared intently at him. "I hear they gave you quite the name." she made a face of disdain. "Nightingale…what sort of name is that…but I suppose poor Myana was working with what she could get." she shook her head in disappointment.

"So you also knew my mother?"

"Ha! Did I know your mother? Dear boy, I helped get your father to talk to your mother! I'm his sister, Deidra! I saw your father and mother through everything! I would have been there to see you born if I could have!"

Thrax's eyes widened as he leaned closer, eager to hear more. "What…was he like? My father?"

"He was a spitfire indeed!" she had a sort of faraway look as she happily reminisced. "That man always had a smile, a jump in his step, and kindness in his heart. He was truthfully the wisest and strongest among us! But Saedon never was one to take on too much responsibility! He enjoyed the basic luxuries of life too much. Of course, he did relax such mindsets a little after Zephrus was born."

Thrax hesitated before deciding to ask his next question. "What is…his story? Zephrus?"

Deidra's eyes turned sad, and her smile flickered. "I wish I could say it was a happy one…Zephrus was born to your father and another Gyrian woman. Camilla was the kindest of all of us. She never had a cruel word to say about anyone, though she would scold you half to death…your father loved her so deeply, you could almost feel it. They got married young and were set to have a child. That was the first time I saw your father so happy. But it wouldn't last. She died on the road giving birth to your brother. We weren't close enough for a doctor, and there wasn't enough medicine. Zephrus was heartbroken. We all helped him care for little Zephrus, and you could see in Saedon's eyes how much he loved the boy. He put all his love for his wife into his son."

"Y-you said that meeting Zephrus's mother was the first time you saw him that happy. What was the second time…?"

"I'm getting there, dear!" she affectionately patted his knee. "After that, we came to Hevaña, just as the time had come for our summer festival! We filled the city square with our caravans and music! Oh, the most beautiful music! We danced and sang like phoenixes finding their partners! That was the day your parents met. Your mother was only a nobleman's daughter then. She hadn't even spoken to the king. They had a whirlwind romance. It was a beautiful thing. They loved each other so much, and how Myana adored Zephrus! We never stayed away for long because the caravan couldn't stand to see those two so sad without her. I only wish things had been able to remain so happy…" her smile fell, and her eyes began to pool with tears.

Inanna hugged her tightly. "We all miss them, mother."

"What…what happened then? If you don't mind my asking." Thrax prodded gently.

Deidra looked at him and shook her head slightly. "I'm afraid that that tale will have to wait. I'm sorry…I can only tell so much…I-…I don't always like to remember."

"Mother, I brought Thrax to learn more magic under us. Majora wasn't able to teach him everything. Is that alright?"

"Well, why didn't you say so, silly girl? Look at me, babbling on when we have work to do!" she quickly wiped her eyes and stood up, straightening her clothes. "Now, Thrax, what are some of your specialties?" Deidra asked, scurrying over to a cabinet.

"W-well…when I last was with Majora, we practiced runic magic."

"Ah, the runes! Let's see…" Deidra threw open the cabinet doors to reveal multiple leather-bound books; their spines cracked and peeled with the once colorful letterings fading with age. "Let's see…do you recognize any of these?"

Thrax peeked over her shoulder. "Few, I'm afraid…" he stopped her suddenly and pointed to some. "There, I had just mastered this set of runes when I last saw her."

"Ah, teleportation runes! They're very tricky. Did you manage to get it to work?"

"Well…" Thrax suddenly remembered being inside Gwen's closet and falling out to see her standing over him with a knife. "In a way…"

"Never mind," Deidra waved her hand. "We'll start from there. Have you ever attempted summoning spells? For a familiar?"

"I've attempted it, but my abilities aren't really in animal magic."

"It's important to have a familiar, at least. Almost all who practice magic do."

"Who's your familiar?"

"A bear. She comes when I need her most or when I need her company. Many keep their familiars close at all times."

"What if it doesn't work?"

373

Deidra gripped his shoulder and gave him a stern look. "Don't be discouraged just because a spell doesn't succeed on the first try. Spells can be tricky, especially runes. Even the most powerful mage can make a mistake. You just…keep going. Keep trying. It's how we learn. Don't be afraid to make a mistake."

"You're right. I apologize. Sometimes I need to be reminded."

"We all do. There's no need to apologize," Inanna assured him and took a piece of charred wood from the fireplace. She dusted off some of the ashes and began to draw on the wood floor, writing out the runes in a circle. "These are the runes for summoning your familiar. The spell you chant is 'Nae fuli mi, bestia terrae.'"

Thrax nodded and knelt, putting his hands on the runes. He took a deep breath and began to chant, "*Nae fuli mi, bestia terrae…nae fuli mi, bestia terrae.*" As he spoke, the runes began to glow a soft orange light.

"Excellent, Thrax. Keep going." Inanna slowly got up and stepped back.

The light shone brighter before a spark formed in the middle of the circle. He gasped, but Deidra gripped his shoulder. "Don't stop. Keep going."

Thrax did as he was told, though he still apprehensively watched the spark as it flickered stronger and soon grew into an enormous flame. "Deidra-!"

"I told you, don't stop!"

The fire grew until it filled the drawn-out limits of the runic circle, growing taller until the flames almost touched the top of the wooden wagon. Slowly, the fire began to split open like a flower and rescinded until it was gone again, leaving in its place a small fiery red fox, sleeping peacefully with its little nose covered by its tail.

375

Thrax gasped as he sat back, staring in awe at the creature.

"You did it, Thrax!" Deidra gripped his shoulder. "The spirits of the earth have given you your familiar."

The little fox stretched out, opening its mouth in a wide yawn. He got up and walked over to Thrax, stepping onto his knees. Thrax stared for a moment, then slowly reached out his hand to stroke his head. "I'll call you…Kitsae."

The little fox perked his ears up at this, and his little tail swished happily across the floor.

"He likes you." Deidra chuckled softly. "What will you do with him?"

"I'm not sure…how do you call a familiar?"

"Well, you can use many ways, but the easiest is to create a whistle to call them to you." Inanna turned and rummaged through a little box before she pulled out a bone whistle carved into the shape of a leaping fox. "Here. You can take this with you, and it's charmed, so he will hear you from wherever you are. He'll be able to use your connection to appear by your side for whatever you need."

"Thank you." He cradled the whistle before putting it in his pocket. "Are there other spells one can do with their familiar?"

"Oh, plenty. But for now, perhaps you should continue practicing your rune magic. Though your summoning was excellent, there's still much to do." Inanna waved a hand over the runes, slowly fading into the wood. "Now, let's begin your next spell."

Chapter 19

Zephrus rode through the streets to thunderous applause with Sigyn by his side, cradling his hand and beaming at him. Zephrus merely scanned the crowd, his gaze lingering on any who didn't seem to be singing his praises.

"All hail, king Zephrus!" His followers cried as they followed his precession.

"The gates are just ahead, my lord." His captain called over his shoulder.

"I know how to get to the gates, Katrulus," Zephrus muttered icily.

Katrulus quickly bowed low in his saddle. "O-of course, my lord…I-I meant no offense."

"Just continue, Katrulus, and keep your mouth shut."

Sigyn reached up and gently wrapped her arm around his bicep. "My dearest, why do you appear so cross? Shouldn't you be celebrating? Look around us; our people are rejoicing! They're cheering your name!"

Zephrus tilted her face towards him, his eyes scanning her countenance. "Oh my darling, Sigyn…how much you still have to learn…look closely. Those who cheer for us are those who took this kingdom with us. Those who do not are those who would see us overthrown. There is no real chance to rejoice when our kingdom is on the line."

Sigyn's smile faltered as she listened to him, and when he released her, she, too, began to scan the crowd. She plastered a smile for appearances, though Zephrus noticed the flicker of doubt in her eyes.

Once out of the kingdom, the group rode to an army camp nearby. When they came into sight, all the men stopped as they were doing and bowed deeply. Zephrus never glanced at them and merely cut straight through to his general's tent, where the older man examined a map with other officers. They soon noticed him approaching and also bowed.

"General Donahue. What news have you?"

"I'm afraid nothing good, sire. We still have yet to locate your cousin's caravan. There is no word of them moving, though we aren't quite sure where they are."

"Then you must send more men. I will not allow them to try and defeat me. We must make examples of them for all who dare oppose us." Zephrus raised an eyebrow at him and lazily slid out of his saddle.

"Y-yes, of course, sir, but we don't exactly know where to send them. If we had that knowledge, we could send our men straight there. It's dangerous to send out too many when we need to defend our hold."

"You focus too much on why you can't get something done, Donahue, and not enough on how to do it." He walked past him and held his arm out, giving a low whistle. After a moment, a loud caw rang out, and a black raven appeared in the sky, swooping down onto Zephrus's arm. "Hello again, Sephtis…" he gently stroked his feathers, and the bird affectionately tugged his shirt sleeve. "Go. Find my traitorous cousin and the vermin that travel with her. Return when you find them." He lifted his arm higher for the raven to launch off, and with another caw, he took off toward the mountains and vanished behind the clouds.

"As I said, Donahue, too much on why you can't and not enough on why you can. When Sephtis returns, you send a faction of soldiers to take them out. I expect you to ensure they will not survive such an attack, and failure to do so will mean that you will have to take their place." he warned and mounted his horse. "Come, my love." He took Sigyn's hand, not noticing her apprehension as she followed him, looking back at Donahue's pale face.

Sigyn rode closer and leaned forward to try and catch his eye. "My dearest, are you sure that was entirely necessary?"

"Whatever do you mean?" He didn't turn to her, still keeping his stony expression.

"I mean, it's not necessarily Donahue's fault if he can't bring them back. After all, not all of our men are exactly skilled assassins or trained mages."

"If they're able to be slaughtered by such a weak excuse for a wizard, then they are of no use to me and deserve to die."

Sigyn's eyes widened. "Zephrus, come now, you don't mean that do you?" she gave a small, nervous laugh.

He remained silent before finally saying, "If that's what you wish to believe, my dearest."

Sigyn felt her heart drop. "Zephrus-..."

"I will speak of it no more, Sigyn. Leave it be." his voice came out with a low growl.

Sigyn clenched her reins and closed her mouth. "O-of course...yes, my love..."

Late that night, Sigyn collapsed back on their bed, panting softly. Zephrus leaned on his side, pushing back his black hair, slicked with a thin layer of sweat. "My beloved dove..." he murmured and pulled her onto his chest, tracing circles on her bare skin.

She gave a rather proud smile as she rested her head on his shoulder, gently tracing his shoulder. "Zephrus?"

"Hm?"

"Do...do you love me?"

He sat up a little to look at her. "What sort of question is this, my dearest? Of course, I love you. You are my queen, after all." He cradled her face and kissed her slowly, but Sigyn put her hands on his chest and gently pushed him back.

"If I were to fail you somehow, would you say I deserve death, like those soldiers?"

"Sigyn, where is this coming from?" he sat up, brow furrowing. "You're not acting like yourself."

"Well, neither are you, Zephrus!" she sat up to examine his expression more closely. "You're...darker. I don't know how to explain it, but it's not you, Zeph. The man I fell in love with wouldn't be so quick to kill his allies like that."

"Oh, my darling Sigyn...how little you truly understand..." he tenderly slid his hand up to cradle her cheek and push back her hair. "We are at war, my dove.

384

We must do all we can to win it. Sometimes, it means

sacrificing a few weak links to emerge even stronger. Their

defeat will guarantee our hold of Hevaña. I do not intend to

let this go. Our people deserve a land to call home, don't

you think?"

"Zeph, you know I do!"

"And that bastard Jarkus deserves to pay for it,

yes?"

"Yes, Zeph, but he already has paid for it. Why

don't we banish the others or something? Is there a need to

kill them?"

Without warning, Zephrus slapped Sigyn across the

cheek with the back of his hand at full force. She gasped

and clung to it in shock. Never in her life had Zephrus ever

struck her.

"Zeph, why-…" she gasped as Zephrus suddenly

grabbed her arm and forcefully dragged her halfway out of

bed, his fingers digging into her arm. She clung to the sheets, holding them against her body, whimpering, "Zeph, please, y-you're hurting me-!" She fell silent as he grabbed a fistful of her hair with his other hand and yanked her head back so she looked up at him and saw the violent, dark look in his eyes.

"You listen well, my queen," he spat the word out like it was filthy. "I am your king and husband. You will obey me. If I say they deserve to die, you do not get to question me. If I were to let them live, they could gather allies that might come to overthrow us. Better to be silent and listen than dead from a broken neck, is it not, my dove?"

Sigyn swallowed hard and gave a slight nod. "Y-yes, i-it is, my king. I-I'm sorry. I meant no offense."

A cold smirk twisted his lips as he released her hair and cradled her face for him to kiss. "That's my girl…" his low, handsome voice that once sent chills of pleasure up her spine now only gave her a chill of fear.

Sigyn laid back on the bed and turned away from her husband, though instead of turning from her as well, Zephrus pulled her close to his chest and kissed down her neck, his hands roaming her body, making her shudder. Something terrible had changed within the man she had loved so dearly, the man who had inspired her to think that their people could finally have peace, the man who had sworn to love her all their lives.

That man was gone. It seemed all that was left was a monster.

Sigyn woke late the following day, long after the sun had risen in the sky. There was a loud thumping at the door, and as she got up, she realized that Zephrus was already gone.

Considering last night's events, this didn't bother her as much as it usually would have.

She opened the door to her young lady-in-waiting. The girl was in one of her fancier gowns with her hair pulled back into a simple knot and a simple gold pin in her thick brown hair. "Oh, your highness!" she quickly bowed before her. "We must get you ready!"

"Ready? For what?"

"King Zephrus has called you to the throne room immediately! We must make haste!"

Sigyn quickly got up and let the girl help her brush and braid her hair and get dressed. Sigyn even took the time to put on makeup and dab flowery perfumes on her neck. The two quickly hurried down the winding tower stairs to the throne room, where Zephrus sat on the throne, resting his chin on his fist, listening intently to the caws of the crow perched on the end of his knee. Even though she had seen him only the night before, there was still a physical change to him. His cheeks seemed more sunken, with deep, dark bags under his eyes. His eyes which once gleamed a beautiful amber had lost their sparkle and seemed dull with exhaustion.

Sigyn made sure her clothes were straight before stepping out and bowing deeply. "You wished to see me, my love?"

"Come, wife, sit by me." he hadn't even bothered to look at her, just lazily gesturing to the throne beside him.

Sigyn frowned but obeyed, taking the throne beside him. Zephrus reached over and took her hand. Though usually, Sigyn would have felt a thrill of joy at this, now she felt nothing. The sting of his strike across her face was still too familiar.

"Sephtis has brought back information on the location of my traitorous cousin and the bastard wizard. I will be sending my men to capture them. We will also be going and bringing the mage. I will draw him and his pathetic friends out and kill him with my own hands.”

Sigyn gripped her skirt in her fist to steady her hands as she tried to speak up again. “Zephrus…a-are you sure it’s really necessary? After all, Inanna is family. This is your father’s son. Can we not at least try to-!” she gasped as he suddenly leaped up. Sephtis flapped up to his shoulder, glaring at Sigyn with eyes like little chips of onyx.

“Why must you be so damn stubborn, Sigyn? What has gotten into you? You are not acting as you once were!”

His accusations made her heart surge with angry courage. “It is you who is not acting as you once were! Something is wrong with you! Where is the Zephrus I once knew, the man I loved? The man I married? What happened to the man who saved me from my mind? He’s gone now! I don't see you anymore, Zephrus! It's like I'm looking at a beast instead of my husband! Ah!" she cried out as Zephrus grabbed her long black hair and threw her to the ground.

"How dare you? You filthy bitch! Whom do you think you're speaking to in such a tone? I'm your husband, your king! I am tired of being disrespected! I am king! Me! I have taken my rightful place! I will make you all bow to me!" He screamed and raged, pacing like a cornered animal, his chest heaving and his eyes wide.

"What is happening to you?" Sigyn screamed, tears of pain welling in her eyes as she clutched her head where it had hit the hard stone. "When was that ever what you wanted? This wasn't about taking over Hevaña to rule! We were trying to make a home for our people! Where did that dream go, Zephrus?"

"Have we not reached that, wife?" he waved his arms wildly, gesturing toward the castle. "Are you not grateful for what I have given you? What the hell am I supposed to do to make you happy, you ungrateful bitch!" He grabbed her hair again and violently shook her.

Sigyn cried out and gripped his wrist, tears leaking from the corners of her eyes. "Please, Zephrus! You're hurting me!"

"Shut up! Shut up! I can't listen to your mundane ramblings any longer!" His eyes slowly began to change to a sort of copper color, with red beginning to form around his pupils. He grabbed her jaw, squeezing it hard and digging his nails into her face. "You will shut your whore mouth, ungrateful wife! You will put on a pretty face for the people while we find those traitors! You will sit by me and keep that pretty face as we watch the mage's neck snap to bring him out, do you understand?"

"Zephrus, you promised, though-!"

"I said silence! Very well, if you cannot keep yourself silent, I will do it myself! I have no use for your stupid, useless mutterings!" he put his hand over her mouth and screamed, "*Vox tal*!"

Sigyn's handmaiden kept her hands over her mouth and squeezed her eyes shut to hold back her tears as she had to listen to her queen's screams of fear and pain slowly fading to nothing, filling the throne room with a heavy silence.

Chapter 20

"I just can't do it, Inanna!" Thrax snapped angrily as he stared at the third failed attempt to animate a raven statue.

"Perhaps it's time to take a break?" Gwen suggested, sitting in the rickety old chair by the fireplace, stroking Deidra's ginger tabby cat as she slept curled up on her skirt.

"There's no time for breaks when learning spells like this. You have to do it, Thrax. You don't get a choice. Zephrus has ensured that. The ability to animate is an essential one. If you're in battle and don't have allies close by to give you aid, this spell could save your life." Inanna gently took his wrists and flipped them, so they were facing him. "Imagine your life force like a ball of fire inside you. Picture the green flames you make and use that to fuel your power. Send that to the statue. Now," Inanna sat back and crossed her arms. "Try again. We won't stop until you've done it right at least once."

Thrax heaved a heavy sigh but did as he was told, imagining a ball of green flame in his chest as he held his hands around the raven statue and chanted, *"Nantum vitae, umi nom vitae."*

As he repeated these words, the raven began to give off a soft blue glow, its stone wings twitching slightly. Gwen and Inanna leaned closer as he chanted louder. The light flickered before going out, ultimately, the statue growing still.

Thrax threw his hands in the air and fell back onto the floor, cursing angrily. "I can't do it!" he growled in frustration.

Gwen got off the chair and knelt beside him, pulling him up to sit up. "Maybe I can help?"

"How?"

"I was just thinking, Inanna, is it possible to have stronger magic if you're fighting for someone?"

"Well, magic is most definitely strengthened by emotion. I would say that perhaps imagining something to invoke such emotion could help."

"So, how about you try imagining one of us? Like me or Aaheer, the only way you can save us is to animate the raven statue. Maybe it'll help strengthen your power!" Gwen offered with a gentle smile.

Thrax thought for a moment and nodded. "It's worth a shot." he rearranged himself and let his hands hover over the raven statue as he began to chant again. He closed his eyes so he could concentrate. He saw Gwen, covered in blood and mud, reaching out to him, silently screaming for help. A rush of anger and fear filled him, his hands growing warm from the spell's power. He felt she genuinely would die if he didn't perform the spell.

Meanwhile, Gwen and Inanna had scooted back as the light around the raven grew brighter before it faded. Its stone wings scrapped slightly as they stretched. It tilted its head toward Thrax and gave a loud caw, making him open his eyes.

"I did it…" he gasped. The bird picked at its wings before hopping up onto his knee.

"Well done, Thrax! It seems you had the right idea, Gwen! What did you see?"

His cheeks went pink, and he turned away, distracting himself by fixing his ponytail. "Nothing. Don't worry about it. Are there any other spells we need to practice?"

"No, that'll be enough for today. Try practicing on smaller objects without using strong emotions and work your way up. I would suggest using Gwen's idea as a last resort. That method can be quite draining. Now, I want you to go and get some rest tonight. You've worked hard these past few days and need to rest your body and mind."

Thrax and Gwen got up and said their goodbyes as they left.

"Bye, Teyana!" Gwen waved to the woman sitting outside the caravan. She smiled and returned it as Inanna approached her, gently kissing her cheek.

"So," Gwen trotted up to Thrax, looping her arm through his. "What did you imagine?"

"It's nothing." Thrax huffed, feeling his face grow warm again and praying she couldn't see him blushing. "Don't be nosy."

"Ugh, you're being weird."

In the distance, the two could hear the call of a hunting horn. The camp fell quiet as it came again, and many jumped up, crying gleefully, "They're back! Tan's back!" Children rushed toward the sound, laughing gleefully as a large group of horses came riding in, burly men and muscular women in leather and metal armor, with weapons strung on their backs and saddles along with multiple animals. The man at the front of the procession had short curly black hair that stuck out of the blue and gold scarf around his head that matched the blue stones set in gold that he wore in a necklace and earrings, brown skin with long scars across his face, and dark brown eyes. He wore a black sleeveless coat, leather breastplate, braces but no shirt underneath, dark green pants, and laced-up hunting boots. His bow hung from his saddle with a sword and axe while his quiver of arrows was strapped to his back. He flashed the young girls a bright grin, making them blush and giggle amongst each other as he trotted past.

"Making a show of yourself again, Tan?" Inanna grinned as she approached his horse.

"Come now, sister, I have to have some fun, don't I? I don't get to be the big leader you are!" he teased, dismounting and pulling her into a hug, making her squirm.

"Ugh, let me go! You smell horrid!"

He threw his head back and gave a deep laugh that made Gwen's heart flutter when she heard it. "That's what comes with spending two weeks on a hunting trip!"

She smiled and giggled, drawing Tan's attention back to her. "Well, I don't think I've seen you here before!" He grinned as he approached her and gave a sweeping bow. "Tan Pryor, at your service."

Gwen gave a little curtsy. "Gwendolyn Grace. You must be Inanna's brother!"

"I am! I rather regret being on such a long hunting trip when I could have been in the company of a fair maid like yourself." He grinned as he took her hand and kissed it gently.

Gwen blushed and giggled sweetly. "I-I don't know what to say. That's very sweet of you, Tan."

Thrax scowled and stepped between them. "I'm sorry, who are you, again?" he raised an eyebrow.

Tan seemed rather startled that Thrax was even there and gave him a friendly smile. "Tan Pryor! I'm afraid I don't know you either?"

"Thrax Nightingale." Thrax put his hands on his hips and scanned over Tan's appearance. He tried to puff out his chest a bit to seem more prominent than Tan, who was admittedly a whole head taller than he was.

"This is Uncle Saedon's son." Inanna piped up.

Tan's eyes widened and suddenly swept Thrax up in a hug. "How could I have missed it! Of course! You're uncle's spitting image! We're so glad to have you back in our family!"

Thrax made a grumpy face at suddenly being caught in Tan's arms. From a distance, Gwen could see Aaheer and Astricus snickering as they approached them.

"So that means the prince is here as well?" Tan asked and caught sight of Aaheer. "Ah, I'd recognize you anywhere! Just like Thrax, you're the spitting image of Myana!" Tan also pulled Aaheer into a hug, though Aaheer seemed gleeful at being so welcomingly embraced.

"I'm prince Aaheer! I'm pleased to be of help and service to you!"

"Tan is known for being rather friendly to newcomers," Inanna whispered.

"You certainly have brought quite some powerful allies with you!" he grinned at Astricus, Dyael, and Borbyr, who came slowly, looking at him with confusion. "Zephrus would be a fool to think he could defeat us!"

"Aye, we'll be stronger with you and your hunters back, brother!" Inanna grinned. "Though he doesn't have magic, he makes up for it in skill with a bow! Tan could hit a squirrel a mile away through the eye!"

Gwen squirmed with discomfort at the thought. "I-…oh…h-how impressive."

"Is that so? My general can hit a mouse from two miles away!" Dyael boasted with a smirk, resting her hand on Borbyr's chest.

"Oh? Is that true, big guy?" Tan grinned up at him.

Borbyr scowled at the hunter. He reached up and gripped his bow slung over his shoulder. "I've trained since childhood with the bow. A human that's barely a man couldn't possibly beat me."

Not noticing Borbyr's quiet aggression, Tan threw his head back and laughed again, making Gwen's heart feel like it was doing summersaults in her chest. "I like you!

We'll have to have a good challenge one day! I'd be honored to learn from a skilled centaur!"

Borbyr blinked in surprise at Tan's friendliness, and a small smile tugged at his lips, almost despite himself.

"Alright, enough out of you! We will celebrate the return of our brother, Tan! The gods bless him with good health and a bountiful hunt!" Inanna called out, and the people cheered before moving to help the men unpack.

"Gwendolyn? Might you join me for a walk?" Tan asked, holding his hand out to her.

Gwen grinned and took it. "Of course! Also, call me Gwen."

Thrax watched them walk away, his face quite hot and his fists clenched tight.

"Seems someone is quite jealous," Astricus smirked, his little tail wagging with glee over watching Thrax steam.

"I am not! Gwen can do as she pleases! I'm not the only man in her life!"

"Of course, you're not, but Tan *is* quite handsome, and it seems he's taken quite a liking to her. If I were you, Thrax Nightingale, I'd watch out, or he may take your girl."

"She's *not* my girl! Gwen can do as she pleases! It's no skin off my back!"

"Of course, darling. That explains why you're redder than phoenix fire. Listen, if I were you, I'd consider telling Gwen how you feel soon, or someone like Tan may come and sweep her off her feet before you even have a chance." Astricus waved his hand toward the two as he went to help Aaheer.

"I-I do not like her!"

"Of course you don't, Thrax."

"So tell me about yourself, Gwen!" Tan was positively beaming as they walked through the green forest, the warm summer sun shining between the thick leaves.

"Well, what do you want to know?" Gwen asked, carefully stepping over a stump.

"How about…were you a member of the prince's court?"

"Oh, no. It's complicated. Thrax accidentally showed up at my house, and I sort of…agreed to join him. The more I've learned about everything, the more I've decided I can't just go back to my old life. I have to help."

"Ah, so your heart is as kind and lovely as your countenance." Tan smiled sweetly and held her hands in both of his. "I have just met you, lady Gwen, and I can tell you are a woman of a good and noble spirit."

Gwen felt her whole face heat up and quickly let go to cover her cheeks. "Now you're just flirting! You're horrible, Tan Pryor!" she teased.

"Oh please, my lady, do not think I intend to dishonor you with empty words!" he laughed and took her hands again. "I intend to learn more about you, and if you have me, I would like to ask your permission to court you."

Gwen's heart leaped again. This was all happening so quickly. She turned away, still grinning, as she walked to climb onto a stone on the bank of a brook. "Perhaps. If you can convince me enough."

"Then may I be permitted to try?" Tan climbed after her, sitting beside her on the rock's edge. "We can meet here again. I will teach you how to shoot. You said you wish to help our people. Then let me help you achieve your wish. I want to teach you what I know."

Gwen thought for a moment. She had been learning much with her knives, but to be able to fight with more weapons would be helpful. She had been meaning to ask Borbyr to teach her anyways, and as long as Tan was offering, she might as well learn from a handsome man who thought she was pretty. "Very well! Tomorrow at midday!"

Tan broke into a giant, happy grin and kissed the back of her hand. "I will wait with bated breath, my lady."

Chapter 21

Gwen woke the following day with butterflies in her stomach, dressed in her brown pants and boots, and a long-sleeved black top. Looking forward to her shooting lesson with Tan, she was so full of joy and didn't even notice Thrax, thoroughly grumpy.

"My, Thrax, if you were any sourer, you would make spoiled milk seem sweet!" Astricus sat on the cushion beside him with a sly smirk.

"Shut up, goat." he snapped.

"And testy, too! I love it!"

"You seem quite excited about trying to make me miserable," Thrax grumbled.

"Oh, not at all. I just haven't had good gossip in so long! Everything has been so serious. It's nice to turn my attention to something else." Astricus explained. "Plus, it gives me a chance to help my friends."

"Help? How?"

"Well, because you're wild about Gwen. Seeing her with someone else makes you miserable. Also, from what I've observed, she's attracted to you."

Thrax blushed deeply as he suddenly remembered something back when they were at the centaur camp, in the bed they shared, holding each other, whispering sweetly. "We talked about us having a relationship…she asked to take some time to get to know each other more. I-…almost told her everything…"

Astricus gave an angry bleat and punched his shoulder. "Are you an absolute dunce, Thrax Nightingale? Why didn't you take the chance to pour your heart out to her?"

"Ow! Because she didn't seem ready for such a thing, you damn goat!"

Astricus huffed and sat back. "Well, I can't blame you for respecting Gwen's space, but that means she's interested in you! Maybe she hasn't taken the first step because she still wants to ensure that *you* want *her*. Try telling her how you feel. How you *really* feel! She'll tire of waiting for you if you don't do it soon!"

Thrax leaned against the table, rubbing his shoulder. His entire face had gone bright red, and he avoided looking at the faun prince. "I'll think about it."

Gwen beamed as she sat on Tan's horse, hugging him around the middle. He led her through the beautiful forest until they reached a rolling green field dotted with patches of vibrant flowers, waving in the soft breeze and towering mountains in the distance, their snowy tops piercing through the clouds where majestic birds could still be spotted circling the peaks.

"Tan, this is beautiful!"

"It's my favorite spot when we travel here. I enjoy the space. It's perfect for beginner target practice." He led his horse a few yards before hopping off and helping Gwen down.

"For you, my lady." He handed her a bow and a leather brace.

"What's the brace for?" she asked, tying it to her forearm.

"To protect you from the rebound of the bowstring. You can use my arrows for now," he took off his quiver, propping it up beside her. "Take your arrow, then notch it in the bow."

Gwen did as she was told, clumsily attempting to pull the string back while keeping the arrow in its place.

"Here, let me show you." Tan stepped closer, so his chest was almost pressed to Gwen's back. His breath tickled her neck as he put his calloused hands over hers and instructed, "Pull back like this…keep your arms and body level…steady your breathing…I can practically hear your heartbeat." he gave a low chuckle, making her blush.

"Well, wouldn't you be if a handsome man was pressed against you like this?" she quipped.

He smirked and leaned closer, having her draw the bow back until her hand reached her cheekbone. "There…now…slow your breathing…aim like this…and loose."

Gwen released the arrow, and it sailed straight into a tree branch.

Tan stood straight and grinned. "Not bad for a first try!" he said and drew another arrow. "Try it on your own, now!"

Gwen drew the arrow back as he had shown, though far more slowly and with more trouble. She eventually released the arrow, which flew into the treetops, falling to the ground with a clatter.

Tan put a hand over his mouth, his voice quivering with mirth, "At least it reached the tree."

Gwen made a face at him. "I'll get it right!"

"Don't work yourself too hard, my lady." Tan drew another arrow, helping her again to aim, his calloused hands tenderly cradling hers as he guided her, leaning close, so his lips brushed against her cheek. "We have plenty of opportunities to practice."

Gwen felt the now familiar summersault of her stomach from his actions. "Is this how all Gyrians flirt, or just you?"

"Just I."

"I'm sure you have all the girls swooning for you."

414

"I care little about how they see me. There is only one girl I have my eye on right now. I wondered if she might want to join me for dinner and dancing tonight. I heard my sister mentioning having a small celebration for my return."

"I'm sure she would be delighted. You'll have to ask her directly, though," she said coyly.

Tan smirked and took her hand, holding it to his lips. "Gwendolyn Grace, will you honor me by joining me for a dance tonight?"

Her coy smile grew, fluttering her eyelashes at him, dramatically holding her hand to her heart. "Why Tan Pryor, you minx! How could I possibly refuse?"

Tan threw his head back to laugh. "You are fascinating, lady Gwendolyn! Then it's decided. I will eagerly await tonight."

"Why are you getting so dressed up?"

"It's a party, Thrax. Am I not allowed to look nice?"

Thrax fumed, sitting on the bed of their shared caravan, arms crossed, while he observed her apply the cosmetics Inanna had given her. She was dressed in a shimmery green and silver skirt wrapped around her waist and a corset top tied in a crisscross pattern down her back. She wore some necklaces and bracelets Inanna gave her and had her hair tied back in braids and pinned to her head with decorative hair sticks.

"Is it just for the party or someone at the party?" Thrax grumbled.

Gwen felt her cheeks grow warm as she sat back. "It's none of your concern. I can dance with whomever I please." She firmly set down the rouge and strode out of the caravan.

Thrax huffed and stood up. "Fine. If she wants to be that way, I'll let her. Why did I ever try to listen to that damn goat?"

"Thrax?" Inanna knocked at the door.

"Oh, Inanna. What is it?"

"I just saw Gwen. She looked rather grumpy. Were you two arguing?"

"Sort of. I think she's quite interested in your brother."

A quick look of understanding crossed her face, and she laughed. "Thrax, I think she's more interested in the attention he's giving her. My brother is sweet and can be quite the charmer, but I feel Gwen would rather get that attention from someone else."

417

"Astricus said the same. Perhaps her interests have changed, though." Thrax said with a huff.

"I think what's changed is you making a fool of yourself." Inanna looked him over. "I have an idea. Why don't we fix you up a bit? Mother says that looking your best helps you feel your best. Maybe that might help you confess to her."

Thrax's face went pink. He hesitated before sheepishly saying, "What if she really isn't interested?"

"I'm quite certain she is, Thrax. But brooding over my brother, rather than showing her how you feel, will do nothing to win her favor. Come on; we still have time."

"What are you going to do?" he asked as she began to rifle through the wardrobe.

"I'm going to try something. You have your father's features. I suspect if I dress you like him, you'll win Gwen's heart as easily as he won your mother's." she pulled out a loose white shirt with an open front and a pair of emerald-green pants. She then pulled out a couple of golden earrings. "Put these on."

"This is what my father wore?" Thrax raised an eyebrow but still began to undress.

"Not exactly, no, but it's quite similar. Uncle Saedon didn't dress up much, but he still managed to show off. Wear those, and don't be afraid to ask Gwen to dance."

Thrax paused as he pulled on the shirt, the tips of his ears feeling quite hot. "I…I'm not much of a dancer."

"Doesn't matter. I'm sure you'll be able to dance well enough, and Gwen, I'm sure, will be more than pleased."

"I seem to be trusting you quite a bit," Thrax grumbled.

"You aren't exactly winning her on your own, Thrax Nightingale, so I'd keep your opinions to yourself now." Inanna glowered moodily. "I don't have to be doing any of this, you know."

"No, you're right, you're right. Thank you, cousin." Thrax apologized quickly. Once he was dressed, Inanna had him sit and began to undo and brush his long, black hair, braiding the sides and then joining it into one thick braid down his back.

"You don't have to do this, you know."

"I know. Frankly, though, I think it'd be more disappointing to your father if he knew his son was too frightened to tell the woman he loves how he felt." her mouth twitched in a playful smirk.

Thrax chuckled softly. "Was father quite a flirt?"

"No, I wouldn't say that. He enjoyed giving compliments, but his heart was never into such things. He was taken by your mother the moment he saw her, though."

"What do you remember of them? When they were together?"

"They were smitten with each other the moment they met. I remember they tried everything they could to stay together. I remember how they wrote letters and danced together…there was no love on this earth stronger than theirs…" she murmured with a sad smile.

"What do you think would have happened if father had lived?"

"Well, I don't think Aaheer would have been born. I think Zephrus would have been different, and frankly, you would have grown up much happier. But we can't change how things are. Uncle Saedon's likely tired of hearing us complain all the time and wondering how things might have been. So, we're going to honor him by looking to the future. We must think about how we'll help our people, stop Zephrus, and get your brother on the throne. Oh, and how could I forget? How to get you in the arms of your lady love." Inanna smirked, making Thrax blush heavily.

"Inanna, please!" Thrax's cheeks went bright pink.

"Come now, cousin. It's time for the celebration." Inanna insisted and helped him to his feet. "You don't want Tan to beat you!" She giggled and led him outside of the wagon.

The caravan had been set up, so the wagons were in a wide circle. A large bonfire was built, and musicians were tuning their instruments. People were scurrying to finish making food piled on the tables, and vines were woven with flowers and hung from the wagons to add decoration. Tan stood by the fireplace with Gwen, laughing and chatting, making her blush. Thrax felt his chest tighten and a bubble of anger heat up in his belly.

"Calm yourself, Thrax." Inanna gripped his shoulder. "There's nothing wrong with what they're doing.

Don't forget, Tan is your cousin as well, and Gwen's allowed to have friends. Perhaps you should get to know him as such before you make sweeping judgments about him." she ruffled his hair and nudged him towards them.

Thrax took a deep breath and stepped forward, trying to calm his beating heart.

Tan looked at him and gave a huge grin. "Thrax! I've been wanting to speak with you!" he pulled him into a rough hug, lifting him off his feet.

Thrax felt the breath leave his lungs as he choked out, "Y-you as well." He caught sight of Gwen's expression as she smirked. Thrax gasped for air and rubbed his ribs as Tan sat him back down.

"So, little cousin, how old are you?"

"Twenty-three this harvest. You?"

Tan's grin stretched wider making Thrax wonder if

it didn't hurt him. "I just turned twenty-three! How about that? We're close in age, aren't we?"

"I suppose we are. So, you don't have magic?" he asked.

"Thrax, that's rude!" Gwen smacked his arm.

"Oh, don't fear, lady Gwendolyn. I took no offense!" Tan assured her, waving her indignation away with a warm smile. "It's perfectly alright! No, I don't have any magic. Inanna took after our mother in that regard. I don't mind, though! My power's in my shooting!" he winked and patted his bow on the table beside him.

"Really? Has Inanna never taught you spells to improve your shooting?"

"Oh, she's tried, but I just don't have that kind of skill, I'm afraid." his smile fell slightly as he spoke. "No, that gift went to her. My father died before I was born, so I couldn't learn skills from him as Inanna could from my mother. So…I found my own skills."

Thrax went quiet for a moment. He knew that feeling all too well. "I never knew my father either. I learned my magic from my master. Mother wasn't allowed to talk to me."

Gwen remained silent, smiling as she watched the two cousins.

"I know from the stories that uncle Saedon would have been very proud of you." Tan gripped his shoulder. "I'm sure your mother is too. You'll have to have mother tell you how they saved my life when I was a baby."

"Really?" Thrax's eyes widened. "I…never knew…"

"Mother can tell you better than I can."

Thrax glanced at Gwen before pulling on Tan's arm. "Can I speak to you, Tan? Privately?"

Tan tilted his head quizzically. "Um…sure…"

Thrax led him away from the party just outside the caravan circle. "I owe you an apology."

"For what?" Tan gave a little chuckle. "You've never wronged me, cousin."

"I did, however. I've been cold to you and unwilling to get to know you as family. I've been jealous."

"Jealous? What on earth for?"

"Well…because you have a life that I wish I did. You have your family, amazing skills, people who love you, and-…you seemed to have lady Gwendolyn's heart…" he admitted, looking away in shame.

Tan snorted. "Have her heart? Hardly, Thrax! Listen, if this is what that's all about, I can tell you that lady Gwendolyn hasn't even allowed me to court her. In truth, I wanted her to myself. I'm ashamed of that now because I can see you love her. I only just met her." Tan smiled tenderly and hugged him. "My time will come. You go to her tonight, dear cousin, and tell her how much you love her. Don't you dare lose her; you hear me? I can tell she's wonderful, even from just meeting her."

Thrax gave a small laugh, his chest tightening with emotion. "You're right…thank you, Tan. I'm…I'm fortunate to have met you…my family."

Tan immediately pulled him closer. "The gods have brought our little family together again, dear cousin…I don't intend on losing that."

The two headed back to the party, and Gwen stood up. "There you are! I thought you might have been whisked away." she gave both boys a teasing grin. "Tan, are we still going to dance?"

"Actually, my lady, sadly, I must retract my invitation for this evening." He bowed low and kissed her hand. "Though it has been a true joy, I will remain your fast friend. I must leave you in Thrax's company."

Gwen's brow furrowed as she watched him leave. "What was that about?"

"Just an understanding between family." Thrax took her hand and smiled. "May I have this dance?"

A coy smile crossed her lips. "I'll allow it." she winked and followed him to the crowd of dancers. The two twirled about, pressed close together, the light of the fire lighting their steps, warming them from the cool night air as they laughed and sang with the others. They danced until their legs felt like jelly, and they ran, laughing gleefully, their faces red with the fire's warmth, and dancing to the tables laden with food. They sat down, giggling at each other.

"Enjoying yourselves?" Inanna asked as she approached with two tankards, Teyana holding her arm.

"Absolutely!" Gwen grinned at her. "It's a wonderful party!"

"You should see our others, then!" She winked, set the cups in front of them, and then took Teyana's hand.

"What's this?" Gwen asked, peering into her drink.

"The finest blackberry mead you will ever find, dear girl!" she kissed Teyana on the cheek, making her giggle softly. "Made by my beloved!"

"Teyana, you made it?" Gwen took a sip, and her face lit up. "It's delicious!"

"Oh, it's nothing!" Teyana looked rather sheepish. "I learned from others. Don't act like it was only me."

"What do you mean? This was made with your tender love and care, my dearest." Inanna pulled her close and kissed her sweetly on her neck.

"Inanna!" Teyana went pink and giggled. "Your mother is watching!"

"We're married, my star. She knows what happens between a married couple!" Inanna teased.

"You two seem very happy." Thrax smiled. "Perhaps you can teach my brother how to court so he can finally make Astricus the happiest goat in all of Hevaña."

"Oh? Does our little faun prince strike Aaheer's fancy?" Inanna smirked. "Perhaps I'll have to teach him how to court."

"Inanna Pryor, you will not!" Teyana tugged her wife away from them. "You give her too many ideas, Thrax Nightingale." she teased as they walked away.

Gwen giggled and took another drink from her cup. "They're quite cute, aren't they?"

"Indeed..." Thrax paused a moment before reaching out and taking her hand. "I must speak to you, Gwen."

"Oh? Is it more questions about why I do the things I do?" she giggled.

"No…no, it's much more serious."

"Oh, serious? My, Thrax, in front of the children?" she gave a scandalized gasp.

Thrax snorted and reached up, holding her face in his hands. "Hey! I'm trying to speak to you on an important matter!"

She stuck her tongue out playfully. "Alright then." she sat up straight and waved her hand over her face, dropping her smile. "Serious."

Thrax smiled and shook his head before taking her hands and gazing deeply at her. The intensity of his look made her look more seriously at him. "I wanted to talk to you about…well, about us. Back in the centaur camp, you said you wanted to…get to know each other more before we discussed courting, right?"

"I did."

"Right. So…about Tan. Do you-…well, do you fancy him?"

Gwen paused at that and took a moment to think about it. "Truthfully? I like looking at him. I liked the things he was saying to me. But I don't know if I'd say I fancy him."

"Then…Gwen…is there someone you do fancy?"

"Yes. He's a bit of a dunce and an ass, but he's quite sweet."

"Astricus?"

"No, you idiot! You!"

Thrax couldn't help the smile that broke across his face, even though he knew her answer. "I fancy you as well…no, I think I've fallen for you, Gwendolyn Grace. I've fallen madly and irreversibly in love with you," he admitted and held her hands tenderly, lifting them to his lips to kiss. "And I've finally gained the courage to say so."

Gwen felt her heart leap in her chest and her face grew hot. Before she realized what she was doing, she stood up, grasped Thrax's face in her hands, and pulled him into a deep, loving kiss. "I love you too, you idiot."

Thrax's eyes widened and broke into an enormous grin. "Why did you not say anything before?"

"Well, we weren't exactly discussing it in depth. We had other things happening." Gwen giggled. "Plus, you had enough on your mind and would make me too mad to confess myself."

"Mad? Oh, you mean like with Tan."

"Yes. You must understand that just because someone else speaks to me doesn't mean I will run away with them. Plus, I was not romantically committed to you when Tan was flirting with me. I choose whom I want to be with just as much as you do, Thrax."

He lowered his gaze and nodded. "You're right…I apologize. I shouldn't have let my temper get the better of me."

She lifted his chin to look at her, smiling sweetly. "We're in this together, Thrax Nightingale. We work things out together. Alright?"

"Alright…" he kissed her softly, holding her cheek in his hand.

When they pulled apart, Gwen grabbed his hands, "Let's dance!" and pulled him to the dancing circle.

With a laugh, Thrax twirled her and spun with her and the rest of the caravan, resting one hand on her waist, the other holding her hand out, chest-to-chest, following the steps of the rest of the group while the music pounded in their chests.

As the moon climbed into the sky, Gwen and Thrax soon collapsed in the grass by their wagon, laughing and gasping for breath, their faces bright red from the fire and the dancing.

"Enjoying the party?" Aaheer asked, sitting next to them.

"Aye, little brother," Thrax said with a chuckle, kissing Gwen tenderly on her cheek. "I would say it has been a most wonderful evening!"

"Indeed! I would think so with how you two seemed to be joined at the hip tonight!" Dyael laughed, trotting over with Borbyr beside her. "Finally told each other how you feel? It's about damn time!"

Gwen blushed more and nestled her head against Thrax's shoulder. "It just…worked out, I suppose…"

"I won't deny it; I'm a bit surprised." Aaheer snickered slightly. "Thrax has never been good at admitting his love. Frankly, I've never taken you for the hopeless romantic, brother."

435

"Oh? You could have asked me how to flirt." Gwen winked at Thrax. "I could tell you all about how to flirt with women. I've done it lots of times."

"You've flirted with women?" Dyael asked, raising an eyebrow.

Gwen went pink and gave an awkward smile. "Well, yes. I don't care about people's gender. I'm drawn to people for who they are."

Astricus's ears perked up, and his little tail wagged gleefully. "Like fauns!"

Gwen grinned and nodded. "Exactly like that."

Thrax blushed and gave a small smile. "Well, perhaps your skills would have taught me how to win you over sooner…" he squeezed her hand and brought it to his lips.

"Alright, alright! I don't need all of that!" Astricus stuck his tongue out, miming gagging like Thrax had done to him many times. "Come, Aaheer, let's dance!" The faun locked his arm with the prince and took off for the dancing circle, making Aaheer yelp at the sudden movement.

"Yes, it's about time for us to retire." Dyael nodded and gestured for Borbyr to follow her. "Sleep well, you two."

"Good night, Dyael! Sleep well, Borbyr!" Gwen waved to them and turned to Thrax, her cheeks growing pink. "Perhaps we should get some sleep as well?" she tenderly drew circles on his hand.

Thrax's face glowed red, and he awkwardly cleared his throat. "I-…u-um…p-perhaps your right…" he agreed. They may have slept by each other's side for weeks, but this new development created something new between them, and Thrax wasn't quite sure how to handle it.

The new couple took each other's hands and wandered to their wagon, closing the door away from the party. Thrax lit a candle or two, bathing their tiny home in a warm orange glow.

"It was a fun party," Gwen said as she reached back to tug off her corset. "Um…Thrax, would you…help me with this?"

"Oh, of course. You looked lovely this evening, by the way."

"Thank you." Gwen reached up and pulled the decorations from her hair. Once the corset was undone, she let it fall to the floor. Thrax quickly averted his eyes for her comfort. After a moment, he felt Gwen's gentle hand hold his cheek and lift to meet her gaze. "It's okay to look, Thrax…I-…I want you to look…if you're okay with it." Her entire face was bright red, right to the tips of her ears, poking out from her blonde waves. Her blue eyes glittered with affection and desire.

Thrax felt his heart leap into his chest as he slowly removed his shirt. "I can't deny I want you, my love…I-…I fear I'll do something indecent if we continue like this."

"Would you be alright with it if we did?" Gwen asked, stepping closer and resting her hands on his shoulders. "I certainly would."

Thrax swallowed harder and snaked his hands around her hips. "I would like it…" he pulled her flush to his body, kissing her deeply and slowly. Gwen hummed into his kiss, sliding her arms around his neck, one hand pulling out his ponytail, shiny black hair cascading down his shoulders.

He lifted her into his arms and put her on the bed, still kissing her with growing desperation.

"Gwen…are you sure? You know you can always refuse me still." Thrax whispered, between their kisses, his heart still pounding.

"You're so sweet, Thrax." Gwen cradled his face in her hands. "I want this…I want all of you."

The wizard's cheeks flushed. He gave a small chuckle and tenderly pushed Gwen's blonde locks from her face. "I'm afraid I may not be a very skilled lover…I don't have much experience," he admitted.

"Don't worry about that…every couple has to work out the kinks…we can discover ourselves together."

"Aye…I'd like that…" Thrax moved to kiss her again, one hand sliding down to rest on her hip while his other hand explored her, squeezing and kneading her breast. His touch was hesitant and unsure, though as their kisses and whispers of affection grew more passionate, his movements grew more confident.

Gwen felt her heart pound against her chest as her hands slid down to the hem of his pants. She pulled back from his kiss to take in the sight of his body, with defined muscles from the weeks of travel and fighting.

"Does my body please you, my lady?" The wizard whispered huskily, lifting her leg around his waist as he kissed down her neck.

"Yes…" she couldn't form more words as her body grew hotter with Thrax's attention. She slid her hands across his chest and rolled his nipples under her thumbs, making him falter.

"A-ah! Devil woman…" he chuckled with a purr to his voice, making Gwen's lower region throb with need. "I'll have to teach you a lesson, I see."

Thrax grasped Gwen's wrists and pushed her back on the bed. He held her arms above her head firmly so she wouldn't be able to touch him, making her whimper. His mind felt fuzzy, but he could still recall the things he had heard from soldiers and their tales of nights with courtesans. He kissed Gwen's body until he reached her breasts. He took one in his mouth, running his tongue across her nipple. Gwen gasped, arching her back, pressing him closer to her breast.

The wizard gazed up at her, eyes burning with lust that made her squirm with passion. "P-please, Thrax…m-more…I-I want you to use your tongue."

"No…I want to tease you some more…" his husky voice made her stomach flip as he moved to the other breast, sucking and licking her nipple, making her moan louder.

She lifted her legs around his waist, rocking her hips against his. His erection throbbed against his already tight pants, making him falter again, giving a shaky moan.

"You don't know when to quit, do you?"

"I thought it's what you liked about me…" she teased, taking a moment to remove her hands from his hold, reaching between them to palm him through his pants.

"Ah! Nngh…i-it's-…fuck…come here…" he grabbed her hands again, holding them down beside her head. He locked his fingers with hers and kissed down her stomach. One of his hands slid away, tenderly caressing down her body, with love in each touch, to the ties of her skirt. His fingers nimbly undid the tie and tossed the garment aside. Thrax felt his mouth go dry and his heart leap into his throat.

"Beautiful…" was all he could mutter as he positioned himself between her legs, hooking them over his shoulders. He kissed her inner thigh, gazing at her with his fiery emerald eyes.

Gwen felt her stomach twist again under his gaze, writhing with desire. "Thrax, you're teasing me…" she whined, using her legs to pull him closer.

"Aye…I thought that was obvious." There was a touch of laughter in his voice as he hummed softly, kissing and experimentally licking at her labia, studying her face.

Gwen shifted to sit on her elbows to watch what he was doing. When she felt his tongue between her legs, she gasped, her face going deep red, holding her thighs around him, pulling him in closer.

"Did you like that, my lady?" he whispered huskily, his hands slowly wrapping around her thighs, his fingers tenderly stroking them up and down.

"Yes…do it again…in fact, do it more…right here…" her fingers slid down and pushed open her folds, stroking at her clit.

"As you wish…" Thrax took her fingers, gently sucking on them, before diving back between her legs, sucking and licking her clit. His movements started slow, making her press her head back into the pillow, moaning with lust, her hands sliding down to tangle in his hair, pressing him closer. With this encouragement, he began moving quicker, watching in reverence as she unraveled under him.

"Thrax, please," she sat up so he could see her face, her eyes wild with lust and her usually pinkish face now quite red and flushed. "Please, take me…I want you to fuck me."

He broke into a wide grin and sat up, licking his lips. "Delicious…" he purred before he got up beside the bed, quickly getting out of his pants and tossing them across their caravan.

Gwen's eyes widened seeing him fully naked, and she swallowed hard, suddenly feeling her mouth go dry as her heart threatened to pound out of her chest. She hesitantly reached out and wrapped her hand around his cock, looking up at him as she began to pump up and down.

Thrax bit his lip and groaned softly, climbing back onto the bed over her. "Are you sure you still want this? We can still back out."

"I want this…please, Thrax…" Gwen assured, releasing him to lean back and hold her legs as open as she could.

"Fuck…okay…I'll go slow…tell me if it hurts." He positioned himself and slowly pushed into her.

She closed her eyes, grimacing slightly. "Shit…hold on, let me get used to it…okay, you can move. Go slow, though."

Thrax set a slow pace, resisting the urge to thrust wildly into her. His overflowing lust fueled his body, legs trembling from holding back, but he wanted to ensure he didn't hurt her. He leaned forward, sliding his hands up to lock her fingers with his again. The two forgot how to speak not long after this, falling into moans and passionate gazes as the pace picked up. Thrax slammed into her, leaning down to bite at her shoulder while she wrapped her arms around him, digging her nails into his back.

Gwen shifted to wrap her legs around his body, running her hands across his shoulders and chest. Thrax growled with desire, grabbing her legs and yanking her closer. She squeaked and giggled before falling back into wordless moans as the new position made her body feel hot, twinging with waves of pleasure at each thrust. Thrax panted heavily, kissing across her shoulder and collarbone. He thrust harder into her, one hand grasping and kneading her breast roughly while the other gripped her hips to hold her steady.

"Fuck…Thrax, yes! Right there! I-I'm gonna come!" she cried, closing her eyes and arching her back as the ecstasy began to build.

"Fuck, Gwen!" he gritted his teeth as he slammed into her.

Gwen pressed her head back into the pillow, arching her back as her body quivered with pleasure, making her cry out his name. Her hips rolled as she rode out her orgasm, saying his name in a weak whimper. She was left a panting, moaning mess as Thrax moved his hand from her breast to the sheets. He tilted his head as he thrust harder before throwing it back, moaning in pure bliss, stars dancing across his vision, his hips jerking as his mind slowly cleared from the intense pleasure.

He collapsed beside his lover, pushing back his black hair and pulling her into his arms. "Was I sufficient, my love?" he purred, kissing her neck and jawline.

"Oh definitely…" she pressed her body to his, her hands lovingly caressing him. Her mind was cloudy from exhaustion as she nuzzled his neck, struggling to speak more than a few words. "I think we'll be doing this much more often."

Chapter 22

Thrax woke with a deep, grumpy groan as the sunlight peaked between the bed curtains. He sat up and stretched, yawning and scratching his chest before hopping out of bed. Gwen was standing by the fire, getting the teapot she'd been heating, dressed in only the shirt Thrax had worn the night before, her blonde hair tied back.

Thrax grinned and walked over to her as she poured tea into mugs. "Good morning, my darling," He whispered, holding her from behind and kissing her neck.

She giggled, scrunching her shoulders from the ticklish feeling of his scruffy beard. "Good morning, love." She turned her head to greet him with a tender kiss. "Sleep well?"

"Like a baby…" he chuckled. "You left me feeling completely drained, you devil…" he teased and kissed her again. "How are you feeling?"

"A little sore, but alright," she assured and handed him a cup of tea. "Let's get dressed. I want to stop by the town today. We need some more supplies."

"Perhaps you should wear my shirt." Thrax smiled tenderly. "It suits you…"

"Flatterer. I think I will." she tied up the shirt more properly before grabbing her breeches and boots Inanna had given her.

"We need to get more food and supplies for weapons. I have a feeling our fight with Zephrus is growing closer."

"I think you're right. Should we have the others come?"

"I'm not sure. I think any of us may be too recognizable, but going with more numbers might be our safest option if a fight breaks out."

"I say we bring them. Maybe even bring Tan. Since he's been gone for so long, he won't be as recognizable."

"He and Borbyr could watch from afar. They would be excellent lookouts."

"You're right." Gwen clasped her cloak and grabbed a basket and her knives, sticking them in the sheathes on her belt. "Come on. We should get there early for the best options."

The couple stepped out into the gray morning, clouds the color of down feathers covering the sun. Aaheer and Astricus stood by the breakfast fire, speaking with Dyael and Borbyr.

"Ah! There's the happy couple!" Astricus called out with a devilish grin. "Was he suitable, lady Gwendolyn?"

"Astricus, please, don't announce it to the whole camp!" she smacked his arm, looking sheepish. "Was I so loud?"

"Don't listen to him, Gwen; he's simply trying to embarrass you," Aaheer assured her, shooting the faun a stern look.

"Are you leaving the caravan?" Borbyr asked gruffly, pointing to Gwen's basket.

"Just gathering some supplies. We wanted to invite all of you and Tan to come with us." Thrax explained.

"Oh, you want me to tag along, dear cousin? What an honor!" Tan popped up behind him, smirking. "All it took was for you to get a pretty girl in your bed to like me, I see."

"Tan!" Gwen cried, holding her face in her hands, blushing furiously.

453

"Alright, come on, now, leave her alone, all of you." Aaheer scolded, putting his hands on his hips firmly. "We'll all go with you, Gwen, and don't listen to their teasing."

"Oh, come now, your highness, we meant no harm! At least now you can be assured no one else in the caravan will try to take your wizard from you!" Tan assured and winked teasingly at Gwen. "Come on, then! To the village!"

The group all walked to the village, but as they got closer, they began to notice the large crowd gathering in the street.

"Something's wrong…" Tan murmured. "Maybe this isn't a good idea."

"No, we need to know what's going on," Aaheer spoke. "Dyael, Borbyr, you're the fastest of all of us. Can you head back to the caravan and tell Inanna something is wrong? We'll likely need backup."

"I can send Ea. It'll be best if he goes. He's faster than even us."

"We can stay on the outside as a getaway. Look out for any of his soldiers." Borbyr grabbed his bow and notched an arrow into it. "You be careful." The centaurs turned and trotted away from the crowd, circling the edge of the village.

"Let's split up. You three go that way. We'll go the other." Gwen pointed them around one side of the crowd and pulled her hood low. She quickly snatched Thrax's hand and pulled him around the group.

"Excuse me…pardon me…" The two pushed past the crowd until Thrax suddenly froze in his tracks, making Gwen pause so she didn't hit him.

"Thrax? What's wrong?" When she stepped around to see his face, he was pale, eyes wide in horror. "Thrax? Thrax, what is it?" she looked out to the crowd and saw a man standing on a gallows platform, the noose hanging loosely around a woman's neck and her dirty hair, her hands bound, and a sad, lifeless expression on her entire being.

The man looked almost shockingly like Thrax, though his face had a sunken appearance and an evil air around him. There was something dark in his eyes and his cruel, twisted smile.

"Thrax…that's Zephrus…" Gwen realized. "But…who's that woman?"

"That's-…my master…" he croaked, his voice cracking with emotion. "Majora…"

"People of Terra Vale! I, Zephrus Saedon, have come to bring you a long overdue message! Here before you, I hold one of the last people of King Jarkus's court, the great mage, Majora Crowe! I am here to tell you that the era of Jarkus is no more! You no longer have to fear him! I will do all in my power to be the kind of ruler the good people of Hevaña need, as well as for my fellow Gyrians! I will create a new homeland for us, where all may prosper! But my trust does not come lightly! I demand your respect as your king, and I will not be afraid to answer those who speak or act against myself and my court! Now, let us celebrate the end of the Thornblade era and usher in the era of house Saedon!" He stepped away, and one of his soldiers pushed Majora aggressively over the trapdoor.

"This is your last chance, sorceress. Renounce the old crown and the old prince. Come to my court, where you will be treated well." Zephrus offered, holding out his hand to her.

The woman lifted her head, and for a brief moment, a spark of hatred came into her eyes as she spat at his feet to the crowd's gasps, yanking on her restraints. "You are no king! Long live prince Aaheer! Your arrogance and dark magic will be your downfall! Long live the prince! Long live Aaheer! Long live, queen Myana!" As she cried, the people in the crowd began to cheer alongside her, chanting, "Long live the queen! Long live the prince!"

Zephrus's expression darkened. "SILENCE!" he threw out his hands, and enormous cracks jutted across the ground, tiny tongues of red flames slipping from them. His smile widened, and he pointed to Majora. "You seal your fate, mage. You will never see your loved ones again." With a wave of his hand, the lever was pulled, and Majora dropped with a gasp. A crack sounded as she strained and struggled, her feet kicking slightly as she tried to breathe.

"NO!" Thrax screamed and rushed out into the circle, blasting fire at the rope, breaking it.

"Thrax, no!" Gwen ran after him, trying to stop him.

"Fools!" The others came from the other side of the crowd.

"Oh, what a surprise! My little brother came to watch his master die!" Zephrus cackled.

"You! You bastard! This is all because of you!" Thrax threw himself at Zephrus, blasting fire at him. The crowd around them screamed and ran away.

Zephrus lazily lifted his hand, blocking the fire with a shield. "You have been training all these long years, and this is all you can produce? Please, this was meant to at least be a challenge." he sneered.

"To hell with you!" Tan cried, releasing an arrow.

Zephrus raised his other hand to catch the arrow, turning it to black ash. "Why Tan Pryor. I wasn't aware you were so interested in such events, cousin. I thought you preferred taking live bodies to your bed."

Astricus ran up to him, ducking low to drill his knife into his side, but just as he got past his shield, Zephrus grabbed the faun's fist in his hand. "Oh? A faun prince? You must truly be desperate, little brother!" He cackled and grabbed Astricus by the horn, shoving him away so hard that there was a crack, and part of his horn was left in Zephrus's hand. Astricus cried out, clutching his head as blood began to soak his hair.

"Bastard!" Aaheer charged him with his sword drawn. "You'll pay for hurting them!" he swung, and Zephrus drew his sword, stopping him.

"And here we have the little prince…such an honor to have you here…we certainly weren't expecting two executions."

Aaheer stepped back, his eyes wide and his hands shaking slightly, but charged again with a roar of fury the others hadn't seen in him, swinging his sword.

Meanwhile, Gwen ran to Majora on the ground. Her breathing was very shallow and rugged. "Majora…don't worry; we're getting you out of here."

"Who…?" Majora gave a violent cough, a bit of blood dripping down her lip.

"No, don't speak. You don't know me. I'm Gwendolyn. I know Thrax. He's alright. We're getting you out of here." With great difficulty, Gwen grabbed Majora under her arms and dragged her through the crowd of screaming villagers to an alleyway.

Once she was safely hidden, Gwen ran to the square, drawing her knives. She charged at Zephrus and jumped from the gallows onto his back. He cried out in shock, stumbling forward, then laughed. "My, you surprised me! That doesn't happen often! Come here, girl, I'll make you my trophy!" he reached back to grab her, but Gwen answered by stabbing his hand and shoulder.

Zephrus cried out, grabbing at his wounds as she leaped away. "Leave, Zephrus! I won't let you hurt my friends!"

Zephrus gave another manic laugh, now shaking slightly, his twisted face paler and sweating from pain. "Oh, I see! You're his little whore! Then I'll have to kill you next! I'll kill all your little friends until you have nothing left, brother!"

"You are no brother of mine!" Thrax shouted and cried, "*Ényo tumó!*"

Zephrus created another shield that blocked the purple lightning that shot at him.

"Please, you must know more than that." The wizard snapped his fingers, and a giant crow swooped down, scratching at Thrax's face, making him shout. A scream-like howl turned their attention to a fox running from the forest. Kitsae leaped up, grabbing the crow in its jaws.

"Damn you! Damn you insignificant little beasts!" Zephrus screamed, blasting ice at the ground. Astricus scrambled back as it began to cover his hooves, Aaheer trying to pull him back more quickly.

"ENOUGH!" Thrax blasted at the ice with fire, making it melt. "That's enough, Zephrus! I won't let you keep doing this! To this country, to the people, and to my father! You don't deserve to call yourself an Arimas!"

"Oh, and you do? Please. You are not yet worthy to kill, little brother. Come to the castle when you are ready. Be prepared to die, as well. You will be an example to this wasteland of a kingdom, and I will put all your heads on pikes outside my kingdom!" He raised his arm, and Sephtis broke from Kitsae's jaws, flying to his master with a loud caw. Once on Zephrus's forearm, the two disappeared in a cloud of black smoke.

"Well done, Kitsae…" Thrax scratched the fox's ear.

Gwen threw herself into his arms, pressing her face into his chest. "Don't you ever do something so stupid again, Thrax Nightingale…" her voice quivered with emotion as he held her tightly.

"I'm sorry, my love…I didn't mean to worry you." When he released her, they went to check on Astricus. "How is he?"

"The bleeding isn't so bad. He'll be alright. The wound is shallow, so it won't take long to heal. His horns may not grow the same, though." Tan explained.

"My horn…will it grow back, though…?" Astricus murmured, his face stained with blood on one side, tear tracks cutting through it.

"It will…don't worry. You'll be just fine, your highness." Tan assured him.

Aaheer knelt next to Astricus, holding his hand and gently cleaning the faun's face. He looked up at his brother with enormous tears in his bloodshot eyes. "Go to Majora, Thrax. Quickly. I won't let anything happen to them."

"She's over here," Gwen took Thrax's hand and led her to Majora's hiding place.

The mage was still breathing, though it was in short, rattling breaths. "Thrax…" she coughed again, blood dribbling from the corner of her mouth.

"Master…" Thrax's voice tightened as he pulled her into his arms. "Gwen, we don't have much time…we have to get her back."

"I'll go find Borbyr and Dyael."

"No need." Dyael walked up to them, dragging one of Zephrus's soldiers, his shirt clutched in her fist. "We were able to cut down his men. Figured saving one could give us information."

"Perfect timing. We need to get back to camp immediately." Gwen lifted Majora with Thrax. "This is Thrax's master. She needs magic healing, or she won't survive."

"Borbyr, take them back. I'll stay here with the others. You be safe, Gwendolyn, you understand?"

"You too. Come back to us."

Gwen and Thrax carefully climbed onto Borbyr's back, holding Majora between them, her head lolling against Thrax's back.

"Please hold on, Majora…I just got you back…I can't lose you…" he whispered as Borbyr took off back for the caravan.

Chapter 23

Thrax sat outside Deidra's caravan, his face pressed into his hands, with Gwen's arms around him. The two had been sitting silently, unable to think of the right words to say to each other for what felt like hours.

Their silence was broken when the door opened, and Teyana came out, leaning on her walking stick, her somber expression telling Thrax everything.

"I'm so sorry, Thrax…there's nothing we can do for her…she has only a few moments left…not only is her neck broken, but her throat is severely swollen, blocking her airways…we'll leave you to say your goodbyes."

Thrax slowly stood up, staring at the caravan. His body felt numb as Gwen took his hand, leading him inside, Deidra and Inanna following Teyana to leave them some privacy.

Majora, once the picture of life when Thrax studied with her, now lay still and dying in Deidra's bed.

"Master…" he choked out, falling to his knees by her side.

"Thrax…my sweet boy…you're alive…" she croaked, struggling for breath.

"Please, master, don't speak. You need your strength."

"Foolish boy…I'm dying…I know it…but I am glad I can die knowing you are alive…you are so strong, Thrax…you are just like your father…you all must defeat Zephrus. You are not alone in this, my dear student…lean on your friends, your family, and your mother…they will guide you and your brother through this…Zephrus will fall, and peace will return…your father will rest easy, then…when I die, I ask only these things; learn your mother's past, so you may finally have a relationship with her…and stand by Aaheer. You have always been each other's greatest allies and friends. Finally, never forget how much you are loved, Thrax." Majora's trembling hand reached out and cradled Thrax's face, now thoroughly soaked with tears as he listened to his master's dying words, too choked to make a sound.

"You and your brother were your mother's greatest treasures…and you were always mine…though I had no children, I saw you as my own."

Thrax closed his eyes and pressed his face into her shoulder. "You were always my family, Majora…" he choked.

"There, my boy…don't cry for me…remember the life we had, not the life lost…let me leave this place seeing tenderness on your face." Majora looked at Gwen, standing back from them, her face red from holding back tears. "Tell me, who is this lovely lass who helped you rescue me?"

Thrax turned suddenly toward Gwen, having somewhat forgotten she was there. "Gwen…Majora," he quickly stood up, gently pulling Gwen closer, holding her to his chest. "This is my beloved…Gwendolyn Grace…"

Gwen gently wiped his face with her sleeve before bowing deeply to Majora. "It's an honor…Thrax has told me so much about you."

"You are his beloved…" Majora broke into a pained but happy smile. "How did my student get such a pretty thing like you?" her laugh turned into a harsh, choking gasp for breath.

"Master, please…" Thrax and Gwen knelt beside her, him grasping her hand desperately. "Please, take care…we wish to have you here as long as we can…we hope you may see our victory one day. Aaheer would want no one but you to crown him. Songs will tell of how you saved us. We'll have statues built for you, master. Whole schools of magic! You will be able to see Gwen and me get married one day if we decide to. You will be able to live peacefully as you have always wanted. Wouldn't that be wonderful, master? Master? Majora? Majora, please, speak to me…don't leave me yet…you can't leave me! Please, I need you! You have so much more to teach me! Don't leave me, please; I can't do this without you, master! You were my only family for so long!"

Gwen had to pull Thrax away from the bed, holding back her tears as much as possible. He turned to her, collapsing in her arms, his choked cries heard from outside the wagon. Teyana, Inanna, and Deidra quickly returned, taking Majora's body to prepare for her funeral. Deidra watched them leave before walking to the young couple, slowly kneeling to hold them in her arms.

"It's alright to grieve…both of you…a brave, wise soul has been lost tonight. Stay here until the funeral tonight…do as you need to grieve. Scream, sob, break anything in here. I know the pain of a broken heart. I need to go now, but I will tell you when it's time…" Deidra slowly stood and left, closing the door, so all that was left was the sound of the fire and the small gasps of breath Thrax gave as he cried.

"He won't get away with any of this…too much has been lost because of him," Thrax murmured, clinging tightly to Gwen.

"No…he won't…we will avenge everyone and protect others from his wrath." Gwen agreed, gently stroking his hair as she let him cry.

"Tonight, we have lost an incredible soul. Our sister and ally, Majora Crowe of Skaobia, court mage to the crown of Hevaña, the bane of darkness. She has saved countless Gyrians alongside our beloved queen Myana, raised our brother Thrax as her own, and rescued our dear queen and prince from Zephrus's wrath. We would not have nearly the strength or advantage to win this war if it was not for her. Many have felt and benefitted from her welcoming heart, kindness, love, and wisdom. Her loss sorely burdens us, but the gods will see her good heart as we have and bless her. We send her from this earth to the realm of the gods so that she may be reunited with warriors of the past like her, and in her name will see this war's end."

Inanna was speaking before the entire caravan in front of the enormous funeral pyre built for Majora, with everyone standing around it. Majora rested on top, draped in the finest fabrics each family could find in their home, sticking flowers and herbs meant to bless the dead between the wood. Someone had even gotten out a book of spells gifted to them by the mage when they still traveled to the kingdom. They all wept quietly as Inanna spoke, heads bowed in prayer that her spirit would be safely returned to the land of the gods.

Thrax stood silently, only a few tears falling as he listened. He had cried so much he could barely even produce more tears. Gwen stood beside him; her head lowered in respect. Aaheer clung to his hand, the two brothers mourning her together. When Inanna finished speaking, they stepped forward, igniting the wood with torches. When they stepped back, Gwen and the others took their hands in silent solidarity for them.

The Gyrians began to chant in another language, waving their arms up as the flames grew taller. When the pyre was consumed by fire, they began singing the most beautiful song they had ever heard. None of them could understand it, but they knew it was a song praising Majora for what she had done for many people.

When the pyre had finally burnt to ash, Aaheer turned to his brother, holding his shoulder. "It's time to sleep. We'll need our strength."

"Yes…we'll all need our strength." Thrax looked amongst his friends. Aaheer, Astricus, Borbyr, Dyael, and Gwen all still stood holding each other's hands, their faces stained with tears. "Thank you…all of you…I know you didn't know Majora as I did, but I cannot express how grateful I am to have you here with me."

"We don't have to have known her." Astricus croaked. "She meant so much to you…it was hard not to feel for you…you are our friend, after all."

"Yes…your connection with her was strong. We are here to be your friends and allies. We mourn with you, Thrax Nightingale. We know she left behind too soon, but she trained one of the most powerful wizards Hevaña will

476

ever know." Borbyr spoke solemnly, much to everyone's surprise.

"Thank you, Borbyr…I couldn't ask for a better group of friends." Thrax gave an exhausted smile and left with the others for bed.

"Deidra. You said you wanted to speak with us?" Thrax, Gwen, and Aaheer approached the older woman the next day as she sat on the steps of her wagon with Inanna.

"Yes. Sit down, you two. I told you, Thrax, when you first arrived, I would tell you the story of your mother and father. I intend to fulfill that promise. I asked Aaheer to join us because he must learn too."

"As I told you and Gwen, your mother and father met at our summer festival. They had a whirlwind romance, and we were staying in Hevaña on a near-permanent basis. We never strayed too far or very long. Well, after two

477

years, Myana was forced to engage and marry king Jarkus, but they didn't let that stop them. Saedon and Myana met secretly as often as possible, planning their escape. It wasn't long before they could no longer hide that Myana was pregnant, and it was no secret that the child was not the king's son. In a rage, Jarkus ordered all Gyrian men and boys in our caravan to be killed simply because he could. Gods bless Myana forever, she warned us, earning us just enough time to begin to get away, but I had just recently given birth to Tan. There was no way we would be able to escape in time. I just wasn't strong enough yet. Saedon helped us escape and get him safely to Myana for the moment with plans to return for my boy and Myana, escaping Jarkus's hold."

"Why did you bring Tan to my mother?" Aaheer asked.

"I was still so weak. My son was only a few days old. Saedon brought him to Myana, who knew of a servant who had recently had a child. She agreed to nurse my son while we escaped, and I returned to health. No other women in our caravan had newborns at the time, so no others could care for him. I wish we had been able to do something differently because then maybe Saedon wouldn't have had to return so soon. Jarkus was still on high alert for any of our caravans. Saedon was too desperate to get Myana away to see the signs that Jarkus had laid a trap. He was captured and hung while Myana was forced to watch and mourn silently. My poor Inanna." Deidra gripped her daughter's hand. "She was in that crowd…she met Majora after his passing and had to carry his body back to us on horseback. Even worse, we learned that you had been born, Thrax, just before his death. We were never able to meet you, and your father was never able to meet you…it broke

479

your mother's heart…I know it did…she loved your father dearly and was so excited when she found out she was pregnant with you."

"What do you mean?" Thrax spat out bitterly. "My mother abandoned me! She let me suffer my whole life and be named a bastard! If she truly cared, she'd have done somethi-!" he gasped as Deidra struck him across the face, her face red with anger.

"Stupid, stupid boy! Have you not been listening? Don't you ever speak of your mother that way! Myana adored you! She did as much as she could without risking your life! Jarkus would have killed you if she tried to escape! She especially couldn't leave after Aaheer was born! You boys had better learn quickly that Myana did everything she could for you two to live the life she knew you deserved, that she wished she'd been free to live! She kept Jarkus back in every way and did everything she could to help all he affected!"

"How do you know this?" Thrax stood up, grasping his cheek.

"Because I knew your mother! She was my dear friend, and I knew how she cared for you! Majora would take Myana's letters, give them to Midra, and Midra would bring them all to me to read. She told me everything she felt. I still have all of these letters." She pulled a large lockbox out. "This was the only knowledge of you I had. I'm giving you these letters to read and understand her. I want you to learn your mother's true nature that she couldn't show you."

Aaheer took the box and opened the latch, revealing the letters stuffed to the brim. He closed it slowly and looked up. "What happened to Zephrus? How did this happen to him?"

"I can only tell you so much," Inanna spoke up. "But I can tell you how it began. Zephrus was bitter and angry for years. Just before he left for his attack, he approached me, trying to get me to join him. I refused. I told him this wasn't what his father would want. Saedon cared deeply for his family. I know if he were still alive, he would even take you in as his son, Aaheer. That's just how he was. Zephrus has somehow gotten the idea that Myana is at fault for all of this. If she had never met Saedon, he wouldn't have fallen for her and been killed. He wanted to take as much revenge against her as he could. I think he's driven himself mad from the thought. I suspect he was even playing with dark magic, which our people forbid."

"Those spells should have never come into existence." Deidra spat. "But, some people will take the gifts the gods have given us and use them for their cruel purposes."

Aaheer looked in the box again, his brow furrowed. He closed the box again, then stood up and bowed. "Thank you, both of you, for telling us this. Come on, you two. We have much reading to do."

Gwen got up and pulled Thrax with her as they went to Aaheer and Astricus's cabin.

"Penny, for your thoughts?" Gwen asked.

"What?" Thrax raised an eyebrow at her.

"Oh, forget it. What's on your mind?"

"Well…a lot…I'm not quite sure what to think…I've had these ideas about my mother all my life, and now I'm learning that I might be misguided…it really might be all Jarkus's fault…he was the center of everything that went wrong in our lives. I guess-…I don't know my mother…I mean, I always knew I didn't know her well, but this is-."

"A whole new level?"

483

"Yeah…that's one way to put it…After this, I have much apologizing to do…I can't believe what an absolute bastard Jarkus was."

"Can we please," Aaheer suddenly whipped around, his face red and knuckles white from gripping the box. "Stop talking about Jarkus? Please? I don't want to hear about him!"

"Aaheer…I-I'm sorry. I didn't mean to upset you,"

"Well, I'm just a little tired of always hearing what an awful person my father is. It's not very encouraging, is it? I was born because of that monster, you know. I didn't have a kind, honorable man for a father; I had an absolute shit stain of a human. I have to go each day learning about more awful things he did, thinking about what I have to do to not only make up for it but prove I'm not like him." his voice trembled the more he spoke. His hands began to shake, making the box rattle slightly.

484

"Aaheer…" Gwen pulled him into a hug. "We're sorry…we didn't even think about how this made you feel."

"She's right. I'm so sorry, little brother." Thrax wrapped the two in his arms.

"If it makes you feel better, you're nothing like him. It only takes a few minutes of speaking with you to know just how kind and intelligent you are. Plus, you're not alone in all of this. We're here to help and stand by you, all of us."

Aaheer's grip around them tightened as he hid his face in their shoulders. "Thank you…both of you…I just- …I didn't want to let on how much it bothered me."

"Those that know you can speak well of your character. You have three kingdoms, our own, Astricus's, Dyael's, and the Gyrians, all backing you up. You are never without friends here, nor will you ever be without your brother." Thrax gently rested his forehead against Aaheer's.

"You know what," Gwen looked between them. "I think I'm going to make myself useful somewhere else. I think you two need to have some time together."

"I think," Thrax smiled at his brother. "That's an excellent idea."

Chapter 24

"Majora would have loved this, you know."

"What?" Thrax looked up from the letter he'd been reading to his brother.

"Us spending time together like this. She would have loved it. We never did get to see each other much as we got older." Aaheer explained, lying on his bed as he read.

Thrax chuckled, leaning back against the bed from the floor. "You're right. Another thing Jarkus did."

"He probably got tired of us hiding frogs in the maids' quarters." Aaheer snickered.

"Or letting the hunting dogs loose in the castle!"

"Remember when we decided to paint the walls in the portrait hall?"

"I thought mother was going to burst from laughing so hard!"

The brothers laughed heartily at the memories. Thrax smiled tenderly at the letter in his hand. "This letter talks about when you broke your leg, falling from that tree. It was my first time successfully using a healing spell…mother said she was so proud…she never got to tell me she was proud…and she also said how sorry she is that she couldn't help you more…you know, the more I think about Myana, the more I realize…I was always too critical of her."

"Well, couldn't be helped, could it?" Aaheer rolled onto his side, propping up on his elbow. "You weren't allowed to spend much time with her."

"Was she ever allowed to talk to you about me?"

"Only a few times. She'd come to visit me in secret before I went to bed. I could ask her anything I wanted. I remember her telling me you and I had different fathers, but she loved us the same. I remember all sorts of things she told me. She made me want to be a better king."

"Really? I didn't know that…" Thrax read on to the following letter, the old, yellowing paper wrinkled and stained from old tears on this one.

"My dearest Deidra,

It's that time again. It's been thirteen long years since Saedon's death. I mourn him more and more each year. Oh, I can't begin to tell you how much Thrax looks like him. You'd be amazed! He even has a talent for magic! Sometimes I wonder if perhaps he would have even surpassed Saedon! I wish I could look at his face more. I miss my sons so much. Last night, I snuck away from Jarkus to go to his room. He was fast asleep, but I didn't wake him. It is the only time I can see him freely, and I knew he

489

wouldn't want to see me. I think he hates me, Deidra. I don't blame him. I wish I could just run away with my boys, but I don't have the skills you do. I wouldn't even reach the caravan before I did something foolish or got caught by Jarkus. Then what would happen? Thrax and I would likely hang, and my poor Aaheer would probably be left alone. Oh, my sweet Aaheer! Never have I seen a kinder soul in a boy! If I didn't know better, I would also think Saedon was his father! Imagine! He resembles me, though, and I thank the gods for that! I know how much it would hurt to see Jarkus's face in my son, but I can take pride in knowing that my Aaheer will not only be better than his father, I know he will be remembered for years to come! They'll have stories about Thrax and Aaheer; I know it! I apologize for this, my friend. I know it must hurt to read sometimes. I wish I could be with you to remember the old days, but one day we will see each other again, my friend.

Be well,

Myana Thornblade"

Thrax felt his eyes burn as he read. There were years worth of letters in the box, and in each one, Myana never failed to mention the two of them and how much she loved them. At that moment, Thrax would have given anything to hug his mother.

"Thrax?"

"Yes?"

"Can I ask you something…well…personal?"

"Um…I suppose."

"Well…" Aaheer turned his head away, though Thrax could see the tips of his ears becoming very pink.

"H-how did you admit to Gwen you loved her?"

"Well, I just sort of…said it, I guess." Thrax broke into a huge grin. "Aaheer Thornblade, are you telling me you have a crush?"

"Don't say that as though it's so surprising!"

"Well, come on, out with it! Who is it?"

"It's-…" Aaheer muttered something Thrax couldn't quite make out.

"What?"

He heaved a great sigh and pressed his palms to his eyes. "It's Astricus…"

"Really? Do you fancy the goat? I thought you couldn't stand him!"

"N-no, it wasn't that! He used to make me uncomfortable with how he always flirted."

"So what changed?"

"Well…he stopped flirting and fawning all the time…we started talking and getting closer, and he started treating me like a friend rather than a crush, and I…I just…started falling for him…" Aaheer's whole face was red by now.

"Don't look so frightened, brother!" Thrax thumped his back, making the younger prince grunt from the force. "This is wonderful news! I'm so happy for you!"

"Truly? Do…you think the kingdom will approve? Or…mother?"

"Myana has no say in whom you marry. Neither does the kingdom. If they fuss for you to marry royalty, Astricus is royalty. If they fuss for you to marry a woman, they cannot fight you there either. One cannot control the gender they are attracted to. If they cry that you cannot continue the Thornblade line or other such nonsense, remind them that you can adopt any child in need to become the next prince or princess. Are we not proof that blood does not necessarily equal strength of brotherhood?"

Aaheer blushed more at the suggestion of marrying Astricus but still smiled. "Thank you, brother. You've always known how to make me feel better."

"Come. Supper should be ready soon, and I'm starved." Thrax stretched as he stood, cracking his limbs. The two brothers left the wagon even closer than they had been in a long time. As he reached for the door, Thrax finally realized he saw himself as Aaheer's brother. He finally felt that they were family.

Chapter 25

The caravan was in a bustle, many moving quickly, eyeing Inanna's wagon warily as they walked past for dinner. Dyael, Borbyr, and Gwen stood to the side, speaking in hushed tones.

"What's going on?" Thrax asked as they approached.

"We have a visitor," Borbyr growled.

"What do you mean? Where's Astricus?" Aaheer asked.

"The faun is with her wife." Borbyr jabbed his thumb toward Inanna's cabin.

"A woman wandered into the caravan today," Dyael explained, her brow furrowed. "According to Inanna, she is Zephrus's wife. She didn't look so good, though."

"Where is she? What are they doing?" Thrax looked at the wagon.

"When she got here, she couldn't speak. Inanna says that it was some dark magic. She's trying to repair the damage." Gwen explained, gently wrapping her hands around Thrax's arm, leaning against him. "That poor woman…when she saw Inanna, she collapsed and started sobbing. I can't imagine what she's experienced."

"Don't consider her so innocent yet." Borbyr glowered at the wagon. "She stuck by him till now."

Dyael smacked his arm and gave him a scolding look. "I'm sure she didn't know exactly what was going on, and I don't consider Zephrus the most understanding person. I bet he would have killed her if she tried to leave sooner."

"How did she get away now?" Thrax rested his hand on Gwen's, running his thumb over her knuckles.

"Well, that's what we're hoping to find out. They've been in there for a long time."

The group looked at the wagon. The anticipation and curiosity were practically palpable.

It was near dark when Inanna finally came out of the wagon. The trees already hid the sun, the dinner fire tall and crackling, bathing them all in its warmth. Children were being put to bed, and the evening meal was being cleaned up. By then, Astricus had returned and was sitting with them in the grass, except Dyael and Borbyr. The princess was pacing slowly, holding Ea to her ear, listening to his trills and chirps, while Borbyr stood protectively by her. They all stood still when Inanna emerged, ragged and pale.

"Is it true?" Thrax stood slowly. "Is she Zephrus's wife?"

"Her name," Teyana followed her wife to them, leaning heavily on her walking stick. "Is Sigyn. Her girlhood name was Sigyn Iduna."

"Was she unable to speak?"

"It was more than that…it was dark magic…" Inanna rubbed her forehead, clearly exhausted. "Her voice was stolen from her."

"What does that mean?" Dyael stepped closer.

"If Zephrus had just stopped her from being able to talk, we would have been able to use a simple spell to unblock her voice. But Zephrus had completely removed her voice from her body. That's incredibly dark magic. I had always been afraid that Zephrus would fall into such magic, but I didn't think he would take it this far. He has reached the ability to dismantle parts of human essence."

"How do you repair that?"

"It's complicated magic. We had to try and reconstruct her voice. We got it done, but I'm exhausted…" she slowly sank onto the ground, leaning against the wagon.

"I will go with them," Teyana assured her wife. "We'll be speaking to her about Zephrus. I think she will be all we need to learn about him."

"Come," Teyana motioned for the others to follow her into the wagon. Gwen gripped Thrax's arm, mentally preparing herself for what would happen.

Sigyn sat on the side of Deidra's bed, the older woman gently patting her hands as she spoke softly. When they entered, she looked at them with a mildly stern look. "This poor flower has finally been returned to us. Do not think ill of her for how Zephrus tricked her."

"Do not worry, mother, I will be watching over them and their question." Teyana held up a reassuring hand. Sigyn looked up at them with wet, doleful brown eyes. Her face was darkened with bruises, one fading from her cheek, a large one by her eye, and one shaped like a handprint across her mouth. Her clothes were ragged and caked with dirt, and her hair was filled with branches and burrs.

"Teyana…" Her new voice croaked slightly from lack of use and holding back tears. "It's so good to see you."

"You as well, Sigyn. These children," she gestured to the group, "are helping to lead this fight. This is Gwendolyn Grace, Prince Astricus, Prince Aaheer Thornblade, and Thrax Nightingale." Each of them bowed to her in turn.

"Thrax…" she stared at him for a long moment. "You do so resemble your father."

"I hear that more often than you think…" he offered her a small smile, making her chuckle softly.

"So, how did you manage to escape?" Aaheer asked.

"It wasn't something I planned…I didn't think I would have the chance. I ran as everyone started to panic. In truth, I'm almost certain Zephrus no longer cares enough to even look for me…" her lip trembled, and she pressed her face in her hands, choking out sobs as Deidra hugged her, trying to comfort her.

"None of this is your fault, Sigyn," Teyana assured her, gripping her shoulder. "But I'm afraid I do have to ask you some questions. Is that alright?"

Sigyn took a deep breath and nodded.

"Alright…first, I need you to confirm, has Zephrus been using dark magic?"

"Yes, but it's more than that…I always knew Zeph enjoyed trying to push the envelope, but it wasn't until he took my voice from me that I realized what he was becoming… he was already going too far with it. The magic is taking over his mind. He doesn't sleep, eat, or feel anything other than rage and a need for revenge."

"Where did he find the materials?"

"I don't know. I think he's collected them over the years, but I can't be sure. When we took over the castle, I remember he had a trapdoor installed in his horse's stable. When I asked him about it, he insisted it was only an escape route if the castle should be breached."

"Did you see what was past that trapdoor?"

"…I did…before we left for Terra Vale, I started searching through his things. I needed one more piece of confirmation to leave him. Though I truly see who he is now, I-…I still miss what we did have…" she sniffed heavily and wiped her cheeks before continuing, "I searched his library, our bedroom, and the armory, but there wasn't much proof. Finally, I remembered the trapdoor, so while he was out of the castle during the day, I went down it and found an entire hidden library filled with gruesome books, spells, and all kinds of potion ingredients. The floor was all black, where he marked it for spells. I saw…body parts…there were so many bodies, but I-I don't know where he got them. They could have been servants, villagers, our people, I-I don't know! I just knew I needed to get away."

"No way…" Gwen's face twisted in disgust. "This guy sounds like a fucking psycho."

"Lady Gwendolyn, please." Teyana held a hand up to silence her. "Was there anything else you noticed, Sigyn?"

"Well…I noticed that he would go down there more often…he wouldn't sleep in our bed anymore…I think he would stay up all night…but I think I've most noticed the…talking. He would sort of mutter to himself. It didn't sound like anything…one night was particularly horrible, however…I was walking back from the garden with my handmaiden, and h-he was on his knees in the hall…he was clutching his head, like this," she pressed her hands to the side of her head, gripping at her hair, "and he looked rather sick…he was frothing at the mouth almost and-…h-he was crying. He couldn't speak. We couldn't figure out what had happened. Any time he tried to explain, it just made no sense."

The group all listened intently. The more she spoke, the less they could even form words to try and speak.

"I-I wanted to help, but I was t-to scared…I hate that I still feel attached to him and want to help him…" she hugged her arms tightly, shuddering. Her lip trembled again, and she seemed to steel herself, gripping her knees. "But I won't. I want nothing to do with him anymore. He's gone too far. I-…I truly don't think he can be helped anymore. There was a time when I would have tried harder, but-…well, I have too many people to put before him…" her hand moved to her stomach.

"Sigyn…are you pregnant?" Deidra gave a small gasp.

"I think so…this is the second month I haven't had my cycle."

"Does Zephrus know?" Teyana raised an eyebrow.

505

"No! And he's not going to know! That's why I came here. If I am pregnant, I especially don't want my baby around him. I could have taken much more of Zephrus, but I'm not putting my child through that." she insisted.

"Oh, my dear…" Deidra hugged her close. "You don't deserve to go through that either…but I'm glad you are here with us. This baby will be raised with love. I swear it." Deidra assured her.

"And-…" Aaheer found his voice suddenly. "When we defeat Zephrus, you will always have a place at the palace."

Sigyn smiled gratefully at them. "I'm glad I was able to meet you all…after seeing your fight with Zephrus, I think you all have a chance against him…you have great potential."

The four of them exchanged awkward but happy smiles.

"Alright, I think that's more than enough from us." Teyana rapped her walking stick against the floor. "Out, you lot. Sigyn needs to build her strength."

Once out of the cabin, Thrax turned to Teyana. "Do you think Sigyn is pregnant?"

"I don't know. But if she is, we can't let Zephrus find out. If he realized she was having his baby, he would stop at nothing to take that child and turn it into his perfect prodigy."

"So now, not only do we have to fight Zephrus, we have to keep him away from his ex-wife, who might be having his kid?" Gwen sighed and shook her head. "As though we didn't have enough on our minds."

"It can't be helped. Besides, Sigyn's information was crucial. I imagine it was a huge relief for her as well. If what she says is true, Zephrus's mind is consumed by the black magic he's been toying with. Though he gains strength from it, he becomes increasingly more likely to make a mistake. That means we will have a greater opportunity to defeat him. You all go rest now. I need to speak to Inanna about what we've learned." Teyana waved them off before going to sit by her wife.

The group said their goodbyes and went to their wagons. Gwen and Thrax changed in silence before Gwen finally asked, "Do you think we will have to kill Zephrus?"

Thrax paused and pondered. "Most likely. Though, I don't enjoy thinking about it."

"Do…you think you'd be able to?"

"I don't know…though he has done horrible things, he is my father's son…frankly, I've never enjoyed the idea of killing before."

"Even after everything, he's done?"

Thrax huffed, turning to her. "What do you want me to say, Gwen? That I can kill him without a thought? Without pause or question? I can't. He's still a human being. He's a human being that has done horrible things, ruined my family, killed my master, yet I still can't bring myself to choose to kill him willingly."

Gwen quickly hurried to him and hugged him close. "I'm sorry…I didn't mean to make it sound like that. I'm okay that you would still hesitate. I know that's just who you are…you're a good person, Thrax Nightingale." she stared up at him with her soft blue eyes. "It's why I fell in love with you."

"I love you too, Gwendolyn Grace." Thrax gently held her face in his hands, kissing the corner of her mouth. "I'm sorry I snapped…I'm just so tired from all of this."

"I understand…soon, it'll all be over, and everything will be as it should be," Gwen assured him before climbing into bed.

Chapter 26

"Again!" Inanna ordered Thrax.

The two of them were in the woods, working on his fighting with his magic. He was currently struggling with the accuracy of his ice blasts.

"We've been at this for hours, Inanna." Thrax panted heavily, pushing back the sweaty hair stuck to his forehead. "If I keep shooting ice, I'm going to get frostbite."

"And each hour, Zephrus gains another soldier. You need to be prepared to fight with magic. It's the only way you will be able to defeat him. Now, start again. If you can, try to perform the spell without speaking it. It keeps the enemy from having an advantage over you." Inanna held up her hand, summoning a manticore.

The beast flexed its mighty wings, roaring furiously, its scorpion tail writhing angrily.

Thrax sighed with exhaustion and tried his best to summon the ice, his fingers stinging from cold. Frost formed on the grass around him as he raised his hands and shouted, "*Mraz ferrum!*"

Cold air, glittering with ice crystals, swirled in his hands before the crystals swirled together to create great chunks of ice, shaping themselves into large jagged pieces that shot at the manticore.

The creature roared and swatted them away with its tail before charging toward the wizard.

"Fuck…" Thrax hissed and ran around him. "Aren't I supposed to learn *without* risking my life?"

"You'll get too used to one style of fighting. You need to work on aiming a spell while you're moving quickly. Not every enemy will kindly wait for you to take your turn to attack." Inanna shouted. "Don't worry; I won't let him seriously hurt you."

"How reassuring…" he grumbled, throwing himself behind a boulder as the beast swiped at him. He looked at his hands, trying to summon more ice. "Shit…" he bit his lip as the spell failed. "I'm so tired. I can barely make more ice."

"Then what do you do? What other spells do you know? If ice doesn't work, how else can you attack? Try something different. Take this time to learn how to think on your feet."

"If I can't create ice, I likely can't make much else…" he muttered in irritation, jumping behind a tree that the manticore bit into, yanking it from the roots. "Damn, what can't you break?" he cursed, charging back into the circle.

"Use your head, Thrax! There are more spells than just ones that create things! Remember what you've been taught!"

Thrax raked his brain to remember his lessons before finally pointing towards the charging manticore. "*Rigescunt indutae!*"

The beast froze, midleap, falling to the ground on its side.

"Yes! Excellent!" Inanna cried, clapping her hand on his back. "Temporary stun spell! Well done, Thrax! I think that can be enough for today. Why don't you go wash up?"

"Yeah, thanks, Inanna." Thrax trotted down to the river, happily peeling off his sweat-soaked clothes. As he approached, he heard a soft humming and relaxed when he saw Gwen wading in the river. She had her skirt tied up to her upper thigh so it wouldn't get wet while she washed clothes in the water, scrubbing and wringing them out.

"So this is where you disappeared to," he said, approaching the bank.

She jumped hard and whipped around, relaxing when she realized who it was. "Finished with training already?"

"Aye. I'm dying for a wash. Care to join me?" The wizard smirked as he waded into the river, slowly untying his pants.

Gwen blushed and turned away, giggling. "You're a devil, Thrax Nightingale! I have chores!" she lifted the basket of clothes onto her hip and scurried past, dramatically dropping her basket to the ground when he hooked her around the waist, pulling her close to his chest so he could lovingly kiss her neck.

"Are you sure you don't want to join me in the river?" he purred, gently massaging her waist.

"Well, if you're going to insist…" she pretended to sigh with the inconvenience as she slipped out of her clothes, following him into the river.

The couple laughed and splashed in the water before falling into each other's arms on the riverbank, kissing while the gentle tide tugged slightly at Gwen's locks.

"You've gotten so strong, my handsome wizard."

"So have you, my Gwendolyn…you certainly aren't the same woman you were when we first met." he laughed softly, thinking of how out of place she looked in his world.

"How long has it been since then?" she asked, her hands caressing his body.

"It's hard to tell…winter will be here soon, so I imagine it's almost a year now…" his hands slid down to her thighs, lifting them around his hips.

"Almost a year…Thrax, where do you think I should go after all of this?"

"What do you mean? Are you not going to stay with us?"

"Would it be okay if I did?"

"Gwen, you've been with us through all of this! We wouldn't be here if it weren't for you! Of course, you can! You can come live with me in the palace. You and I…together."

"Together." she broke into a huge grin and pulled him into a passionate kiss. "Just more bedrooms for us to defile." she grinned deviously, making her lover blush and grow hard at the suggestion before breaking into a vast wolfish grin.

"You tricky minx! Come here!" He laughed and pulled her closer as he kissed her feverishly, his hands squeezing her thighs.

Gwen gasped and giggled, wrapping her arms around his neck. One of her hands slid up into his hair, tugging lightly as his hands traveled up to her breasts, massaging them slowly.

The sound of a branch snapping suddenly stopped their moment of passion. The two looked up quickly, seeing Astricus and Aaheer stumbling towards the river, entangled in a passionate kiss, both quickly and feverishly trying to remove the other's clothes. When they noticed the other couple, all four went completely red. Thrax promptly dropped down to cover Gwen's body, and Astricus hid his face sheepishly in Aaheer's chest.

"Well…this is awkward…" Gwen murmured.

"Yes…um, I think we'll be going now." Aaheer murmured, shuffling with Astricus from the bank back towards the caravan.

Once they were gone, the couple looked at each other and burst out laughing, settling to finish their bath before returning to the caravan.

Gwen sat on the floor of their wagon, sharpening her knives on a stone, while Thrax lay in bed, reading a map to the firelight. She leaned back against the bed, where Thrax moved his hand to brush against her hair.

"Since the caravan is stuck in Hevaña for the winter, we'll need to move the group further from the cold. If we head here," Thrax pointed to the map. "we'll be close enough to villages to get more information while staying far away from Zephrus."

"Do you think this will be when we start planning to beat him? Like…a final battle, sort of?"

"If we can, that would be best. Starting the new spring under new leadership would be beneficial. Aaheer's rule would come with new hope. The people would plant their crops and begin to get used to him as the new king. Full bellies can always make people more interested in what you have to say."

"Alright. We need to start moving people and getting ready for a fight. Do you think he'll attack us along the way?"

"Oh, certainly."

"We'd better make sure our weapons are sharp, then. I'll go tell Inanna and ask for some armor."

"Armor?"

"Well, you don't think I'm going to sit back with the children, do you?" Gwen gave a slight smirk as she got up.

Thrax chuckled and kissed the top of her hand. "My darling, I would never suggest such a thing. You've grown so much, and I think you'd string me up before the sentence was completed." he laughed.

Gwen laughed and turned the knife she'd been sharpening, so the back of the blade rested under his chin. "That's exactly right, my love," The power in her stance, hand on her hip, gazing through hooded eyes, tilting his chin up with her knife, made his heart flutter in his chest. "And you'd best remember that. I may be a woman, but I won't go quietly…" her hand caressed his face and neck as she leaned down to kiss him before pulling away her knife and walking out of the wagon.

Thrax put a hand to his chest and laid back on the bed, his heart racing with desire. "Oh my…this was certainly unexpected…"

Chapter 27

Gwen and Thrax rode at the head of the group with Aaheer, Astricus, Borbyr, Dyael, and Inanna. Teyana, Tan, and Deidra rode just behind them, with the rest of the caravan following and their strongest fighters on all sides to watch out for enemies.

"How far will this likely take?" Gwen asked Inanna.

"A few days. We'll remain on the paths and travel to the village of Bonewell."

"Where's that?"

"You've been there before, my lady," Aaheer smiled. "It's where mother and I were hidden. I'm sure she'll be pleased to see us. I can't imagine she's left Orag's inn since we last saw her."

"Damn, how long has it been since then?" Gwen giggled softly, remembering her first meeting with the queen.

"Too long, for sure." Aaheer sighed with a look of homesickness on his face.

"Imagine the shock she'll get," Tan chuckled from behind. "Watching her two boys and a strange girl run off only to return months later with an entire army."

"That reminds me," Astricus turned to Dyael from where he sat on Aaheer's horse. "Can Ea make the journey to our villages? We'll need all hands available for the fight."

"Aye, he should make it just fine," she promised, stroking his feathers. "We can send him off when we arrive."

"Could he look ahead for us for trouble?" Inanna asked.

"Aye, no trouble at all," Dyael promised and had her bird take off. Ea gave a warbling call and glided over the trees down the path ahead.

"He's such a clever thing. We haven't seen many phoenixes, but I remember one country we visited where they were as native and common to the land as rats on a ship." Inanna explained with a smile. "It was beautiful. We woke up to phoenix song every morning, especially when they realized Teyana would feed them."

"That does sound lovely…did they burn things, though?" Gwen asked.

"No, they had developed a sort of oil that they smeared on their buildings and the branches of the trees that kept them from burning from phoenix fire by accident. It mixed just fine with water, so their plants were also resistant. The luck is since it was in the desert, it wouldn't burn by the sun's heat or if they were attacked and their enemies tried to burn their crops."

"Do you still have it?" Thrax asked, looking at the wooden wagons that were pulling behind them.

Inanna looked back before answering, "I should have some. We can make more, but I will need your help, Thrax. It'll take much magic to make, and mine isn't enough."

"Of course. Do we have the ingredients?"

"We'll be able to get more in Bonewell. Mother knows the recipe; I know the spell."

"Excellent. We can also have the villagers put it on their buildings if we have enough."

"If not, we should put it on the largest buildings like the Keep and the inn, so people have a safe place." Dyael insisted. "I can use Ea's old feathers to test whether it is successful."

"Perfect. Now, with your armies," Thrax nodded to Astricus and Dyael. "How many will that give us?"

"With my village, at least fifty men. With the other faun villages…I want to say about three hundred."

"Our men will increase that number by another one-hundred and fifty," Borbyr answered.

"Then, with ours, we'll have at least another fifty. If we have injured and sick healed in time, and if some women are willing to fight, we should have another hundred." Inanna said.

"Six hundred men…will that be even close to enough?" Aaheer asked.

Inanna pursed her lips. "If he has been able to take over the entire kingdom of Hevaña with soldiers to spare in other villages within its territories…he'll crush six hundred men before the day is over."

"Dammit all…then what do we do?"

"I say," Gwen piped up. "We talk to the people of Bonewell and other villages we pass by. If your mother is still there, Aaheer, do you think she'll have any other allies she can contact?"

"I think so. Her family was merchants and sailors. They would answer her if she could contact them, and they might have their allies to assist."

"Well, there you go! Would the sailors have water access?"

"Yes." Aaheer's grin grew. "There's a harbor along the east side of the central city. If ships come in and start attacking, it will take many of Zephrus's men to handle it."

"Leaving us a chance to come from the other sides and close in with whatever other soldiers we can get." Thrax beamed at Gwen and leaned over to kiss her. "You're a genius, my love."

"Wait, I just thought," Aaheer piped up again. "What about lady Midra?"

"Yes! I'd almost forgotten all about her! She'll have all sorts of spies and helpers!" Thrax's shoulders relaxed with this knowledge.

"The dark elves!" Astricus added. "We almost forgot about them as well! They'll answer our call as well!"

"Yes! Yes, you're right! We still have a fighting chance."

Gwen smiled at his reaction, knowing the plan would bring him comfort. Ea returned and gave a soft warble, landing on Dyael's shoulder and preening his feathers.

"All clear."

The caravan was quiet that night. After so much travel, no one seemed quite in the mood for stories or speaking. The six friends also sat silently around the fire, unsure of what to say.

"Everyone is silent as corpses," Tan murmured as he sat beside them with his food.

"I guess they're just tired and nervous," Gwen said, glancing over to some of the mothers, holding each other as they spoke in hushed voices, wiping tears from each other's faces.

"Aye…Inanna won't say it, but she is too. The idea of our people going into such a risky battle weighs her heavily."

"I'm sorry." Thrax ran his fingers through his hair. "I wish I didn't have to involve you all."

"Don't start this shit, Thrax." Tan rolled his eyes. "You're our family, and Zephrus is a prick trying to destroy us. Of course, we're going to help. Don't start some savior complex bullshit now when we're already in this. Family helps each other out."

Gwen smiled and took Thrax and Aaheer's hands. "That's to both of you, by the way. You don't need to treat this like you need to shoulder all the burden alone. We're here for you. Let us help you."

Aaheer gave a small laugh and squeezed her hand in return. "Wouldn't dream of it, my lady." his gaze drifted to Astricus across the fire, the two staring at each other longingly.

"Get a room, you two!" Dyael scolded, throwing a piece of her bread at the side of Astricus's head, breaking the awkward tension as they all laughed at the blushing faun and began to relax.

"You know," Dyael spoke up again. "This would be an excellent opportunity to practice our fighting skills while traveling. We could practice at night, before the evening meal."

"I think that's a great idea!" Gwen grinned and pointed to Borbyr, who jerked back at the sudden attention. "I want to challenge you to a shooting match, Borbyr!"

"Aye!" Tan stood up, beaming devilishly. "I'm still owed a match with you as well!"

Borbyr relinquished a small smile. "I suppose I will have to humble you both then."

"Gwen, I'm surprised we haven't had a duel to see who has the swifter blades." Astricus grinned as he patted his sheathed dagger at his waist.

"Are you challenging me, goat boy?" she had a devious glint in her eye. "Because I accept! Hope you're ready to get your fuzzy butt beat!"

"I suppose that means I'll be practicing magic with Inanna." Thrax leaned back and looked up at the stars.

"Then we'll have to practice with swords," Aaheer said to Dyael, who punched her fist into her hand.

"I won't go easy on you, prince-y!"

"I wouldn't ask you to!"

"I'm so excited now!" Gwen wiggled in place, beaming and flapping her hands happily. "I wanna go train now!"

"I wouldn't advise that." Teyana walked over, leaning heavily on her cane as she held a small sleepy toddler on her hip. "You start training tonight, and you'll be too tired to travel tomorrow."

"Oh yeah, I forgot for a second." Gwen pouted and sat back beside Thrax.

He smirked and wrapped an arm around her shoulders. "Take a night to rest, my little warrior. Even you need to rest." He leaned over to kiss her neck, making her scrunch her nose and squeak with laughter.

"I wanted to come over and thank you, kids." Teyana hobbled over to them, leaning on her walking stick. "Everyone's been so nervous about traveling closer to Zephrus, but seeing you kids so hopeful and determined," she beamed tenderly back at the others in the caravan, who had all relaxed more and were talking a little more merrily. "It gives them hope. We can use all of that that we can get."

"Teyana, you act as though we're doing something impressive." Tan chuckled. "We're just talking about training."

"Well, this will be a big battle, Tan. Mothers and fathers do not take the risk of losing their children lightly; you know that. Inanna is barely eating from nerves."

"Aye, I know. I don't think us talking like this is that big a deal."

"Perhaps you don't, or any of you, but to us, it

means hope. Seeing young, strong fighters like you filled with confidence makes people feel we have a fighting chance. Now, no more talk of training. You lot need to be well-rested."

"I think that's an excellent point to end this discussion." Thrax chuckled and stood up. "Let's all get some rest."

They all nodded and got up to disperse for the evening.

Chapter 28

Zephrus loomed over the spell book that sat before him on the table. His forehead was lined with sweat as he studied the pages.

"Damn, these spells…they take so much energy…" he scowled, rubbing sleepily at his eyes which had grown sunken and bloodshot from long hours in the dim candlelight.

The table was covered with a pile of bodies with rotten gray skin and rancid dark red muscle exposed. Some of the parts showed yellowing bone or skull. It took just as much of Zephrus's concentration to keep the smell magically disguised as trying to animate these parts into a moving body. He approached the corpse and raised his hand, which had already been sliced open. The other held his knife and stabbed it into his forearm, slicing it down with a pained grimace, letting the blood drip onto the body.

"Ah!" he cried, stumbling against the table, clutching his fresh wound. He straightened up and shuffled back to the book, grabbing a bandage to wrap around the cut. "Dark forces aid me…*with my blood, may you rise, from dirt and death, be alive. Everlasting sleep begone and rise with the morning song! Artum mortem, artum mortem, artum mortem!*"

The corpse glowed purple light as the body parts were fused. The creature rose with an almost irritated hiss. It looked to Zephrus, who gave a wild grin. "Excellent…to the others with you."

The corpse gave another hissed as it slid rather clumsily from the table and shuffled off to a side room built off the laboratory.

537

"Excellent…yes, yes…now to call upon my father…" he threw together the ingredients and chanted the spell, smirking as the shadowy figure of Saedon Arimas formed. The spirit lifted its head and turned away from his son.

"Release me, Zephrus. I have nothing to say to you."

"Oh, come now, father," Zephrus chuckled and held out his arms. "You're disappointed now because I've grown my army and am one step closer to defeating that whore? When did the great Saedon grow so soft? I suppose I shouldn't expect you to understand, however. You were a fool to chase her in the first place. This wouldn't have happened if you hadn't climbed into her bed."

Saedon whipped around and flew in his son's face, his smoky face growing darker. Zephrus's cocky smirk slipped, and he took a step back, studying his father's spirit carefully.

"How dare you. How often will I have to tell you that you're wrong, my son? Myana loved you like her own. No matter how much you deny them, her sons are our family. Even with a family that loves you and want to help you, you have fallen for the temptations of darkness. You know what you are doing is wrong. It goes against everything I ever taught you about magic. Everything our people taught you."

Zephrus sneered and stormed away to his bookshelf. "Everything *you* taught me…why should I care what you taught me anymore? You weren't here long enough for me to learn anything significant. I don't need your opinion anymore, father. I don't need any of you! I've become stronger than I could ever imagine without you-!" He whipped around to yell at his father's spirit but found

nothing.

He was alone.

Chapter 29

"For a human who hasn't fought much, you're light on your feet!" Astricus grinned as he and Gwen went at it with their daggers.

"So are you, for a clumsy goat!" she quipped.

"Clumsy?" He cried in mock indignance before rushing past her and jumping onto a tree. He used the tree to leap forward, rolling behind Gwen, grabbing her closest ankle, and sweeping her to the ground with a yelp. "Who's clumsy now?"

"Still you!" she laughed, turning to the prince, who squealed with surprise. Gwen wrapped him in a headlock and twisted her legs tightly around his waist. "I don't go down so easily, goat-boy!"

"Gwen, release the goat before he passes out!" Tan called from where he was practicing shooting some makeshift targets of bales of hay with a painted-on red mark. "I don't think he can take much more humiliation!"

"Who says I'm humiliated?" Astricus called, getting up and beating the dirt off his fur. "I'm quite proud of our little Gwendolyn! She's gotten so stwong! Isn't that wight, wittle Gwen?" he cooed, squishing her cheeks.

Gwen swatted his hands away playfully. "Shut up!"

"I'm not kidding, however. You have gotten so much better!"

"Well, I guess it's to be expected! I've had to fight with you guys more than ever in my world."

"Hey, Gwen, why don't you come to practice your shooting?" Tan called.

"Oh yeah! I've been neglecting that!" she admitted as she trotted over to him, scooping up a spare bow by his feet.

542

"Alright, let's have a little fun with this! How close can you get to that bullseye?"

Gwen pursed her lips as she readied her arrow. "Just don't laugh if I miss…" she drew the arrow back to her cheek. The chill of an autumn breeze sent a shiver up her spine. After a deep breath, she finally released it. The arrow lodged itself into the hay, sticking from within the center target.

"Hey! Not bad! You're quite the sharpshooter!" Tan praised, retrieving her arrow.

"Thanks!" she gave a huge grin. "I wasn't expecting it to be so close!"

"You've done very well so far, but now is the time we start working on your speed. It's key to have a sharp eye that moves quickly. The enemy doesn't give you time to sit still and aim."

"Understood!"

They were distracted by the sound of running hooves. Inanna rode over the hill, her gaze scanning the tree lines. "Pack it up, everyone. We're back on the move."

"So soon? What's wrong, sis?"

"Dyael spotted one of Zephrus's scouts while hunting. They're too close for comfort, so we're moving now."

"Where are the others?" Astricus asked.

"Don't worry; they're with the caravan. Get your things and come on. We've no time to lose." Inanna waved her hand and the large target they had been using levitated and followed her as she rode back over the hill.

"Well, orders are orders." Tan sighed, slinging his bow over his shoulder.

By the time they reached the caravan, most of everything had already been quickly stored away. Children had been shoved into wagons, and almost everyone was either on horseback or ready to walk the long journey.

Gwen grabbed her horse and quickly rode to the front with Thrax, whose shoulders slumped in relaxation when she joined his side. "We're starting as soon as we can. Aaheer nearly had a cow when he heard about the scout. I think he's more worried about it than Inanna is."

"I don't blame him. Zephrus's presence has always meant someone getting hurt to him."

Their conversation was interrupted as Inanna faced them all at the head of the group. She raised her hand for quiet, and almost everyone fell silent to listen, aside from a few nervous horses and the sounds of the forest. "Everyone needs to stay as close as they can to each other for today's journey. Zephrus's men have been spotted not too far from us, so we must move quickly and carefully. All children, sick, and elderly are to stay in the wagons. No one is to leave the group without another to guard them. We stop only at nightfall. If we are attacked, those with wagons or who do not fight will ride ahead as fast as possible. We will stay behind to fight and catch up. Everyone, move out."

Everyone followed in grave silence. All hope that had been sparked the evening before was lost. The fear of Zephrus had put everyone on edge. Dyael trotted up to walk by Gwen and Inanna while Thrax and Borbyr fell to the back of the caravan. Tan flanked them to the left, Aaheer and Astricus to the right. The rest of the warriors circled the procession to protect the more vulnerable.

"What did the scout look like?" Gwen asked her friend.

"He was an archer, meant to fight from a distance. I expect the rest of the troops weren't far behind. He wasn't even on a horse."

"Do you think they found us?"

"I doubt it. Ea and I were gone before he even spotted us. Still, I imagine if we aren't careful, they'll catch up quickly." she looked back behind her. "We aren't exactly the faster group."

"It can't be helped." Gwen reminded her. "We're moving an entire village. Not all are as fast as centaurs, nor are they as skilled."

"Aye, you're right on that." Dyael gave a wolfish grin. "You two legs couldn't even outrun us on a horse if you tried."

"Those are fighting words, princess." Gwen returned the grin.

"Now is not the time, girls." Inanna flashed them a sharp glare. "You need to keep your wits about."

"Well, what if Gwen and I rode ahead to look out for trouble?"

"Can't Ea do that?" Inanna nodded to the phoenix.

"Aye, but we have a system. When I lead a scouting party, Ea and one of our fastest hunters goes ahead of us sometimes. Ea flies farther out to alert our scout and distract the enemy. Helps them be able to ride back and warn us while keeping the enemy in place for us to shoot them down."

Inanna sighed and rubbed her temple. "Alright, fine. You two ride ahead. If you spot trouble, come back, and warn us immediately, alright?"

"Aye, you needn't worry about us," Dyael assured her and took off.

"Hey, wait up!" Gwen laughed, kicking her horse into a gallop after the princess.

"Hurry up, Gwen! You humans should have no problem catching up!" she snickered.

"You got a head start!"

The girls slowed down to a walk as they examined their surroundings. "Doesn't seem like anyone else is around," Gwen noted.

"You can never be too careful. Ea, fly." Dyael held her arm out. Her phoenix hopped from her shoulder to her forearm and used it to take off ahead of them. "He'll be able to alert us of danger."

"So, where are you planning to go after the war?"

"Back to my people. It'll probably be time for me to take my father's place as queen. Might even look for a wife."

"Won't he object?" Gwen made a face, remembering king Cyrian and his less-than-kind way of speaking to his daughter.

"Probably. My father has fought many wars and kept our people safe. Not to mention, he's as stubborn as a mule and can be more vicious than an angry boar. I'm sure he'll even join us himself in the final fight. But my father is also growing old. Losing my mother, all the fighting, raising me, and ruling, it's all taken a toll on him. I want to take what I've learned and use it to lead my people and give my father a few years of rest before his spirit leaves for the next world."

Gwen gave a small smile. "I think that's quite sweet…that you still look out for your dad like that."

"What about you, Gwen? What will you do?"

She paused and swallowed, tightening her hold on the reins. "Well…I honestly haven't tried to overthink it…considering neither Thrax nor I know how we got to each other, I fear I might not even be able to get back home…if I can't get back, I don't know what I'll do."

"Have you not thought of living with Thrax?"

"What?" Gwen's whole face glowed red. "W-well, I'd like to one day, but come on! We just started…well, courting. Plus, we're only in our twenties. In our world, that'd be way too early to start living together."

"Well, where else would you live if not with him?"

"Hmm…maybe I could live at the castle. If Thrax plans on going back there, I guess I could too. I could join Aaheer's court. I don't know what I'd do, though."

"Maybe Astricus will make you his companion. Like a lady-in-waiting."

"Huh? Why would he do that? Wouldn't he go back to his village?"

"Oh, come now, Gwen, you don't think Astricus would abandon his lover, do you? I bet the second we end this, Astricus and Aaheer will marry, and Hevaña's central city will be shared with humans, Gyrians, and fauns alike." She giggled. "I've known Astricus since we were children. He's been madly in love with Aaheer for years. There's no way he's giving up a chance to be with him if he can help it."

Gwen giggled as well. "I guess you're right. I'm sure Astricus would make it fun to be part of the court. It'd be nice to have us all together. Do you think you'd move your village closer?"

Dyael's smile turned sad. "I'd love to, but I also must think of what's best for my people. I'll try to move them as closely as possible, but we must follow our food. I'll still try my best."

Gwen frowned at the thought of being without her friend. "I bet we could find a way to help. Maybe Astricus will start like a royal herd of deer or something, so you don't have to travel away from us."

"I appreciate the offer, Gwen, but I wouldn't do that. Not for my people or myself. That'd be an essential part of who we are away from us. It's easier for people like you who can farm, forage, and hunt. I will try to stay near you but staying in one place would completely undermine who we are."

"You're right. I'm sorry, I didn't even consider that."

"It's alright. I know you want us to remain close." Dyael took her hand and squeezed it. "Even if I'm not close, you will still be a dear friend. We can have Ea bring us letters."

"Right!" Gwen smiled, feeling much better.

At that moment, Ea came back with a chirp. He landed on his master's forearm and leaned forward, cooing in her ear and tugging her curls with his beak.

"What? What the hell does that mean? How did she even do that?" The bird cooed again and ruffled his flame-colored plumage. "Well… alright then." Dyael looked at Gwen with a confused look. "Ea says he spotted someone.

Not a scout, but not a villager either. He said she spoke to him and claimed to be your friend.”

“A friend of mine? I can’t possibly think of who that would be.” Gwen’s brow furrowed, and she looked down the path at the cloaked person approaching. She was holding a staff, and her face was hidden from them. Once she pulled it back, Gwen gasped.

“Lady Midra!”

“Gwendolyn! I knew our paths would cross again!” Her hazel eyes glittered with the same look of delight Gwen remembered when she was first introduced to the mage. Midra’s face seemed much more tired, with grayish shadows under her eyes and a streak of gray in her sleek black hair.

“You know this woman?” Dyael raised an eyebrow.

“Yes! What are you doing out here? I thought you left Bonewell ages ago! I took you for long gone!”

"I came back to find you all. I had heard rumors that the caravan had left Terra Vale. It just took trying to figure out where you might go. I went to the first place I could think of."

"So I'm guessing we can trust you, yes?" Dyael asked.

"Oh! Yes, Dyael, this is lady Midra, master Majora's sister. Lady Midra, this is princess Dyael."

Midra beamed at her. "Wow! You're more imposing than I thought you'd be! Despite all my travels, I haven't gotten to meet many centaurs. Would it be alright to ask you about centaur customs?"

"Uh-…" Dyael's cheeks went pink, and she turned away awkwardly. "S-sure, but we should get back for now."

"Yeah, Thrax will be over the moon when he sees you! Come on!" Gwen reached down and lifted the mage onto the back of her saddle. The three women rode back to the caravan, Gwen trying to hide her massive grin as she caught sight of her lover.

"Everything go well?" Inanna called, noticing the extra companion.

"Aye, but we had an unexpected visitor," Dyael explained, gesturing to Midra.

"It's good to see you again, Thrax!" The mage grinned at him.

The young man's eyes went wide, and he pushed his horse forward to them to pull her into a hug. "Lady Midra! How did you find us?"

"I ended up stumbling into Terra Vale after I heard about your fight with Zephrus!" she explained, holding Thrax's face in her hands and looking him over. "My…you look so different from when I last saw you."

"Is…that good?"

"Yes, yes! You look like you've grown up so much…" her smile turned sad as her eyes went misty. "I wish my sister was here to see how you've grown."

"So you heard?" Thrax took her hand and swallowed hard to keep tears out of his eyes.

"I'm afraid so. I hope you haven't been blaming yourself, Thrax. My sister's spirit would never rest if she thought you blamed yourself for her passing."

"No, don't worry," he relinquished a wry smile. "I know it wasn't my fault. It was Zephrus."

Midra gave a firm nod. "And that's why we need to get to Bonewell. Apologies, my lady," she bowed to Inanna. "I didn't mean to take up time."

Inanna waved her hand. "Don't worry, lady Midra. Any family of Majora is welcome company to us. We're happy to have you."

Midra and Thrax spent the rest of the journey catching up on what they had been doing all that time. Thrax caught his master's sister up on their trip to Terra Vale, his and Gwen's relationship, and what they had learned about Zephrus over time. Midra went into a story about how she got captured by pirates but ended up befriending the captain and asking him to help in the fight, then getting lost in a forest that held the fae and had to give them her boots with gold buckles in return for her freedom.

"Sounds as though you've had many adventures, my lady," Dyael noted.

"Aye, it hasn't been easy. Since you first told me about what happened, Thrax, I've been trying to find recruits for fighting with us. I have quite a few, but I don't know if it will be enough."

"Your help is more than appreciated, Midra. We need all that we can get. Where are the rest of your crew?"

"They're in Bonewell by now. We got there early, but I wanted to try and meet you along the way. You haven't met any trouble with Zephrus's men, have you?"

"Not much. Did you run into some?"

"No, but I'm not sure how much better this will be…you see, when we got to Bonewell, there was a rather large squadron from Zephrus's army. We chased them out with the villagers, but I feared they had run into you and caused trouble."

"Maybe that was where the scout we saw was from?" Gwen asked Dyael, who shrugged.

"Perhaps. If you run from a scout, I hope that means they aren't too close to you all at the moment. If not, I'm afraid there's a real chance they went for reinforcements." Midra said somberly.

The group fell silent as they contemplated this. The sun began to sink behind the trees, and Inanna stopped the group. "Let's go ahead and set up camp."

The caravan immediately began to move about, murmuring amongst themselves as they set their wagons for the night and began to prepare for the evening meal.

"Lady Midra," Inanna pulled up beside her and Gwen. "I must ask that you refrain from discussing Zephrus as much as possible this evening. We have a woman in our group, Sigyn, who was his former wife." she pointed out Sigyn carefully climbing out of her wagon with another man helping her. She rested a hand on her belly, which had begun to grow, and sighed as she sat on a rock to rest. "She escaped his hold and has had a rather dark experience with him. I don't want to distress her, especially with her child."

Midra studied Sigyn for a moment before slowly dismounting Gwen's horse. "Don't worry, lady Inanna, I'll make sure she's comfortable," she promised and walked to Sigyn's side, smiling softly as she introduced herself.

"Out of all the people whose paths I thought we'd cross," Thrax smiled as he dismounted. "I didn't think it'd be Midra."

"I didn't either! It's a pleasant surprise!" Gwen agreed.

"I don't think this is a good thought, but…it's almost like having Majora back."

"Thrax…Midra isn't Majora…you can't let yourself compare them."

"I know, I'm trying not to…it's…hard, in any case…I always associate Midra with Majora. She's like a second teacher to me."

"Maybe looking at her as your next teacher is better than thinking of her as a replacement for Majora."

"Yeah. That's probably the best way for me to go about it. Thank you, love." Thrax leaned over and kissed her tenderly before tying their horses to their wagon.

Chapter 30

Thrax lay with his arm around Gwen as she slept on his chest. He stared up at the roof of the wagon blankly. His gaze traced the grain of the wood, dimly lit by the single candle on the side table that night. Buzzing thoughts bounced around in his skull like angry bees, making it ache.

He shifted Gwen off his body and slowly got up, running his fingers through his hair. He snuck quietly outside and sighed softly as he sank onto the steps.

"Can't sleep either?"

Thrax jumped and looked over to the dying embers of the evening fire where Sigyn sat quietly, the bags under her eyes even heavier than before.

"Lady Sigyn…I apologize; I didn't see you were there…"

"Don't fret. I appreciate the company." she patted the ground beside her. Thrax quickly got up and sat beside her.

"How…how are you feeling?"

"I've been better…" she gave a wry smile. "I've been getting sick every morning."

"Oh…I-I'm sorry to hear that."

"Don't be…" she rested her hand on her belly. "This little one has given me much to hope for. At least with you all, I know they will live a happy life."

"You still seem so tired, though," Thrax noted.

Her lips pursed as she thought for a moment. "Understand that my heart still aches. I know it's hard to believe, but there was a time when Zephrus was kind and loving…at the time, I had fallen for him so hard. He gave me hope that one day our people could be given a home that we deserve and would be able to destroy king Jarkus's cruel reign. I'm ashamed to admit even I had been drawn in by his manipulation and cruelty…" she pressed her forehead to the palm of her hand. "When I finally noticed the change in him, I couldn't bring myself to stay and watch him torture people. His attacks on me made me want to get away even more. Finding out I would have a child was the final nail in the coffin. I had to get away and stop him. I want my baby to grow up in a world of peace with a family they can be proud of, like you, Thrax."

Thrax felt his face grow warm at her kindness. "Thank you…do you still want to live in the kingdom? Once this is all done? Maybe Aaheer can get you a home in the Aristocratic quarter."

Sigyn thought for a moment. "Well…maybe. I'd have to think about it. Not every Gyrian wants to live this life forever, but I'm not sure I'm ready to leave them again. Not yet, at least."

Thrax nodded. "I'm certain you'll always be welcome in Hevaña, no matter what you decide."

Sigyn smiled and pulled him into a hug. "Thank you, Thrax. You and your family are very kind."

Thrax could feel the heat radiating off his face from embarrassment. "Ah- i-it's not a big deal."

Sigyn chuckled and nudged him gently. "You should go to bed. We still have a long way to go, and you need your rest."

"Yeah…you should get some rest too. Good night, Sigyn."

"Good night, Thrax."

The next few days moved quickly and with relative silence. They left early before the sun had risen above the trees and took camp just after it sank into shadows. People were not so inclined to stories or light chats. There was a gloomy cloud that seemed to hang over them all.

"Most of our journeys come with joy and no hurry to it. I don't think we'll be getting much desire to relax until we reach Bonewell." Inanna explained.

"I wouldn't either. Dyael, is Ea still not seeing anything?" Aaheer asked.

"All clear. But we shouldn't take our guard down. Inanna, will we pass the faun village?"

Astricus perked up from Aaheer's horse and looked over hopefully.

"That will be our best option, yes. We need to avoid the Eternal Night. It will take much longer, but cutting through it would be infinitely riskier."

"My people," Astricus piped up, trying to resist the vast grin tugging at his mouth. "Would be more than happy to welcome you to our village. I'm sure they'd be willing to join us as well. I have someone looking after them; they can remain with those who cannot fight."

"Thank you, Astricus. We're always grateful to you. I'm sure you miss your people greatly."

"I do…" he agreed and hugged more tightly to Aaheer. "I don't think I've ever been away from them so long…but it's alright now! Once we get there, I'll bring all those who can fight to join us and send word to the other villages to join the fight!"

"We're close enough to my people that I could send Ea to my father and ask for his aid," Dyael noted.

"Yes, thank you, all of you. Do what you must, and hopefully, we'll reach the village soon, Astricus. Just a few more days."

The journey grew more exhausting each day. It took a week to go around the forest to the faun village, but once there, a collective sigh seemed to come from the weary travelers as they all collectively relaxed. This would be, though briefly, a moment for them to rest and recuperate. Astricus grew giddier the closer they got, and the second the village came into view, he leaped from Aaheer's horse and ran to his home.

The fauns cried out and ran to him, happily throwing their arms around him and breaking into tears of joy.

"Everyone!" He stepped back and smiled at his group. "I have something vital to say. Our Gyrian brothers and sisters and my traveling companions will be joining us for a few days of rest before we continue our journey. Once we leave, though," his smile fell slightly as the topic grew more serious. "I will need all who can fight to join us as we journey closer to Hevaña. We are growing closer to the time of battle. It is time we fulfill our role as allies."

The fauns gasped softly and began anxiously whispering amongst each other, causing Astricus to call for silence. "It will not be easy, I understand. But we need to support our brethren in the fight, and we need all the hands we can get. Terna," A tall, muscular faun woman looked up. "I need you to send messenger birds out to other villages to call for those who can fight to join us in Bonewell. Once we leave, I will also need you to stay and watch over our village again."

"Of course, my prince." she turned and hurried to a larger building to do as asked.

"Now," he smiled at the travelers and held his arms out. "My friends, come rest and be merry with us! We've spoken enough of sad things. Now we will celebrate!"

The fauns cheered and rushed forward to pull them into the village and began to cook, pouring wine and playing music. The children quickly gathered together and, before long, were running around gleefully.

Gwen laughed softly and hugged Thrax's arm. "I've missed this!"

"Why don't we change and dress for the celebration?" Thrax offered.

"Yes! I want to dance!"

"Are you going to make me again?"

"Come on, Thrax! You're a great dancer! We haven't gotten to dance since-…" she paused and blushed, holding the door of their wagon.

A devilish smirk crossed Thrax's face. He stepped closer and tilted her chin to look him in the eye. "Since what, lady Gwendolyn?" his voice came out in a flirtatious purr that practically made steam come out of her ears.

Gwen quickly opened the door to the wagon and rushed to the wardrobe, her heart pounding as her mind raced with memories of their first night together. Thrax chuckled from the doorway before following her inside.

Once changed, the two went out to join the party. Dyael trotted in a dance step with the fauns, all laughing gleefully around the large bonfire that had been built. Borbyr was blushing and smiling softly as one of the faun ladies flirted heavily with him. Inanna and Teyana sat and drank, singing to the music. Aaheer and Astricus sat together, weaving some flower garlands with many of the young faun women who were all talking to them excitedly and giggling. Young fauns danced around as they served food and wine, humming to the music. The hollow had changed from lush green to a brilliant red, orange, and gold array. The vines that hung along the cliff's edge had begun to turn brown, but there was still greenery amongst the fiery leaves as hemlock trees, junipers, and spruce trees lined the hollow's border. The evening autumn breeze made Gwen hold closer to Thrax, who took a deep breath.

"Isn't it wonderful, Gwen?"

"Autumn is my favorite season. It looks so pretty here."

"Now we have a chance to enjoy it. Let's take some time to forget our troubles."

"Yes. Now, come on, Thrax! Let's celebrate!" She grasped his hands and pulled him to the bonfire. She twirled happily and began stepping around the fire, clapping with the other dancers in time to the music. Thrax hurried over and grasped her hands, scooping her up in his arms. He lifted Gwen off her feet, kissing her neck sweetly. She squealed in delight, wrapping her arms tightly around his neck as he set her down. He wrapped one arm around her waist, the other tenderly holding her hand, and danced around with her. He twirled her under his arm as she lifted her skirt to avoid tripping.

The fauns clapped along as they all danced. Dyael trotted by and smirked at them. "Nice fancy steps, Thrax!"

573

"Don't deny you're jealous, Dyael!"

The princess laughed and kicked her heels happily, whooping with the others. They didn't stop dancing until Astricus stood on a table, calling for everyone's attention.

"First, I want to thank Inanna and her people for welcoming me amongst them as their family. Our people have always been friendly, but I am grateful nonetheless. You truly made me feel like I was welcomed into your family."

The Gyrians raised their goblets and cheered.

"To my people, I also thank you for letting me join my friends and patiently waiting for my return. I couldn't imagine being without any of you. You are my family and home. As long as I am with my people, I am home, truly."

The fauns cheered, a few of them wiping their eyes and sniffing.

"Finally, to my friends, Thrax, Gwendolyn, Dyael, Borbyr, and Aaheer. You have all become my dearest friends. We haven't always had an easy journey but we have come together as friends. I can trust you all with my life, and I can't ask for better friends to join on the battlefield. I hope I can provide as much support as you all have provided me."

"Get on with it, goat!" Thrax yelled, causing a few chuckles as Gwen elbowed him in the ribs.

Astricus laughed and picked up a goblet filled to the brim with wine, some sloshing over his hand. "The point is that we are here to unite to overthrow the threat that is Zephrus Arimas. Right now, our forces are small, but with our strength, and the strength of our allies, we will be victorious, for all of our sakes! We will take on the battlefield with ferocity and courage! To our rebellion!"

Everyone cheered, raising their cups of wine and taking heavy swigs. Astricus drained his cup and staggered as he threw it to the ground, shattering it to the cheers of the villagers. "Now, let us continue celebrating our reunion and preparing for our trip to Bonewell!"

When he hopped down, he stumbled, falling into the arms of Aaheer. He chuckled as he carried his lover over to their friends.

"Damn, Astricus, how could you drink so much wine without getting sick?" Gwen asked.

"It is tradition for the leaders of fauns and even centaurs to drink heavily and hold celebrations in preparation for a battle. It is believed to bring good luck and a strong victory. The drunker the leaders become, the more likely to succeed." Borbyr explained, looking over to Dyael, who had begun her third cup of wine, and the fauns encouraged her as they drank from their cups.

"Sounds like a party!" Gwen grinned. "Now I'll have to come back to join you guys for a centaur party!"

Borbyr broke his gaze from the princess to look at Gwen. "So this means you're going to stay?"

Her smile faltered as the group all looked at her questioningly. "Well...I-I-..."

"You can't leave us, Gwen!" Astricus slurred with a wail as he threw his arms around her, slumping against her. "We love you, and we'd miss you!"

She gave a sad smile and hugged him tightly. "I'd miss you too, Astricus."

"We don't have to talk about this, Gwen," Thrax assured, gripping her shoulder.

"No, it's about time for us to discuss it. I've already been here so long. You all have truly become my family. We have fought, traveled, and lived together for months. I...don't even know if I could go back. Frankly...I don't know if I could return in good conscious. This…has become my home. I couldn't leave any of you. I…I couldn't leave Hevaña even if I had the chance."

Thrax's grip tightened on her shoulder as Astricus gave a whimper and wailed again, hugging her tighter. "I couldn't imagine you leaving us, Gwen! Don't ever leave us! We love you, Gwen!"

Aaheer awkwardly pried him off and laughed softly. "I should get him to bed before he makes a fool of himself. Gwen, I'm delighted to hear you're going to stay with us. You know you'll always be welcome at the castle. If you'd like, I'd love for you to join us in the court."

"Thank you, Aaheer."

Thrax took Gwen's hand when they left and pulled her away to the forest's edge.

"Thrax?" Gwen tenderly took his face in her hands, pushing his black hair from his face. "What's wrong?"

"You… want to stay here? With us?" he met her gaze, eyes wet with tears slowly building.

"Thrax…I love you so much. You and I are meant to be together. I don't think it was anything less than fate that you fell into my room." she giggled at the memory of him sprawled out on her bedroom floor. "I could never leave you; leave us."

He grasped her face in his hands and pulled her into a deep, tender kiss. "You are my starlight, Gwendolyn Grace…" he pressed his forehead gently to hers. "I want you to make me a promise, however. If this battle…if something should go wrong, don't try to stay. Don't try to…" he swallowed hard. "Don't try to avenge me or anything. I want you to promise me you'll get out of there. You'll try to get back home to safety. Can you promise me that, Gwen?"

579

Her blood ran cold at the thought of Thrax's death, her hands moving to grip his sleeves tightly. "I can't promise that, Thrax, because that's not going to happen. He is not going to beat us. We will win and will live our lives together here. He will not take us away from each other."

"Gwen," his voice grew firmer as he reached up to grasp her hands. "I appreciate your conviction, but please, my love, I need you to promise this. I need to know that if there's even the slightest chance we won't be able to succeed, you will still be safe."

Gwen felt like a lump was forming in her throat as her eyes burned. She pressed her face into his chest and murmured. "I-…I promise…but please promise me we will fight, so that doesn't happen. I can't let that happen, Thrax."

"Of course, my love…" his fingers tenderly ran through her hair. "I will fight all I can to ensure we will remain."

Chapter 31

Zephrus fell to the bed, his hands on either side of the woman beneath him. She had him locked in a feverish kiss, her fingers fumbling as she tried to undo his clothes. Zephrus growled with impatience, quickly tearing off his clothes and throwing them aside. He hoisted her legs up, pushing her dress up at her waist, and yanked her closer, his hips pressed to hers. She gave a little squeal but still grinned up at him. Her face was flushed as she undid her bodice, so her breasts were let free.

Zephrus groaned and began leaving kisses down her neck as one hand massaged her breast. The other caressed her body and slipped under her skirt, slowly touching her. The woman arched her back against his hands, moaning and tangling her fingers in his hair. "Your highness…"

"Sigyn…" he moaned longingly.

"What?" The hands that had just been entwined in his black hair were now pressed to his shoulders.

"What? What's wrong?" He sat up, looking irritated.

"You…called me Sigyn, my lord."

"I-…no, you heard wrong…I-…" he stared down at the woman in his bed. When his wife shared his bed, this woman had been one of her ladies in waiting. He was not foolish to her longing gazes ever since Sigyn left. Looking down at her now, though, Zephrus felt his face scrunch. Her desire to get into his bed, to take advantage of the absence of his wife, disgusted him. He loathed her. Zephrus leaped up and walked to the other side of the room.

"Get out."

"M-my lord?"

"Are you deaf? I said get out! Get out, now!" he grabbed the bodice of her dress and threw it at her.

She yelped and grasped the clothing, haphazardly

holding her clothes to keep herself covered as she ran out,

whimpering softly as her eyes filled with scorned tears.

Once left alone again, Zephrus sank into the chair at

his desk, pressing his eyes against the palms of his hands.

"Sigyn…my Sigyn…gone…I've lost you because of that

bastard child…" he felt his eyes burn with tears that he

quickly blinked away.

The candlelight flickered around him, making

goosebumps appear on his arms. He turned and was met by

a black beast towering over him, thick and dripping in

black ooze, its gaping mouths open in a haunting moan.

Before the wizard could react, the creature grasped his

shoulders and howled, drowning out Zephrus's cries. He

immediately grabbed a knife from the desk and slashed its

hand off. The beast moaned in pain, and Zephrus took a

moment to stab its other hand, making it wail and pull

away. He created balls of red fire and threw them at the creature as it slithered back into the shadows.

Zephrus panted as he sat back, wiping his forehead. He hissed as pain surged through his arms. One had a nasty slash, while the other had a stab wound. "Fuck…what IS this thing?" he cursed as he cleaned and dressed the wounds.

"What caused this creature? I've never seen anything like it. Can't it be a ghost? Some ghoul? Fuck. I need some fucking answer." He flipped angrily through his books, tossing them more aggressively across the room each time he got no answer.

He eventually gave up and slammed his fists against the desk, clenching them till his nails stung his palms from cutting into the skin. He ground his teeth in frustration. "All of this…is him!" He roared, throwing his hands across the desktop to knock its contents off and kicking the desk onto its side. He grabbed the chair and threw it to the wall, screaming. The books were burnt, and the luxurious wine-red curtains ripped from the wall. An inkwell was chucked, splattering black stains across the floor, and smashing against the wall. A candleholder was sent flying at the windows, crashing through them. Sephtis flapped his wings from his perch, cawing in irritation at all the noise.

Zephrus fell to his knees in the center of the destruction, his chest heaving. "No more…I won't let anyone control me anymore…never again." He clutched his head as it throbbed, screaming curses as he pressed his forehead to the ground. "No more! No more! I can't stand it any longer! This battle, this thing I'm seeing, I want it all gone!" The wizard clenched his fists to the side of his head and slammed them to the floor, taking some chunks of dirty black hair with them. "It's that family! Those damn Thornblades and that bastard child! It's them! Everything!

Everything is them! I want them dead! I want their heads mounted on my wall and their bones fed to the dogs!" he slammed his fists repeatedly against the floor until they became scrapped and bloody.

"If I kill them, this will all be over…yes, yes, yes…this will all be over! I have to kill them! Ha! Once they're gone, this will all be mine! Mine, mine, mine! I'll rule this wretched kingdom! I'll bring Sigyn back! I'll make her my wife again, and we'll have enough children to rule this kingdom and more! We'll start an empire! A dynasty! The house of Arimas will live forever! I have to kill them! I have to wash my hands in their blood! I'll watch the eyes of that fucking prince lose their light! I'll slit open the bastard boy's belly myself! I'll throw his bitch to my soldiers! Inanna and her traitors will be my slaves! Yes, yes, it's all coming into place!"

He gave a maniacal laugh and leaped to his feet. He raced to the shattered windows and threw them open, scattering broken glass. "Sephtis, hunt them down. I'm not waiting for them any longer. I will have my men destroy them. Report back when you have found them."

The bird cawed again before swooping out the window, flapping over the forests. Zephrus watched as the sound of the bird's caws and his shape became a faded black spot in the sky. "Prepare, *brother*. You and your little friends will meet their end soon."

Chapter 32

This next departure did not feel quite as solemn, despite the crackle of tension in the air. As they prepared their wagons, the fauns chatted with each other and the Gyrians. Weapons and armor were piled in amongst the supplies. Children ran around the food barrels, chasing dogs and climbing over stacks of clothes.

Once prepared, they all left to the goodbyes of the remaining villagers. Astricus rode with Aaheer, smiling a little more than he had when he first left the village at the beginning of their journey.

"You seem quite chipper, your highness," Borbyr noted as he walked alongside them.

"Aye. It's not a joyful journey, but having my people by my side makes it feel not so bad. It makes me feel more hopeful."

"That's always good. Anything that can provide more hope is encouraged." Dyael nodded. "I have a feeling our battles are fast approaching. We'll need all the hope we can get."

"How do you know that?" Tan asked, turning to look at them.

"The trees were speaking as we left. They can feel it as well. They spoke of Zephrus's men cutting through their sacred forests."

"Right! The forest near Astricus's home would be filled with magic, wouldn't it? With it so close to the eternal night?" Gwen asked.

"Aye, they are, but trees have always spoken with each other. We centaurs, and fauns, can listen to their voices more easily. What may sound like the wind to you sounds like voices whispering secrets to us. We are connected to nature and animals in a way that many others aren't. We can hear the voices of many."

"Can humans learn to hear them too?"

"Well, you can, but there are many limits, and it takes many years of practice. In Thrax's case, it would be easier because he comes from magic and has a familiar. The voices of familiars are far easier to understand. Thrax, have you been able to recognize Kitsae's voice yet?"

"I admit, I haven't tried. Perhaps I should. I could ask him to help look out for Zephrus's men with us."

"Aye, you must continue to practice your magic!" Inanna nodded. "Any knowledge you can take in gives you a little more leg-up against Zephrus. Since that time to fight is approaching, you'll need it for sure."

"What can I do to help, Inanna?" Gwen asked.

"You are doing just fine as you are, Gwen. We appreciate any help anyone can give in training, caring for

591

soldiers, gathering information, or anything like this. All will be expected to play their part in this fight.”

“Then we’d better make sure to keep going. The sooner we get to Bonewell, the better.”

They all settled into camp that night with relative ease. Gwen led a group into the trees to search for food. She and the elder children listened intently as Teyana instructed them on what mushrooms in the area were safe to eat. They returned, tired and dirty, to the warm glow of the campfire. Thrax was standing over the cooking pot, stirring while instructing Kitsae to fetch him ingredients every once in a while. The fox chattered happily at his praise.

Gwen sat on the steps of their wagon and heaved a heavy sigh as she unlaced her boots and massaged her aching feet.

"All settled, my love?" Thrax turned to her, wiping sweat from his forehead.

"Just about. You'd think my feet would be used to so much walking after all this time."

"It never gets any easier." He gave a low chuckle before scooping out rabbit meat, cooking in a creamy broth with carrots and diced mushrooms. Thrax began pouring it out into bowls while animating a knife to slice some nearby loaves of bread, then carefully levitating the bowls to the people within the camp.

Gwen took her food gratefully and smiled proudly at Thrax. "You certainly are getting good!"

"Thank you!" He sat beside her and pulled a wrapped rabbit's leg from his cloak to give to Kitsae, which he snatched up happily. "I'm grateful for all I've been able to learn. I wish I didn't have to learn it so quickly, but here we are."

"I know what you mean. I certainly didn't expect to be so good with a knife or a bow."

"And you're a natural with them," Thrax assured her. He reached into his pants pocket and pulled out a map. He studied it a moment before pointing to a spot within the woods. "Here. Since we're following the traditional path, this should be about where we are, considering how many days we've traveled with relatively no trouble. We should get to Bonewell before nightfall if we move quickly tomorrow."

"What do we do from there?"

"Well, we," he gestured to the two of them, then over to Astricus and Aaheer. "should meet with my mother first and give her a full explanation of what's happened. The next step will be getting the word out and gathering our army. We'll send letters to the centaurs, villages, the dark elves, mother's family, whomever we can reach."

"Do we need to work on our letters? I remember I learned about how to encrypt letters in school. I could show you how so we can make sure it's not so easy to figure out what we're saying."

"That sounds like an excellent idea. I didn't think schools in your world would teach such things!"

"We learn all kinds of stuff though I certainly don't think it's as cool or as useful as what you lot learn here."

"Well, don't forget, we live in two very different worlds. I don't think what we learn here would be so useful in your world."

She shrugged and began stirring her food, looking down into the bowl. "I don't like thinking about it…it makes me sad…" she admitted.

"You miss your father, don't you?"

"Yeah…I wish I could tell him where I am…I'm sure he's been looking all over for me. At least, I hope he has…I dunno, I think it's nice to think he might care enough to look."

"Do you think he wouldn't?"

"I dunno, he probably would. But since my mum died, it's hard to tell with him sometimes…our relationship has been a fucking mess."

Thrax nodded solemnly. "I remember you telling me you two argued often."

"Yeah. Honestly, I thought of how things were between you and your mum. He loves me, but sometimes I wonder if he sees me as his kid. He still treats me like I'm one, at the very least."

"I am sorry you won't get that closure. But I'm certain he'd be proud if he could see you now." Thrax gripped her shoulder, tenderly rubbing circles with his thumb.

"Thank you, Thrax." Gwen slid her hand up to hold his.

"Oi, sad sacks," Dyael called over from the fire. "Quit skulking in your corner, and come over here!"

The couple went to sit with the others in their group. "Astricus suggested we try to have some song to lighten the mood. What do you think, Thrax? Does that wizard voice know how to hold a tune?" Dyael snickered.

"If by 'hold a tune' you mean shattering glass from how bad it is, then yes," Aaheer smirked.

"Alright, smartass, why don't you give it a try, then?"

"An excellent idea, Thrax! One of the few you've had since I've known you!" Astricus grinned at his lover, clapping in delight. "Yes, please, darling! Give us a song!"

The others cheered as Aaheer's face slowly turned a deep red. "I-I…I don't know, I-I'm not sure I can remember anything right now."

"Sing 'The Faerie Queen'!" Someone shouted.

"I remember that one. Mother used to sing it. Come on, then, Aaheer, give it a go." Thrax insisted, smiling.

"I-…o-oh, alright then…" Aaheer shifted in his seat and cleared his throat, closing his eyes to concentrate.

"The fair faerie queen comes out to play,

With the sweet silver moon on her wings.

Her voice is soft as a cloud,

Her eyes were as bright as the stars.

The playful pixie watches from afar,

His heart beats loud for his queen.

Each night he comes to watch her dance,

His mind fell prey to her elegant trance.

The pixie and queen,

Forbidden to meet,

But this sprightly pixie

Does not easily take defeat.

He comes out and bows before the queen,

He says, "I know I am no prince,

I am no creature of refinement,

But my lady, I cannot stop my heart.

It sings at the sight of you,

It craves to make you smile.

Though I know I will be forward, I must ask,

My fair lady, would you care to dance?"

The queen laughed like a soft summer breeze,

To the pixie's delight, she did agree.

They danced and danced to the light of the moon,

But the faerie queen left too soon.

The queen and pixie met there each night,

They could hardly leave each other's sight.

Their hearts pined when they were away,

They could barely wait for the end of the day.

But one evening, the two had been found.

It was the faerie king!

With great rage, he roared at his wife,

But the sprite would not let him harm his love!

That night, the pixie passed in her arms,

For he could not stand to see her harmed.

The queen cried the sweetest tears,

And their love would be remembered throughout the

years.”

As Aaheer's melodic voice sang, the camp grew quiet as

they listened. When he finished, Astricus grinned happily.

“I never knew you could sing so well, my darling!”

“Aye, imagine how it feels to hear it almost every

day, though!”

“Don't tease him, Thrax! It was beautiful, Aaheer!”

“Thank you, Gwen…” Aaheer gave a sheepish grin.

“With that, though, I think it would be wise to retire. We

still have plenty of traveling to do tomorrow.”

Everyone murmured in agreement before all rising

and going to their separate wagons for the evening.

“You know,” Aaheer murmured to his lover as they

stepped into their wagon. “I never really noticed how much

that song reminds me of my mother.”

"You have a point…but I guess the story wasn't too bad. Your mother certainly is as sweet as the faerie queen."

"I suppose you're right. I hope I can tell her that soon."

Chapter 33

The ride into Bonewell was quiet and tense. Everyone was looking for any sign of an ambush. They didn't breathe easily until they settled near the inn with the familiar sign above its door; "The Runaway."

"Are you two ready?" Astricus and Gwen held their partner's hands comfortingly.

They nodded, and the four of them walked inside together.

There was the everyday hustle and bustle within the inn. The older man behind the bar, Orag, was still wiping down tankards and talking with patrons. Men in corners were laughing and cursing over card games while a bard stood to the side, playing music by the fireplace.

"Coming through!" cried the barmaid, lifting a pair of tankards in one hand and a plate of food as she squeezed between a table of men. "Here you go, boys. How's fishing today?"

"Dismal, Myana! This might be the driest year I've seen in a long time!"

"Oh, chin up! I'm sure the gods will give us a big rain soon!"

"Mother?" Aaheer gasped.

Queen Myana, dressed in an old barmaid outfit and muddy boots, whipped around to face her sons. Her green eyes filled with giant tears, and she screamed with joy. To the dismay of the patrons, she tossed aside her tray of food and drink and lifted her skirts. She ran to them, pushing past tables and patrons, throwing her arms around them for a tight hug.

"My boys! My boys! You're back! Thank the gods; you're alive! You're alive!" She kissed their cheeks and began to weep. Thrax and Aaheer hugged her tightly, pressing their faces into her shoulders so others couldn't see them as they started crying.

"Mother…" Thrax whispered, his voice choking at just saying the word. He couldn't remember the last time he'd called Myana that and truly meant it.

She wailed happily at this and hugged them even tighter. "Oh, look at me! I'm just a mess!" she stood straight to wipe her face. "Oh! Gwen and Astricus! Thank goodness you're all okay! Come on. We should go upstairs so we can talk. I'll be down later, Orag!"

"No worries, Myana! Take all the time yeh need. These folks can stand to wait a few minutes for beers."

"What? But we've been waiting for ages!" some men at the bar whined.

"Ah, quit yer bellyaching. I can serve yeh just fine!" he grumbled

As they climbed the stairs, Thrax couldn't help his smirk. "So, a barmaid?"

Myana gave a sheepish grin as she led them into her room. "Well, I certainly couldn't just sit up here and worry, could I? Orag and the villagers have helped me so much, so I started doing what I could to help them."

"I think it's wonderful, mother." Aaheer grinned at her.

"Thank you, my dear. Now, tell me, what all happened while you were gone? I can already see in your faces that you two have grown so much, but I need to know more. Oh, I've missed you so much. Tell me everything that has happened."

Thrax and Aaheer looked between each other, smiling, before going into the full story with her; their journey to the fauns, the centaurs, then to the Gyrians.

"My! You two have been on quite the adventure!"

"There's much more, though, mother. The Gyrians we found?" Thrax felt his eyes burn with happy tears again. "They were father's family. The Pryors."

Myana's hands clenched her skirts. "They're…they're here? Oh, gods…I-I haven't seen them in…" she broke into a huge smile. "I can't wait to see them after we finish talking. Now, tell me what else happened."

"I'm afraid the next part isn't so happy." Aaheer put a comforting hand on his brother's shoulder. "We…sadly were there when Majora passed…Zephrus…hung her…"

Myana's knuckles turned white as her grip tightened, and she gave a choked sob. She quickly covered her mouth and swallowed hard. "I had hoped-…oh, Majora…I'm so sorry, Thrax, that you saw that. I know it must have meant the world to her to see you safe one last time…" she reached over and grasped his hand, which he gladly took. "I only wish I could have been there for you boys."

"The day after, though, we had…well, an unexpected guest." Aaheer continued. "Zephrus's wife."

"What? Zephrus had a wife?"

"Apparently. She's carrying his child now. She escaped to us because Zephrus had become crueler. He even put a spell on her that took her ability to speak."

"I-…that's…very powerful magic…" her brow furrowed. "If what you say is true, I'm afraid Zephrus has already dug himself into his grave. I'm glad he can no longer drag her or that little one down."

"Well…there is one more thing," Thrax admitted and pulled his hand from Myana's to hold Gwen's. "Luckily, this one is much happier. Mother, you remember Gwendolyn, right?"

"Of course! You look very well, my dear!"

608

"Thank you, your highness." Gwen smiled and curtsied.

"Mother, Gwendolyn, and I are courting now."

"And," Aaheer took Astricus's hand and tenderly kissed his knuckles. "I've begun courting Astricus."

Myana's mouth fell open as she looked between her sons before pulling the four of them into a hug. "Oh, I'm so happy for you boys! Oh goodness, lady Gwendolyn, prince Astricus, I'm so glad to have you as part of our family! I'd been waiting for you two to get together finally! I knew it was only a matter of time!" she laughed at Astricus, gently holding his face in her hand. "And you, Gwendolyn! I'm so glad Thrax found you. I just know you've been good for him. I'm so happy to have you in the family!" she cried, grabbing Gwen into another hug.

Gwen squeezed her eyes shut and practically melted into Myana's hug. "I can't express how much that means to me, your highness."

Thrax gave a sad, knowing smile. He still remembered her story about losing her mother.

"Please, call me Myana, my dear! You're family now!"

"Thank you! You can call me Gwen."

"Oh! Wait, we need to go downstairs! I want to see Deidra again! She is here, isn't she?"

"Yes, she, Inanna, and Tan are here. We even crossed paths with Midra!"

"Oh, Midra! She's so kind, Gwen, you'll love her! Astricus, join us! I want to know you both better now that you are family, No more formalities!" The trio chatted happily as they walked downstairs, leaving Thrax and

Aaheer alone. The brothers looked at each other with big smiles.

"I never thought I'd be so happy to see her." Thrax's voice cracked from holding back tears.

"I hadn't either. I'm happy we found those letters."

"I am too…I'm-…glad that we can talk to her now. I think my father would have wanted that."

"I know mine would have hated this…and that makes it feel so right."

Myana grinned gleefully as she hugged Deidra tightly, the two crying softly.

"I've missed you so much, sister! I'm so glad you're safe!" Deidra held Myana's face in her hands, wiping the tears from her cheeks. "Saedon would be so proud of you and what you have done."

Myana gave a choked sob and pulled her into another tight hug. Gwen smiled and looked to Thrax as he and Aaheer walked over.

"Oh my goodness, is this Tan?" Myana grinned, turning to Tan and resting her hands on his shoulders. "Look at you, all grown up!" she kept wiping her eyes, unable to stop crying. "It seems like just yesterday I was holding you as a baby! Oh, you look so much like your father!"

"You knew my dad?" Tan's eyes widened.

"Of course! He and Saedon were great friends. I'm so happy to see you two!" she cried, pulling Inanna over to hug them.

"Myana, you need to meet my wife!" Inanna insisted, motioning her over. Teyana shuffled over with her cane and shifted so she could take Inanna's arm. "This is my beloved, Teyana." Inanna cradled her wife's hand and kissed her cheek.

"It's an honor to meet you, your highness."

"You got married!" Myana gasped, pressing her hands to her mouth, releasing a fresh sob. "I've missed so much…I can't believe I didn't get to watch you all grow up."

Thrax and Aaheer approached their mother, hugging her around her shoulders. "It's not your fault, mother," Aaheer assured her.

"Myana…" Midra approached, pulling her into another hug. "Please, don't you ever blame yourself for any of this. Majora would never want you to feel this way."

Astricus covered his mouth to hide his sad smile. "I'm just so glad to see this," he murmured to Gwen.

"Did you get to see what their relationship was before?"

"Sadly...Aaheer always had a turbulent relationship with his mother. Seeing how he and Thrax have grown...watching them reunite with her...it's wonderful. I knew she always loved them but never blamed them for not having a good relationship with her."

Gwen nodded in agreement. "I still remember when I first met her and Aaheer. Thrax barely even wanted to look at her."

"It's all because of Jarkus..." his fists clenched in anger. "He ruined everything about their lives."

"It does make me wonder if Zephrus hadn't killed him, would someone else have done it?"

"I have no doubt. The thing with Zephrus, though, is that he wasn't exactly doing it out of the good of his heart. I mean, he's after all of them! I don't think he would even want the current people of Hevaña to stay."

"I think we're going to have to take a more serious look at what we need to do to take him down. We need a plan."

"At least one of you humans is talking sense," Dyael grumbled, walking up to them.

"What do you mean?" Gwen asked.

Dyael sighed and crossed her arms. "Look, I've held my tongue because I'm here as an ally, but we need more of an idea of what to do than gather allies. With so many camping near this village, it's bound to attract attention. We'll need to figure out how to guard them and for an inevitable fight."

"Our people have answered our plea for aid," Borbyr spoke up, holding a few letters. "But that won't be enough. It will take them a few days to reach us. I suggest we set up camp a bit farther from the town. Have those that won't be fighting stay back. The town will act as a hub for our injured and things like that. All who are fighting can join us at camp."

Dyael nodded. "We need to start making this plan as soon as possible."

Gwen glanced over to Thrax and Aaheer. "Why don't we wait until tomorrow? I…think we should let the boys have this."

Dyael huffed slightly, but her grumpy exterior lessened. "Alright. But we should start as soon as possible tomorrow."

Gwen nodded and walked over to her lover to speak with the others. Astricus grinned as he hugged Aaheer's arm, tail wagging gleefully as he talked to Myana about his and Aaheer's relationship. Dyael shook her head again but walked over with Borbyr to join in the conversation, almost despite herself.

Gwen fell back onto the bed, pulling her lover down with her. She whimpered and moaned as Thrax kissed down her neck, his hands sliding down in a sloppy attempt to remove her blouse.

"Thrax…" she whined, her leg sliding up to hook around his waist. "Touch me, please…"

He growled against her skin as his hands traveled up to her chest, squeezing and kneading. Gwen's top was tossed aside, and he immediately latched onto her breast, his tongue circling her nipple, sucking, and grazing his teeth lightly, causing shocks of pleasure to run up her body.

Gwen tugged his ponytail loose to grasp a fistful of his thick black hair, pressing his head closer to her skin.

Thrax hummed in pleasure, pushing up her skirt with one hand, sliding her legs open with the other, his fingers tenderly grazing her skin. "Gwen…god…I can't resist you…" he murmured, his lips brushing her skin in light, tender kisses down her body.

"I love you, Thrax." Gwen moaned.

Thrax paused to sit up with a loving smile before giving her a sweet kiss. "I love you too." he returned his descent down her body, nipping and pinching her skin to leave light love marks before throwing her skirt over his head and burying his face between her thighs, hugging them close around his face.

Gwen quickly slapped her hand across her mouth to keep from crying out to avoid disturbing the others in the other rooms. She arched her hips to press them closer against his mouth as Thrax's tongue flicked across her clit, humming in pleasure as his hands slid to grip her ass.

"Th-Thrax…f-fuck…I-I c-can't-!" she whimpered, her legs trembling as his tongue pushed into her vagina, swirling around. She threw her head back, biting on her hand to stifle her moans as her body was wracked with pleasure. His hums of joy sent little shivers up her spine.

The wizard pulled his head back to catch his breath, licking his lips clean. "My beautiful Gwen…" he moaned before pressing his face between her legs again, his tongue starting a second attack on her clit.

Gwen wrapped her legs around his body to pull him closer, her hand stinging from biting down to stifle her cries of pleasure. She pulled it away to croak out, "Thrax, s-stop-!"

His eyes widened, and he pulled his head out from under her skirt. "Gwen? Are you alright? Did I hurt you?"

"No, no…I -…hold on," she pressed her hands to his chest and sat up on her knees. Thrax paused, his brows furrowed in concern that he may have done something wrong. Gwen leaned in for a slow kiss as her hands slowly pulled off his clothes. Once he was naked, she laid back and hooked her arms under her knees to hold her legs open for him. "Please…fuck me, Thrax. I need you."

Thrax's eyes widened at the display and gave a shaky moan of pleasure, licking his lips in anticipation. He gripped her hips and slowly pushed his cock into her, tilting his head back with a low groan. Gwen pressed her head back into the sheets, trying to stifle her moans as Thrax set a steady pace. One hand slid from her hips to grip and massage her thigh.

He thrust into her, cursing and moaning softly, lightly smacking her butt. "Fuck, Gwen, you're so gorgeous…you take me so well."

His hand slid up to pull her hand away from her knee. He hooked her leg over his shoulder, kissing her ankle and calf.

Gwen shifted, lying on her side, still holding her legs open. She turned to press her face into the sheets to quiet her. The new position sent waves of pleasure through her body and a shiver up her spine.

Thrax gave a guttural growl and clung desperately to her leg over his shoulder and her hip as he began thrusting wildly. Gwen tried to form words of praise, but her mouth hung open, unable to speak. She tried to haphazardly move her hips to meet his thrusts, desperately chasing for more.

"Gwen…oh fuck…fuck! Gwen, I-I'm gonna come!"

"Come in me!" She turned her head just enough for him to hear her.

Thrax gritted his teeth; his thrusts slammed into her, body shaking as the pleasure wracking through his body made his head spin. "Oh god…oh god…"

Gwen whimpered as he kept thrusting, screaming into the sheets as her orgasm left her body trembling, stars dancing across her vision, and tears springing in her eyes.

Thrax collapsed beside Gwen and pulled her into his arms. He pressed his chest to her back and left a trail of tender kisses on her neck and shoulders. "You are amazing…"

"So are you…" she snuggled against him, nestling her head against his shoulder.

They lay in each other's arms, cuddling closer. Gwen felt Thrax's breathing slow as he began to drift off. Her heart pounded as her thoughts ran away with her. Despite him falling asleep, she couldn't stop herself from speaking, "Thrax, I wanted to mention something to you…I know it's an awkward time to bring it up, but it's important."

"What is it, my love?" the wizard grumbled, propping himself up on his elbow. He blinked his eyes slowly and gently, pushing her hair back from her face.

"Well…Astricus and I were talking to Borbyr and Dyael earlier."

"Were they talking about battle plans too?"

"Did they already talk to you about it?"

"Briefly. I told them we could start first thing tomorrow. I want to enjoy this moment…" he kissed her jaw and hugged her closer.

Gwen turned to face him, holding his cheek in her hand. "Good. I didn't want them to disturb you and Aaheer. I know this is the first time you've seen your mother since we left. I wanted you to enjoy tonight."

"And enjoy it, I have." his hands slid down to grip her butt. "I'm the luckiest man on the entire continent…to get to share my bed with the most beautiful woman I have ever met."

"Flatterer." she giggled, nuzzling his neck.

"And what kind of lover would I be if I didn't remind you how much I love you or how beautiful you are?"

"Well, you're already one who's quite self-assured of his skills." she teased.

Thrax's eyebrows shot up at that. "Oh? Do I need to prove my skills to you again, my love? I wouldn't mind hearing that pretty voice call my name again."

"Pervert!" she pressed her hand into his face to hide her blushing cheeks.

He laughed and held the hand to kiss her palm and pull her closer. "Come here, my darling. You need rest. We don't want your legs to be too sore tomorrow." he gave a devilish chuckle as he pressed his face into her neck.

"You truly are insufferable, Thrax Nightingale."

"Then it's a good thing you love me.

Chapter 34

"Again!" Borbyr screamed, pawing at the ground in irritation. "We are going to continue until you get this right!"

Gwen wiped the sweat from her brow as she turned her horse again and notched an arrow in her bow. "Can we not take a rest? We've been at this for hours!"

"Oh, and do you expect Zephrus or one of his men to give you a rest? You've fought them before, Gwen. You should know better. Now, again! We rest when you get each target just right!"

The group had all woken early to drag their supplies to a nearby moor and set up camp. They were closer to the shade, setting up tents, cooking fires, and making makeshift forges. Meanwhile, Gwen had been dragged away by Borbyr to practice her archery, and she was ready to shoot an arrow through him from how long they had been going and how much he had been yelling.

"Start again!"

Gwen took a deep breath and kicked her horse into a gallop, aiming for the row of targets. She shot her first arrow, quickly drawing her next for the second target and down the row of five haybale targets.

"Not bad, but not enough." Borbyr huffed, pointing at the arrows just within the target's edge.

"I can't keep going all day, Borbyr! My fingers are going to bleed, and my horse is going to collapse!"

"And we will keep going until you lose your fingertips, princess!" he snarled. "You are a human with little fighting training; a centaur toddler would beat you in a fistfight! This is a war, Gwendolyn! I thought you knew that! Again!"

"Hey, I've gotten through my share of fights now! I know what's at stake with this war!"

"Scrambling through a few fights doesn't make you a warrior! If you know what's at stake, then prove it. Become that warrior."

Gwen glowered and yanked her horse back around. She took off and shot at each target. The arrows landed with a thump just outside the ring of the bullseye.

Borbyr's stiff posture noticeably relaxed. He let out a sigh and nodded. "Much better. That's enough now, Gwen. Take that breather."

Gwen walked her horse over, still shooting Borbyr an irritated look. "I hate the way you get when we're training. You get mean."

"It works, though, doesn't it?"

The camp had raised the tents, and everyone was moving around to prep. Thrax stood with Aaheer as a blacksmith fitted them with armor. Thrax was visibly uncomfortable as he adjusted the chainmail under his leather breastplate that was branded with the sigil of Hevaña.

"Nice armor." Gwen's gaze roamed his form as she dismounted her horse and puckered her lips for a kiss.

He smiled and pecked her lips. "Thank you. You're sweaty."

"Thank you for stating the obvious, dear." she teased and adjusted his armor. "Hm…looks good on you."

"We'll need to get you armor as well," Aaheer said. "You will be joining us, yes?"

"Of course. I wouldn't have it any other way." Gwen grinned and turned to the blacksmith. "What will I need?"

"Let my apprentice take your measurements, miss." The middle-aged man waved a hand to a young man who hurried over with measuring tape. "We will get you fitted with all you'll need."

Gwen let the teen move her body to take her measurements and looked at Aaheer. "Any word about Zephrus?"

"Nothing new as of late. Last I heard, he was still gathering soldiers in Hevaña. They've set up camp outside the city walls."

"I suppose no news is good news in this case. What about our allies? Any responses?"

"A few nearby villages are sending soldiers over. Cyrian has sent his soldiers as well. They all should be here within the next two days. Fauns and more centaurs aren't far behind. Some other forest creatures are joining the fight."

"Really? What do you mean by that?"

"Midra mentioned some allies of hers coming to our aid. She didn't say much. It could be anything from more elves, orcs, and fae."

"What would make them want to help us?"

"The fauns are heavily connected to the creatures and protectors of the forests. They tend to join in the fights of their allies for the sake of being allies. Some also think that if fauns are fighting, that must mean the forests are in danger, so they're going to join."

"I say we should take what we can. Father's sent word to other centaurs. They're not far behind." Dyael walked over, tightening the ties of her leather armor. "They've also called for aid from their allies."

"That all sounds fantastic." Gwen lowered her arms as the apprentice finished taking her measurements. "What else do we need to do to prepare?"

"Weapons, medicines, training, food…standard stuff." Aaheer pointed to the medical tent nearby. "Those who have some skills with herbs or magic are trying to help make sure we have plenty prepared for any injured. Midra has been a gem helping them."

"Is there anything I can-…" Gwen was interrupted as a horn sounded in the distance. The camp flew into action, gathering armor, weapons, and horses.

"What's happening?" Gwen grabbed Thrax's arm.

"That's one of our scouts! They spotted Zephrus's men! We're being ambushed!"

"Let's move!" Aaheer grabbed his sword in its scabbard and ran to grab a horse, Gwen and Thrax close behind.

Aaheer mounted as Astricus ran over and grasped his hand. "I'm staying behind to help. Be careful, my love. Come back to me."

Aaheer leaned down and kissed him, promising they'd return before taking off.

Soldiers charged toward Zephrus's men, who released a volley of arrows once they crested the hill. Thrax threw his hands up and yelled a spell that produced a blue shield of light to many soldiers around him.

Gwen kicked her horse into a gallop and notched an arrow, aiming it at one of the soldiers. The arrow flew and hit the soldier in the chest, knocking him back to the ground.

The battlefield became filled with cries and the clanging of swords. Blood flew in arches, splattering the ground and shields.

Thrax charged through the field, waving his hand at them. *"Bo'nim duhn!"*

Black smoke shrouded his hand as the shadows of the enemy turned into black tendrils. The tendrils wrapped around them, breaking or choking them to death. Their bodies fell into bloody heaps as Thrax leaped over them.

"Oi, there's something wrong with these things!" Tan called, repeatedly shooting at a soldier that had latched onto his horse's saddle. "These bastards aren't dying!"

"Hold on! *Bo'nim duhn!*"

The shadows entangled the soldier, but as they squeezed, its body fell into a pile of severed limbs.

"What?" Tan's eyes widened in horror at the single arm hanging off his stirrup, cleanly cut at the shoulder. "He's a corpse! There are walking corpses in their army!"

"Go warn the others! I don't think they'll be able to take them out without magic! Look out for Aaheer!"

"Don't have to tell me twice!"

Gwen and Dyael were by each other's side, cutting through the enemies as Tan ran over.

"Oi, we've got a major problem! There are undead in their army!"

"What? What are we supposed to do then? How could they even do that?" Dyael cried, embedding her axe in someone's skull.

"Does it matter right now? I'm going to help Aaheer! You two stay together!"

"This is bad! If there are too many, we'll be overpowered! Those things are nearly impossible to kill without magic!" Dyael kicked the new body off her weapon.

"Send Ea out to Thrax! He can burn them up!" Gwen sent off another volley of arrows into the cluster of enemies.

Dyael grinned with pride as she stomped on a fallen enemy. "Excellent thinking! Look at you, strategizing!" she whistled for Ea and pointed toward Thrax, struggling as he was surrounded. The bird screeched and swooped overhead, his fiery wings growing brighter as he dove into the throng, sending burning soldiers screaming.

"With those two, we'll be through this quickly! Come on, Gwen, let's finish this!"

"See if you can keep up with me, then!"

"Is that a challenge?" There was a glint in Dyael's eye at the prospect.

Gwen grinned. "What, scared princess? Think you'll get your ass handed to you by a human?"

"Oh, you're on! Whoever gets the most kills is the winner!"

The exhausted fighters shuffled back, heads hung. Their faces were dirtied by sweat, dirt, and blood. The bodies of the dead were piled onto horses to be buried while the injured limped alongside them.

Astricus ran into the crowd, looking for Aaheer. When he spotted his lover, he threw his arms around him, ignoring that he was covered in sweat and his armor was stained with blood.

"Thank the gods…you're back…you're all back…" his voice warbled a bit. "You were all gone so long-…" he fell silent and pressed his face into Aaheer's shoulder.

The prince gently shushed the faun, hugging him close. "It's alright, my love…it was a tough fight…we had some unexpected trouble."

"You could say that again." Gwen huffed, holding Thrax close as he leaned on her for support. He had a deep gash in his leg as he hobbled into camp with her.

"What happened?" Midra walked over and took Thrax from Gwen, leading them to the medical tents.

"It was Zephrus's soldiers. They weren't just regular men. Some of them were undead!"

"What? If this is a joke, Thrax, it's a very sick one!" his master's sister scolded.

"Why would I joke? I saw them with my own eyes! I think Tan still has the arm of one on his horse."

Midra pursed her lips as she sat him on a cot, grabbing a potion and dabbing it on a cloth. "If what you say is true, then that's extremely dangerous."

"Tan told me on the way back that it's dark magic. Does that mean Zephrus gathered some other wizards?" Gwen asked, sitting beside her lover. He hissed in pain and grasped her hand as Midra cleaned the wound.

"Not necessarily. While I'm sure Zephrus has many wizards who delve into dark magics, this is not the same.

Necromancy, reanimating a body, is a banned dark art, but it is much simpler. This wasn't that, though." Thrax explained with a grimace. "No, these were the bodies of the dead built into a whole soldier that doesn't die from a simple axe or arrow or even a sword. They die by destroying the body. Fire and magic will be your best option in that case."

"It's an extremely complex and dangerous spell. It has been known to drain the life force of the user. Dark magic has already been known to drive the user to madness. From what I've heard from Sigyn, Zephrus has already been delving into this, so it's no surprise he's taking this further. It just means much more trouble for us."

"Why would he do something like that?"

"When you've gone too far, eventually you stop caring…I imagine Zephrus isn't even fighting this to prove any point. By doing this, he's trying to cause as much harm as possible."

Gwen pursed her lips and gripped her lover's hand. "Thrax…I don't know if we have enough to stop him…if this is true, we'll need much more help…much more than we have. What if he has more of those things? What if he has other wizards to help him too?"

Midra held a hand up to quiet her. "Don't fret, Gwen. I've already sent word to many of my companions to aid us. They will be here any day now. There. All better, Thrax." She pulled the cloth away to show his wound slowly closing into a white scar. "That'll fade over time."

Gwen's body relaxed a little bit. "Thank you, Midra…I don't know how confident I feel in all of this anymore."

"I understand. We still must do what we can to help the kingdom. We have more allies coming to help than you may think. Don't forget, her majesty has also sent for her family across the sea as well."

She nodded and looked away. "I should go help the others."

Thrax watched her go with a sad look. "I wish I could do more to ease her worries."

"I don't know if anyone can do much, Thrax. We are all worried. I don't think that will stop until this war is over."

Dyael and Gwen sat together by the evening fire, resting beside each other. Gwen leaned back as Dyael braided her hair into many little braids.

"…so what kind of women have you met, Dyael?" Gwen asked.

"Oh, not many. Centaurs don't usually bring their herds together very often. But, I did meet a charming princess from a nearby herd." The warrior's cheek broke into a sheepish blush.

"Oh, tell me about her!" Gwen clapped her hands with a devious grin.

"She's charming…shorter than most centaur women, but still quite strong. She's not much of a fighter but a great hunter. She also loves reading and learning. She's brilliant. Very sweet, as well. She always has a smile and a laugh like a bird song."

"Oh my god, you are absolutely smitten! What does she look like? Is she curvy?" she teased with an eyebrow wiggle.

"Gwendolyn Grace, you are terrible!" Dyael laughed and carefully wrapped some of the braids around her head. "But…yes, she is…very curvy…she has a body like a fertility goddess…she has a cute chubby tummy and-…"

"Big tits and hips?" Gwen gave a devilish grin.

"Y-you're as bad as a bachelor stallion!" Dyael shoved her shoulder. "But, yes. That's what she looks like…with a beautiful dapple-gray coat and eyes like the ocean…and her hair is a gorgeous dark brown…she keeps it long and braided…her handmares keep it decorated with flowers…" her blush spread across her entire face as she described her. She clapped her hands to her cheeks to try and hide it.

Gwen wolf-whistled playfully. "I have never seen you talk about someone like this, Dyael! You like her! You should tell her how you feel when you get back!"

Dyael paused as she finished pinning Gwen's hair in the fancy style. "H-how do you do that?"

Gwen sat up and patted her head. "That's a good question, honestly. How do centaurs show their interest?"

"Well, usually, we show off our battle skills and bring back prizes of war, but she has no interest in those things."

"You said she likes books, right? We could help find a book for her, and you could tell her while you give it! Try saying how you want to learn more about her, too! I'll look for books with you, too! Is there something she likes to study?"

Dyael broke into a huge grin and pulled her into a tight hug. "Gwen, you are a wonderful friend! She likes studying other cultures. She says it helps her to rule with more understanding. Maybe we could find her something like that?"

"Of course! I hope we will still be such good friends after this! I want to spend more time with you!"

"If you don't stay at the castle, I'll steal you away!"

"You know, I always said I'd make a good centaur!" The girls broke out in giggles, laying back in the grass. Gwen rested her head on Dyael's waist, where her human body met her horse body, and looked up at the stars. "I love the night sky here so much…do centaurs have any stories about the stars?"

"We believe our best warriors become stars when they pass so that they can watch over our young warriors. Sometimes they gather in clusters to chase off monsters that bring nightmares."

"That sounds lovely…I know some humans have similar beliefs. My dad and I don't believe in that sort of thing, though." she admitted with a heavy yawn, shivering against the cold wind. Her eyes were growing heavy with sleep.

"Don't worry, though…my ancestors will look out for you too," Dyael promised with a kind smile and pulled her close to rest against her, warmed by each other's presence and the soft glow of the dying fire.

Gwen smiled and curled up closer to her friend. Despite all the fear, she was glad to have at least a small moment of peace with her.

Chapter 35

Zephrus paced down his camp, men falling quiet as they watched him. No one dared to speak as he passed. The only sounds around him were distant animal calls and the clanging of the blacksmith's forge.

He didn't glance about but headed straight for the tent where General Donovan was standing over a map of Hevaña, talking with two officers. The second they noticed Zephrus, they stopped and stood straight.

"Gentlemen…" his ice-cold voice came out with a slight croak. "Tell me, have you finally worked out how to fix your incompetence?"

"I-…p-pardon, your highness?" Donovan swallowed.

"Your *incompetence*. In defeating the little wizard and his prince?"

"Oh, o-of course! W-well, we've thought of spreading our camp completely around the city and creating a proper blockade along the harbor. We'll set up signal fires on the ships and have officers at each corner to get word quickly in the case of an attack. W-we've already ordered for any men in the city that can hold a sword to come to serve. W-what are your thoughts, sire?"

Zephrus glared down at the map of Hevaña and the territory around the kingdom. "Hmph…very well…and what of my new soldiers? What is being done with them?"

"Th-they have been put into cages, as you ordered, highness. They're being f-fed with meal scraps."

"Good…good…and my wife? Have you found her?"

"N-no, sire…we've found no sign of her."

Zephrus pursed his lips at this but quickly spoke to hide his feelings, "What of the squad we sent?"

"Most are dead, I'm afraid. The undead was enough trouble to let some of our living come back."

"Perfect. That means they're working as they should. Send word to the ships to prepare some batches of phoenix fire. I have the materials for them to make more."

"Why phoenix fire, sire?"

"If I know those little roaches, I'm sure they'll have found some way to have ships on their side. We don't want to take the risk. Since phoenix fire burns stronger than regular flames, our ships will use it to set any enemy ships aflame."

"Right…we'll get right on that, sire."

"Good. Don't delay. We need to ensure we're thoroughly prepared. I won't give up my crown. Am I clear?"

There was a flurry of flapping wings as Sephtis burst through the tent flaps and landed on his master's shoulder. The bird cawed in his ear, and Zephrus narrowed his eyes. "Hm… alright," he pointed to a village on the map. "Sephtis says they're camped near Bonewell. They'll likely try to come from the side, then," he dragged his finger to the side of the castle facing the forest. "So keep our men there most alert. Have an extra officer or two. Keep the men on permanent alert at all hours. We can't risk an ambush. I want guards around the camp day and night. Is that understood?"

"Of course, sire."

"Good. When they get here, don't kill those little trouble-making runts. Bring them to me. I want to hear their screams while I kill them myself."

"U-understood, sir…"

"Have we gotten any answers to our requests?"

"Some, sire. Two of the orc tribes have agreed to join. I'm afraid the other two have refused. One was celebrating a royal wedding, and the other was mourning the death of the chief's wife."

"Hm. Anything else?"

"Yes, my lord. We have spoken with the sirens that have migrated to the port. They have agreed to sink any enemy ships they can. The high elves have answered our call, but I'm afraid they will take a while to make that journey. But we have more Gyrian boys coming in. It seems some have a collection of harpies with them as well."

"Harpies? I see. How old are these boys, general?"

"They're young blood, my lord. Many are men, but most of them are young boys. Barely even men. Sire, if we let them fight, they will surely die."

Zephrus shrugged. "So be it. They will be dying for honor and securing our new home if they are to die. They can distract these rebels long enough for one of our men to kill them. Let the land be slick with their blood. It will nourish our new ancestral grounds.”

“I-…yes, sire…”

“Very good. I must be off. I’m glad you aren’t as incompetent as I thought, general.”

The soldiers all bowed to him, waiting for him to leave before they exchanged concerned looks.

“What should we do?” one officer asked Donovan. “This has gone too far.”

“He’s too far gone…who knows how much worse he’ll get after this is all over…” the second officer whispered, glancing around as though Zephrus was still hiding in the corners. “I think he’s mad by now.”

“There’s nothing we can do…would you rather keep under him or risk your and your family’s lives?” Donovan hissed quietly.

"I think we'll have to fear for both either way…" the first officer swallowed hard. "This isn't the man I first considered my king…we'll all be suffering because of him when this is all over."

Zephrus sat at his desk, scribbling furiously. His hands were stained with ink from how many attempts he'd made at writing a letter to his beloved Sigyn. His eyes were sore from staring at the parchment. The candles were burning low and dimming the room in its fading glow.

His hand ached, and his head nodded every once in a while. Eventually, his body gave up, and his head fell to the desk, face plastering into the wet ink.

A chill crept up his spine. Zephrus slowly opened his eyes, staring down at the desk. The candles were barely lit from how low the wax had gotten. Long strips of wax had hardened down the edge of the candlestick and created little piles on the wood. Between the flits of light, Zephrus spotted eyes staring at him from the shadows.

The black beast gave low, guttural moans as it slowly reached its long, spindly fingers towards him. The black ooze dripped from its body, mixing with the white candle wax. Zephrus's heart pounded in his chest. He felt like his body was encased in ice. A feeling like he would throw up made its way to the back of his throat.

The beast pulled itself closer and onto the desk. Its body slunk closer, each inch making Zephrus feel like his body was going to cave in on itself. The beast was so close to his face that Zephrus thought he would feel its breath, but the creature wasn't breathing.

It opened its mouth slowly, stretching the ooze to show a gaping black hole. The shrieks were hollow and filled his ears till nothing else could penetrate the sounds of the screams. Zephrus lay there, feeling like his body was dying. He felt empty and shattered inside. Tears suddenly began falling down his face. Zephrus wanted to scream, run, attack, anything! He felt like he couldn't even breathe.

The creature stopped screaming and stared at him with empty black eyes. It oozed across the table and Zephrus's letter before backing away and fading into the darkness. A few moments passed, and Zephrus felt air rush back into his lungs and sat straight up. He panted, clutching his chest, staring down at his writing. The ink was smudged and stained his face. The tears had made splotches and turned the wet ink into little pools.

Zephrus rested his elbows on the desk and put his head in his hands. His head pounded as he tried to collect his thoughts. Slowly, he got up from his chair, walked to his bed, and crawled under the covers, watching the candles extinguish themselves while he tried to fall asleep.

Chapter 36

Gwen, Astricus, and Aaheer sat at grindstones as Tan showed them how to sharpen their weapons.

"…and make sure to clean them thoroughly. A blade that's well-cared for will always give you a higher advantage in battle."

"When do we know to replace them?" Gwen piped up.

"Well, if you take care of your blade well enough, you can hopefully make it last for many years. Although, I think the centaur method of keeping at least a second weapon on you is always wise."

Astricus glanced at the little dagger he was sharpening and pursed his lips.

"Oi, goat, don't look so worried." Tan teased, tapping his blade flat on the stone's side. "You've got another weapon on that head of yours!"

Astricus flushed and looked back down at his weapon as though he couldn't remove his gaze from the grindstone. "M-my horns haven't even finished growing in…" his hand ran along the broken horn that still hadn't fully healed.

"I still wouldn't want to go against those." Aaheer teased, making the faun relinquish a small smile.

"That's right! Besides, we may need your horns if those other soldiers don't get here."

"Sounds like I arrived just in time." Midra grinned as she walked over. "I just came to relay a message from Inanna. Some of our allies have just arrived."

"Excellent!" Aaheer leaped up. "Who's come?"

"The centaurs. They said the fauns aren't far behind. I'm sure they'll be here any minute if not here already."

"I need to be there to greet them! I can't believe I wasn't there to greet the centaurs!" Aaheer fussed and grabbed Astricus's hand. "Come, love, we need to be there!"

"Wait for me!" Gwen jumped up, sheathing her dagger as she ran after them.

Dyael and Borbyr were standing with Inanna and Teyana at the entrance to Bonewell in deep conversation with the large centaur army. Cyrian and three other kings towered over them, looking down at Inanna.

"Your highnesses! My…h-humblest apologies!" Aaheer panted as he ran to them and bowed deeply. "I-I'm prince Aaheer of Hevaña. This is my lover, prince Astricus."

The faun prince bowed just as deeply.

"The human finally arrives." One of the kings snorted derisively, pawing angrily at the ground. "You'd think the one who started all this trouble would at least have the courtesy to greet his allies."

"Silence yourself, Yarel," Cyrian growled, tail flicking in irritation. "Do you think I would be foolish enough to entrust my daughter with a human I wasn't certain of? If our ally Astricus trusts this human enough to take as a mate, then he is trustworthy."

Dyael broke into a huge grin at her father's praise of her friends.

"Hmph! You always indulged your daughter too much, Cyrian…" the king called Yarel spotted Gwen and sneered. "Who is this? Some new lover of your daughter's?"

Gwen glared back. "No, but I *am* her friend and Aaheer's sister-in-law!" her face burned at the words.

"Allies and friends with humans! You've gone softer than I thought, Cyrian!"

"Enough!" another king piped up, pushing back Yarel. "This is no way to handle this. We are here to fight a common enemy and answer our vows as allies."

"Then remind me why exactly we're here again. I still don't understand how the affairs of humans affect us." the third king challenged.

"I can answer that." Dyael stepped forward. "If Zephrus successfully takes over this kingdom, who's to say he'll stop there? We have seen his cruelty firsthand. I have no doubt he'll continue spreading his terror over many others. Though we are strong, a vast army like his can still overpower us. Even if he didn't attack our herds directly, he could take our forests, our hunts. We might have to travel far to be able to find new, suitable land to travel to. We have to protect our people, allies, and forests. I, for one, will fight alongside them no matter what you all say."

The kings looked toward Borbyr, who stood with a stern glare and crossed arms. "I will stand by my princess. That is my oath as her general and friend. I have also seen this man's cruelty and the more than capable abilities of these humans."

This seemed to be the last push the other kings needed. They all nodded and motioned for their soldiers to set up camp.

"I hope you know I'm putting much trust in you, little princess." Yarel hissed.

Dyael gave a strained smile, though her eyes still burned with hate. "You won't have to worry about a thing, my lord."

Once he was gone, she huffed, stomping her feet in irritation, and tossed her head. "I've always *hated* that man! He's worse than father!"

"We don't have the luxury of pickiness, I'm afraid." Inanna put a calming hand on the princess's arm. "We need all the help we can get."

Dyael's anger was distracted by rustling in the trees as fauns began pouring out. Astricus couldn't help his bleat of happiness as he ran into the arms of his allies. The leaders of the other herds embraced him warmly, their tails all wagging happily. He led two kings and queens to the group, all bearing the same wreath necklace as him.

"Everyone, these are my dear allies! Queens Thedra, Dwyna, and kings Quintus and Za'ah!" the queens smiled and bowed deeply while the kings nodded to each of them.

"This is my lover, prince Aaheer of Hevaña!" Astricus ran to Aaheer, gleefully wrapping his arms around his waist while introducing everyone else.

"We're glad we could offer our aid to you all." Queen Thedra's voice was warm and gentle. "I'm so sorry to hear what happened to your family, prince Aaheer. You and your brother have our deepest condolences."

"You're very kind, my lady. Thank you."

"We will go ahead and set our camps up." King Quintus gently took Za'ah's hand and pointed for their army to set up near the centaurs. "Our soldiers need rest. We can speak later."

"Right, of course. We were told dryads would be offering their aid as well. When should we expect them?" Inanna asked.

"I'm afraid we can't say." Dwyna gave an apologetic smile. "The dryads don't tend to give us much other than telling us they'd be there."

"Right…thank you, your highness."

Dwyna nodded and took Thedra's hand, leading their soldiers to set camp.

"I suppose that went as well as we could hope," Gwen spoke up. "Do you think it's enough?"

"Frankly, it's more than I thought it would be." Inanna sighed, finally relaxing. "I'm just glad some of them came. Before you all got here, Yarel was threatening to leave."

"You don't think he will, right?" Aaheer's eyes widened in horror.

"Yarel is an absolute ass, but despite his many flaws, he is also extremely loyal. He promised my father to fight with us, and he won't break that, no matter how much he threatens it." Dyael promised.

Thrax ran up behind them, panting. "Sorry, I was practicing my spells! Did I miss them?" he put his hands on his knees to catch his breath.

"Sorry, brother, they just left to set up camp." Aaheer patted his back.

"Fuck!" he groaned. "Sorry I wasn't here to help you, brother."

"Don't worry, it all worked out," Gwen assured him. "Why don't we go get some herbs for medicine?"

"Good idea!" Teyana reached into a pocket in her long skirt. "I have a list with me of things we need. You shouldn't need to look too far from camp to find them."

"Perfect! We'll make sure we find all we can, Teyana!" Gwen took the list and Thrax's arm and whisked them away to hunt for herbs. Thrax nearly tripped over his own feet as he followed her.

Once they were away from camp, Gwen relaxed and took a deep breath. "It's nice to get a break, huh? Those centaur leaders were scary!"

"Really? What were they like?"

"One of them, Yarel, made Dyael's dad look positively feminist! He barely even listened to Dyael until Borbyr spoke up. Not to mention, he was so disrespectful to Aaheer!"

"I'm not surprised. Though centaurs have fierce warrior women, some are stuck in old ways and mindsets."

"Pfft…I'll never understand people who think like that. It's not so different in my world either."

"What a deplorable thought that such thoughts are carried even across worlds."

"We get by. Now, let's focus on these herbs."

The two worked silently, searching through the grasses and around the trees. Thrax glanced at Gwen every once in a while as she bent down to pick some plants. "Gwen…what do you plan to do when we reach Hevaña?"

"What do you mean? I'm going to fight with you guys."

"Well…I was thinking, what if you-" he hesitated, trying to find the right words.

Gwen turned towards him with the fiercest look she'd ever given him. "Don't you fucking dare suggest I should stay behind."

"Look, it's just a suggestion."

"Well, it's a dumb one! What, am I going to sit behind and play nursemaid? I don't think so! I'm in this fight as much as any of you!"

"Now, Gwen, listen for a moment, alright? Almost a year isn't exactly what I'd consider enough to prepare for a full war."

"I've been handling my own so far!" the plants became crushed in her fist.

"Those were just skirmishes by comparison! Please, Gwen, just…consider it?"

"No! We've been over this before, Thrax! I've been in this since the beginning! I'm going to fight with you! How many times am I going to have to say it?"

"Lots of people are going to die, Gwen! I can't risk you getting hurt!"

"So, are you going to ask Aaheer to stay behind? What about Dyael? Inanna? Borbyr? Tan? Midra? I was joining in to help you out, but it's more than that now. It's so much more. This is my home too, Thrax. I have people I care about. The caravan isn't just your family now; they're mine too. I'm one of them at this point. I'm not doing this just for you, and if you want me to stay behind because of "risks," you'd have to ask all the others too. You'd have a pretty damn small army by then."

Thrax pursed his lips silently.

"I'm not going to stay behind, Thrax. I know you want me to be safe. But you can't expect me to sit quietly. I could ask the same thing of you, but I won't. We're fighting together. I know I don't know as much about fighting as you, but I'm not a baby. I can hold my own." she reached up and gently cradled his face.

Thrax leaned into her touch with a grimace. "I hate when you're right."

"I know. But we're in this together. In every way. I don't want to argue about it anymore, alright?"

"… alright."

"Good." She kissed him softly. "Now, we need to get these herbs back. I feel there will be lots of us getting patched up soon."

Thrax and Gwen delivered the herbs and went to practice and train for the rest of the day. The evening came, and the camps gathered in relative silence and soft discussions for the evening meal.

"Silence again…" Aaheer murmured, scooping his stew with a thick slice of bread. "I wonder how much longer until we fight properly."

"We could always talk to Inanna about it." Gwen shrugged. "I'm sure she has a proper plan. We could ask."

"How can you be so calm, Gwen? I figured you'd be just as nervous about all this."

She shrugged. "I don't know, honestly. I just…accepted it. I'm not exactly fearless, but I'm here. I want to help as much as any of you. If you don't mind, I'd rather not mention it."

"What do you mean?"

"Well, when you remind me that I'm not from here, it makes me feel rather shitty. I've been with you all for almost a year at this point. I've started to build a life with you all. I'm with Thrax; I've begun to learn much more about being a Gyrian; by now, I'd even consider myself a Gyrian. I want to be seen as one of you and not just a tag-along. I'm tired of sticking up for myself so much."

The others broke into grins as she spoke, and Aaheer held up his cup. "I can drink to that. I apologize that I made you feel unwelcome. You certainly are one of us."

"That's right; you're stuck with me." They laughed, but Thrax still grimaced.

He got up and walked to the edge of the caravan. His hand reached up to fiddle with his earring before jumping hard at the snap of a branch.

"Borbyr! What the hell? Are you trying to stop my heart?"

"Apologies. I was attempting to hunt, but there are slim pickings right now. What are you doing away from the others?"

"I just needed to think, I guess."

"It is lady Gwen, yes?"

"That obvious?"

"Your mind is often on her these days."

"I'm afraid it's getting worse. I don't know, Borbyr. The idea of her going into this battle terrifies me. If she were to get seriously hurt or-…" he paused and swallowed down his following words. "If she were to get seriously hurt, I don't know if I could forgive myself."

"Have you spoken to her about your fears?"

"Yes, but she still insists. She won't consider anything else." he huffed and leaned back against a tree.

"I find it fitting that she and the princess are friends. They are very much alike."

"Loud, stubborn, and snappy?"

Borbyr relinquished a smile and even a slight chuckle. "A bit. But there's still more to them. They are loyal and enthusiastic. Gwen has learned so much. Even I can see it. I know what you fear. I feel it too every time Dyael goes into battle."

"But Dyael is different. Centaurs train for battle practically from birth."

"Doesn't matter. When you grew up together as the closest of friends, no amount of training will stop me from worrying."

"How do you deal with it?"

"Well, I consider a few things. If I doubted her skill, I think Dyael would be incredibly hurt because I've seen how hard she works. If she were to be taken from the battle, it would seriously hurt her morale because she's so confident. If she is sure of herself, I can usually be sure of her, particularly in battle. Perhaps you should use that thinking for Gwen."

"Huh…thanks, Borbyr. I've spoken to the others about this a few times, but they didn't get it. Even Gwen."

Borbyr nodded solemnly. "I recognize this is a problem you two have been working on for a while. I hope my council was helpful. I want you both to succeed."

"I think it was exactly what I needed to hear."

"I'm here for you as well, my friend."

"You consider us friends?"

Borbyr snorted and pawed at the ground. "Do you think I would go through all of this if I didn't consider you a friend by now?"

Thrax grinned. "No, but it's still nice to hear."

"If you wish to help her feel better and make up for it, I'm sure one of the others might have a suggestion. Perhaps your cousin or Astricus? They know her better than I do."

"Yeah, I think I will. Thanks, Borbyr. Why don't we go back together?"

"Aye."

"So you said there's not much food around?"

"No. The rabbits were too young and scrawny. I didn't see a deer the whole night."

"This is more of a fishing village. That might have something to do with it."

"Could be. Centaurs don't usually eat fish, though." His nose wrinkled, and he looked somewhat disappointed.

"No worries, big guy. I'm sure you won't have any trouble when we get on the road."

The others waved them over to sit by the dwindling fire.

"Nothing?" Dyael asked Borbyr.

"Afraid not, your highness."

Dyael groaned and pouted. "I can't understand how you humans can eat fish. It's so…fishy."

"What did you expect, candy floss?" Gwen snickered.

"What's that?"

"Oh, it's a sweet where I'm from."

"What's it like?" Aaheer asked, leaning closer.

"Well, it's all soft and sweet. It melts in your mouth, and all the sugar gets crunchy. It's also pretty sticky and gets the color all over your fingers." She moved her fingers like there was something stuck on them to demonstrate. "It's delicious, though!"

"It sounds delicious! Do you know how to make it?" Astricus piped up, tail wagging enthusiastically.

"I'm afraid I don't."

"That's a shame. Your world sounds so interesting, Gwen."

"It's alright. Honestly, I prefer it here."

"Well, we're glad to have you here!" Dyael gave her a big grin.

Thrax sat back as they talked, smiling softly to himself. Though his fears hadn't entirely been quelled, it was nice to have people around whom he cared so much for.

Chapter 37

"You want to know how to make Gwen feel better?" Inanna raised an eyebrow at Thrax, pulling her attention from the map before her. When he entered, she had been in Myana's room going over battle plans.

"Yes. We fought yesterday, and Borbyr suggested I make it up to her. I want to do something nice for her. But…well, we haven't talked about stuff we like."

"Hm…Gwen always seems interested in exploring. Why don't you take her somewhere nice?"

"Like where? I don't know this place."

"I know," Myana spoke up and pointed to a spot on the map. "There's a faerie fountain not far from here. The faeries are moving to warmer climates for the coming winter, so I bet if you take her tonight, you'll surely see some before they leave."

"But," Inanna quickly jumped in with a severe expression. "Do not forget to warn her about them! Wear your wards, no stepping into faerie circles, no taking faerie food, and don't touch the faeries. The last thing we need is to worry about Gwen disappearing into the faerie realm."

Thrax nodded firmly. "Don't worry, I'll warn her."

"You should go this evening. The faeries come out at night, and it's a full moon. It'll be so lovely. I'm sure she'll adore it. I know I did." Myana sighed happily.

"You've been there, mother?"

"Oh well…yes." She suddenly went bright red and put her hands to her cheeks. "I first went with your father to a faerie fountain and…well, Orag offered to take me to the one nearby."

"Orag? The innkeeper? Myana, I'm surprised!" Inanna grinned and crossed her arms. "Though, of all people who deserve to find romance, you certainly are top of the list.”

“Oh, stop teasing, Inanna! It’s not romance!” Myana giggled like a schoolgirl, her whole face brick red from embarrassment.

“Well, if you two are done trying to make me vomit thinking about my mother courting again, I’ll be going. I appreciate your help, mother.” Thrax hurried down the stairs. “The faerie fountain…now I need to figure out where that is.”

He got to the bottom and turned to the bar where Orag was serving a young man. “Hey, Orag! I need your help!”

“Hello, master Thrax! How can I help you?”

“No need to call me master. Can I ask you something?”

"Anything for Myana's boys." He gave a wide grin, a rosy blush forming under his thick silvery whiskers.

"I was wondering if you could tell me how to get to the faerie fountain. I want to take Gwen. Mother couldn't tell me where it was."

Orag gave a smug grin and chuckled. "I was wondering when you'd come to ask me about the fountain. Myana told me you and miss Gwen had begun courting. All the young couples in Bonewell take a trip to the fountain. It's beautiful. Here, let me map it for you." The innkeeper grabbed a napkin and began mapping the camp and forests nearby. He showed him a particular stream leading to a clearing where the fountain rested. "Take her before the full moon is at its peak. That's the best time. She'll love it."

"Thanks, Orag." Thrax took the napkin and read over it. "I appreciate the help."

"It's no trouble, my boy."

"Oh, I want to mention that if you hurt my mother, my brother and I will have no hold-ups about finding a way to make you pay."

"O-oh, she…told you about that?" Orag's face was red as a tomato.

"She did. I don't mind you two courting. I want her to be safe. I'm sure you can understand."

Orag broke into that wide grin again. "I can. Don't worry, lad. I wouldn't let anything like that happen to her."

"Good." Thrax gave a smile and shook his hand. "Thank you again. I'll keep all of this in mind."

"Good luck, lad!"

"Where on earth are you taking me, Thrax Nightingale?"

"It's a surprise." Thrax beamed as he pulled Gwen along through the woods. He followed the stream as Orag instructed, careful to avoid slipping or tripping over roots.

"Could you at least light the way? It's pretty dark."

"Don't worry; we're almost there. Besides, I have this and have no intention of letting go of your hand." He gave a cheeky wink as he hoisted a blanket under his arm and kissed Gwen's knuckles.

She rolled her eyes but smiled anyways, following along.

They followed the stream to a clearing in the trees where an old stone fountain sat, nestled between two large moss-covered boulders. The fountain was made of pale stone, cracked and covered in moss and vines. The water flowed into the stream from a spout and over the fountain's edge. The land was lush with little wildflowers and a ring of mushrooms surrounding the fountain's edge.

"Oh, Thrax! This is beautiful! Is that a faerie ring?"

"Yes. It's called the faerie fountain. There are a few out there, but mother told me one was nearby. I wanted to surprise you with it. I wanted to make up for our fight."

"Thrax, this is so lovely!" She held his face in her hands and kissed him sweetly.

"Wait, there's more. Here," he unraveled the blanket onto the grass and patted it for her to sit. She plopped beside him, snuggling into his side to lessen the chill of the evening breeze.

"What other surprises have you plotted for me?"

"Wait. When the moon is overhead, you'll get a lovely surprise."

"Oh, will I? Well, until then, why don't you come here," she shifted, straddling his lap and kissing him deeply and slowly.

Thrax hummed into the kiss, resting his hands on her body to keep her steady. When they pulled away for air, he couldn't help his smirk. "Why Gwendolyn Grace, I believe you're trying to seduce me."

"Now, what could give you that impression?" she purred, running her hands across his chest. "I was simply returning your kindness."

"Well, you know the saying, good things come to those who wait?"

"Yes?"

"I think you'll want to wait on this. Trust me; the surprise will be well worth it."

Gwen couldn't help but laugh. "It must be good if you ask me to wait! Alright then," she shimmied so she was sitting between his legs, leaning back against his chest. "I'm ready."

Thrax looped his arms around her waist and rested his chin on her shoulder. "Any moment now, you'll see something wonderful."

Moments after he spoke, the moon was overhead. Its reflection shimmered in the pool of the fountain. Everything around them began to change. The stone of the fountain began to glow with a soft silvery light. The wildflowers around them also started to glow in pinks, purples, and gold. The petals unfolded to reveal tiny faeries. They had pointed ears, beady black eyes, and large sparkling wings of many colors. Some flittered up from the grass, while others crawled from the cracks in the fountain or the moss on the rocks. They flew around each other in the ring of mushrooms, whispering, and chittering in their language.

Gwen sat with her mouth tightly closed, watching wide-eyed silence. Thrax beamed and leaned closer, whispering in her ear. "Those are pixies…they won't disturb us if we don't disturb them." A shiver ran up her spine at feeling his warm breath on her neck, but she nodded, pressing closer into his arms.

After a minute, some of the little pixies pulled out tiny instruments and began to play the music that reminded Gwen of music boxes she saw as a kid. The faeries started to whirl and dance, fluttering from one mushroom to the next around the ring while others skimmed across the water like ice skaters. Pixie couples floated into the air with glittering wings shining in the moonlight, making little rainbows on the water.

Gwen watched in reverence as she snuggled against her lover. Thrax was only half paying attention to the little creatures' dance in front of them. His attention was more focused on Gwen's joyful smile and how the moonlight made her blonde hair look silvery.

Eventually, the moon moved just enough that the fountain and flowers stopped glowing, and the faeries stopped their moonlight dance. Slowly, they yawned and began to crawl back into their homes and rest for the night. Gwen stayed still and quiet until she saw all the little pixies were gone.

"You knew that would happen?"

"Mother told me it would. I knew about faerie fountains, generally, but I hadn't seen one before either."

"Really? Well, I'm delighted you showed me." She fell silent for a moment before turning to straddle his waist again. "Thrax, I want you to make love to me."

"Uh…well, I can certainly fulfill your request, my love," his brows knit together in confusion. "But why so serious all of a sudden?"

"I know you're afraid I'm going to get hurt. I'm afraid you will too. I don't know what will happen, and I'm trying not to think about it too much. I'm still going to fight, and nothing will stop that," she began to roll her hips and leaned in to whisper in his ear. "But in case something does happen, in case we don't make it, I want to be able to share one more night with you. I want to remember you ravishing me again and how much I love you."

Thrax groaned at the friction and pressed his forehead to her shoulder. "I…I don't want you to get hurt…and I don't want you to feel like I doubt you…but I will not accept you talking like that." He looked up to meet her gaze. "We are going to succeed. We are going to make it. And when we do, I'll make love to you all night as I will tonight."

Gwen felt her heart thundering in her chest. Without another word, she pulled Thrax into a heated kiss. He moaned into it, his hands beginning to roam her body. She rolled her hips, making his erection grow from the friction.

"Fuck…Gwen…you're getting me all wound up."

"I certainly hope so…" she couldn't help her chuckle as she pulled away, despite her lover's protests. She placed her hands on his chest and laid him back on the blanket. Still grinding against him, her hands slid down to grab the hem of her blouse, pulling it over her head to expose her breasts. With one hand, she kneaded her breast while the other began to slip off her skirt. Thrax stopped her hand and pulled her forward. She gasped and planted her hands beside his head. Thrax took the opportunity to take one of her breasts in his mouth, immediately sucking on it and teasing her with his tongue. She gave a low moan, panting softly as his tongue rolled against her nipple, sucking and running his teeth against the sensitive skin.

His hands traveled down her body to her skirt and slipped under, cradling her body as he pulled it down, tossing it on top of her blouse. His hands roamed back up to hook on her thighs below her butt. He moved to the other breast, sending a fresh wave of moans and shocks of pleasure through Gwen's body.

"God dammit, Thrax," she whimpered, her eyes burning with lust and thighs rubbing together with need. "Stop teasing me."

He pulled away from her breast, his mouth making a little pop. As his hands slid up to squeeze her butt, he broke out in a wolfish smirk. "That's half the fun, dearest."

Gwen pouted and sat up again. "Fine. Then I'm at least going to get in on it too." She turned so her back was facing him and shimmied back, so his face was between her knees. Thrax felt his face grow warm and his erection strain in his pants. She leaned forward to undo his trousers and push them down, so his cock sprang free. She took his cock in her hand and began to pump him slowly, leaning down to take him in her mouth, sucking quickly.

Thrax pressed his head back against the blanket, moaning. After regaining some of his senses, he wrapped his arms around her hips and pulled her closer to start licking her clit. She was soaking wet and gave off a heady scent that made Thrax's mind feel clouded and lose every thought except his desire. He pushed his nose into the curls of coarse blonde hair and began to flick his tongue against her clit, making Gwen falter. She moaned against his cock, creating extra stimulation.

Her tongue ran along it and teased at the tip, making it twitch and leak precum. Thrax's licking and teasing made her thighs tremble from the sensation as he held her closer. Eventually, she sat up, gasping for air. Thrax pulled away and looked at her.

"Gwen? Is everything alright, my love?"

"Oh, more than alright." She turned and straddled his lap again and positioned herself over his cock. "I'm going to ride you until dawn." She slowly sank down, tilting her head back with a low moan.

Thrax gasped and gripped her hips, nails digging into her soft flesh. Once she was entirely on top of him, she began to grind on him.

"It's my turn to do the pleasing…" she purred before bouncing up and down, her hands pressing against his chest.

Thrax snaked his arms up Gwen's body, cradling her waist. He looked up at her as though she were the most precious thing in all the land. Gwen felt her face grow hotter under his gaze. Something in his eyes made her stomach flip with joy, and her heart beat faster. She leaned back a bit, propping her hands up against Thrax's thighs, and began to roll her hips, making him press his head against the blanket and let out whimpering moans of intense pleasure.

When he could compose himself enough, Thrax lifted his head and pulled Gwen to sit up straight. She squeaked in surprise at the sudden movement. His hands quickly grasped her wrists and propped up his legs.

"Don't think I'm letting you have all the fun,"

Holding her arms to keep her in place, he thrust his hips as quickly as possible. Gwen threw her head back, moaning, her eyes rolling back. The clearing was filled with the sounds of slapping skin and intense moans.

When Thrax released her wrists, Gwen collapsed against his chest, gripping his shoulders. But Thrax wasn't done. He wrapped his arms around her and pressed his face into her neck. Ensuring he had a firm hold of her, he kept thrusting even faster and harder. A sheen of sweat broke out across his forehead and neck. His breath came out in sharp gasps as he kept going, feeling his body grow hotter with lust.

"Gwen…Gwen…fuck, I'm gonna come-!"

"Yes, Thrax, yes! Come for me, baby. I want you-…" she couldn't finish and buried her face in his neck as he hit just the right spot.

Thrax grasped Gwen's shoulder in his teeth, biting firmly to muffle his loud moans. He reached his orgasm with waves of heat coursing through his body, his eyes rolling back from the intense pleasure. He bucked his hips, chasing after that last bit of pleasure and wanting to ensure Gwen got her fair share of the fun.

Gwen whimpered, digging her nails into Thrax's skin until it almost bled. She rolled her hips, and it didn't take long before her vision was blinded by stars, her body shaking as it convulsed in waves of pleasure. Her knees squeezed at Thrax's hips to keep her in place. She pressed her face harder against Thrax's skin as she rode it out before collapsing onto his chest.

Their bodies were hot and sticky. Another breeze made them shiver and cuddle closer. They both took one end of the blanket and wrapped it around themselves. Gwen snuggled against Thrax's chest while he wrapped his arms lazily around her, tracing the length of her spine with one hand.

"Was the surprise worth it, my love?" he murmured, already half asleep.

"Absolutely…thank you, Thrax." she shifted to kiss him, slowly and lazily, before flopping back onto him. The two held each other under the moonlit sky and twinkling stars, asleep in moments.

Chapter 38

"Gwen! Thrax! Horny fuckers! Wake the fuck up!"

The two lovers were woken by a wave of freezing water from the stream. Gwen squealed and sat up, holding the blanket to her chest. Thrax cursed and sputtered, pulling her close on instinct.

"The fuck is wrong with you?" he roared, wiping the water from his eyes. "Haven't you ever heard of privacy, Astricus?"

"I'm not the one fucking in the middle of the damn woods!" Astricus's face was bright red with anger. His ears were laid back, and one of his hooves stomped on the ground.

"What the hell has gotten into you, Astricus?" Gwen demanded.

"It's Zephrus! His men are here! He knows where our camp is!"

"What?" The two immediately sat up straight, listening much more closely.

"Inanna spotted his damnable bird! She put a spell over the camp so our allies were the only humans that could find it. But that doesn't apply to non-humans! He sent his bird, and it found us! And when we realized you weren't at camp-." Astricus's eyes welled up with tears, and he angrily wiped them away.

"We're sorry we scared you, goat." Thrax grasped his forearm.

"Come on; we don't have time to chat." Gwen waved for Astricus to turn around.

He faced the trees while the lovers pulled their clothes back on, then the three raced back to camp. Teyana was ushering the sick and injured into the village with some of the healers. Inanna was shouting orders while Dyael helped to guide people. Borbyr and Ea were carrying enormous amounts of supplies in a wagon for the healers to drive.

"Astricus!" Teyana waved for him to follow her.

"Wait, Astricus, why is Teyana calling you away?" Gwen paused.

Astricus hesitated and looked away. "I'm…not going into battle." He admitted.

"What? But Astricus, you've been training with us this whole time!"

"I know, it's just…if I die, I have no one to take my place. My people would be left with no one. You all have family and friends you could turn to if, gods forbid, something happened. I want to help, so I will stay with Teyana to care for the injured. I'm sorry I won't be able to fight beside you."

Thrax gripped his shoulder with a solemn expression. "Don't beat yourself up over this. You're doing what's best for you and your people. Remember that. We'll make sure to stay safe too. When this is over, we'll have the grandest royal wedding the continent has ever seen, and your people will never have to want or worry again."

Astricus gave a hearty sniff and wiped his eyes. "That's the kindest thing I think you've ever said to me, Thrax."

Thrax went pink and huffed. "Don't act like I've never been nice to you, goat."

"There it is." Astricus hiccupped and smiled. "That's the Thrax I know." He threw his arms around Thrax, who became sheepish but hugged him close.

"Don't worry, Astricus; it will be okay." Teyana shuffled over and gripped the faun's shoulder. "There's no way we can be defeated. We have a good army and excellent healers. You've been doing very well with your practice, as well. We'll win back our home for sure."

There was a brief pause, and between the four of them, a snowflake slowly fluttered to the ground. Everyone looked up to a growing white flurry descending on them.

"Is that bad?" Gwen asked.

"Well…it's not ideal," Teyana admitted. "But if it's not good for us, it's surely bad for them as well. Come on. We need to move."

Despite hundreds of soldiers moving across the dirt road, now crunching with the buildup of snow, not a word was spoken. The tension in the air could be cut with a knife, but instead, it was cut by the icy winds blowing white flakes in their faces.

Aaheer looked like he might be sick but tried to keep his face as stoic as possible.

Astricus sat in the healer's cart next to Teyana. His face had become blotchy with ruddy red cheeks and swollen eyes.

Inanna stared straight ahead as she rode at the front of the group. It was like she didn't dare to look back.

Thrax was staring at his hands, silently muttering what seemed like spells to himself.

Gwen and Borbyr stuck close to Dyael's side. She had a crease in her brow, and even Borbyr's eyes darted with fear. This did little to settle Gwen's nerves. She clutched her reigns so tightly that her knuckles were white and indents formed in her palms.

That first night was filled with silence. There were no talks of encouragement. The most warmth came from the fires, and everyone huddled together in tents against the snowy night.

That snow didn't stop by morning. It grew harsher as they got closer. The horse's hooves sunk deep as they walked, and they would need to pause and pull a cart from the muddy banks. The little army faced a week of traveling through deepening snow.

When it eventually stopped, it felt like a breath of fresh air. The air was crisp, and Gwen smiled as she blew little clouds of breath. The sun began to break through the clouds more often, and little songbirds flitted between trees, pecking at frozen berries in bushes or digging in the muddy earth for bugs. This breath of life in the last half of their travels was just the perk the little army needed. They walked with more pep and rode with straightened backs.

After another week of prolonged travel, they reached the edge of the forests surrounding Hevaña. While everyone set up camp, Aaheer stood at the forest's edge, staring at the kingdom.

Thrax approached his brother and stood beside him.

"It's strange," Aaheer murmured. "I never thought I'd feel so happy to see this place. Even in the state it's in."

The kingdom seemed dull compared to the last time they saw it. The once beautiful, clean domain appeared to have a layer of gray. White tents surrounded the outer walls protecting the central city from Zephrus's army. Dark gray smoke billowed in the sky from forges and fires hard at work. The harbor had large naval ships with black sails.

"It feels wrong, though…it's not….home." Aaheer's shoulders slumped.

"I never thought I'd call this place home. But seeing it like this, you're right. It's not home."

"Thrax, when this is all over, and we have our home back, I want you to come live in the palace. Not up in the towers, away from everyone. I want you to live the life you deserve. You're my brother, Thrax. You're a prince of Hevaña too."

Thrax snorted. "What a way to start your rule as king. Declaring the disgraced bastard child a prince? Come on, Aaheer, I'm better off as just a court wizard."

"…is that what you want, however? To be a court wizard?"

"Well…what else would I be?"

"You can be my brother. You can live with us instead of hiding like something to be ashamed of. We love you, Thrax. You're our family. I want your support. I need it. We don't have to live apart anymore. If you want this, you know it's open to you."

Thrax pondered, then smiled. "You know, I've just wanted to feel seen all my life. Like people would recognize me. It sounds silly, but I always felt like people saw right through me—even you. The only person who didn't feel like that was Majora. But this year…this long year has been something else. I lost the one person that felt like my only family. I found my father's family. I…have cousins. I feel like I finally got to have my brother. I fell in love. I made friends. I got to learn about mother. Even with Zephrus getting in the way, I feel I've gained everything. I've gained a family.

"I'm not letting anything get in the way of that ever again. You're stuck with me, little brother. I think I'll continue to fill the role of court wizard. But I guess now you can call me a wizard prince." He snorted softly. "Sounds kind of silly, huh?"

Aaheer chuckled and shook his head. "A little. But I like it. It's fitting."

Thrax wrapped his arm around Aaheer's shoulder in a hug. "It's time we start to repair the damage, eh?"

"Yes. You know, I'm not as upset thinking about my father anymore. He feels like a distant memory. I'll still have to prove myself, but the older we get, the more people will see me, not my father." He gave Thrax a huge grin. "By the end, they'll finally see us for us, not our parents."

"I think you're right." Thrax looked back at Gwen and Astricus, who organized the supplies in the healers' cart.

"You know," Aaheer turned to look at them as well. "I'm going to marry Astricus after all this."

"Good. I think the goat's good for you."

"Thrax?"

"Yes?"

"I'm glad you're here. I don't think I could have made it without you."

"That's not true. You always had a strength you never saw in yourself. We helped push you in the right direction to let it out."

"What? You're telling me the scrawny bookworm has strength?"

"Don't pretend you aren't still a bookworm."

"Alright, brute," Aaheer smirked, hands on his hips. "Let's settle with neither of us could have made it without each other, and we probably would have all been dead in the first week?"

"Yeah…except Gwen…"

"Are you still on that? Thrax, Gwen's happy here. I don't think we even could get her back."

"But if we could, don't you think she'd want to? Her father's there. Everything she knows."

"I think that's for her to decide. If she went back, she wouldn't have us. She wouldn't have you. She's built a life here and has grown like the rest of us. Do you think it'd be good to take that from her too?"

Thrax pursed his lips. "I don't know."

"Hey," Aaheer gripped his shoulder. "There's still time. You two can talk about it together. I'm sure we'll be able to figure something out. Come on. Let's focus on what's coming and get our rest. We want to be prepared when we take back our home."

"Yes. Let's collect our little worker bees."

Gwen stood straight and stretched her back. She groaned and rubbed her eyes. "If I look at another bunch of leaves again, I might collapse."

"Imagine how us healers feel!" Astricus smirked.

"I never was into the plants and all that. It's impressive you can even do this."

Astricus shrugged. "It was something I was trained to do as I started leading the village."

"I guess that makes sense since you're all living in the forest."

"Out of all the things I'd find out about you, Astricus, knowing you're a wild plant creature doesn't surprise me." Thrax snickered and slipped an arm around Gwen's waist.

"Good to see you still have the energy to mock me." Astricus gave a dramatic pout.

"Don't worry, my love," Aaheer pulled him close and took his hand. He turned it over and kissed his lover's inner wrist. "I'm proud of you and all the things you know."

"Are you proud of *me*, Thrax?" Gwen batted her eyelashes up at him.

He chuckled and pulled her close to kiss her shoulder. "Of course, darling."

"You're all disgusting!" Tan called from a campfire, making gagging noises. "Get a room, you horny bastards!"

Everyone around them laughed, and Thrax pointed to Tan. "I don't want to hear it from you, cousin!" he smirked. "I know when this is all over, you will be flirting with every woman in the taverns, telling them all about your 'war stories'!" he said with air quotes.

Laughs rang out again as the couples approached.

"Well played, cousin!" Tan winked and motioned for them to sit amongst the other soldiers.

Aaheer held up a hand. "I'm afraid I can't join tonight. I'm going to speak with Inanna and Teyana before dinner. I want to go over some strategies before I forget."

"You're leaving?" Astricus frowned.

"Just a few minutes, my dear." Aaheer kissed Astricus between his horns. "I will be back before you know it." He left; despite the pitiful look the faun gave.

"Don't worry, your highness." One of the soldiers piped up. "We don't mind having you here."

"It's not that. I want to make sure Aaheer is alright."

"I spoke to him before we came over. He's certainly worried and has a lot on his mind. I think he'll be okay, though." Thrax nodded.

"I think we all need a good night's sleep tonight," Gwen added. "We've been traveling for many days, and I'm sure we're all exhausted and concerned."

"Aye. I don't know if I can even eat tonight." A soldier admitted.

"Don't," Tan quickly pointed at her. "Start on that. You need to take care of yourself and eat. Fuel your body, and you'll be perfectly ready for the fight."

"In fact," Gwen stood up, stretching again. "I'm going to go take a nap before supper. I'm exhausted."

"Excellent idea, Gwen! You get good sleep, alright?" Tan smiled.

"Don't worry, I'll be sleeping like a rock!" she waved as she walked to her tent.

"I'd better wake her when we eat, or else she'll sleep till morning," Thrax said, making everyone chuckle softly.

Chapter 39

Zephrus paced in circles around his tower as the candle flames made the shadows flicker around the room.

Occasionally, he stepped over to the window to stare at the pinpricks of firelight amongst the trees.

"He's here…he's so close…" He licked his lips in anticipation.

Sephtis gave a rumbling coo, fluttering his wings occasionally. He hopped to the end of his perch and cawed at his master.

"Yes, you did excellent, my little friend," he held out his arm for the crow to hop on. "And soon, we will be victorious. Our time has finally come."

"Your highness," General Donahue knocked. "May I enter?"

"Yes, come in, Donahue. I hope you're bringing me good news?"

"Yes, Highness. Our allies have all finally arrived. The sirens have taken their places in the harbor, and the others are in their tents, preparing."

"Good, very good…" He turned his back to the general, staring out the window as he moved his bird to his shoulder. "Donahue, speak honestly to me, friend. Do you think we will win?"

The general fell quiet, opening and closing his mouth. "I-…y-you wish me to speak bluntly, sire?"

"Did I stumble on my words? Give me your opinion."

"I-…well, I don't know, sire. Our numbers are large, but if the rumors are true, we may be at least equally matched to the enemy. I have no doubt it will be difficult to defeat them."

Sephtis turned his head and glowered at him before leaning closer and clicking his beak in Zephrus's ear.

"You're right, my friend." He stroked his feathers slowly. "He does seem doubtful. How shameful that our general wouldn't have faith in his soldiers. I suppose our men will die under his incompetence, then."

"P-please, sire, th-that's not what I meant-!"

Zephrus whirled around with a glare like spikes of ice. "Oh, then tell me what you mean, general? Please! If I'm to believe that you don't have faith in our men, whose fault would that be? My own? The servants? If you say our commanders, remember that they are under *your* orders, Donahue!" he jabbed his finger angrily into his chest, making him stumble back against the wall. "If they are making poor decisions, it is because *you* cannot give them the right orders! If our men die, know that their blood is on your hands! I might as well have your throat slit now for your foolishness!"

He turned and stormed through the room, screaming obscenities. He grabbed the curtains on the walls and ripped them so violently that the entire curtain pole fell with it, then threw the chair at his desk across the room into the stone wall. Sephtis cawed angrily and flew up to the rafters. He cawed and flapped at the destruction Zephrus left.

"P-please, my king!" Donahue begged.

"I ought to execute you! I could burn you! Drown you! Yes, I-I'll feed you to the sirens! I'll-…I'll-…" Zephrus eventually stood still. His knees wobbled then he crumbled into a heap on the floor.

"Your highness! Page boy, call the healers! The king needs help!"

Zephrus groaned as his eyes slowly opened. He blinked hard to focus his gaze, trying to make out the faces of the people standing over him.

"Ah! There you are, your majesty." The healer said, "We've been waiting for your return."

The wizard groaned, rubbing his head. "What…happened?"

"It seems you had a collapse. I'd say from exhaustion. You have not been sleeping or eating, have you? Shame on you, sire. What kind of example does that set for our people if our king doesn't take care of himself?" The healer pressed a cool rag to his forehead.

Zephrus scoffed. "What am I to hide away? I have duties and obligations. Enough," he pushed the healer away and got up on shaky legs. "I must go speak with my men. I've had enough of this."

"Sire, please, you need to rest."

"Enough! You're dismissed." Zephrus waved dismissively and stumbled out of the room like a newborn foal trying to stand. Sephtis swooped down from his perch to follow his master.

He straightened his hair and clothes as he went down the stairs, rubbing at his eyes. He cut through the hallway and out of the castle to the stables. He took out his horse and began to saddle him up.

"It's time for war, Sephtis. Fly to the camp. Let them know I'm coming." The bird bobbed its head and squawked as it took off.

"You look tired, Zephrus."

He paused as he grabbed his horse's bridle. "Finally deciding to show yourself, traitor?"

Sigyn tilted her head. "Zephrus. You know I wouldn't do that to you."

"But you did. You left me. You abandoned me."

719

"No, Zephrus. You pushed me away. You know you're better than this. Where is the man I married? You aren't yourself." She held her hands to her chest, head bowed.

"What could make you believe that? I'm finally getting what I've fought for all my life. You saw my journey. This is my true path."

"Oh, Zephrus, you know that's not true. You've let this consume you. You're just hurting yourself now."

"Why do you care? You left me. You hate me."

"No, Zephrus. I love you. I still do."

He felt his lip tremble before throwing the bridle. "Leave, you witch!"

The bridle landed limply in the hay. Zephrus was all alone now. He panted heavily, and his knees trembled again, falling to the ground. His eyes burned as he lay on the ground, quietly sobbing. "I don't care…I don't care…I don't care."

Zephrus walked with Donahue pleading behind him. They approached the new camp set up along the other side of the city. Orcs milled about, fixing their armor or training or talking amongst themselves. They fell quiet as Zephrus passed, scowling at him. He walked straight to an enormous tent, where four orcs stood around a table.

When he entered, they all turned to look at him with scowls. Three women and a man were tall, with enormous muscles and broad shoulders. The largest was a woman with grayish-green skin, fangs poking out from her lower lip, yellow eyes like poison, and long black hair in a ponytail.

"Zephrus Arimas." She crossed her arms and towered over him. "It's about time you showed your face to us."

"My apologies, lady Hela. I'm afraid my mind has been quite preoccupied lately."

She scoffed and looked over at the other orcs. "Humans always were so frail." The other three snickered.

Zephrus tried to keep his sneer from showing. "I appreciate your willingness to leave your homes and come to our aid. I assure you, you will all be rewarded handsomely."

"I would certainly hope so. We don't do this for charity."

"Of course. I am here, though, to discuss something important. It has been brought to my attention that you have brought a particular weapon to aid our cause. I am most interested in learning more."

Hela broke out with a sinister grin. "Yes. Our fellow orcs disapprove of our methods, but I've found them quite useful. Come, I'll show you." Hela led them out of the tent to another right beside it. She pushed open the flaps, and in the dim light that flooded in, Zephrus saw an enormous cage. There were loud hisses and shrieks as clawed arms, covered in feathers, reached out, slashing angrily. Sharp eyes pierced through the dark with a look that could kill.

"Harpies…" he whispered. "My general had mentioned you had some. How did you come across these fine specimens?" Zephrus gave Hela an approving smirk.

"What, and tell you, our secret? Just know, Zephrus, these things are hungry and angry. They will attack and kill anything they can get their claws on. These aren't our only ones, either. You'll find they'll give us quite the advantage on the battlefield."

723

"That's all I needed to know. Donahue,"

The general snapped to attention. "Your majesty?"

"Send a message through Sephtis to our guests in the forest. They get a day to prepare. We battle at dawn on the second day."

Chapter 40

Inanna read the letter around the fire at the evening meal. "Zephrus has declared a time of battle. We spend tomorrow properly preparing, then battle at dawn. I suppose he's finally done waiting."

"It's awful soon. Do you think we're ready?" Aaheer asked.

"Your mother's allies have been notified, yes?"

"Yes. They should arrive on the second day."

"Excellent. Dyael, Borbyr, how are your soldiers?"

Borbyr straightened and pawed at the ground. "Our men are on standby and ready for anything."

"You say the word, and we're ready." Dyael agreed.

"Midra? What about your allies?"

She glanced between everyone, chewing on her lip. "Well…I should have some arriving tomorrow, but I'm not sure if all of them will be able to arrive on time."

"That's alright, Midra. You've done plenty. Astricus, Teyana, are the healers ready?"

"We've got enough herbs for everyone and. the younger ones have been wrapping enough bandages to cover all Hevaña. We've been practicing spells, and everyone is doing excellently."

"This is all very good. I'm very proud of our progress. I don't think we will need to worry about whether we're prepared. We are a force to be reconned with. We have a purpose, a focus, and a drive. We are fighting for the greater good of our continent. We are a beacon of hope for all fighting tyrants and traitors like Zephrus. We will not be defeated without a fight. If we are to die, may we die with swords in hand and the bodies of enemies at our feet."

"Here, here!" Cried Dyael, and the others around them cheered.

Gwen sat silently, gripping Thrax's hand. They didn't even have to look at each other to know what the other was feeling. But when everyone went to bed, Gwen sat on the edge of their cot, staring at her hands.

"Gwen, talk to me, my love. Tell me what worries you." Thrax asked, sitting beside her and tilting her chin to look at him.

"It's just…well, I'm having trouble wrapping my head around the fact that this is happening. This isn't like in Terra Vale. I'm not fighting a couple of men with Dyael. We could die out there. I guess I'm just scared…" she admitted.

"Oh, Gwen…I am too…" Thrax assured her, wrapping his arms around her. "This is something we knew was coming, but it's still difficult when it gets here. But know I will be by your side as much as possible. I won't let anything happen to you, my beloved. You are my world, Gwen. I won't let anything break us apart. Not war, not even death. I will always find my way back to you. We are going to win and live together as a family. We are going to be married, and you will want for nothing ever again."

Gwen felt her lip tremble as she wrapped her arms around him, clutching his shirt. "I'm holding you to all of this. I want a wedding in the castle and a big party in the woods with all our friends and family. Don't you dare die and ruin our life plans, Thrax Nightingale."

"Of course not…" he couldn't resist a slight chuckle. "We will grow old together and live the life we've both wanted…because I can't imagine sharing that life with anyone but you."

"I don't know what brought us together. Maybe it was chance, or maybe fate. Either way, I'm so grateful you fell through my wardrobe."

"And I'm glad that my spell failed, so I did. Even though you did try to stab me…" he chuckled.

Gwen sniffled and pressed her face into his chest, giggling weakly. "That was payback for you kidnapping me."

"You did that before we even got here."

"Semantics."

"Look, why don't we think more about these things in the morning? We have a lot to do tomorrow and want to ensure we're ready. Come sleep, my darling." Thrax laid back and motioned for Gwen to lie on his chest. She obeyed and buried her face in his neck.

"We're going to get through this."

"Ugh! You've got to be fucking kidding me!" Gwen roared, holding her bow and covering the stinging mark that had been left on her bicep.

"What happened?" Tan turned away from his target practice.

"I just broke my bow." She lifted the weapon to show the snapped string.

Tan chuckled and shook his head. "Well, we can't have that, can we? Come on. We need to make sure our archers have fresh bowstrings anyways."

As they walked to find some bowstrings, there was a commotion from within the forest as people leaped up and ran toward the edge of camp. That's when Gwen spotted the tops of antlers. She felt her heart leap as she dropped her bow and took off after the others.

"Gwen, where are you going?"

"The elves are here, Tan!"

"What?"

She shoved through the crowd to the line of dark elves riding deer, looking around the camp.

"Seems like we got here just in time." Ethera gave a soft smile from her deer at the head of the group.

"Aye. We heard there are already plans of battle tomorrow." Gunnalf looked out across the field.

"Gunnalf! Ethera!" Gwen grinned at them.

Gunnalf's eyes crinkled at the corners from how wide his grin was. "Hello again, lady Gwendolyn! You look well! You seem stronger!"

She glowed with pride at his praise. "Stronger than when you last saw me! We're so glad you're here!"

"We're glad we got here in time. What others have arrived?"

"You're the tail-end of the others coming. We have a few others that should not be far behind you. Zephrus has declared battle tomorrow at dawn."

Ethera pursed her lips. "That certainly isn't much time for us to get settled."

"I know it's sudden, but we knew this would happen sooner or later."

She heaved a sigh and rolled her eyes. "The least he could do is let his allies prepare." She joked before motioning for the elves to follow her. "We'll get set up and prepared right away. It was good to see you again, Gwen."

Gwen grinned as they rode off. She turned to the Gyrians and beamed at them. "Come on, everyone. You heard her. We don't have much time to prepare, so let's ensure we're as ready as possible to show Zephrus that we won't be pushed around!"

The others murmured in agreement and split up. Gwen trotted back to her bow with Tan and followed his instructions to get it strung.

"You should name your weapon. Every good weapon has a name." He informed her as he watched.

"Really? I don't know; I've never really thought about that stuff. Does yours have a name?"

"Of course! This bow has gotten me through many battles and hunts. I call it Woodpecker."

Gwen snorted. "Woodpecker?"

"It's precise and can pierce even the smallest creature from afar. I'd like to see you come up with something better."

Gwen paused and studied her bow's smooth wood and leather handle with its freshly taut string. "Hmm…I think I'll call it…Falcon."

"Falcon?"

"Because it can kill from afar. Like a falcon."

Tan gave a slight scowl. "That is better than Woodpecker."

Gwen laughed and took out a knife. "I think I'll try and carve a bird on it too. Why don't we do it together? I'll make a falcon; you make a woodpecker."

"Alright, then. Maybe they'll bring us good luck." The two sat cross-legged with their weapons on their laps and began to cut. When they were done, Gwen held her bow up with pride.

"It looks more like a duck than a falcon, but at least it's mine!"

Tan, meanwhile, held up a bow with a beautifully crafted woodpecker, making her scowl now. "Well, mine might have a better name, but yours has a better bird."

Tan laughed and helped her to her feet. "In that manner, we are evenly matched. I'm glad to see you feel so certain about tomorrow. It's good for morale and will give you more courage on the battlefield."

"I've been working on this for over a year. I'm ready to prove myself and fight for my family." She nodded firmly.

"I'm even more proud to see your progress. You've become quite a force of nature."

"I never thought I'd get the chance to be. Back home, I go to school and study all day. I never thought I'd do much outside of academia. I never thought I'd get a chance to. I'm glad I'm here. I feel like I can be anything."

"Good. This is your home too. You deserve to have a place in it."

Gwen turned to look out across the camp and the field to the silhouette of the kingdom. "My home too…I've always said it, but it just feels more real…I don't ever want to leave this place."

They heard more voices call out and turned to see Midra talking to a bunch of men, women, elves, orcs, and what seemed to be a griffin.

"Looks like Midra's friends are finally here. We're all accounted for."

"Not much we can do now other than wait."

Chapter 41

The army rose with the dark gray sky overhead. A freezing wind cut them to the bone as they changed into armor and readied weapons. They hadn't even mounted their horses when the first few snowflakes began to fall.

"What do you make of it, sister?" Tan stared at the clouds as they slowly grew lighter from the rising sun.

"We will have to make do. There's nothing we can do about the weather. Zephrus won't stop for cold."

Ethera and the dark elves lined up on their deer while others rode horses. The orcs remained on foot, and a few griffins stood by their sides.

Gwen stayed close to Thrax, clutching Falcon, waiting for Aaheer, who was saying one last tearful goodbye to Astricus. He rode over and looked between Thrax and Inanna. "After you, my lady."

"No, Aaheer. I think you should be the one to lead us. This is your kingdom, after all. They need their true king."

His eyes went wide, and he looked at everyone who smiled in agreement. "I-…thank you. It would be an honor. Move out!" He called, turning his horse to the edge of the field.

Everyone followed him through the trees as the snow began to pick up. The harsh wind whipped at their hair and sent shivers down their spines. When they reached the edge of the tree line, Aaheer pointed ahead of him. "Form rank! Prepare to charge!"

Everyone immediately followed his orders. He rode to the front to join his friends and the other leaders. They were all staring across the snowy ground at the rows of Zephrus's soldiers. He sat at the head, and even from their distance, Thrax could practically feel his half-brother's gaze burning into his skin.

"You should speak to them," Dyael said. "Encourage them."

"Oh…right…" Aaheer suddenly looked very sick.

"Breath, brother." Thrax gripped his shoulder, still staring at Zephrus's shape. "We're in this fight together."

Aaheer followed his gaze and sat there for a moment before finally turning to face their vast army. Their faces were grim, and their animals danced on their feet, tossing their heads at the tension in the air.

"My friends, today is the day we have all been preparing for. Today, we fight a united threat. We fight for honor, for glory. We fight for friends and allies. For family and lovers. We fight to defend those that cannot defend themselves. We fight to stand up to those that don't wish to rule; they wish to control. They wish to become the new heel to push our people under. Well, we will not let that happen! Today, we will fight! We fight for honor, love, and glory. We fight to protect our continent and our homes!"

The army cheered and raised their fists.

"Weapons at ready!"

Swords and spears were drawn, and Aaheer drew his own, riding down the line. "Fight for truth! For righteousness! For home! Today, we fight or die trying! Fight on! Fight on! Fight on!"

"Fight on!" They roared.

"Fight on!"

"Fight on!" Gwen and Thrax screamed, raising their bow and sword.

Aaheer drew his horse up to Thrax's side. "Ride with me, brother. Today, we take back our home. Forward charge!" He pointed his sword forward, rearing his horse.

They all roared and kicked their animals into motion. Thrax and Aaheer led the charge, urging their horses to move faster.

As they raced forward, Zephrus's army cried out and charged. Gwen felt her heart pounding in her chest, the blood rushing in her ears. Snow and wind stung her eyes as she tried to keep up with the others. Before she knew it, their forces collided, and she lost her friends in the chaos.

Thrax pulled his horse as close to Aaheer's as he could. His hand filled with green fire as he sent blasts into the crowd of soldiers. Aaheer's sword swung and scraped against the armor, cutting into flesh and bone.

"Don't you dare leave my side, brother," Thrax demanded.

"Wouldn't dream of it."

An orc surged at him with a roar, raising his axe. Thrax pointed at him, and a red lightning bolt shot at him, piercing the orc in the heart. His eyes widened in horror as he collapsed to the ground, immediately trampled under the hooves of charging horses.

Above their heads, griffins dove into the fray while phoenixes shrieked, filling the air with smoke from their burning fire.

Thrax took his sword and spun his horse around to stab another enemy. He froze when he saw the peeling and rotting flesh under the leather armor. "Fuck! He has more of those undead soldiers!"

"What?" Aaheer turned to watch Thrax produce shadows that split the body into pieces. "Fuck! Don't let it get to you too much! Come on!"

Between fights, Thrax saw Inanna making enormous vines grow, dragging enemies down into the dirt. Dyael reared up, crushing the skull of a man beneath her hooves. Gwen was shooting arrows left and right. They caught each other's gaze, and she relaxed at his sight.

She charged her horse into a hoard racing toward Borbyr and shot an arrow into the neck of one. Borbyr, without hesitation, notched two arrows and took out two others. The last raised his sword to strike, but Gwen got there just in time. She turned her horse to kick his, knocking them to the ground.

Borbyr's eyes widened before he gave a proud grin. "Glad to see you've been listening to me."

"Who do you think you're talking to here?"

"Have you seen the others?"

"Yes, Thrax and Aaheer are still alive. Dyael's with Inanna."

"Good. Find the elves. I'm going to find Cyrus!"

Gwen turned to do as he said. She scanned for the sight of deer antlers. Before she could find them, her horse collapsed with a squeal. It rolled over her, knocking the breath out of her. A woman stood over her with a war axe stained with blood.

"Say goodnight, little girl."

Gwen lifted her arms to protect her face, but she didn't need to. Midra reached her in time, grabbing the woman by the throat. "I don't think so." Ice stretched from her hand, rapidly encasing her and immortalizing her horrified expression. She threw her to the ground with a hard shove, shattering her to pieces.

"Are you alright?" Midra grabbed Gwen's hand, pulling her up.

"Yes. You just saved my neck. Have you seen the elves yet?"

She shook her head. "I'm sure they're around somewhere. I'm heading to the docks with some men to go after the ships. I spotted some of Zephrus's men heading for them."

"I'll go with you!"

They waded through the sea of falling bodies and enemies. Bright red blood stained the snow that crunched under their feet as they pushed through to the group of warriors Gwen had met a little over a year ago in that tavern she and Thrax had stumbled across.

"They're setting up catapults on the ships." The large man covered in lacerations pointed as they loaded something into the catapults.

"Are they sailing?"

"No, it looks like they're staying, but I'm sure whatever they're planning is bad for us."

"Then we need to get to work. Gwen, you and Enara stay back and shoot them down. Ragnar, Vega, and I will go on board to attack."

"You can count on us. Fight or die trying." Enara said, drawing their bow as well.

"Fight or die trying." Midra and the others took off for the ships.

"Aim for the sails first, Gwen. Take out their access to the water." Enara raised their bow, notching an arrow. They whispered a spell that gave it a golden glow. They shot it into the main sail of the closest ship. The hole the arrow made began to smolder and spread. Enara shot three more arrows at the sails, making the men panic and race around. A few tried to shoot at them, but all they had to do was take a few steps back.

"How did you do that?"

"Enchanted arrows. Here," they took some of Gwen's arrows, casting a spell on them as well. "This will ensure they reach their mark and do more damage. Shoot well. We need to draw their attention from the others."

Gwen stared at the glowing arrows. They felt warm in her hand, like a hot summer day. She notched an arrow and shot it at another ship. The arrow went straight through the center of the main sail.

"Amazing!" Gwen laughed.

"You're a natural." Enara smiled before looking over her shoulder. "Uh-oh. We have company." The two turned their horses to run from the ships, leading the enemy soldiers away from the docks. Enara shot one of their burning arrows, catching an undead. It burst into flames, letting out a guttural cry before falling into ash.

Gwen shot off her regular arrows at the living soldiers. "We need to lead them away from the docks!"

"It looks like Midra and the others have already gotten there!"

Gwen could see bursts of fire, enormous waves, and crackling lightning coming from the ships. "Can we give them some sort of extra cover?"

"I think so. Stay back here and cover me. I have an idea." They reached into a satchel around their waist and pulled out a perfectly round white stone. They took off for the docks, and Gwen was forced to stay behind, fending off any soldiers seeking to chase them down. She took a chance to look back at what Enara was doing. They stood at the bank, and a massive plume of mist appeared before them, stretching out to shroud the boats, so they were nothing but a faint silhouette in the cloud. They turned and raced back toward the fight.

From in the mist, Gwen spotted a giant ball of bright light. Her eyes widened as she recognized it as a ball of fire heading straight for them.

"Enara, look out!"

The wizard spotted it just in time. They shouted and threw themselves off their horse as the fire crashed into the ground, sending the animal flying with the debris. Gwen jumped down and ran to help them up.

"Are you okay?"

"In a relative sense. Come on; we have to get away." They pushed her to get away as the fire began to spread, despite the snow and mud.

"What is that? What kind of fire burns in the snow like that?"

"It's phoenix fire. It's stronger than regular fire. We'll be caught in it if we don't get out of here. I don't think this is the only one they have!"

They ran from the banks just as another burning rock launched into the air, landing further into the battlefield. Soldiers and horses were sent flying and screaming into the air.

"How do we stop it?"

"We need more magic for this! You'd be out of your element, I'm afraid!"

"I'll find Thrax. He'll know how to help! You need to get to safety! Try to get back to camp!" Gwen grabbed her horse and hoisted herself up before galloping back into battle.

Chapter 42

Thrax swung his sword against another soldier, trying to break through his blocks.

"Give up, little wizard!" He sneered. "You won't be able to stop our king!"

Thrax felt an angry fire burn in his belly. "He is no king!" He drew his sword back and cut through his leather armor, plunging the blade into his stomach. He wrenched it free and turned to attack again. To his surprise, an enemy rode by, slamming her shield into the side of Thrax's head. He was sent flying off his horse, his ears ringing as he tried to focus.

Someone stood over him and helped him to his feet. "On your feet, brother. You're not going down that easily. Not on my watch." Aaheer pulled him up, letting Thrax lean on him for support.

"What are you doing? Get back on your horse and get away. It's too dangerous for you to linger around me."

"Did you suddenly forget all that talk about sticking together?"

Thrax pursed his lips. "Alright, but you'd better not leave my side."

"Wouldn't dream of it."

The brothers pressed their backs to each other, lunging and slashing with their swords. Thrax used his magic to make giant pillars of rock that sent enemies flying into the air. Any undead that came near were crushed by Thrax's shadows, tearing apart their decaying bodies. Aaheer swung with a precision Thrax hadn't yet seen in his younger brother. As they dueled, there was a pause in the fighting as everyone looked to the sky. Cutting through the dark gray and flurrying snow like a shooting star, an enormous ball of fire flew overhead, landing just feet away from them. The explosion shook the ground, making them stumble.

"What the hell?" Thrax cried, getting to his feet. "What was that?"

"Thrax! We need you!" Gwen rode over and pointed to the burning rock. "They're lighting the rock with phoenix fire! We need magic to help stop it!"

He gritted his teeth. "Fucking hell…"

"Go. I'll be fine." Aaheer promised.

Thrax hesitated before finally jumping up on his horse. "I'll get Inanna and the others. Get the centaurs, as well! They can help stomp it out!" He turned and rode off towards the flames.

As they got closer, his horse tossed its head and danced nervously. "Easy, boy. We'll be alright." He spotted Inanna racing toward the flames as well. He rode over to her and pulled up by her side. "What do you think?"

753

"We need water and ice. I'll try to freeze it if you drench it. Watch out for any more they may send."

"I'm on it." He turned to ride off as Inanna ran along the spreading flames, blasting frosty winds to slow the spread. He turned wide around the path of another round of burning rocks hurtling at them. He stopped at one of the fires and held his hands in front of him.

"*Nsao van tey…nsao van tey…*" A bubble of water formed in his hand, slowly growing. He lifted his hands above his head so it could continue to grow before throwing his hands apart. The bubble burst, dousing the phoenix fire in water. Mixed with the wet mud from the snow, he managed to extinguish the flames. Others were using their magic in similar ways to stop the spread. Satisfied that others were handling it, he turned to reunite with his brother.

Aaheer was lying on the ground, using his sword to block a woman's battle axe from embedding in his skull.

"Aaheer!"

The woman looked up just as Thrax's sword sliced into her neck, cutting off her head. He dismounted and helped his brother up.

Aaheer immediately grabbed his brother's arm and pulled him behind him so he could lunge at a man trying to sneak up on him.

"Nicely done."

"You're not doing so bad either."

"Oi," Dyael called, lifting her arm for Ea to land again. "Take a break from the banter and help us cut off some heads!"

"Is Ea able to do anything about the fire?"

"I'm afraid not. He can only create more."

"Why don't we send him and the other phoenixes up to attack the rocks?" Aaheer pointed up toward the clouds.

"That," Dyael grinned. "We can do! Ea, fly!" The phoenix shrieked as it took off again. From across the battlefield, more phoenixes took off into the air, following him toward the docks.

They watched before a dark shadow was spotted in the clouds. Harpies with long claws, their bodies covered in feathers and mouths opened to show enormous, dripping fangs, burst through the snowy sky to attack the phoenixes. The birds screeched and blasted fire, locking in their combat.

"Damn! They'll be too distracted by those things to watch out for the rocks!"

"Zephrus thought out more than we anticipated," Thrax growled, watching them.

"No time to worry about it now. Someone will be able to help shoot them down." Aaheer insisted, pulling their attention away.

The snowfall was growing heavier. The wind was picking up and blew clouds of dusty snowflakes in their faces. Mingled with the quickening fall, it was becoming harder to see what was happening around them.

"*Míthas simo laúdas*." Thrax's hand was filled with green fire.

Dyael cried out as a rope wrapped around her throat. She reared up, kicking furiously. The man holding the rope smirked and lunged with a sword. Borbyr burst through the storm to kick the man away, throwing him to the ground. He grabbed the rope off Dyael's neck and wrapped it around the man.

"You think you can get away with attacking a centaur princess?" He growled and threw the man across the field.

"Excellent arm, Borbyr." Thrax nodded, shielding his eyes to watch the man fly off.

"This is no time for jokes, Thrax. Our men are dying quickly. For every man of Zephrus's we kill, they take ours in equal numbers or more. We cannot hold out much longer."

"We have to," Aaheer said firmly. "We have no choice. The snow must be our problem."

"Then we cannot guarantee that we will even be able to make it till then. We may need to retreat or die if the storm continues at this rate." Borbyr pawed at the ground in frustration.

"If we retreat, they will guarantee we die before we get away! We fight or die trying!"

As they bickered, Thrax's attention was drawn back to the sky. Sephtis came swooping down, cawing angrily. The crow clawed and pecked Thrax, pulling at his hair and reaching for his face.

Thrax angrily swatted at the bird, and Dyael finally managed to whack it off him with her shield.

"Well done, little wizard." Zephrus slowly clapped right behind him, making them all jump. "You've managed to survive our little game. Now, we are united." Against the snow, Zephrus looked gaunt and sinister. His dark skin was dull, and his sharp eyes held only malice. "Are you ready to die, Thrax?"

Chapter 43

"But first, before we continue this little game, I think we could use some privacy." He waved his hand, sending Aaheer, Dyael, and Borbyr flying back. He pushed his hands out, and all the soldiers around them got forced away, so they were just in a clearing on the snowy battlefield.

"I've been waiting so long for this. I was curious to know what this little wizard holding my father's ire was like. What could the queen's bastard possibly be like? Frankly, I'm underwhelmed."

Thrax gritted his teeth. "Well, I thought you'd be more frightening. You look more like a dead tree."

"Oh, what wit. You're so clever. But enough of this banter. It's time for you to die. No, I think I'll keep you alive. But just long enough for you to watch me slaughter your friends.”

Thrax filled both hands with green fire. “I’d like to see you try. I’m not the man I was one year ago.”

“I’m sure you aren’t. But we’ll see if you’re enough to stop me.” Zephrus blasted blood-red fire at him. Thrax rolled out of the way, swinging his arm to send a green fire into the side of his head. Zephrus raised his hand, stopping the flame and smoldering it to an ember.

“Come now, little wizard. You can surely do better than this.” He lunged at him and planted his palm firmly on Thrax’s chest. A blast of force sent him flying, knocking the wind out of him. He scrambled to his knees, trying to catch his breath. Zephrus walked toward him and sent a kick right to Thrax’s face, blood gushing from his nose and splitting his lip.

He pulled himself up and pointed at him. "*Ényo tumó!*" A purple lightning bolt shot at him, but Zephrus stepped to the side.

"You're boring me, little wizard."

Thrax slammed a hand to the ground, and brown vines shot out of the mud, wrapping themselves around Zephrus. His eyes widened as he struggled against them. Eventually, he was able to collect himself enough to burn them away. He laughed and sneered at Thrax.

"Now that's more like it!"

Thrax threw up a shield as Zephrus blasted fire at him. Thrax managed to pick up a handful of snow and throw it at him. It turned to water and drenched the other wizard completely. He sputtered and shivered against the cold.

"Is that all? Making me a little chilly?"

"No." Thrax took another handful of snow and blew it at him. It created a spinning tunnel of flakes, trapping him inside. The snow flew in his face, hindering his vision. Thrax took the opportunity to blast frost at him, watching it climb up and stick to the water on his clothes. Zephrus struggled, kicking to break up the climbing ice. Finally, with a roar, he broke through the spell.

"Enough!"

With a flourish of his hands, the snow began to pick up around them, trapping them in their private battlefield. Zephrus held his hands out, and the ground started to rumble. It cracked and slowly began to split apart around Thrax. He jumped to get out of the way, but the cracks followed him. Long, skeletal fingers started reaching out as moaning skeletons and decaying bodies grasped his clothes, trying to drag him into the earth. Thrax blasted at them with blinding light, scrambling back. The corpses crawled out, chasing after him. He touched the ground again, and the vines reappeared. They wrapped around the bodies and pulled them back down. They locked over the cracks and sealed the earth back together like sewing a torn cloth.

Zephrus gasped as he lost control of his spell, panting and sweating. "Not bad…you've certainly been improving…"

Thrax glared at him and held his hands together before slowly drawing them apart. A large portal began forming, and a huge black dog with shackles on its paws stepped out. It snarled, blue flames flickering between its fangs. The creature roared and lunged at Zephrus. Sephtis swooped down, grabbing the beast's face. Zephrus took the opportunity to cast a spell on his bird. The crow grew larger, and its feathers began to drip in black shadows. Its eyes burned red as it attacked. The dog managed to pull away, to snap and growl. Thrax quickly closed the portal, and the dog disappeared in a burst of blue fire, making Sephtis startle.

"After him, you beast!" Zephrus roared, and Sephtis turned its attention to Thrax, swooping at him again.

Before Thrax could devise a spell, Kitsae broke through the snow and jumped up to grab the crow's belly, shrieking in anger. The little fox clawed and clamped its teeth firmly.

Thrax cast his spell, making the fox grow, its fur giving off tongues of red fire.

"So you have some little runt, I see. No matter. You can't stop us, little wizard. You might as well give up while you have the chance."

"I don't think so. You know what I think, Zephrus? I think you're afraid. You're afraid you can't beat me. You're afraid that everything is finally turning on you. You've already lost Sigyn. Your army is dying around you.

You can't even defeat an apprentice. You're scared you can't beat me-!"

With a scream of fury, Zephrus lunged, drawing his sword and forgetting all magic. Thrax quickly drew his blade and knocked away his swing.

"How dare you think you can defeat me?" He snarled, walking forward and dragging the tip of his sword along the dirt. "You are nothing. You are a bastard. You got my father killed. You are *nothing*!" He raised his sword above his head to strike him, but Thrax stopped his swing again, kneeling on the ground and trying to hold him back.

"I," He spat, glaring at Zephrus with pure hatred. "Am Thrax Nightingale. Son of Saedon Arimas and Myana Thornblade. My brother is prince Aaheer. This kingdom is my home. This castle is my home. And I won't let you take another step into my home!" He shoved Zephrus back, and the two locked in a fierce sword fight.

Gwen did her best to guard Midra and the others from anyone that tried to ambush them. She and Enara rode along the field, shooting them down or cutting them off with magic.

"We can't keep going like this!" Gwen cried.

"We can because we have to!"

A giant harpy burst out of the clouds and shot down to snatch them. Before either of them could register, an arrow went straight into its chest, killing it in moments. Borbyr pulled up beside them, scanning them for injuries.

"I am here to help."

"Good. We need to protect Midra. They're taking out the ships, but they need support. Can you see to that?" Enara asked.

Borbyr put a hand to his heart. "I will make sure I succeed."

When Gwen turned to watch him run to the docks, she spotted a shadow crawling through the mist and snow out on the water. She squinted before breaking out into a huge grin. "Enara! It's our reinforcements! Myana's allies have arrived!" Sure enough, long boats emerged fully into view. The front of the ships was carved and shaped to look like enormous fish. Men shouted orders as they rowed to block Zephrus's men so they couldn't retreat from the docks. Spears were chucked and embedded into the boats with ropes connecting them. Myana's allies leaped over the edge of their ships to climb across to the enemy boats and begin their attack.

Gwen's burst of hope didn't last long. From under the waves, she saw a faint glow. Even from there, she could hear the soft warbling of music.

"How in the hell did he get sirens here?" Enara cried. "We have to help them!"

"But won't we get caught in the spell too?"

"Not if we stop them. Listen, this won't be easy to pull off. I'm going to give you some of my arrows. If something should go wrong, use them. These," They pointed out, the ones with tips stained in red dust. "Are enchanted to explode. Shoot them at the enemy ships."

"But it might kill you!"

"That's a price we are willing to take to end this." Without another word, Enara turned their horse and galloped to the docks. They ran along the wood, casting ice spells to cover the water and stop the sirens from pulling the soldiers in or preventing the bewitched sailors from jumping to a watery tomb. Even with Enara's help, there wasn't much they could do without more magic. The harpies were still swiping men off the boats, carrying them away or dropping them to their deaths. The sounds of their pained screams could be heard across the water.

"Fuck…" Gwen gritted her teeth before riding over. She jumped off her horse and raced onto the largest of Zephrus's ships, drawing her knives.

"What are you doing here?" Midra demanded. "We told you to stay on land! It's too dangerous!"

"Well, I've lasted this long, haven't I?" Gwen ducked from a punch and knocked the man's leg out from under him, causing him to topple. She grabbed his hair and cut his throat as deep as she could. She rolled away to stab at the thighs of a man trying to ambush Midra. When she got to her feet, she gripped the handles of her knives and punched her next attacker straight in the nose.

Midra raised a brow and nodded in approval. "I think you'll be just fine."

"Look out!" Gwen threw her knife over Midra's shoulder, catching a soldier in the face.

Midra grinned. "More than fine, I'd say."

Gwen ran past her, grabbed her blade, and propped herself on the ship's railing. She drew her bow, Falcon, and began shooting into the water. Sirens quickly ducked their heads under the water, hissing. Gwen saw some of their shadows swim below the waves toward her before grabbing at the wood and clawing up the ship's sides to reach her. She shot at the creatures closest while the others continued singing songs to drag down Myana's allies.

Midra appeared by her side, shooting lightning down into the water. The sirens gave blood-curdling screams before collapsing into the surf.

"Can you get across? The men need your help on the other ship."

"I can't shoot as well from there; I need to stay here."

They quickly ducked as a roaring sound passed overhead. Zephrus's men had launched another rock burning with phoenix fire, but instead of sailing into the battlefield, it shattered into the wooden ships of their allies. The sailors cried out and leaped for their lives as the boat splintered and was engulfed in flames. Sirens took the chance to grab whom they could and drag them into the depths. Blood slowly blossomed around them as bodies floated to the surface.

"Shit…Midra, get to land. I have an idea."

"What? Gwen, what are you doing?"

"I'm going to destroy the ships!"

"Are you crazy? You could get killed!"

"There's no time! If we don't destroy them, we'll be overrun! Get to land and help Thrax and the others! I'll be alright!"

Midra hesitated before grabbing some of the arrows and putting another enchantment on them. "Here. This should help delay the blast so you can get away. Don't stay longer than you should. Come back to us."

Gwen gripped her hands. "I will. Go, they need you. Get the others off the boats as well!" She turned and ran to the other side of the ship. She took the enchanted arrows and aimed at the farthest one. She released her arrow and managed to catch it right at the railing.

"Shit…come on, give me something good."

Her next arrow caught the railing as well. The next ship got an arrow to the main mast. She drew her next arrow and aimed. Before she could shoot, she felt a pair of hands grab her. The man dragged her away from the railing. She kicked and screamed, biting his hand hard. He yelled and released her. Another man quickly appeared and stabbed her in the thigh with a dagger. Gwen screamed and fell to her knee.

"Not so mighty now, are you, little girl?" They sneered. One grabbed her by the hair and yanked her head back. He took his knife to cut her neck, but Gwen quickly threw her head back into his nose. She scrambled to the railing as another fell on her, trying to hold her down. She kicked and bit at him, stabbing at his hands with her arrow. A white-hot pain ran up her side as his knife carved into her back and his fingers wrapped around her neck. She gasped and struggled under his grasp, slowly lifting Falcon and notching the arrow.

"Stop her!"

Before they could reach her, she released it. The arrow embedded itself right in the center of the boat's side. She grinned and grabbed two more enchanted arrows. She stabbed one into her captor's shoulder, getting him to release her. She took the chance to get to her feet and run off the boat. She got the other arrow to stick to the main mast of this last ship and shoved through the fight, hands grabbing at her clothes and blades nicking her skin. She climbed onto the railing to jump into the water and the bank when the arrows exploded. The ships rose quickly in a cloud of fire, smoke, and splintering wood. Gwen could barely register when the boat she was on also exploded.

She didn't remember even hitting the ground. Her ears were still ringing with the sounds of the blast. Her whole body ached, blood dripping down her face and body. Slowly, she crawled to the grass, away from the water. She could hear screams and the crackle of the fire. As she forced her eyes to focus, she turned and saw all Zephrus's ships reduced to a mass of rubble. The bodies of sirens floated in the water, and those that had survived were hoisted onto her allies' boats.

She had done it. Then, she collapsed onto the ground.

"There she is!"

"Oh gods, she's hurt bad!"

"Quick, get her to camp!"

She barely had the strength to open her eyes as Midra, Enara, Ragnar, and Vega hoisted her onto Dyael's back.

"What-…what are you…doing?"

"Gwen! Thank the gods!" Dyael's face was pale with worry. "I need you to stay awake. We're getting you to safety!"

"What? N-no, I can't leave…" she gritted her teeth as she tried to stand.

"Oh, no, you don't!" Ragnar, the man, covered in scars, grabbed her and put her firmly on Dyael's back. "You don't need to keep proving yourself, Gwen. You're truly not the young girl I met you as. You are strong, brave, and clever. But you need to take care of yourself now. It would be best if you got to safety to stay alive. Stay alive for your friends and family if you won't do it for yourself."

Gwen stared at Ragnar blearily. "But…"

"No buts. I want to have more tavern drinks with you and Thrax together. Promise me we'll all get to spend time together, like that day when you and Thrax met us in the tavern. I want us all to be able to celebrate together. It won't be the same without you. Dyael, get her back safely."

"You can count on me." The princess set off into a canter, trying to keep herself steady so Gwen wouldn't fall.

"I can't stay, Dyael…I have to help."

"You've helped enough, Gwen. Now, we need you to live."

As they ran, Gwen stared out at what remained of the battle. Amongst the fighting, she could see a wide circle towards the center. In the center was Zephrus, bearing down on…

"Thrax!" she cried, rolling off Dyael's back with a hard thud to the ground.

"Gwen!" Dyael turned to get her friend to her feet.

"He's going to kill him! We have to save Thrax! Please, Dyael, help me save him!" She begged, tears cutting through the blood on her face.

Dyael followed Gwen's gaze and gritted her teeth. "Fuck… alright, let's go!" She lifted her friend back up and took off.

Thrax kicked at the dirt, trying to gain his footing. He was battered, bruised, and bleeding. He had grabbed a shield, but it was currently the only thing protecting him from Zephrus's blade.

Zephrus had a foot planted firmly on his chest, pressing into him as he swung his sword, trying to catch Thrax off-guard.

He laughed maniacally as he swung. "How does it feel, little wizard? Knowing you're about to die? You've come so close! But it wasn't enough!"

Thrax gritted his teeth and shoved hard with his shield, knocking Zephrus back. "Why…are you doing this?" he wheezed, trying to catch his breath. "I still don't get it…I did nothing to you."

"You were born. Your existence took everything from me! So, I'm going to kill you and everyone you love. I think I'll even stick your head outside the gate. At least you'll be home. Isn't that what you wanted?"

"I never asked to be born! My mother didn't do anything; it was Jarkus! You already killed him! Just stop this!"

Zephrus swung again with a roar. Thrax raised the shield just in time to block it, but it still broke in half and sent him stumbling back.

"If your mother had kept to herself, kept her legs closed, and stayed away, my father would still be alive, and we wouldn't be here! You disgust me. You don't deserve my father's name. You don't deserve to call yourself a wizard." Zephrus kicked Thrax in the chest again, making him fall, coughing violently. He stepped on his chest again, making Thrax wheeze and kick, clawing at Zephrus's leg. "It's time for you to die. Say hello to Jarkus and Majora for me, won't you?"

Thrax lifted his hand, trying to summon the strength to stop him. Before he could even form a spell, though, Zephrus was thrown to the side. Gwen had leaped toward them, yanking Zephrus to the ground with a roar. She pinned him down and, screaming with rage, raised her dagger and stabbed it to the hilt in Zephrus's shoulder.

He roared and threw her off, scrambling to his feet and racing towards the kingdom's gate.

"Gwen!" Thrax ran to his lover, helping her to her feet.

"Let go, Thrax! We have to get him!"

"Gwen, you're hurt! Please, let me take this!"

"You're not going to convince her!" Dyael ran over and knelt down. "Get on, or he's going to get away!"

"Take Gwen and get the others. I'm going after him!" Thrax demanded.

Gwen carefully climbed up her friend's back, and once she was safely mounted, Thrax turned and ran after Zephrus.

Snow stung his eyes and skin as he weaved between the soldiers, pausing to shove off passing enemies. He forced himself to run faster through the mud, despite his legs beginning to ache with exhaustion.

He saw Zephrus's cloak whipping into view between the crowd of soldiers. He desperately forced his way through to reach him. He eventually burst through and ran straight toward him.

"Zephrus!"

Zephrus looked over his shoulder, eyes widening when he saw the wizard getting closer. He stopped one of his soldiers on horseback and yanked him off, hoisting himself up and racing for the gates.

"You can't run for long!" Thrax cried, forcing himself to keep running. He pushed through the wooden doors of the gate, following the clopping sound of horse hooves.

"Thrax!"

He paused as Dyael and Borbyr flanked him with Gwen and Aaheer on their backs.

"I think Zephrus is heading for the palace! You're more likely to reach him before the rest of us." Aaheer said. "We'll flank him on the right and left. We could corner him at the palace doors if you can reach him."

"Sounds fine by me. I think I know exactly what to do. Let's end this." They all nodded solemnly before splitting up.

Thrax ran toward the square, his eyes darting back and forth. He crouched and put his hands on the ground. "*Caeli*!" A burst of wind propelled him into the air. He used the gust to land on the nearest rooftop and began his race again, using the wind spell to launch himself over the gaps between buildings. It didn't take long for him to spot the other wizard flying down the road.

"Zephrus!"

His head jerked up in surprise. He pointed at him and sent a ball of fire flying toward him. Thrax swept it away with a blast of wind.

"I told you; you can't get away!"

"That's what you think, little wizard! I am eternal!" He urged his horse to go faster.

Thrax looked up at the castle growing closer, then to either side, and spotted Dyael and Gwen to his left, Borbyr and Aaheer to his right.

He kept throwing spells at Zephrus, trying his best to catch him off guard. Neither fire, ice, wind, lightning, or even stone and earth had been enough to stop him. They were getting closer to the castle steps, and in a moment of stupidity, Thrax leaped from the rooftops toward his horse. He grabbed the back of the saddle with one hand while the other clenched Zephrus's stirrup. The horse stumbled in surprise, nearly throwing them. Zephrus pulled his foot up and slammed it into Thrax's face. He clutched his nose as he tumbled to the ground, then sent a vine shooting after them.

The spell was fast enough to reach the horse and wrap around its back leg. The animal shrieked as it fell, and Zephrus was sent flying into the castle steps.

Still grasping his nose, Thrax stumbled to his feet and jogged toward him. Zephrus was breathing heavily, clutching at his chest. He screamed as he threw another blast of red fire at Thrax, though he was able to step out of its path.

"It's over, Zephrus. You've lost. Give yourself in."

"Never! I will never bow to you!"

"Then perhaps you can bow to us!" Aaheer cried as he and the others rounded the corner, pointing their weapons at him.

Zephrus's eyes darted back and forth, and Thrax finally saw it. Real fear. It was like watching a cornered wild cat.

"No…no! This can't end like this!" Zephrus slammed his fists into the ground, sending enormous cracks spider-webbing across the stone.

Dyael and Borbyr reared back in shock. Zephrus took a moment to throw open the castle doors and ran into the throne room. Thrax jumped across the new-formed chasms and ran in after him.

"Enough, Zephrus; it's over! This doesn't have to end in more bloodshed!"

"Do you think I'm a fool? This can only end one way, little wizard! One of us will die, and I will ensure it's not me!"

"No!" An arrow sailed through the air and into Zephrus's shoulder. Gwen stumbled to Thrax's side, bow drawn. "I won't let you take him from us!"

"Fuck! You filthy little whore! How dare you! I'll cut open your bellies and feed you to the dogs!" He roared, drawing his sword and rushing at them with a roar.

Thrax aimed and lunged. Perhaps divine intervention, pure luck, or fate made it all happen. By all accounts, he should have missed. Nonetheless, Thrax's sword plunged into Zephrus's belly, the point sticking out of his back, dripping red with blood.

Zephrus's eyes went wide as he coughed, blood splashing out of his mouth and onto the floor. He sank to his knees, sliding off Thrax's sword.

"No…no…this can't be it…!" His voice cracked as his breathing became rattled.

"And yet, here we are."

"No…no…!" He turned over and began crawling, pulling himself against the polished floor. A thick trail of blood followed him. They all watched silently as he pulled himself to the throne, desperately reaching up to grasp its seat. "N-no…th-this wasn't…f-father, I-…h-help…f-father…p-please…" he fell slowly onto the ground, gasping for air until he let out a last rattling moan of pain and became still.

Everyone was silent before Thrax walked up to the throne and kicked at Zephrus's body, pushing it off.

"Say hello to Jarkus for me, you filthy bastard."

Gwen fell to her knees with a heavy sigh, unable to keep standing from the pain. Thrax pulled himself away from the scene to run over to his lover.

"Gwen…Gwen…look at me…" he pulled her close and rested her head on his lap. He pushed her hair from her face, spotting the large gash on her head and the wounds on her leg and side. "Gwen…darling, look at me."

She took slow, shallow breaths, clutching the wound in her side. "Thrax, is he dead?"

"Yes, yes, my treasure. We did it. He's dead." He whispered, cradling her closer.

Gwen gave a weak laugh. "We did it! I-…I'm so proud of you, Thrax."

"Please…we should be proud of each other…we did it, Gwen."

"You're right…I can't believe I just did all of this…" her laugh turned into a raspy cough that sprayed blood down her chin.

"Gwen!"

"Come on, missy. You're going back to camp now. I can't believe I let you convince me to bring you here." Dyael trotted over and lifted her onto her back.

"Will she be okay?"

"She should be fine if we get there quickly. Come on; you need to be looked over too. I'll take you both."

"I thought you weren't ever letting humans ride on your back again." He teased.

"I can make an exception here for my friends."

"I think," Aaheer jumped down, putting his hand on his brother's shoulder. "We'll walk back. You two go ahead of us and make sure everyone knows Zephrus is dead."

"Have it your way." Borbyr shrugged and followed Dyael out of the palace.

Aaheer smiled and left the castle, leaving Zephrus's body behind.

"Don't you want to get rid of him first?" Thrax asked.

"I'll ask someone else to handle him. All I want right now is to know we're all okay and fall asleep without being afraid."

Thrax looked at Zephrus's body, then turned to follow Aaheer. "How are you feeling?"

"Like a weight the size of a giant has been lifted. What about you?"

"Like I was stomped by one."

He chuckled. "I'm just glad you're safe. I'm proud of you, brother. Grateful, too. Because of you, we have our kingdom back."

"Don't sell yourself short. You had as much a hand in this as I did."

He laughed again. "Fine, then. *We* did it. Together." He hooked an arm around Thrax's shoulder and pulled him in close. "You are truly my brother, Thrax. No one will ever be able to take that from us again."

Thrax's heart ached, and his eyes stung. He hugged his brother back and ruffled his hair for good measure. They stepped outside and blinked hard. The sun had begun to pierce through the clouds, and the snow had slowed to a few lazy flakes drifting to the ground.

"Right. Brothers."

Chapter 44

Gwen felt aching pain shoot through her body, making her sit upright before clutching at her side with anguished moans.

"Woah there, little spitfire." Warm hands held her hand and shoulder, pressing close to her back. "Don't open up those wounds after Teyana did so much for them."

"Thrax?"

"Aye." He gave a wide grin. His green eyes sparkled with delight. He was bruised and had a few patches to cover wounds, but he was in relatively good condition. "You sure made a name for yourself out on the battlefield! Enara told me everything. I'm so proud of you, my love." He gave her a big, sloppy kiss, making her giggle.

"What about you? You faced down with a dark wizard and took him out!"

He rolled his eyes. "If you didn't show up, I'd have died. By the way, I'm still mad at you for that. You were practically on death's door from all that blood!"

"What was that? Sorry, I couldn't hear you over the fact I saved your life, even when I was half dead." She smirked.

"Ha. Well, I won't let you take any more big risks like that, young lady." He smirked and pulled her into a deep kiss.

Gwen closed her eyes and leaned into it, wrapping her arms around him. "I needed that." She looked at her surroundings. They were in what seemed to be an attic room with a soft feather bed. "Where are we?"

"We're in mother's room at the moment. In the Runaway."

"We're back in Bonewell? Have I been out for two weeks?"

"Closer to three. Your body was healing." Thrax looked away to hide his frown.

Gwen turned his face so he would look at her as she kissed the corner of his mouth. "Good thing I had such a wonderful caretaker." This made Thrax perk up a bit, beaming at her.

"Ah, Gwen! Glad to see you're recovering well!" Myana pushed open the door with a tray of food. Behind her was a tall, slender man with broad shoulders, sunkissed skin, and bright blonde hair. He had a big smile and Thrax's green eyes. "Gwen, this is my brother, Nereid Steel-Sea."

"Steel-Sea? That's your maiden name?"

"Aye," Nereid stepped forward with a sweeping bow. "And may I say it is an honor to meet the woman that saved my crew. You have done us a great service and honor, Gwendolyn Grace." He stood straight, still grinning from ear to ear. "My sister tells me you are courting my nephew."

"Yes." She took Thrax's hand and squeezed it.

"How wonderful! You two seem as fine a pair as my sister and Saedon were! Full of love for each other! I wouldn't suppose there are any wedding bells on the horizon?"

Gwen felt her face go warm to the tips of her ears. "I-…w-well-…"

"Uncle," Thrax quickly stepped in. "I don't think now is the time to think about such things. Gwen needs her rest."

"Oh, of course! How rude of me! I'm very sorry, my lady," he bowed deeply again. "Please take all the time you need to rest. I hope when you are well enough, we can celebrate in honor of our victory!" He punched his fist in the air as he left.

Myana sighed and shook her head. "Don't mind, my brother, dear. He's always been quite eager. Our family hasn't seen much joy these days. Now, they meet not only their nephews but also celebrate a major victory! Thrax and Aaheer told me everything. I'm so proud of you and even happier that you are alive."

"Are they alright?"

"Oh," she waved her hand. "They're fine. Aaheer hurt his leg and is still limping, but he can remove his bandages soon. Borbyr's wounds are already scarring. I don't know if Dyael even got more than a few scratches. Everyone will be just fine. As will you." Her warm smile made Gwen's heartache.

"I'm glad we could come home." She took Myana's hand. "Thank you, mother."

Myana's eyes went wide before tears filled, and she hugged her. "Oh, look at this! You've gone and made me all weepy!" She whimpered. "You and Astricus are too sweet, calling me mother before either of you is even married! Oh, look at me!" She pulled away and wiped her eyes, sniffing heartily. "Yes, I-I should go help the others. Please, take your time, darling. Enjoy the food. Thrax, darling, please bring the tray when she's done. Rest well, my darling!" She scurried out of the room, still wiping her eyes.

"Did you do that just to get her to leave?" Thrax teased.

"No, I meant it. I haven't had someone care for me like that since I was a little girl. I'm sure I'll be around for a while."

"Oh?" Thrax's smirk grew. "Already thinking about those wedding bells?"

"Pfft!" She shoved him to disguise her blush. "What? At least wait till I can walk again!"

"Well, that's alright, then, isn't it? I don't mind getting to rest with you."

"How long did you sleep after we got back to camp?"

"I think we were about two days into the journey to Bonewell when I woke up."

Gwen snorted with laughter. "Well, I can't blame you, considering I've been out for a fortnight."

"No, I suppose you can't. But it'll be much nicer together, won't it?" he shimmied over, cradling her in his arms and laying back on the bed with her.

"It will…why don't we let your mom take her room? We can go to our old room."

"What? But it would be better to keep you in one place. I can't imagine walking right now will be comfortable for you."

"Thrax…I don't want to fuck in your mom's bed."

"Oh…oh! Oh! R-right, I-I'll get Astricus to help us!" He rushed off, his cheeks bright red.

Gwen watched him go, blushing and giggling.

Another month passed before Gwen could genuinely go out on her own. During her recovery, every few steps had been met with searing pain, opened wounds, gasping for air, and a couple of times where she hit her head trying to go down the stairs on her own. Once she was at her full strength, she could enjoy the beauty of early spring.

The riverbank was frosty, and the water was gray like the sky. The weak rays of the morning sun were barely beginning to peek from under the downy-gray clouds.

Melting frost dripped from trees as birds chirped and fluttered around for breakfast, and little pink and white buds started to open with fresh green leaves. Gwen took a deep breath of the sharp, crisp air, then let out a cloud of warm air.

"Up so soon?" Midra carefully stepped down the bank to sit beside Gwen on the cold sand. The two were wrapped in thick, woolen dresses with shawls.

"I like it. It's peaceful."

"I thought you were going to tell me Thrax snores."

"Come off it; I'm serious!" Gwen giggled. "I haven't gotten to …enjoy this place. I've gotten to see so many things, so many wonderful things. But each new thing I would try to enjoy still came with a cloud of death and dread."

"Well, it's gone now."

"Right. So, I'm taking it all in now."

"Well…surely you'll have plenty of time, right?"

Gwen pursed her lips and looked down at the small chunks of frost and ice melting off the sandy dirt. "I-…I do miss home," she admitted. "But I can't stand the thought of leaving this place. I love it here. I'm a hero. I've become such a better person. There's so much for me to see and learn. Back home, I was just Gwendolyn Grace. My father barely spoke to me. All I did was read books in Latin or Greek, pet my cat, and watch Coronation Street."

"What's Latin?"

"But here, I'm lady Gwendolyn Grace. I'm the woman who blew up a navy. I went from barely remembering how to sit on a horse to shooting arrows like I've done it my whole life. I've traveled across a kingdom and learned to fight, sew, and cook good food! There are so many interesting books, too! This world you all live in is so different from mine. It's beautiful. It's new. But…I wouldn't want to stay so badly if I didn't have the others. Midra, I don't think I can try to give this up. Would I- …would I be wrong for staying here? Instead of going home to my father?"

Midra pursed her lips. "Well, it sounds like, despite everything you've said to the contrary, you aren't firm on a decision."

"It's just-…"

"It's where you grew up. Where your family is."

"Or what's left of it."

"I think," Midra gently squeezed her shoulder. "You think about where you're happiest and go there. You can still be sad about the place you've lost, but you will be much better off staying where you feel the happiest. Does that make sense?"

Gwen nodded and rested her chin on her knees. They watched the sun rise over the trees in silence, then watched it hide behind the clouds, turning them into a much lighter, misty gray.

"Midra," Gwen suddenly got to her feet. "I've made up my mind." Before the mage could respond, Gwen scrambled over the bank and raced into the village, hoisting her skirt to her knees. Passersby, beginning their day, stared as she raced past. She barely acknowledged the inn as Myana opened the door for new guests. She ran past it to the camp where their allies were still staying. She ran by the centaurs, the fauns, the dark elves, the wizards, and the humans until she spotted Thrax coming out of the trees with a bundle of firewood.

"Gwen?"

"Thrax!" She threw herself into his arms, knocking him to the ground and sending the wood flying.

"Ow! Gwen, what the?" She silenced him by pulling him into a deep kiss.

"I've decided, Thrax! I've decided I'm not going to go back home! This is really, truly my home! I want to stay here with you!"

Thrax's eyes widened, and he laughed heartily, pulling her in for another kiss. "Good morning to you, too!"

They went around the camp and village, telling everyone that Gwen had decided to stay.

"Oh, how perfect!" Myana clapped. "Now we can celebrate Gwen staying and getting our home back!"

That night, they set a glorious festival at the village square. Everyone came to celebrate with food, music, and drink. Everyone was dressed in their most extravagant clothing, and those that didn't have much were gifted other fine things by many. Lovers gathered to either share one last night or stayed in whichever place they would call home. Children ran underfoot, screaming joyfully, splashing in the river, rolling down hills, or sneaking sweets.

Thrax and Gwen had never seen something so beautiful. Thrax wore the same black and green clothes he'd met Gwen in. Gwen was wearing a regal dancing gown from Myana that had been "sitting for too many years in an old wardrobe." The dress was a beautiful ocean blue and accented with a shimmery copper brown.

They danced, drank, and ate all night, talking, laughing, and sharing stories with friends. Gwen had honestly never felt so happy.

As the moon climbed higher into the sky, she noticed Thrax fidgeting and looking like he was going to be sick.

"Is Thrax okay?" She whispered to Aaheer, pointing to him as he spoke to Myana across the square.

Aaheer gave a knowing smile. "Oh, I think he'll be just fine."

"What's that supposed to mean?"

"I think you're about to find out." He pointed as Thrax approached, his forehead shiny with sweat and a look like he was still on the verge of vomiting.

"Gwen, will you come with me?"

She narrowed her eyes as she took his hand. The wizard led her to the edge of the square, mostly out of sight.

"Gwendolyn Grace, these past months have been…the most stressful, most eventful, most frightening, but most importantly, the most wonderful months of my life. Before meeting you, I had never felt as happy, healthy, or loved as I do now. I don't know what brought us together, be it magic or fate, but I will thank the gods every night for introducing me to you. You taught me how to love and be a better me. You got me to see the world as you do; the beautiful, incredible, wonderful world around us. There is darkness and danger here, but I know we can get through anything together. And now, you're staying too! And…w-well, I guess I should get to the point, shouldn't I?"

"It's okay." Gwen grinned. "I like hearing you talk."

Thrax chuckled, swallowing hard. "I guess the point is, well, I don't want you to just…like…live in the castle with us or something. I-…well, I want you to be one of us. I want you to be part of the family. If you'll have us. I mean," he knelt on the ground and pulled out a ring. The metal was made from glittering silver and set with a gem that glistened gold, purple, and red. "Gwendolyn Grace, will you do me the honor of letting me marry you?"

Gwen opened her mouth to speak, but no words came out. She felt her eyes burn and her throat grow tight.

She barely registered the tears as they fell. "Thrax…oh god, yes, Thrax! Yes, yes, I will marry you!" She threw her arms around him, and they suddenly heard hundreds of people clapping. The cheers and whistles of joy made them realize the whole party had paused to watch them.

Gwen blushed, and the two giggled, holding each other close. Thrax took Gwen's hand and carefully slipped it on her finger.

"Mother and the blacksmith helped make this happen…this was the ring my father proposed to my mother with…a fire opal."

Gwen felt her eyes flood with fresh tears and her heart swell with love. "It's gorgeous, Thrax…I couldn't have asked for anything better."

After a few weeks, they were all finally back in Hevaña. Repairs to the city had already begun and even expanded.

More houses inside and outside the walls were built for new homes and families. Astricus had brought his entire village to come and live amongst his new people. Gwen and Thrax stood beside them as they watched Aaheer and Astricus marry and be crowned as the new kings. Gwen and Thrax were then crowned as prince and princess. Just as Thrax had promised, Aaheer and Astricus were given a royal wedding to rival any other. The party went on for days. The kingdom had entirely run out of wine.

Myana retired to Bonewell with Orag. They had found love and comfort in each other. Both were too tired of living in the city. They preferred the peace of running the inn together in Bonewell.

Aaheer's first order as king was to have a monument built in honor of Myana and Saedon. It would be placed in the center of the kingdom, where they first met. Next, he helped Gwen and Thrax secure land outside the forest, behind the city's walls. They could create a resting place for traveling groups like Inanna's caravan. He even ensured Thrax's old workshop was kept so he could have a private workplace.

Gwen would either work at the manor, prepping gardens and stables and decorating their new home with servants and family, exploring the kingdom, and meeting her new neighbors, or enjoying the time she had with her new family. She became particularly close to Sigyn. She was even there to support her while she gave birth to her son. The little boy was named Jorick. Gwen and Thrax would be declared his godparents.

Eventually, Inanna's caravan had to leave; Gwen and Thrax sobbed. He hugged Tan, Inanna, and Deidra, whispering to them through his tears. Gwen clung to Sigyn, weeping into her shoulder.

"Why don't you just stay with us, Sig?" she begged. "We have more than enough space for you and Jorick!"

"You are so sweet, Gwen," She choked, "But this isn't the life I want for my son. I want him to know who he truly is. I won't be gone forever, my dear sister. Inanna has agreed to return here to spend at least one whole season with you yearly. You'll get to see Jorick, and he'll know well of his aunt and uncle."

Gwen blubbered as she forced herself to let her go. "I don't want any of you to leave..."

"Neither do I," Thrax confessed. "I've finally gotten to be with my family. It feels like I'm losing you all again."

"You will never lose us, Thrax." Teyana grinned and handed him a fresh pile of paper and new quills. "You didn't think we'd leave without making sure you still wrote to us, did you?"

He chuckled and sniffed. "No...no, you're right."

"Don't you dare stop practicing your shots, alright? I want to have a good match when I come back!" Tan grinned to hide the fact that he was close to tears as he hugged Gwen.

"Oh, I'll beat you into the ground!" She hiccupped.

When they finally had to stop hugging everyone, Gwen and Thrax watched everyone wave and ride off into the woods. They stood in the grass, clinging to each other until the last waving hand and the final melody of songs faded with the wind.

Epilogue

"But if we don't include the kingdom, we won't have many people at the wedding." Gwen insisted.

"What do you mean? We're having mother's family, Astricus's people, the dark elves, the caravans, and Dyael's herd. How many more people do you expect us to get in the castle?" Thrax chuckled, scratching at his beard, which had become much thicker.

"I know, but we're not close to every single one of them. Wouldn't it be nice to also have the people of our kingdom there to watch?"

"We're planning to have the feast in the square. Why don't we try keeping things easy for ourselves?" Thrax reached over their dining hall table, strewn with papers that were scrawled with notes, lists, and drawings, to take her hand. "I know you're excited about this, but I don't want you to work yourself too hard."

She pouted and dramatically turned away. "You don't want me to be happy." she teased.

Thrax huffed and smirked, taking her hand again. "You know that's a complete lie." He chuckled and pressed his lips to the back of her hand.

She grinned and gently cradled his cheek. "I know. Now, what flowers do you want to use for decorations?"

"Mother always had black petunias planted in the garden. They were always my favorites. What if we use those?"

"I like that! We could use those and flax flowers. We can make them the centerpieces."

"Very well. That's fine." Thrax scribbled it down on a piece of paper.

"Have you made a list of whom you want to be your groomsmen?" she asked, tapping on a paper that was covered in scratched-out names.

"No, not quite. I was thinking about asking Borbyr and Astricus, but you're having Astricus and Dyael be with you. I suppose I could ask Tan, but he and I just aren't very close. I could ask Inanna, but if I asked her, I think it would hurt Tan's feelings. I don't think it would bother her in the same way."

"I think you should ask Tan. It would be a good chance for you two to become closer."

"I suppose I could." The two fell into silence before Gwen eventually spoke up again.

"Are you still alright with having Aaheer be the head of the ceremony?"

"Of course. Why wouldn't I?"

"Well, he's your brother. I figured you would want him to be beside you."

"He will be. He'll just be the one marrying us."

"But I mean, we could always change it. Why not have your mother do it? Or Midra? It'd be like having a piece of Majora with you."

Thrax went stiff, and Gwen immediately knew she shouldn't have said this. "No." he crossed his arms and leaned against the table. "If Majora were still alive, I would want her to marry us. But she's not. I don't want to feel like I'm replacing her."

"I understand. I'm sorry, darling. I know it'll be hard without her." She murmured, gently holding his shoulder.

"I'll be okay." He rested his hand on hers and smiled softly. "I'm marrying the love of my life, after all. Nothing's going to spoil that."

"That's what I like to hear." She teased and kissed his cheek.

Thrax yawned and leaned back, putting his hands behind his head. "What about you?"

"What do you mean?"

"Well, we don't have anyone from your side there."

"I don't know if you've noticed, Thrax, but there isn't anyone from my side here." She giggled.

"I mean…we could try."

"…What do you mean?" Gwen stared down at the paper she'd been making notes on.

"What if we tried that old spell again? Maybe we could get back. You could ask your dad to come."

"No. Thrax, my dad-…no. It's best not to even try that. I don't think I'd want him there."

"Alright," he held his hands up in appeasement. "Alright. No dads for us."

She rolled her eyes again. "Besides, I still have a family. They're just not blood family. That's alright too."

Thrax grinned and leaned over to kiss her sweetly. "That's my girl."